mlc   *A. S.*

Praise for Lynette Eason

"[A] suspenseful mystery and a great love story of personal discovery."

—*RT Book Reviews* on *A Silent Fury*

"Fast-paced scenes and a twist...keep the reader engaged."

—*RT Book Reviews* on *Her Stolen Past*

Praise for *USA TODAY* bestselling author Laura Scott

"A page-turning combination of suspense and second chances."

—*Harlequin Junkie* on *Primary Suspect*

"*Primary Suspect* by Laura Scott is truly enjoyable from start to finish... An excellent choice for fans of law enforcement heroes, medical drama, and run-for-your-life romantic suspense!"

—*Reading Is My SuperPower* blog

SEEK THE TRUTH

LYNETTE EASON

Previously published as *Her Stolen Past*
and *Proof of Life*

Recycling programs
for this product may
not exist in your area.

ISBN-13: 978-1-335-40647-7

Seek the Truth
First published as Her Stolen Past in 2014.
This edition published in 2021.
Copyright © 2014 by Lynette Eason

Proof of Life
First published in 2011. This edition published in 2021.
Copyright © 2011 by Laura Iding

This edition published by arrangement with Harlequin Books S.A.

For questions and comments about the quality of this book, please contact us at CustomerService@Harlequin.com.

Harlequin Enterprises ULC
22 Adelaide St. West, 40th Floor
Toronto, Ontario M5H 4E3, Canada
www.Harlequin.com

Printed in U.S.A.

CONTENTS

Lynette Eason is a bestselling, award-winning author who makes her home in South Carolina with her husband and two teenage children. She enjoys traveling, spending time with her family and teaching at various writing conferences around the country. She is a member of Romance Writers of America and American Christian Fiction Writers. Lynette can often be found online interacting with her readers. You can find her at Facebook.com/lynette.eason and on Twitter, @lynetteeason.

Books by Lynette Eason

Love Inspired Suspense

True Blue K-9 Unit

Justice Mission

Wrangler's Corner

The Lawman Returns
Rodeo Rescuer
Protecting Her Daughter
Classified Christmas Mission
Christmas Ranch Rescue
Vanished in the Night
Holiday Amnesia

Military K-9 Unit

Explosive Force

Classified K-9 Unit

Bounty Hunter

Visit the Author Profile page at
Harlequin.com for more titles.

HER STOLEN PAST

Lynette Eason

Repent, then, and turn to God,
so that your sins may be wiped out,
that times of refreshing may come
from the Lord.

—*Acts* 3:19

To my wonderful, crazy family.
I love y'all so much. I couldn't do this without you.
Thank you for being willing to put up with my
deadline frenzies and take-out food.

To my awesome editor, Emily Rodmell.
It's been a while since I said thanks in a dedication,
so here you go. Thank you for pulling me out of the
slush pile back in 2007 and giving me
a shot at my dreams. :-)

To my Lord and Savior, Jesus Christ.
I love you more every day. Thank you for my gift
of writing. Thank you for letting me do it for you.
May you continue to bless me with stories
and ideas so I can reach others for you.

Chapter 1

Sonya Daniels heard the sharp crack and saw the woman jogging four feet in front of her stumble. Then fall.

Another crack.

Another woman cried out and hit the ground.

"Shooter! Get down! Get down!"

With a burst of horror, Sonya caught on. Someone was shooting at the joggers on the path. Terror froze her for a brief second. A second that saved her life as the bullet whizzed past her head and planted itself in the wooden bench next to her. If she'd been moving forward, she would be dead.

Frantic, she registered the screams of those in the park as she ran full out, zigzagging her way to the concrete fountain just ahead.

Her only thought was shelter.

A bullet slammed into the dirt behind her and she dropped to roll next to the base of the fountain.

She looked up to find another young woman had beaten her there. Terrified brown eyes stared at Sonya and she knew the woman saw her fear reflected back at her. Panting, Sonya listened for more shots.

None came.

And still they waited. Seconds turned into minutes.

"Is it over?" the woman finally whispered. "Is he gone?"

"I don't know," Sonya responded. "Let's just stay here for a while longer."

Screams still echoed around them. Wails and petrified cries of disbelief.

Sonya lifted her head slightly and looked back at the two women who'd fallen. They still lay on the path behind her. *Oh, Lord, help me help them.* She reached for her cell phone. Had anyone called 911? Surely they had, but one more call wouldn't hurt.

Her trembling fingers refused to hold the device and it fell to the ground in front of her. She curled her hands into fists, desperate to control the shaking. She'd done this before. She could manage the fear. But never before had she been caught by surprise like this.

Sirens sounded.

Sonya grabbed her phone and shoved it into the armband she wore when running. She took a deep breath and scanned the area across the street. She'd been in dangerous situations before, working the streets first as a paramedic, then as a trauma nurse on an air-ambulance helicopter.

Later, she'd shake her head at the irony. All those times she'd been in the midst of the flying bullets and had come out unscathed. Now she was a hospice nurse on her day off and she got shot at. Slowly, she calmed and gained control of her pounding pulse.

Her mind clicked through the shots fired. Two hit the women running in front of her. Her stomach cramped at the thought that she should have been the third victim. She glanced at the bench. The bullet hole stared back. It had dug a groove, slanted and angled. He was shooting down, which meant he was higher up.

She had no idea which building the shots came from, but if she had to guess, she would pick the one directly across the street. The office building? Or the clothing warehouse?

The police would figure it out. She checked her watch. No more shots had sounded in the few minutes she'd lain next to the cement fountain, her mind spinning. There were wounded people who needed her.

Heart in her throat, Sonya darted to the nearest woman, who lay about ten yards away from her. Expecting a bullet to slam into her at any moment, she felt for a pulse.

Brandon Hayes heard the gunfire through the open window of his third-floor part-time office at Finding the Lost and automatically reached for his weapon as he spun in his chair.

A police detective by profession and a Finding the Lost employee on his days off, he didn't have a lot of downtime. Nor did he want any.

The Glock felt natural and comfortable in his right hand. He stepped to the side of the window and looked out.

Chaos reigned in the park below.

Two people lay on the ground and appeared to be injured.

Erica James, his sister and founder of Finding the Lost, bolted into the office. "What was that?"

"Bullets. There's a shooter nearby and people are hurt."

She pulled out her cell phone. "Someone's probably already called, but—"

Brandon heard her reporting the incident to the 911 operator as he tried to pinpoint the location where the bullets originated from.

His gaze shifted from the horror below him to the building beside him. Nothing. Not a flash, no movement, nothing. He grabbed the phone from his desk. Rachel, his cousin and secretary for Finding the Lost, picked up. "Get this building locked down now."

"I already did. I heard you say something about bullets fired and immediately called security."

"Good." Her office was just outside of his.

He returned to the window and watched the craziness unfold in the park, assessing the situation, planning the best way to help. Go after the shooter or help the victims?

Movement by the fountain caught his eye. A woman trying to pull one of the injured ones to safety.

Wait a minute.

"Hey, isn't that Sonya Daniels? What's she trying to do? Get herself killed?" He raced from the office, Erica's protests ringing in his ears. "Stay here!"

Brandon hit the glass door, swiped his card that would allow him to exit, but would lock the door behind him. Then he was on the sidewalk. Within seconds he was at the park. Police officers who'd been nearby started to arrive on the scene. To the nearest one, Brandon flashed his badge and yelled, "I think the shooter was in the building next to the bank."

Law enforcement now swarmed the area and he kept his badge in plain sight. He stuck his weapon back in the shoulder holster and headed for the fountain. Sonya Daniels had shown up at Finding the Lost a little over a week ago with a birth certificate for Heather Bradley. She'd hired him to find the person. And now she was rescuing joggers in the park. His heart thudded as he kept his attention tuned to the area around him.

No more shots sounded. He hoped that meant the shooter was on the run and not aiming at any more innocent people.

Brandon rounded the back of the fountain and found Sonya doing CPR on the woman she'd pulled out of harm's way. He dropped beside her. "What can I do?"

Surprise and relief flickered across her face when she saw him. "She needs an ambulance. Her heart's stopped." Sonya did more compressions. "Feel for a pulse."

Brandon did as ordered. He looked up and shook his head.

Sonya gave a growl of frustration and slammed a fist onto the woman's chest. "Beat!" She pressed and released, pressed and released, unrelenting and breathless, with determination etched on her features.

Brandon felt a faint flutter under his fingers. "Keep going. I think I felt something."

Hope blazed in her eyes as she continued her efforts. "Come on, please. Please." An ambulance pulled up next to the fountain and two paramedics rushed over. Sonya looked up. "I think she has a pulse now. She coded about thirty seconds ago."

"You have medical training?" the first paramedic asked as she dropped beside Sonya.

"Yes. One semester short of being a doctor."

Brandon shot her a look. He hadn't known that.

He moved aside as the other paramedic joined them. Sonya fell back out of the way and let them take over. He grasped her arm. More medical help surrounded the other woman. "She's dead," Sonya whispered to him. "The bullet went straight through her head." Grief coated her words. "The one I was helping was shot in the back. Please let her make it, God." Brandon wondered if she even realized she'd whispered her prayer aloud. He hoped God listened to her more than He seemed to hear Brandon's prayers.

He watched the officers doing their job and knew Sonya needed to give a statement, but for now, he needed to get her someplace where she could sit and let the adrenaline ebb. He cupped her elbow and started to lead her away. She resisted. "No, I want to watch them."

Finally, one of the EMTs looked up, caught Sonya's eye and nodded. They moved the woman to the gurney and slid her in the back of the ambulance. The female paramedic looked back and gave a thumbs-up.

Sonya blew out a breath and leaned back against the bench.

An officer approached them. "Has anyone talked to you two yet?"

"No," Brandon said. "I heard the shots from my office window across the street and ran over to see if I could help."

Sonya looked up, then pointed to the hole in the bench. "That's the bullet that had my name on it."

Two hours later, after giving her statement and reliving the nightmare, Sonya was exhausted. Brandon had disappeared about an hour ago to offer his services to the investigation even though she knew he wasn't officially on the clock.

The officer next to her flicked a glance behind her and she turned to see Brandon approaching. He touched her arm and she shivered. "Are you all finished?"

"Yes, I believe so."

"Why don't we go over to my office so you—we—can decompress?"

She nodded, noticing the sparks his touch set off. In spite of the terrifying situation they'd just lived through, she was still aware of everything about him. From the moment she'd walked into Finding the Lost last week, every time she was in his presence, her attraction meter spiked. So far she'd been able to ignore it, telling herself she didn't have the time or energy for a relationship.

Especially not with someone she couldn't read.

Brandon's green eyes hadn't revealed anything to her and she hadn't figured out how to discern his moods or thoughts. That threw her off kilter. Of course, she'd known the man only a week. "Are you finished helping here?"

"For now."

They walked across the park toward the office buildings. Sonya averted her gaze from the blood still staining the jogging path. "How long will they keep the park closed?"

"Until a crime-scene cleanup crew gets here and removes all traces of the tragedy."

She nodded, grateful for his easy manner and unhurried gait. "You hear about these kinds of things on the news almost every day, it seems," she said. "But you never really expect it to happen to you, to find yourself fighting to survive in the midst of something so awful."

She wondered if the shooter was gone. Or if he'd managed to avoid detection so he could linger and watch. She wondered if he was reveling in the chaos he'd created. A shiver slithered up her spine and she offered up a silent prayer that he'd be found and unable to hurt anyone else.

Brandon put an arm around her shoulders and she looked up, startled. He dropped his arm. "Sorry. You looked like you needed a friend."

His gruff voice and averted gaze grabbed her. She touched his arm and gave him a smile. "I do need a friend. Thank you."

He nodded but kept his distance. Regret filled her and she wished she'd just leaned into him and accepted the comfort he'd been offering. She had a feeling he didn't do that very often.

"How's the job going?" he asked as he opened the glass door for her.

She stepped inside the cool interior of the lobby. "It's going fine." She'd been at Spartanburg Regional for only three weeks.

"And your mother's house?"

"Coming along." Her mother had died a month ago. Sonya had moved to South Carolina to settle her mother's affairs. She took a seat. She understood what he was doing. Talking about nothing to get her mind off the shooting. She wished it would work. "Did you find anything about the birth certificate?"

In the process of cleaning out her mother's house, she'd come across a box of baby items. Including a birth certificate for a Heather Bradley.

He nodded. "I did. Interesting enough, Heather Bradley, daughter to Don and Ann Bradley, was kidnapped from a church nursery twenty-eight years ago."

Sonya processed that bit of information and swallowed hard. "Why would my mother have the birth certificate of a kidnapped baby?"

Brandon leaned forward and narrowed his eyes. "That's a very good question. What do you think?"

She reached up and rubbed her forehead, trying to hold the headache at bay. "I don't know. Maybe she found it. She was a yard-sale junkie and something of a hoarder. What if she bought the box, stashed it and never thought about it again?" It had been known to happen. Hadn't it?

"It's possible." He looked doubtful.

"Are you saying you think my parents kidnapped a child?" she scoffed. She pictured her gentle father. A pastor with compassionate eyes and warm bear hugs. Before cancer had stolen his physical body. Cancer had robbed her of both of her parents. A lump formed in her throat. The illness may have taken his body, but his spirit had stayed strong to the end. "No way."

"I'm not saying that at all, but it does raise questions for sure." He paused. "Did anyone live in the house before your family?"

"Yes. The house was a parsonage. My father was a pastor for the church next door. When the church hit some hard times financially, my father decided to buy the house to help them out."

Brandon frowned. "How could he afford to do that if the church was having a tough time?"

Sonya blinked. "I don't know. I never really thought about it. I was only a child. Maybe ten or eleven when it happened."

Brandon tapped his chin and sighed. "Hmm. Well, I'll keep digging."

"Was Heather Bradley ever found?"

"No."

"Oh." Her stomach twisted into a knot.

"But I did locate her family. They actually live about thirty minutes from here, practically across town."

"How was Heather taken? Why would her birth certificate be in her diaper bag? Don't people usually keep those in a safe place?"

He gave her a slow smile that made her heart trip all over itself. His eyes crinkled at the corners. "What?"

"You ask good questions," he said. "I'm impressed. According to Mr. Bradley, his wife had decided to go shopping Saturday afternoon. She checked the mail, and the birth certificate had arrived. She slipped it into the diaper bag so she wouldn't lose it. She said she forgot about it until after Heather was taken."

"Which was the next day. So the kidnapper took the baby and the diaper bag?"

"Right out of the church nursery."

She nodded. "Right. So how did that happen? Where was security? Wouldn't someone see the person taking the child and stop him or her?"

He held up a hand at her rapid-fire questions. "Let me explain. Mrs. Bradley said there were two rooms in the nursery. A room that held cribs for sleeping babies and a monitor. The door was shut so the other children could play without waking the ones sleeping. There was a window in the door, but..." He shrugged. "You have to remember this was almost thirty years ago. Security in church nurseries was nothing like it is today. If they even had security."

"So no one knew Heather was missing until a worker went in the room to check on the other babies."

"Exactly."

"And I found the diaper bag with the birth certificate in my mother's closet." She paused, her mind racing. Then she looked at him and swallowed hard. "Do you think I'm Heather Bradley?"

Chapter 2

Brandon saw the weariness on her face—and a sort of horrified curiosity mixed with embarrassment that she would even consider asking the question. When he didn't answer right away, she pushed him. "Well?"

Brandon shrugged. "I can't say the thought hasn't occurred to me. I think it's a real possibility. We'd have to prove it—or disprove it—of course."

"Of course," she murmured then gave a disbelieving laugh. "I really don't think I could possibly be her. I mean, it just doesn't make sense. I'm not adopted." She swallowed hard. "At least I was never told that I am."

"I understand that you'd feel that way, but I think it's something we need to consider and look into."

She bit her lip and gave a slow nod. "So where do we start?"

"Let me think about it." He rubbed a hand down his

face. "You need some rest. Is there anyone that could stay with you tonight?"

She shrugged. "I'll be all right."

"I really don't think you should be alone. Today was traumatic, a tragedy that's already playing on every news channel in the country. You probably have the media camped out on your doorstep."

Sonya froze. "I hadn't thought of that."

He knew she hadn't. "So. Is there anyone you could stay with?"

"I could call Missy Carlisle, I guess."

"Who's that?"

"A friend from work. Even though I haven't been there very long, we've become pretty close."

"Close enough to spend the night?"

"Of course."

He nodded to the device still strapped to her arm. "Is that your phone?"

Sonya looked at her biceps as though she'd never seen it before. "Yes." She released the device from the strap and dialed her friend's number. While she talked, Brandon watched her. When she'd first come into the office, he'd seen her with Erica and wondered about her.

Erica had caught him watching. Later she'd patted his arm and said, "Don't worry, she's the real deal. She's not here to gawk at our resident hero."

Brandon had rolled his eyes. "Cute, sis. I'm not the one who worries about that and you know it."

"Well, you have to admit, thanks to the media, we've had a few loonies looking to become your next girl-friend."

He couldn't help the wry twist his lips took.

A hero.

Just the thought made him shake his head. He wasn't a hero; he'd just done his job. But the media had dubbed him a hero for being a part of bringing Molly home. Erica's three-year-old daughter had disappeared while on a field trip with her preschool class.

Brandon had been a detective with the police force in Spartanburg. Banned from working the case because of his relation to Molly, he'd resigned and come on staff full-time with Finding the Lost. They'd brought Molly home three years later. Longer than he'd intended, but at least she was finally home with her mother.

And then he'd been in the right place at the right time two months ago. He'd caught and subdued an abusive husband trying to kidnap his child in the grocery-store parking lot. The media had gone nuts. Grudgingly, he admitted Erica had a point. Put the word *hero* on a guy and things got interesting—and extremely embarrassing. Not too long after the story broke he'd started getting marriage proposals via mail, email and even text messages.

Women. He'd never understand them. And frankly wasn't sure he ever wanted to after the fiasco with his fiancée leaving him. All he'd learned was that most women weren't to be trusted. The only exceptions he knew of were Katie Randall and Erica. He had no doubt they were a different type of woman.

But there was something about Sonya that made him wonder if she fell into the same category as his sister and friend. He also wondered if she ever smiled. A genuine smile, not strained or sad or worried.

She hung up and looked at him. "Missy said that would be fine. I need to go home and get some things, though."

"I'll take you."

Sonya stood. "It's not necessary."

"Maybe not, but I want to."

She tilted her head, and her ragged ponytail flopped onto her left shoulder. She studied him for so long, he almost started to squirm. "Okay."

Her quiet acquiescence stirred his heart. And his mind. Was her innocent little-ole-me an act? Or was Erica right and she was the real deal? He decided he'd have to keep his distance until he figured it out.

Sonya sat in Missy's living area and debated whether or not they were close enough friends for her to share her heart. She noted the Bible on the end table and the plaque on the wall that stated, *As for me and my house, we will serve the Lord.*

Neither one of those necessarily meant Missy practiced what she displayed, but chances were she wouldn't have the items if she didn't.

"What is it?" Missy handed Sonya a mug of steaming coffee flavored with vanilla.

Sonya blew on it, then took a sip. She smiled. "My mother always said one little puff isn't going to make one bit of difference in the temperature."

Missy laughed. "Well, she's right."

"I know but I do it anyway."

Missy sat in the recliner and curled her legs beneath her. "Are you sure you're all right?"

The television played in the background on mute. Fox News carried the latest about the shooting, and Sonya shook her head. "I'm all right. Still shaken up, of course. The whole thing is surreal and I'll probably have nightmares for weeks, but I'm just grateful to be alive."

She took another sip of the steaming brew. "How is the woman who was brought in?"

"Still alive when I left an hour ago, but critical."

Sonya leaned her head against the back of the couch. "I don't understand people who can do that kind of thing," she whispered.

"I don't, either, and I don't want to." Missy paused. "So who was the good-looking guy who followed you here?"

Sonya felt the flush creep up into her cheeks. "That's Brandon."

"And? You haven't talked about him at work."

That wasn't her style, but she didn't say that. "I hired him to look into something I found going through my mother's things after she died."

"What'd you find?" Missy turned serious, her brow creasing.

So Sonya spilled her story. Missy stared wide-eyed, her flavored coffee forgotten. Sonya finished with "The shooting happened just across from Brandon's office with Finding the Lost. He heard the shots and came running."

"That's just crazy. And this Heather Bradley was kidnapped twenty-eight years ago?"

"Yes."

"And Brandon works for this company."

"Yes."

"Tell me more about Brandon. You blushed when I asked you about him."

Sonya groaned and gave a half laugh. "I can't figure Brandon out. On the one hand, he's kind, concerned and obviously very good at his job. On the other, he comes across aloof and—suspicious." She'd been aware of his intense scrutiny while she'd been on the phone with Missy, but had pretended not to notice. He'd walked her back to the park and waited while she'd retrieved her car. Very serious, very businesslike. "I don't know." And she didn't. Which meant it was time to change the subject. "I think I'll grab some sleep. What time is your shift tomorrow?"

"Seven A to Seven P." Meaning seven in the morning to seven at night. "What about you?"

"The same, but I'll have to go home and change before I go in."

"I have some clothes and scrubs you can use if you want to borrow them."

She almost took her friend up on the offer. Instead, she said, "I'll just go home early in the morning and get ready. My house is on the way to the hospital, so it's no big deal. And besides, I have to feed Chaucer."

Chaucer, her cat, independent and aloof until it was time to eat, but she'd filled his bowls before her run earlier and he would be physically fine for the next few hours. His temperament would leave a lot to be desired, but she'd deal with that later.

Missy shrugged and yawned. "Okay. Well, if you need anything, feel free to ask or browse."

Sonya smiled. "Thanks. Shampoo and conditioner are all I need for now."

"All right. See you in the morning."

Sonya sat on the couch for a few minutes after Missy padded down the hallway to her bedroom. She stared at the clock on the mantel and listened to it tick.

Each click of the second hand felt like fingernails on a chalkboard.

Now that she was alone, the thought that she could

have died today ate at her. "I don't know why You left me here, Lord, but I thank You for that," she whispered. She knew she'd die one day, and she was ready for when it happened. Meaning she knew she'd go to heaven, but until that time, she wanted her life to count, to mean something.

She saw death on a daily basis, but coming face-to-face with the fact that a bullet could have so easily taken her out made her shudder.

And made her all the more determined to find out what had happened to little Heather Bradley. To find out if Brandon's hunch was right and she *was* Heather. Because if she was, her entire life had been a lie.

From his deck, Brandon sat in the darkness, ignoring the humidity that caused sweat to bead across his forehead. He stared at the half-moon and allowed his mind to process the day. At two in the morning, he sipped a soda, a rare drink for him, but one he enjoyed on occasion.

Living in the middle of downtown had its advantages, one of which was proximity to both of his offices. When Jordan Gray had looked him up after his last tour in Iraq, at loose ends and grieving the death of his brother, who'd recently died of an overdose, Brandon had offered him the spare bedroom.

And now Jordan was getting married to Katie Randall this summer. A June wedding Katie admitted she'd dreamed of since she was a little girl, but never really thought would happen. They'd bought a small house about fifteen minutes away and Katie was moving in tomorrow.

After the wedding, Jordan would join her, and Brandon would be left alone. He could afford the payment, but had to admit he'd be a little lonely. Not that things would be much different than they were now. Jordan spent every spare minute with Katie, coming home only to sleep and shower.

First Erica and Max had tied the knot, now Jordan and Katie. Brandon wondered if he'd ever meet someone. Someone real, someone who didn't want to be with him just because the media had labeled him a hero.

His jaw tightened. Then relaxed as Sonya came to mind. She seemed so likable and genuine. He hoped that was the case, but would keep his guard up. His ex-fiancée had seemed quite likable and genuine—until she'd met someone who didn't come with as much baggage attached to him.

Brandon knew he had issues that stemmed from his family situation—and he was working on them. It had hurt when Krystal had decided she didn't want to work on them with him.

Brandon turned to head back inside. The lamp in his den went out. He stopped. Looked at his kitchen window. The light over the sink was off, too.

For a moment, he stood silent, letting his eyes adjust to the darkness. The town house to his left had power. So did the one to his right.

A blown fuse?

Maybe. But in his line of work, he wasn't going with that assumption.

Brandon set his drink on the small table next to the chair and reached for his weapon. The one that wasn't there because he'd left it on his kitchen counter. Next to his cell phone.

Wary, Brandon slipped to the edge of the deck and waited. Watching through the French doors. Even though it was dark inside, the moon offered a bit of light, coming through the open blinds and into the den.

His patience paid off when a thin shadow moved into his line of sight. The person paused, then moved to his desk. A thin beam of light came from a small penlight. Who was it?

Itching to confront the intruder, Brandon held still, waiting and watching. A weapon appeared for a brief moment, and the large barrel on the end said this was no random break-in.

His gut twisted as he mentally moved into battle mode. His right hand twitched, wanting the comforting feel of his Glock against his palm.

The town house had two levels. Right now, they were on the bottom level. Upstairs he had three bedrooms. One for him, one for Jordan and one he used as an office. The antique desk in the living area simply served as decoration.

But his intruder didn't know that.

Did the person not realize he was home?

The weapon said yes. The leisurely search of the desk said no. Or he wasn't worried about it.

Brandon waited for a lull in the traffic, then slid the glass door open and slipped inside. He closed the door with a quiet hiss.

The figure at the other end of the town house paused. Lifted his head as though listening. Brandon stayed still, his only thought to get to his weapon. The person moved toward him, his weapon held expertly in front of him.

Brandon took note. Weapons training. Breaking-and-entering training. What else? Not wanting to be caught unprepared and while the element of surprise was still on his side, he moved on silent feet through the darkness to the kitchen.

The intruder's gun popped, flashed. The bullet slammed into the wall next to Brandon's head.

So much for being quiet.

He dived for the kitchen and rolled as another bullet burned a hole in his newly laid tile floor. Anger fizzled. His back hit the cabinets. He lifted his hand and snagged his Glock from the counter, keeping his head low.

He'd been shot before. He had no intention of letting it happen again. With his other hand, he reached up and grabbed his phone.

"Come around the corner and you get shot. Tell me what you want and you might keep breathing." He kept his voice steady. Controlled. He didn't want to shoot anyone. Not even this person intent on killing him. He did, however, want to know who it was. But he wasn't going hunting blind.

Brandon listened as he punched in 911 and pressed the phone to his ear.

Silence from the den. The 911 operator's voice on the other end of the phone sounded incredibly loud. He lowered the phone.

A whisper of movement from the living area reached him. Brandon stilled. Moving closer or moving away?

Brandon tried again. "Get out while the getting's good." He pressed the phone back to his ear and whispered his address.

"Yes, sir. I got it. What's the emergency?"

He didn't answer, just listened.

Still the intruder said nothing and made almost no sound. Brandon waited, nerves bunched, muscles quivering with his tension. A low voice finally came to him. "Stop looking for Heather Bradley."

And then the quiet snick of the door shutting.

Brandon stayed still, ignoring the adrenaline rush racing at fever pitch through his veins. Was it a trick to get him to show himself? He moved and peered around the kitchen cabinet, into the den area. No movement, but it was so dark, someone could be hunched down and he'd never see him.

Brandon flattened himself on his belly and kept his weapon in front of him. Army crawling, he moved toward the den, eyes probing the darkness.

He could see nothing. He heard nothing. He turned the volume down on the 911 operator frantically trying to get him to answer.

The sirens in the distance caught his attention and he figured they were headed for him. If the intruder was still in his house, he was going to be trapped.

No one spoke. No more shots came his way.

Brandon's adrenaline ebbed as he finally decided he was alone. He stood, still cautious, watchful. He flicked on the small light above his sink, not wanting to turn on the bright kitchen light after being in the darkness for so long. He needed to let his eyes adjust slowly.

Still keeping himself protected from anything that might come from the den area, he waited to make sure.

Then slowly, methodically, he swept each and every room, weapon ready.

The place was empty.

Only now he knew someone didn't want him looking for Heather Bradley. The question was: Why?

That someone had just made a very bad mistake because now Brandon was more determined than ever to get answers to all of his questions. All of them.

Chapter 3

Somehow Sonya made it through her twelve-hour shift without collapsing. She didn't like working on Sundays, but it was part of the job. She was fortunate she had to take only one Sunday a month.

Now she had one more thing to do before she went home to collapse.

She knocked on the door to room 412.

"Come in."

Sonya stepped into the room and saw the woman in the bed. "Hi, Dineen, my name's Sonya Daniels. I was in the park when you were shot."

"You're the one who saved me," she whispered and held up a hand.

Sonya took it and squeezed. "I'm glad you're going to be all right."

"I am, too." She coughed and winced. Sonya handed

her the cup of water by her bed. After Dineen took a small sip, she set it aside.

"Is someone staying with you?"

"My husband. He went downstairs to get something to eat. He'll be back soon."

"Good."

"Did they catch him?"

"No, not yet."

She nodded. "I figured I would have heard something if they had. It's still all over the news."

"They'll catch him."

Her lids drooped. "I'm sorry. I can't seem to stay awake very long."

"It's the pain medicine. I just wanted to check on you. Go to sleep and heal."

"Thank you."

Sonya smiled and left. Exhaustion swept over her. All she wanted was to go home and crawl into bed. Even the thought of her empty refrigerator couldn't tempt her into stopping at the grocery store. She would make do with peanut butter and crackers and a bottle of water. Sleep was all she craved.

"Hey, Sonya," Missy called.

Sonya turned. "Yes?"

"Are you going home? Do you need to stay another night at my house?"

"I think I'm all right." She'd managed to dodge the reporters this morning. Security had kept them from her while at work. She wondered if they'd be waiting for her at her car. The thought made her grimace.

"Well, you're welcome to stay if you need to. Just let me know."

"Thanks." Sonya gave her a small smile. It was all

she could muster. However, she decided Missy was the real deal and hoped they could build their friendship. She missed having a close friend.

"I'll see she gets home all right."

Sonya turned at the deep voice and found Brandon standing in the small foyer. He looked as tired as she felt. "What are you doing here?"

"I'm fine, thanks. How are you?"

Sonya felt the heat in her neck start to rise and cleared her throat. "I'm sorry. How are you?"

"I'm just teasing. I thought I'd stop by and see if you could use a bite to eat?"

Sonya was amazed to feel energy start to seep back into her tired body. His mere presence jump-started her pulse and made her heart pound. She swallowed hard. "I could eat."

"Great. I want to talk to you about something."

"Like what?"

"Don't mind me. I was just leaving," Missy said.

Sonya felt her flush deepen and she shot Missy a look that said to stop. Missy grinned, waved and headed out the door.

Sonya rolled her eyes and turned back to Brandon, who smiled, his eyes dark and mysterious. She wished she could read him.

"Come on. I'll drive and bring you back when we're done."

She hesitated. "Do you mind if I just follow you?"

He shrugged. "Sure."

He walked her the rest of the way to her car. She slid into the driver's seat and clicked on her seat belt.

Twenty minutes later, she found herself sitting opposite Brandon at one of her favorite cafés about a mile from her mother's home.

Brandon rubbed his coffee cup between his palms. Sonya took a bite of her chicken panini. With food in her stomach, the strong black coffee racing through her veins and the handsome man across from her, she felt as though she'd just had eight hours of sleep. Her watch said it was pushing eight o'clock. If she was in bed by eleven, she would be good to go for tomorrow's shift. "What did you want to talk about?"

"Heather Bradley."

"What about her? Did you find out if—" She bit her lip, unable to voice the question.

"If you're her?"

"Yes. I can't even believe I'm asking. It's just too bizarre."

"Unfortunately, bizarre stuff happens all the time." He smiled. "I've talked to Mr. Bradley once. He's open to meeting you. Would you be interested in taking the baby stuff to them?"

Sonya paused midbite. "Me?"

"Well, it was in your mother's house where you found the stuff. Mr. Bradley said they'd love to have the bag and other items back."

"But…but…" she sputtered. "Won't they think my parents had something to do with their daughter's kidnapping?"

"He asked what I thought about your parents and how they might have come by the items."

"What did you say?"

"Just that you had come to me with this story and the items and were as confused about them as everyone else."

Sonya took another bite, chewed and swallowed. The distraction gave her time to think. "I'm okay with returning the stuff, then."

"Good. He wants to talk to you. Said he had questions for you."

Sonya shrugged. "I feel sorry he's lost his daughter, but unfortunately, I won't have any answers to his questions."

"I told him that. He wants to see you anyway."

She paused. "Did you tell him we were pondering whether I might be Heather?"

"No. But I think the thought crossed his mind when I told him about you."

"I see." She thought for a few more minutes then nodded. "Well, then. When do we go?"

"As soon as you get off your shift tomorrow night? Or will you be too tired?"

"I'll be tired, but I still want to go. The sooner we get this resolved, the better I'll feel. And I'll ask if I can leave a couple of hours early if that would help."

"It would. So around 5:00?"

"Okay. I don't think it'll be a problem."

"Yo. Brandon, my man, what up?"

Sonya jerked at the voice to her left. She turned to find a tattooed young man with more earrings in his ears than she had in her jewelry box.

Brandon stood and held a hand out to the kid. "Spike. Haven't seen you in a while. How are you?"

"Hanging, dude. Just hanging."

"Staying out of trouble?"

"Of course."

Sonya almost had to laugh at his attempt at an innocent look.

Brandon rolled his eyes, but the smile on his lips was genuine. He turned to her. "Sonya, I'd like you to meet Landon Olsen, aka Spike. Landon, this is Sonya."

"Pretty lady, dude." He elbowed Brandon and winked. Sonya could feel the flush inching its way up her neck and into her cheeks. Brandon gave a gentle slap to Spike's head. The boy laughed and said, "Sorry. I'm kidding you." He made a formal bow in Sonya's direction. "Pleasure to meet you, ma'am."

"Well, thank you, Spike. It's nice to meet you, too." She shot a glance back and forth between the two. "So how do you guys know each other?"

Spike stuck out his well-muscled chest. "I'm one of his more successful projects."

Sonya lifted a brow at Brandon and he groaned. "He's a pain in my side most of the time."

Spike grinned. "Dude, you know you're my hero." He looked at Sonya. "I'm gonna be a detective like him one day."

"That's a wonderful goal, Spike," she said. "I have a feeling you'll be one of the best and brightest."

Spike's eyes lit up and she could see he took her compliment seriously. Just the way she meant it. He turned to Brandon. "I like her, man. Don't mess it up." Before Brandon could say anything, Spike announced, "Hey, I gotta go, dude. See you Saturday?"

"I'll be there."

"I'm going to beat you so bad, you're going to need a doctor to put you back together."

"Don't count on it. Your head's getting so big, it's going to weigh you down."

Spike barked his laughter, gave a two-fingered salute and slipped out the door.

Sonya sat back. "What in the world? Beat you?"

Brandon blew out a sigh. "I help out at Parker House. It's a place that takes in young men who've had some brushes with the law and rehabilitates them. Or at least tries to. It's part that and part recreation center. When he said he was going to beat me, he meant he was going to win our game of three-on-three this weekend."

"Basketball?"

"Yes."

"Sounds like fun."

He studied her. "You like basketball?"

"Love it."

"You want to come watch?"

She did. "What time?"

"Nine o'clock."

She groaned. "As in a.m.? On a Saturday morning?"

He laughed. "Not a morning person?"

"Not in the least. I mean, I have to be for work, of course, but on my days off…"

"You almost smiled."

She frowned. "What?"

"You don't smile much."

"I haven't had much to smile about lately." She tried to force her lips into one and he shook his head.

"I'm not talking about a fake smile. I'm talking about a real one." Before she had a chance to respond or even try to find a "real" smile, he said, "But you'll come?" His voice softened and he leaned forward. She caught a look in his eyes that made her gulp.

"Sure. I'll come."

He nodded and looked away. She wondered what he was thinking, but couldn't tell. Did he regret asking her?

He cleared his throat. "Anyway, tomorrow after your shift, we'll go see Heather's parents."

So it was back to business. "Yes. That's fine."

Brandon studied Sonya and wondered what had come over him that he would invite her into a place that he kept as his. His home was his haven. Parker House was his escape, his passion. And he'd just invited Sonya to come. He must be more tired than he thought. "I wanted to talk to you about something else. Someone broke into my house last night."

She gaped at him. "Broke into your house?"

He nodded and told her what had happened.

"But why?" she asked.

"To tell me to stop looking for Heather Bradley."

She paled and sat back. "What?"

He took a sip of his coffee. "I think it's extremely weird that you were shot at yesterday and then someone breaks in my house the same night. It could be just a crazy coincidence, but I've been in this business a long time and I'm just not sure I'm going to buy that theory."

"I don't know, Brandon. The shooter wasn't really going for me personally. He was shooting at others in the park, too."

"True. I've thought about that. And maybe I'm just grasping at straws trying to link the two things."

"What else did the person say?"

He shook his head. "Nothing. Whoever it was didn't get to stay long enough. When he realized I had a weapon, he took off. The cops got there and we searched the area, but came up empty."

He saw her swallow. "I'm so sorry."

"I am, too."

"Do you have any enemies?"

"I think a better question is, do we have any enemies in common?"

"But we've only known each other a couple of weeks."

Brandon lifted a brow. Had it been such a short time? It seemed as if he'd known her a lot longer. "Exactly. The only thing we have in common is your case."

"Heather Bradley."

"Yes."

"So someone doesn't want us looking for her? But who would even know?"

He shrugged. "I honestly don't know, but it's the only reasonable explanation I can come up with. But most likely you're right. The two incidents probably aren't connected."

"You don't have an alarm system?"

"I don't."

"I'm surprised."

He gave a low chuckle. "I never really felt the need for it. I don't have anything worth stealing and I have a gun on my nightstand and know how to use it." He paused. "After last night I might reconsider, though."

"So what now?"

"Now we watch our backs."

"But we keep looking for Heather?"

"Absolutely."

She nodded, relief in her eyes. "Good. I really want to know who she is—or was." Her jaw firmed. "And prove it's not me."

It hit Brandon that Sonya didn't have a deceptive bone in her body. The realization allowed him to relax a fraction. She wasn't after him because of some silly hero status that had been dumped on him. And she wasn't interested in him romantically.

The sharp pang of regret surprised him. Made him look at her a little closer. And he decided that if she wasn't a client, he'd be asking her out.

He drew in a deep breath at the silent admission.

"Are you okay? You have a funny look on your face."

Brandon cleared his expression. "I'm fine. Are you ready to go?"

Her brows knit but she nodded. "Sure."

Together they walked out of the restaurant and he escorted her to her car, his nerves alert, senses sharp. At her car, she started to slide in the driver's seat when he noticed a small square of paper about the size of an index card under her windshield wiper. "What's this?"

He handed it to her and leaned in to read along with her. "'Stop looking for Heather Bradley. She doesn't want to be found.'"

Chapter 4

Sonya gaped. "Well, I guess we're making someone kind of nervous."

"You think?" A muscle jumped in his jaw as he stared at the note.

"So what do we do?"

Brandon lifted a brow. "Do you want to stop looking for her?"

"No way."

"Do you have a paper bag in your car?"

"No, I don't think so."

"All right, let's go back in the restaurant and get one."

Sonya shut her belongings in the car and followed Brandon, who carried the note between his thumb and forefinger. She figured he wanted to get the note tested for fingerprints. She glanced around the parking lot, wondering if the person who'd left the note was watching. Shivers slid up and down her spine.

Spooked, she stayed close to the person who seemed to represent the only security she could find in a world that had shifted on its axis once again. First the death of her father, then her mother and now someone was sending her threats.

She didn't like it.

Sonya waited by the door while Brandon requested a paper bag. The waitress handed him one and he slipped the note inside and folded the bag over. He held it up. "All right, I'm going to take this over to the lab."

"Tonight?"

He shrugged. "Why not?"

"But it's late. You've had a full day and need to rest." She sighed. "And I sound like your mother. I'm going to be quiet now, get in my car and go home."

His lips pulled into a smile. A smile he seemed to struggle with. Almost as though he didn't do it very often and his lips had forgotten how. She knew exactly how he felt. Smiling seemed to take more effort than it was worth these days.

"I'll follow you home before I take this over," he said. "I have a friend who works the graveyard shift. He'll probably be able to take care of this pretty quick. Depends on what else he has in the lineup."

"Okay. Thanks." She walked to the door and stepped outside. Her eyes immediately scanned the area for any threat. "And I think after today's craziness, I would appreciate you following me home." She paused. "And going through my house to make sure no one is inside would be nice, too."

"My pleasure."

His hand slipped under her elbow, and warmth danced up her arm. What was it about this man at her side? It was rather crazy the feelings he'd stirred up in her. And the feelings had her curious, too. She'd felt attraction before. Had even dated a doctor at the hospital before she'd moved to South Carolina to be with her mother during those hard final days of her life. So why now? Why would her heart suddenly decide that it was time to be attracted to Brandon, a man so tightly closed emotionally, a crowbar wouldn't get him to open up?

A hand waved in front of her face. "Where are you?"

Sonya blinked and found herself at her car. "I was lost in thought."

"I could see that. About what?"

She shrugged. "Everything. How confusing my life has suddenly become."

"We'll get to the bottom of this," Brandon said. "I promise."

She smiled. "I know you'll try."

"Well, that smile's not fake, but it looks a little sad." He held the door for her while she slipped into the driver's seat.

"Thanks."

He closed her door and she waited for him to get into his car. He flashed his lights when he was ready and she pulled from the parking lot.

She kept an eye on her rearview mirror and couldn't help wondering while Brandon was following her, was someone following him?

Brandon was concerned. The shooting in the park could have been a random thing. As unfortunate as it was, that kind of thing happened and made the news all the time. Okay, maybe not all the time, but often enough that people were no longer shocked when they saw reports on the news. Saddened, angry and frightened that their world could be such a dangerous place, but not shocked.

But the break-in at his house and the note left on Sonya's car both pointed to the fact that someone didn't want them looking for Heather Bradley. That was one fact he had no trouble figuring out.

By the time they pulled into Sonya's driveway, he'd mapped out his plan of action for the next day.

She pulled into her garage and he met her as she climbed out of her car. "Nice place."

"Thanks. My mother was originally from South Carolina before she and my father met. Then she went to college in Virginia and my dad swept her off her feet." She gave a small smile and led him into the house via the back door. "At least that's her version."

"Your father had a different one?" He stepped into her kitchen. Cinnamon and another spicy scent hit him and he drew in a deep breath.

"Absolutely. He said Mom swept *him* away." The fondness in her voice got to him.

He stopped at the table and looked into her eyes. Which made him crave chocolate.

At the same time, a long-rooted bitterness he'd thought he'd managed to suppress rose up strong and hot, taking him by surprise. "My parents never felt that way about each other."

Something in his tone must have caught her attention. Her gaze sharpened. "I'm sorry."

"So am I." Now he wanted the subject dropped. Him and his big mouth. "I don't know why I told you that.

Forget it." He moved away from her. "Stay here while I check out the house."

He could tell his abrupt departure confused her but he had to get away. He felt his walls slipping, crumbling before her sweet disposition and compassionate eyes. *She's a client, Hayes, remember that. You don't date clients.*

With his weapon ready, he checked the den, the three bedrooms and three bathrooms. He opened doors and peered in every potential hiding place, taking note that she kept a clean house. The glass on the nightstand, the T-shirt over the footboard of the bed and the flip-flops tossed into the corner of the room said she wasn't obsessive about everything being in its place, though. "It's clear, Sonya," he said. He returned to the kitchen to find her staring out the window over the sink. "Sonya?"

She jerked and spun, a pretty cat in her arms. She stroked the animal's head and blinked. "Oh. Sorry. I was lost in thought. Again."

"It's okay. I just said your house is clear."

She let out a relieved breath and set the cat on the floor. "Thank you. Once I lock the door behind you I'll feel all right."

"Who's your friend?"

"That's Chaucer. He's a pretty independent little guy, but when I'm gone for a long time, he likes to be held for a few minutes when I first walk in." The cat sniffed Brandon's shoes and must have decided he was okay as he rubbed against Brandon's leg.

Brandon leaned over and scratched the cat's ears while he debated whether Sonya should feel safe behind her locked doors or not. How serious was the person who'd left the note on her car? Pretty serious if it was the person who'd broken into his house to deliver the same message.

She must have sensed his hesitation. She walked over and patted his arm. "I'll be fine."

Brandon still paused, wondering if he should leave. Finally, he said, "All right. I'll see you tomorrow?"

"At five."

"At five." Brandon forced himself to walk away and climb into his car. He gave the area one last sweep and didn't see anything that made his nerves spike into alert mode.

But that didn't mean it wasn't there.

Sonya twisted the dead bolt. The lock clicked and silence descended. She shuddered as the house took on an ominous feel now that she was all alone. "Stop it," she muttered.

Exhaustion swamped her. She had to get some sleep. Seven in the morning would come fast.

And yet, how could she sleep knowing someone felt threatened enough to leave a note on her car? And to break into Brandon's house…

All of a sudden, she didn't feel so safe. Her locks looked flimsy and she couldn't remember if her bedroom window was latched.

Swallowing hard against the fear that wanted to take hold of her, she headed to her bedroom. At the entrance, she paused. "He said it was clear. There's no one in there."

Saying the words out loud helped, but still…

She stepped over the threshold and went straight to the window, felt the latch and found it locked. Her breath whooshed from her lungs. "Get a grip, girl."

After a quick shower, she threw on a T-shirt and cotton shorts and turned the air conditioner down a notch. She kept her cell phone close. A glance at the clock made her grimace. Almost ten o'clock. The thought of falling asleep and having someone break in while she lay unaware made her stomach turn.

For the next thirty minutes, she paced and prayed. And listened. Nothing happened. No one tried to get in.

She sank onto the couch, pulled a blanket around her and rubbed her bleary eyes. She leaned her head back and sighed. Chaucer hopped up in her lap and nuzzled her chin. She rubbed his ears and he purred.

A noise from the kitchen.

She jerked, breath hitching. Chaucer jumped to the floor with a protesting meow.

Then Sonya realized it was only the ice maker. She got up to pace again, angry with herself and the fear she couldn't seem to kick. She had to sleep if she was going to be worth anything tomorrow at work.

Sonya sidled up to the window and looked out. Then blinked in surprise. A strange car sat snugged up next to her curb. She drew back, fear flushing through her once more. Was there someone in the car? Another peek through the window confirmed someone in the driver's seat. Okay, someone in the car was watching her house. Why? Who?

Had the other incidents not happened, she wouldn't have jumped to that conclusion, but at this point and after everything she'd been through, she was going to go with that first thought. Someone was watching her.

Sonya pulled her phone from her pocket and hit the number to speed-dial Brandon. She hated to wake him, but needed him to know about the car.

"Hello?"

"Hi, this is Sonya."

"What's up? Are you okay?"

"I'm sorry to call you so late, but I wanted you to know there's a car parked out in front of my house on the curb and there's someone in the driver's seat."

"Ah. That's Frankie Lee. He's a buddy of mine. He's a detective and also helps out at Parker House. I didn't feel right leaving you all alone and called him to be your backup."

Relief and a smidgen of anger swept through her. "That would have been nice to know."

A slight pause. She thought she might have hurt his feelings. "Sorry. I thought you might have gone on to sleep and I didn't want to wake you," he said, the stiffness in his voice making her wince.

The anger faded as fast as it had surfaced. "No, it's fine. Wonderful, in fact. I'm sorry I snapped. The truth is, I was having trouble settling down. Now that I know someone is watching out for me, I'll be able to sleep."

"Well, good." The stiffness was gone. "I'm dropping this letter off at the lab, then I'm heading home for a couple of hours of sleep. I'll see you after your shift."

"Sounds good." She paused.

"You need something else?"

"No, no. I guess I just wanted to say thank you."

"You're welcome, Sonya." His low voice turned husky and warm, and shivers danced up her spine with the three words. And the way he said her name. She liked it. It made her feel—cared for. Something she hadn't felt since her mother died.

She hung up and with one last relieved glance out the window headed for her room to get some much-needed sleep. And while glad for the security outside her home, she couldn't help the niggling of unease that inched up her spine. Somehow she knew that while she might sleep easier tonight, the person watching her wasn't far away.

He was waiting—and planning—for the next moment to strike.

Chapter 5

Monday morning Brandon glanced at the clock on his desk at the police station and rubbed his chin. He'd snagged only a few hours of sleep last night, yet they'd been enough to refresh him.

Knowing Sonya was at work and under the watchful eye of Frankie, Brandon had felt comfortable enough to come in and work on his cases without worrying himself to death about her safety.

Brandon knew Frankie would call him if something came up. He hoped nothing did, of course. And now, in an hour, he'd pick up Sonya at the hospital and take her to meet Heather Bradley's family. Time had slowed to a crawl and he had to force himself to focus. However, excitement stirred inside him, distracting him.

He wasn't sure if it was the thought of seeing Sonya

again or the possibility of discovering she was a missing child from twenty-eight years ago.

He stopped to consider that. Wariness rose as he realized seeing Sonya rated higher on his excitement meter than finding out if she was a Bradley. He'd have to add another layer to the crumbling wall around his heart.

His phone rang as he kept up the internal dialogue about why he couldn't allow a romantic interest in Sonya to grow. "Yeah?"

"Tough day?"

Holt Granger, his buddy at the lab. Finally. "Not especially. Why?"

"You sound grumpy."

"I'm not grumpy."

"You sure? Because you sound grumpy."

Brandon sighed. "I'm sure."

"Whatever."

"And no, my day has not been especially hard. I was just thinking about something."

"Something that put you in a bad mood obviously."

Brandon felt his lips twitch. Holt never had a bad day. Or if he did, he didn't let on. "Do you have something that's going to improve my mood?"

"Thought you weren't in a bad mood."

"I said I wasn't grumpy. I didn't say anything about my mood."

Holt laughed and Brandon's small smile curved higher. "Well?"

"I got a print off the letter."

"You're right. My mood just got better. Any matches?"

"No, sorry. Whoever the print belongs to isn't in the system."

"You just tanked my mood."

Holt chuckled then turned serious again. "Nothing from your condo, either. Your intruder had on gloves."

"Yeah. I know."

"I'll stay in touch and let you know if anything else comes up."

"Thanks."

Brandon hung up and looked at the clock again, realized what he was doing and rolled his eyes. His uncharacteristic impatience had him cranky and irritable in spite of his denials to Holt.

But he finally admitted his impatience stemmed from his desire to see Sonya again. He grabbed his keys and his phone and headed out the door. He'd be early, but at least he'd be moving instead of staring like a lovesick schoolboy at the clock on his desk.

At 4:55 in the afternoon, Sonya waved to Frankie Lee, her subtle bodyguard who leaned against the wall and pretended to read a magazine. He returned her wave with a nod and she gathered her things. He sauntered over and pushed the door to the locker room open. "Anyone in here?"

"Just me." Gerri Aimes exited the locker room and gave Frankie the once-over. He seemed to meet her approval because she winked at Sonya. "It's all yours."

"Thanks." Sonya didn't bother to correct her coworker's misunderstanding about who Frankie was. Instead, she stepped into the empty room where she'd change into her street clothes and freshen up a bit before heading down to meet Brandon. Just the thought made her smile. In spite of Brandon's observation that she didn't smile much. She'd noticed lately that when she thought of him, her lips automatically curved upward. She had to admit, too, that while on the job, she occasionally used the smile Brandon called fake. Even that was better than a frown. Or an expressionless facade.

Hospice could be such a heavy place. No one who came to hospice left alive, and families were grieving—some openly, some hiding it well. Others were angry that the medical staff couldn't miraculously heal the dying loved one.

Sonya didn't take it personally, but dealing with them didn't make it any less emotionally draining. And while smiling usually came naturally to her, lately, it had been hard to find something to smile about. She was glad to let her lips relax in the privacy of the locker room.

Not everyone could do her job. She knew that and took comfort in the fact that she was needed even if being needed did come with a high emotional price tag. But she loved what she did and the families she worked with. So she coped with prayer and offered comforting embraces and empathetic tears.

Watching her parents die had given Sonya the desire to reach out to others, to let them know she knew exactly what they were going through. And offer genuine smiles when she could find them.

Some days she saw the results of her efforts. Other days she just prayed she'd made a difference.

Today was one of those days, so she prayed while she changed.

She would see Brandon in five minutes. Give or take a minute or two. She'd gotten permission to leave early, stating she had a personal issue to take care of.

Her nerves hummed and her brain whirled. Who were the Bradleys? What if she was Heather? Her throat tightened at the thought. No way. There just *had* to be a reasonable explanation for everything. Didn't there?

She finished changing and closed the locker door. Another locker door shut with a click.

Footsteps to her left.

The lights went out.

In the dark, Sonya froze and listened. The inky blackness pressed in on her. "Hello?" She thought she was the sole occupant of the locker room since she was the only one leaving two hours before the shift ended.

Had the entire hospital lost power? But why hadn't the generator kicked in?

She moved with shuffling steps toward the door, not wanting to bang her knees on the benches.

Another footfall landed somewhere in front of her, between her and the door. She stopped, her heart picking up speed. "Who's there?"

When she didn't get an answer, but knew someone was definitely in the room with her, her heart kicked it up another notch. With all of the strange things that had happened lately, she wasn't taking any stupid chances.

Sonya shut her mouth and moved sideways. She hit a bench and set her bag on it. She wanted to reach in the bag and search for her cell phone, but didn't dare make the noise she'd have to make in order to find the thing.

So, making no sound, she twisted the strap of her purse around her fingers and stepped around the bench, her soft-soled tennis shoes quiet on the tile floor.

With her pulse pounding in her ears, she moved toward the door once again, hoping whoever had been there seconds before had moved. Another muffled scrape reached her. The person still blocked Sonya's exit.

She slipped back and into one of the bathroom stalls. And wondered if that was possibly the dumbest thing she could have done.

At ten after five, Brandon started to get a little nervous. Where was she? He was parked at the top of the circle next to the front door where she said she'd meet him. Maybe she'd gotten held up. He tried her number and frowned when she didn't answer. He called Frankie. "Where's Sonya?"

"She's changing in the locker room. Taking her a while, though. I was just getting ready to check on her."

"Did you clear it before she went in?"

"I did. Another woman was in there and came out when Sonya went in."

Brandon waffled. "Give her another minute then knock on the door." He should have put a woman on her. Would have made it easier to keep tabs on her in the bathrooms.

"Of course."

Brandon waited for all of fifteen seconds, then got out of his car and headed for the entrance. He was probably overreacting but he'd rather play it safe. He couldn't believe how worried he was. Telling himself he was being silly, that Frankie had it under control, he nevertheless hurried to the elevator.

Sonya held her breath then let it out in a slow, soundless hiss. She'd lost track of how many seconds—minutes?—had passed since she'd stepped into the stall. Two? Three? And yet, she heard nothing. No footsteps, no one breathing. Nothing.

She was beginning to think it really was her imagination after all, but her gut said it wasn't.

She opened the stall door and stepped out.

From behind her, she felt movement. She started to turn and gasped when something hard, cold and sharp touched her throat and pressed. Sharp, stinging pain froze her. "This is your last warning. Stop looking for Heather Bradley." The knife dug a little deeper. Sonya felt a warm trickle of blood begin to slide down her throat. She let out a whimper, lifted up on her tiptoes. She couldn't speak, was afraid to move. One wrong slip of his hand and the blade would end it all.

The knife lowered and she shoved back against her attacker. The figure stumbled. She heard the knife clatter to the tile floor. Sonya spun away and lunged for the door. A hand gripped her collar and yanked her back.

A knock on the door made her attacker pause. Sonya swung around with her fist and connected with a cheekbone. He cried out and cursed, but let go.

"Sonya? Are you in here?"

"Missy! Get back!" Sonya moved and slammed into the bench. Pain shot through her knee and she heard Missy scream as the man raced through the open door. Sonya spun to see Missy shoved against the door and the dark-clothed figure disappear around the corner. Commotion escalated like a cresting wave. She thought she heard Frankie holler, then pounding feet.

Sonya sank to the floor and lifted a hand to her bleeding throat, wondering how deep the wound was. Weakness invaded her. Mentally, she knew she needed to get up and get help, but her body wouldn't cooperate with her. Shock held her in a tight grip.

Then Brandon was beside her. "I need a doctor in here!" To Sonya, he said, "Let me see." He removed her hand and she thought she saw relief flash in his eyes. "I think it's just a surface wound."

"It stings," she whispered, "but doesn't really hurt. My knee hurts worse." She tried to laugh but wasn't sure she succeeded when he grimaced.

"Sonya?"

She glanced up at Dr. Eddie Ryan's concerned voice.

"Hey, Eddie," she whispered. Security and police officers were already on the scene. They must have been close by. The observation almost made her laugh. She'd just had her throat cut and she was thinking about the proximity of law enforcement. Too bad they hadn't been around when she'd been attacked.

Brandon moved back and let Eddie take his spot.

"Who did this?" Eddie asked without taking his eyes from her neck.

She shrugged. "I'm not sure. Someone who's decidedly unhappy with me. Is Missy okay?"

"I'm fine."

Hearing Missy's shaky voice sent relief pouring through her.

"Unhappy with you?" Eddie snorted. "I'll say." He looked up and spoke to one of the nurses. "Let's get her into a vacant room. Looks like she might need a stitch or two. Call the pharmacy and get me a prescription for an antibiotic." He wrote the script, then looked back at Sonya. "I'm assuming your tetanus vaccination is up to date."

"Yes."

"Good."

She looked at Brandon. "Where's Frankie?"

"He went after your attacker," he said. "Security is helping him. We should hear in a bit that he's in custody. Now, let's get you taken care of."

Then hands were helping her into the wheelchair that had been called for. "I don't need this. I can walk."

"Sh." Brandon laid a hand on her shoulder. "Sit."

Since she didn't think she could stand, much less walk as she'd said she could do, she bit her tongue on any further protests.

Thirty minutes later, she had two black stitches in the worst part of the cut, had downed the prescribed antibiotic and was waiting impatiently for Brandon to reappear. Thankfully, the wound was numb and she wasn't in any pain at the moment, but she was grateful for the little bottle of pain pills in her purse for when the numbing medicine wore off.

She wanted to go home and sleep, but more than that, she wanted to head over to the Bradleys' house. Brandon had wanted to cancel the meeting, but she'd asked him to just postpone it if that was all right with the Bradleys. She didn't want to wait a moment longer than necessary to talk to them.

Doubtful, he'd done as she'd asked and now she itched to go. To get the visit over with. To determine once and for all that she was *not* Heather Bradley.

Chapter 6

Brandon's phone rang as he turned onto the Bradleys' street three hours later than their original appointment. When he'd called to tell the Bradleys what had happened to Sonya at the hospital, Don Bradley had expressed his concern, but made it clear that he didn't care how late it was; he and his wife wanted to see Sonya. As long as she felt up to it.

She'd assured him she did.

Brandon grabbed his cell on the third ring. "Hello?"

"Got some information for you." Hector Gonzales, his partner. Brandon had called him shortly after the attack on Sonya and asked him to help with the investigation. His boss, Sergeant Christine Adams, had given them the green light.

"Let me have it."

"We reviewed the hospital security video footage. Basically, it tells us nothing. Everyone who entered looked like they were supposed to be there. There's no one running away except for when he pushed his way out of the locker room and disappeared in all the chaos."

"Down the stairwell that was right next to the locker room," Brandon muttered.

"Yeah."

"But how did he get in the locker room without anyone noticing?"

"He wore a wig. We found it in the trash on the next floor. Holt has it and will test it for any stray hairs from the attacker's head. I'm hoping for some DNA to match up to any suspects we're able to haul in. I think I've found the guy in the security video. He wore that nondescript brown wig and was dressed in blue scrubs."

"Just like everyone else in the building."

"Exactly."

"And the other cameras?"

"Not much. If I've got the right person, on his way out, the figure was dressed in black with a hood pulled up obscuring his face. If that's not him, we've got nothing. I've checked and double-checked the footage of people leaving the hospital shortly after the attack, and other than that one possibility, there's nothing. I mean, people are leaving work and they carry large bags. He could have stashed a bag somewhere, went to it and stuffed his clothes in there."

"Or he ditched them." Brandon paused as he thought. "Okay, so the attacker either got rid of the clothes and left looking totally different or..."

"...he didn't leave right away," Hector said.

"But he might have still tossed the clothes."

"I have a team still going through the trash." He

sighed. "And I'll have the hospital send out an emergency email to be on the lookout for blue scrubs in a trash bin."

"With orders not to touch, but call us immediately."

"Exactly. I'll be in touch."

"Thanks."

He hung up and found Sonya watching him. He filled her in on the conversation and she nodded. "I didn't expect it to be very easy to catch this person."

"No, not easy. But not impossible. No one is perfect, and as soon as he makes a mistake, we'll get him." He tapped his fingers against the wheel, his brain whirling. "Are you sure it was a man?"

She blinked at him. "Yes, pretty sure. If it was a woman, she had a pretty deep voice." She rubbed her head. "And when he had me held against him, he felt muscular. Like he worked out. His chest was like a brick." She paled and swallowed hard. "I couldn't move, he was so strong."

He could see the memory shook her. Brandon parked in front of the Bradleys' house. He reached over to grasp her fingers in his. "It's okay. You're safe now."

She nodded. "Right. For now." Her eyes flicked to her surroundings. He'd pulled to a stop at the top of the horseshoe-shaped drive. Brick with white columns, the front porch ran the length of the home. White rockers and a swing gave it a comfortable appearance. Homey. The manicured yard glistened from the sprinklers that had shut off as they drove up the drive.

Their wealth didn't take him by surprise. He'd done his homework, but Sonya's openmouthed stare said this wasn't what she'd expected. "They have money."

"A lot of it."

"From what?"

"Ann's family owns a textile business that's employed by the government. Don works for her father. Their company supplies a lot of the thread that makes uniforms for the armed forces."

"Wow."

"Yeah. What's really wow is that they live very much below their means."

The front door opened and a man with sandy-blond hair stepped onto the porch. If he had any gray, Brandon couldn't see it. Don Bradley's wide smile clearly displayed his pleasure that they'd arrived. The sun still hung low in the sky, but in another fifteen minutes it would be dark.

"You ready?"

"I'm ready." He saw her pull in a deep breath, and then she opened the door and stepped out.

Brandon did the same. Deep breath and all.

Mr. Bradley headed for them, hand outstretched. "Brandon Hayes?"

"Yes, sir. Nice to meet you."

The men shook hands and Brandon was impressed with the man's firm grip and eye contact. "Thanks for coming."

"Of course."

And then he turned to Sonya. The two locked eyes and studied each other. Brandon swallowed hard.

Even he could see the resemblance.

Same dark eyes, same blond hair. Or maybe he was just seeing things. Just because they both had blond hair and dark eyes didn't mean she was the man's daughter.

Don Bradley held out his hand to Sonya, who took it. "Hello, Sonya."

"Hello, Mr. Bradley." Her voice shook slightly and Brandon wondered if she was seeing the same thing he was. Possibly.

"It's Don. For now. Come in, come in." He waved them toward the front door. Brandon gripped the brown bag that held the baby items Sonya had given him when she'd first hired him and followed the two of them inside.

The foyer held a grand crystal chandelier that illuminated the area. The staircase to the left led upstairs. Don led them into the living room to the right. "Have a seat. My wife should be here soon. She went to the gym to work out." He shook his head. "World War Three could break out and she'd still be at the gym. She never misses her workout. She texted and said she was about ten minutes away." He eyed the bag in Brandon's hand and swallowed. "Is that it?"

"Yes, sir."

He nodded. "Might be best for me to take a look before she gets here anyway."

Brandon handed him the bag.

The man clutched it and took a deep breath. A fine tremor ran through his fingers. He looked up. "You know, I never gave up hope that she would come home. I figured anyone who would kidnap an infant wouldn't kill her." His Adam's apple bobbed. "So, I've always believed she was still alive, still out there. We finally adopted. We have a son who's twenty-two. He just graduated college last year and is working as an accountant in Texas."

So, if she was Heather, she would acquire a brother. Brandon's eyes met Sonya's. Her lashes fluttered as she blinked back tears.

Then Don's face hardened. "We've had people who

claimed to be Heather, you know. People who've actually knocked on our door and said they were our daughter." He cleared his throat. "Can you believe there are people who go looking for unsolved missing-children cases? Children who belonged to wealthy families and were never found? They take that case, research it, learn it and build an entire story about how they are the missing child?" He shook his head. "It's unbelievable. We investigated each and every one, of course, but they were all frauds."

"That's awful. I'm so sorry," Sonya whispered.

He nodded and opened the bag. When he pulled out the brown Gucci baby tote he gasped. His eyes widened and he stared at Sonya. "It's her bag."

Brandon frowned. "I told you it was."

"I know, but I mean, you really have it. I didn't expect—" He spun it around. "And the pen mark is even there," he whispered. "I was writing a check and juggling Heather at the same time. My pen slipped and I hit the bag."

The front door opened and a woman in workout clothes stepped into the foyer. She dropped her gym bag on the floor and slipped off her tennis shoes. Her ponytail swung around her head. Brandon thought she looked amazing for being in her mid-fifties. In fact, she really didn't look a day over forty.

She turned to see them in the living room and gave them a smile. "Hello."

The smile faltered as she caught sight of the bag in her husband's hands. She paled and actually swayed. Brandon moved fast and caught her by the upper arm. She let him lead her to the sofa and help her sit. And still she never took her eyes from the bag. "How?" she whispered. "Where—"

"My mother had it in her closet," Sonya said.

The woman's stunned gaze turned to Sonya. "And you think you're Heather?"

"Actually, no. I don't."

That seemed to take Mrs. Bradley by surprise. Her perfectly arched brow lifted and some of the shock slid from her face. "You don't?" Suspicion clouded her gaze and she scowled. "Well, that's a new approach."

"Ann—" her husband cautioned.

She ignored him. "Do you know that you're not the first person to come to us and claim to be our long-lost daughter?"

Sonya swallowed hard. "I'm sorry. But I'm not claiming to be your daughter. If anything, I'm here to prove I'm not. My parents were wonderful and I had a lovely childhood, but ever since I've started looking for Heather Bradley, I've been attacked and threatened."

"What?" Mrs. Bradley jerked. "What happened? Attacked and threatened by who?"

Brandon filled them in on the incidents. Mrs. Bradley paled even more if that was possible. "Oh, dear. That's simply awful. And you're sure all of that happened because you're looking for our daughter?"

Sonya shrugged. "The person was pretty specific about how I needed to stop looking for Heather Bradley."

Mrs. Bradley lifted a hand to rub her forehead. "This is giving me a headache." She sighed and brushed away a tear. "Of course, no one wants Heather found more than I do, but I'm afraid you're wasting your time. We've looked for her for years and have come up with nothing. What makes you think you can find her now?"

Sonya stared at the woman and pondered her question before it hit her. "Because someone who knows we're looking for her feels threatened enough to lash out and tell us to stop."

The room fell silent. Mrs. Bradley nodded and ran a hand over her messy ponytail. She picked up the bag she'd dropped upon entering the foyer. "I'm going to take a shower. I can't deal with this right now." Her voice cracked and she cleared her throat. "I've tried to accept that she's gone, and every time someone brings her up, it just opens up that old wound. It's like pouring alcohol over it. And I can't do it anymore. I just can't," she whispered and ran up the stairs.

Sonya winced. "I'm so sorry."

Mr. Bradley shook his head and she caught a glimpse of his own tears before he blinked hard. "It's all right. I suppose I shouldn't have gotten her hopes up by telling her you were coming. I should have just found out for sure before saying a word." He looked at Sonya. "But you do look a little like me. I wonder if there's a reason for that or if it's just dumb luck."

Brandon clasped his hands in front of him. "There's one way to find out."

Mr. Bradley lifted a brow. "How's that?"

"DNA testing. We can test you and Mrs. Bradley against Sonya or if you have something of Heather's from when she was born. A lock of hair or—"

Mr. Bradley shook his head. "No. I don't have anything."

"Yes, we do." Mrs. Bradley had returned and now stood at the bottom of the steps.

"What?" Don asked.

"A lock of hair taken the day she was born."

"But—" he started to protest, and then his eyes widened and he nodded. "I know what you're talking about. I'll get it."

"No. I'll do it." She jogged up the stairs.

"I can take it over to my buddy at the lab and see what he comes up with," Brandon said to Mr. Bradley. "It may take some time depending on what he's working on now, but it would give us a definite answer as to whether it matches Sonya."

"Fine. We've waited this long. I don't suppose a few more days—or weeks—will matter much." He looked toward the stairs and frowned. "Let me check on her. Whenever she starts going through Heather's baby book, she gets so upset."

"That's understandable," Sonya murmured, sympathy etched on her face.

"I'll be right back." He ascended the stairs and Sonya met Brandon's gaze.

"Maybe this was a bad idea," she murmured.

"No, I don't think so. If you're Heather then you need to be reunited with your family. If you're not Heather, I'd really like to know why someone doesn't want her found." He paused. "I'd actually like to know that regardless."

"I would, too. But did you see Mrs. Bradley's face? This is really painful for her."

He drew in a deep breath, then let it out through his nose. "I saw. And I hate it for her, but—"

"Here we are." Mr. Bradley stepped into the living room and held out a small envelope. He glanced up the steps. "I gave it to them, dear. Go on and take your shower." Sonya heard receding footsteps. "Ann isn't coming back down. It's simply too much for her."

Brandon took it, held it gently. "I'm sorry this is bringing your pain back." He tapped the envelope. "This isn't all of it, is it?"

"No, no. I kept some." He gave a sad smile. "Heather had a head full of hair when she was born." He studied Sonya's head. "Lighter than yours. But your eyes—" He held out a hand as though to touch her, then fisted his fingers and dropped his arm. "Your eyes—"

"What about them?" she asked.

"It doesn't matter." He forced a smile and Sonya exchanged a confused look with Brandon. He shrugged. Then Mr. Bradley blurted, "Your eyes look just like hers."

"Do you have a photo?"

"Of course." He walked to the mantel and pulled a small photo from behind another picture. "We don't keep pictures of Heather on display. It's just too painful for my wife." He handed the picture to Sonya. "That's Heather. She's sleeping in that one. If you want one of her awake, I'll have to go find an album."

Sonya stared at the picture, sucked in a breath and let it out slow. The baby looked a lot like some of the pictures she'd seen of herself as an infant. Of course, a lot of babies looked similar when that young. She forced a smile and handed the photo back. "Thank you."

Brandon tucked the envelope into his pants pocket. "We'll let you know something as soon as possible."

"I would appreciate it."

Brandon took her arm and she tried not to notice how natural and right it felt to walk beside him. How her head came right to his shoulder and how his subtle cologne made her draw in a deep breath and savor the spicy scent. She liked this man, but didn't have any business doing so. However, that didn't seem to matter to her heart. She wanted to get to know him better, find out what made him tick, but knew she shouldn't.

On the other hand, he had secrets, a hardness about his eyes that made her wonder what he'd seen, what he'd lived. Getting behind that wall scared her even while the idea intrigued her.

She shut the thoughts down. Finding out what the baby bag and items were doing in her mother's house was her priority. Romance wasn't even on the table as an option right now.

The thought made her frown.

And then Brandon was holding the car door open for her. She slid in and leaned her head back against the headrest.

"Are you okay?"

"I'm tired. Just plain exhausted." She lifted a hand to her throat. "And sore." She tossed him a weary smile. "But very glad to be alive. If that's all I have to complain about, I'm far better off than some people." She thought about the women in the park. "Far better off."

He smiled back. "I know what you mean. I'll drop you off at home. Frankie's exhausted. I've got a buddy who's going to keep an eye on you while I run this to the lab."

"I'll be fine."

"I want someone with you twenty-four-seven until we find out who's threatening you."

She shivered. "You're right. I think I want that, too." The thought of being alone, being the prey of an unknown stalker who wouldn't hesitate to kill her, filled her with a fear like none she'd ever felt before.

"What about your friend Missy? Would she let you stay with her?"

"I'll text her and see." She glanced at the clock. "It's getting pretty late. Almost ten o'clock." She tapped out the text to Missy and asked if she could stay at her house.

Almost immediately the reply came. Of course. Come on over.

"All right, I'll take you home to get your stuff."

She nodded and felt relieved. Being at Missy's would take a little of the fear away. Having someone else listen for danger would be a big help. "Do you think he's following us? Watching and waiting to strike again? Tonight?"

He glanced in the rearview mirror as he drove and shook his head. "I can't say no, but I've been watching and haven't seen anyone following."

She heard what he left unsaid. Just because he hadn't seen anyone didn't mean no one was there.

She shivered. "I hope your friend can get the results back from the DNA pretty quick."

"Holt's a good guy. He's kind of like me and works all the time. He'll run it for us as soon as he gets a chance. When I drop this off, I'll really stress the necessity for speed."

She studied him. "Why *do* you work all the time, Brandon?"

He shot her a frown. "What do you mean?"

"You just said you work all the time. Do you have any hobbies?"

He shrugged. "Not really. Unless you count the mentoring work I do with at-risk kids."

"Like Spike."

"Yes. Spike's one of them. And I like basketball, but mostly I work."

"Why?"

"Does it matter?"

Well, he knew how to shut a person out, didn't he? To her surprise, she wasn't hurt, just curious.

"Yes. It matters, but you don't have to tell me unless you want to."

"My fiancée left me." His fingers flexed on the wheel as he pulled into her driveway and put the car in Park.

"Oh."

Sitting outside her home, silence descended, blanketing them as completely as the dark of the night. Only a small streetlight provided a bit of light. Enough to see his profile and the wrinkles in his forehead. Then the wrinkles smoothed and he let out a small laugh. "'Oh'? That's it?"

Sonya felt the heat flood her face and was grateful for the darkness. "I'm sorry. I just wasn't expecting you to say that."

"I wasn't, either." He sounded almost bemused.

"Why did she leave you?"

"She found someone who didn't have as much baggage, didn't work as many hours and had money to spend on her." The bemusement was gone. The flat, hard statement told her how much his fiancée had hurt him. "We were supposed to meet for dinner one night. I arrived at the restaurant. She didn't. When I called to see if she was all right, she didn't answer. I went to her house and she was having a candlelit dinner with my accountant."

Silence reigned in the car for a full minute.

"Well…" She drew the word out, thinking of a response.

"Well, what?"

She gave a small shrug and struggled to find the right

words. Unable to think of any, she settled on "That really stinks."

More silence, and then he gave another low chuckle. "Yes. Yes, it does. It did." He finally turned his head toward her and she could see his eyes. Eyes that didn't look hard or flat. Eyes that looked confused and maybe held a hint of surprise.

She gave an embarrassed cluck of her tongue. "That was a dumb response, wasn't it? I'm sorry. I just wasn't sure what to say."

"Your response was absolutely perfect. Most people just offer platitudes or they get embarrassed and don't want to talk about it." He took a deep breath. "Or they tell me they know how I feel and I'll recover with time. That last one is the one that bothers me most."

Puzzled, she cocked her head and frowned at him. "Well, I certainly wouldn't say that. I *don't* know how it feels." She hesitated briefly. "And I don't want to, either," she blurted.

This time he threw his head back and let out a belly laugh. She stared at him, wondering if he'd lost his mind. Then he leaned over and placed his lips on hers. Stunned, she didn't move. The kiss was light, almost like a thank-you, yet with something more, something deeper, something that made her blood hum and her heart sing.

When he lifted his head, he cupped her chin. "You never say what I think you're going to say."

"And you just did something I never expected you to do."

A grin pulled at the corner of his lips. "I really like you, Sonya Daniels."

The present slammed her. She bit her lip. "Sonya Daniels? Or Heather Bradley?"

Chapter 7

Brandon sat back with a jerk. What was he doing?

"This is where you apologize, right?" she asked softly.

He sighed. "Apologize? No. I won't apologize for the kiss. I don't know that I can explain it, but I won't apologize for it."

She gave him a slow smile. "Good. And it doesn't need an explanation."

"But we can't let this go anywhere. Not yet."

"What?" she asked.

"Huh?" He blinked.

"Let what go anywhere?"

"This. Us. You know what I'm talking about." He felt the heat creeping into his cheeks. How had he found himself having this awkward conversation? He didn't do awkward. He didn't kiss clients, either.

"Yes, I do." She patted his hand. "Don't worry about it, Brandon. I'm a big girl."

"Sonya—"

"I'm going to get some stuff. I'll be right back."

"I'm coming with you. I don't want you going anywhere alone unless you just absolutely have to."

She climbed from the car and stopped. Stared. "That's weird."

"What is?"

"It's dark and I know I left lights on. You think the power went off?"

He frowned as he took in the house. No porch light, no soft glow coming through the blinds from the inside. Then he glanced around the neighborhood. "Your neighbors have power. Let me take a look."

He placed his hand on his weapon and unsnapped the safety strap. She walked up the front porch and unlocked the door. He slipped around her. "Stay back."

She stayed back. Slightly.

He made his way into the foyer, senses alert to anything that didn't belong. The house smelled of a mixture of lavender and chamomile. Like her.

He moved into the kitchen, feeling her presence right behind him. He didn't hit the light switch, not wanting to be blinded by the sudden brightness. Instead, he let the moon filtering through the kitchen blinds guide his way.

The front door slammed shut.

Sonya let out a yelp and spun to face the noise.

Brandon raced to the door, stood to the side and flipped on the porch light. He looked out, blinking, letting his eyes adjust while he stayed out of the line of fire.

With the door cracked, he listened. Heard a scrape.

He peered around the edge of the doorway, the porch

light illuminating all the way to the driveway. Sonya stayed behind him. Good—he wanted to know where she was at all times. His adrenaline pulsed, keeping his senses sharp. Acutely in tune with everything around him, he probed the darkness beyond the reach of the light.

Movement at the back of his car, the trunk area. He lifted his weapon. "Police! Freeze!" The figure obeyed but stayed bent over. "Show me your hands!" The intruder hesitated. "Hands, hands! Show them to me!"

Two gloved hands reached up from behind the trunk. No weapon in sight. Brandon started toward him, his gun held ready, adrenaline pumping through him. Finally, he was going to get the person who didn't want Heather Bradley found.

As he got closer, the intruder darted across the street and into the neighbor's yard. Brandon took three steps to follow then stopped. Sonya raced past him. "Hey!" He shook off his shock and followed her. "What are you doing?"

She didn't answer, just kept up the pursuit. He trailed hard and fast on her heels, as determined to protect her as she seemed to be to put herself in danger. They were going to have to have a serious talk when he caught up with her.

And then she stopped. Spun in a circle and slapped both palms against her thighs in frustration. "Where'd he go?" He noticed she was barely out of breath. Even after everything she'd been through that evening.

"Are you crazy?" he asked. He drew in a lungful of air and scanned the area. The intruder was gone. At least out of sight. Who knew if he was still watching them? Taking aim?

"I want to know who keeps threatening me. I want to catch him." Frustration filled her voice and she kept clenching and unclenching her fingers.

He gripped her hand and pulled her back toward her house. "Come on. No sense in giving someone a perfect target." Once in the safety of her house, he called it in. Officers were on the way, although what he hoped they'd find, he couldn't say. The person had been dressed in black and wore gloves. If the front porch light hadn't been on, Brandon never would have seen him.

Back inside the house, he looked at Sonya. "What in the world were you thinking, taking off after him like that?"

She ran a hand through her tangled hair. "I knew you wouldn't chase him if it meant leaving me behind."

He blinked. And stared. She was absolutely right. "So you decided to run after him."

She shrugged and touched her throat with a wince. "I knew you'd be right behind me."

"You're fast."

"I run a lot."

He lifted a brow. "I can tell."

"I wasn't fast enough, though, was I?" she murmured.

"That might not be a bad thing. Don't do that again, okay?" He shuddered to think what might have happened had she actually caught up with the guy. "How's your throat?"

She lifted a hand and touched her throat with a grimace. "It hurts."

Two police cars pulled up, lights flashing. Sonya winced. "Could they at least turn their lights off? All of my neighbors are going to be over here within seconds."

Brandon walked out and flashed his badge. He asked

them to douse the lights then started his explanation of what had transpired over the past hour.

Sonya called Missy and let her know she'd be a little late, then went to pack her bags. When she came back into the den, the officers were gone and Brandon thought she looked exhausted. "It's a good thing you don't have to work tomorrow."

"Tell me about it."

"I hope you plan to sleep late. Just in case, I'm still going to have someone watching Missy's house."

She nodded. "Thank you."

The frown between her brows didn't bode well. "What is it?" he asked.

"I'm just wondering if I'm putting Missy at risk by staying with her."

Brandon wanted to reassure her, but he didn't want to tell her anything that wasn't true. He sighed. "I don't know. We're not telling anyone where you're going and we're going to have someone tailing us to make sure you get to Missy's house unobserved."

"Okay. That sounds good." The frown remained.

"What else?"

"What if whoever is after me knows I'm friends with her? The person wouldn't have to follow us. He could just be there waiting for me to show up."

Brandon pursed his lips then blew out a sigh. "Well, that's a possibility, of course, but I'm hoping with the two guys I've got watching you, if anyone is planning any more mayhem, these guys will scare them off."

Again she nodded. "Two guys?"

"Yes. One for the back and one for the front."

"Okay." The frown finally faded.

"So are you ready?"

"I guess so."

He held the door open for her. The two buddies he'd asked to stay on her tonight sat in their vehicles. He pointed to the red truck. "That's Max Powell." She waved. Max waved back. Brandon pointed to the black Explorer. "That's Peter Hayes, my brother."

"Your brother?"

"Yeah. He needed a job and I told him he could help out tonight."

"Oh. Okay. So he works for Finding the Lost on occasion?"

"On occasion. Sort of on an as-needed basis. It's a long story, Sonya. I'll tell you about it one day, but not tonight. Suffice it to say, Peter will do a good job, I promise."

"All right. If you trust him, I trust him."

Her simple faith in him made him swallow hard. He decided to tell her a bit more. "There's a lot of history with Peter. I'll be honest with you. He's a recovering drug addict, but he's been clean for months. He's doing his best to get his life back on track and I want to help him do that."

She shot him a warm smile. "I understand."

Peter got out of his car and walked to the back of Brandon's sedan. He leaned over and picked something up. Studied it.

"What is it?" Brandon asked.

"I'm not sure." He carried the item to the front porch and held it up to the light. "Looks like some sort of wire."

"What made you notice it?"

"When I backed up a little, my headlights swept across it. Thought it might be a nail and didn't want you to pick it up in your tire."

Brandon looked at the wire. Flashed back to the person behind his car. His gut tightened. "I've got a bad feeling about this."

Peter lifted a brow. "Why's that?"

"I need some light."

Sonya set her bag on the ground. "I've got a flashlight in the garage." She hurried to get it while Brandon moved to the back of his vehicle. Peter followed. Max got out of his vehicle. "What's going on, guys?"

Sonya returned with the flashlight. Brandon took it from her. "I want to check under my car. Someone was right behind it. If there's a tracking device, I want it. Or if someone was messing with any wires, I want to know which ones." Brandon stretched out on the driveway behind his car and shone the light underneath it. He looked at his brother. "Do you have a mirror?"

Peter shrugged. "Yeah, in my truck. Hold on a sec." He got it and returned to Brandon, who scooted a little farther under. His gasp jerked Sonya's head up.

"Max?" Brandon said.

"Yeah?"

"Can you take Sonya over to your vehicle and wait a minute?"

Max's gaze sharpened. Without another word, he motioned for Sonya to join him. Confusion on her face, she snagged her bag from the ground and walked over to Max. "What's going on?" She looked from one man to the next.

Peter's hands fisted and he stepped back. "Brandon, what do you see?"

Max gripped her upper arm and gently led her farther away. Brandon maneuvered out from under his vehicle, his face pale in the porch light.

"It's not a tracker."

"What is it?" Sonya asked.

Brandon continued walking toward her. "A bomb. We need a bomb squad."

Chapter 8

Sonya watched the bomb squad go to work. She wanted to scream, to give in and promise to quit looking for Heather Bradley. She didn't want people she cared about to be in danger because of her. She looked at the muscle jumping in Brandon's jaw and knew even if she decided to stop looking, he wouldn't.

The twitching muscle, narrowed eyes and hands on his hips shouted his determination to figure out who had just tried to blow him—them—up.

The clock pushed eleven-thirty and she texted Missy and told her friend to just go on to bed. Missy told her where to find the key, but made her promise to tell her everything in the morning.

Sonya agreed, but wondered if she'd even make it to her friend's house by morning. At this rate, she didn't know if she'd even be alive come morning. She swallowed hard and forced those thoughts from her mind. "Please, Lord, let us figure out who Heather Bradley is and who doesn't want us to know. I really don't want to die over this."

The whispered prayer echoed through her mind even as she walked over to hear Brandon ask, "How would it be detonated? It was under the back of the car. The person didn't have time to attach anything to the ignition."

"It wasn't going to go off until the person wanted it to."

"Remote detonation?"

"Yeah."

Brandon cocked his head. "I don't understand. We were all standing around the car at one point. Whoever had the remote could have blown us all to our final reward."

The bomb-squad member held up two wires. "These weren't attached. In order for the bomb to be remotely accessed, these wires have to be attached. My guess is you scared him off before he got them connected." He shook his head. "You guys are one lucky group."

Sonya swallowed hard. "I don't really care why. I think I'll just be grateful it didn't go off."

"I sure would be."

The man walked away and Brandon stepped over to Sonya. She looked up at him, thankful he was still here with her. She moved toward him and wrapped her arms around his waist and hugged him. He patted her back and gave her a hug. She stepped back. "Please don't ever put yourself in danger like that again."

He sighed. "I didn't realize I was in any danger until I saw the bomb." He paused. "And I guess I wasn't really in any danger if the bomb wasn't going to go off. Sure spiked my adrenaline when I saw it, though."

Neighbors crowded their porches and people moved into the street to get a better view of the happenings at her house. Sonya groaned. Just what she needed. An audience and an endless parade of neighbors with offers of help. Not that she didn't appreciate their kindness, but—

"Sonya?"

She turned. Doris Talbot. Her mother's best friend. The woman barely topped five feet and she was as wide as she was tall. Her heart was just as big and Sonya loved her dearly. She walked over and gave the woman a hug, inhaling the scent of mountain-fresh fabric softener and Pine-Sol. "Hi." This was one neighbor she didn't mind seeing.

"Honey, what's going on?"

"It's a really long story."

Mrs. Talbot glanced around at the flashing lights and milling law-enforcement officers. "I'll say." Her gaze lasered in on Sonya's throat. "What happened to you?"

"I had a little incident at work." Sonya had an idea. "Mrs. Talbot, did my mother ever say anything to you about a baby named Heather Bradley?"

"Heather Bradley?" She wrinkled her brow. "No, not that I recall. Why?"

Sonya forced a smile. "No reason. Mom just seemed really upset in her last few days and I can't figure out why."

"And you think a baby had something to do with it?"

"Maybe." Sonya sighed. It was late and Mrs. Talbot had sweat dripping into her eyes. As much as she'd like to continue questioning the woman, she knew she had heart issues. Being out in this humid heat and all the excitement of having law enforcement practically in her backyard probably wasn't good for her. She placed a hand on the woman's upper arm. "Why don't we talk tomorrow? I can explain a little more then."

"That's fine. What time? I'll make a dessert."

Sonya mentally went through her day tomorrow. She didn't have to work, but she did have to pick up her car. "Now, don't go to any trouble." She knew she would regardless of the admonition. "How about we make it lunch? I'll pick up some sandwiches. My treat."

The older woman's eyes lit up. "That sounds lovely."

Sonya gave her another hug. "Why don't you go home and cool off? All of the excitement around here is getting ready to come to an end anyway."

"Oh, yes. What happened?"

Sonya hesitated. "I thought I saw someone lurking outside my house." No way was she going to tell the woman about the bomb under Brandon's car. If she didn't recognize the bomb-squad vehicle, Sonya wasn't going to fill her in.

"What?" Mrs. Talbot placed a hand against her chest. "Oh, my. How dreadful. I won't sleep a wink tonight."

Sonya sighed. "Really, I don't think you have a thing to worry about. Please, get some rest. You're not in any danger. If there was someone here, he's long gone by now."

Mrs. Talbot looked uncertain. Then she gave a slow nod. "Guess I'll just have to trust the good Lord to keep me safe, eh?"

"Exactly." *Trust in the Lord with all your heart...*

"All right, I'll see you tomorrow, dear."

"Tomorrow."

Mrs. Talbot waddled home and Sonya turned to find

Brandon watching her. He smiled. "You ready to go to Missy's?"

"Yes, but I have one question."

"What's that?"

"You've got people who are going to be watching out for Missy and me, but who's going to be watching out for you?"

He trailed a gentle finger down her cheek and she shivered at the heat his touch evoked. "You don't need to worry about me. I can take care of myself."

"Not if someone decides to blow you up," she said. She knew it was blunt, but the fact remained that less than thirty minutes ago he'd had a bomb under his car.

He nodded. "Good point. But now that I know the attacks aren't limited to just you, I'll be more aware and on guard."

Sonya ran a hand through her hair and sighed. "Okay." She told him about having lunch with her neighbor tomorrow.

He nodded. "Do you mind if I join you?"

"Of course I don't mind." She gave him a small smile. "But I'll warn you. Mrs. Talbot is an outrageous flirt. Anytime there's a good-looking man around, her flirt radar is triggered."

His lips tipped upward. "So you think I'm good-looking?"

Sonya felt the heat arrive in her cheeks with a rush. "Um…well. Uh…sure."

He laughed. A laugh so full of amusement that it caught the attention of the other men. Peter raised a brow and Max sent a bemused grin in their direction.

Sonya allowed her own grin to spread. "Oh, wow, you really took advantage of that one, didn't you?"

"Sorry. I couldn't resist." Brandon snickered one more time, then traced her lips with a finger. "Now, that is a genuine smile."

A sweet tingling sensation spread through her. She snapped her lips together, but knew her eyes still held her laughter. He snagged her fingers with his. "Come on. I'll take you to Missy's."

The lighthearted moment felt strange given the seriousness of the situation, but she needed it. Desperately. Even though she was a tad embarrassed. Still, she could laugh at herself and decided that was a good thing. When he met Mrs. Talbot tomorrow, he wouldn't be laughing so hard.

But she probably would be.

Brandon walked into the office at seven-thirty the next morning. He found his sergeant, Christine Adams, drinking a cup of coffee and staring at the fax machine. His boss was a short woman, not more than five feet two inches, with dark brown hair she wore pulled up in a bun. She wore her makeup like body armor and he'd never seen her without it. "You have a minute, Sarge?"

Christine lowered her mug and lifted her dark eyes from the machine. "I guess standing here isn't going to get me the information any faster. Come on in my office."

Brandon followed her and shut the door behind him. Christine took a seat behind her desk and motioned him to one of the vacant chairs along the opposite wall, where he sat. "What's up?"

Brandon leaned back and crossed his legs. "I guess you heard about the excitement last night?"

"Some of it. Someone planted a bomb on your car?"

"Exactly."

"Who are you making mad?"

"Good question."

Christine pursed her lips and steepled her fingers in front of her as she studied him. "You need some time?"

"I think I do."

"I think you may be right. Someone planting a bomb on your vehicle is pretty serious stuff. Nothing to play around with."

"That's kind of the way I feel about it."

She nodded. "What can we do to help?"

He shrugged. "Hector said he'd cover our cases for me. If he needs help, it would be good to have another detective available."

"We can do that. What else?"

"Can I let you know as things come up?"

"Of course." Christine frowned. "Keep me updated, Brandon. You're a good detective and I don't want to lose you."

"Thanks, I appreciate it. And the time."

She nodded. Her phone rang and she lifted a hand to wave. His dismissal. He didn't take it personally. He liked Christine and respected her. She was good at her job and she took care of her detectives. He appreciated that.

Brandon went to his office and found Hector at his desk. "I'm taking off a few days."

"If someone planted a bomb on my car, I would, too."

"That's not the only reason, but I'm going to need your help."

"You name it."

Brandon sat down. "You got a minute?"

"All day."

"Then I want to tell you what's going on."

For the next few minutes, Brandon brought his partner up to speed on everything that had happened from the time Sonya had walked into his office until he'd found the bomb under his car.

Hector shook his head. "And you have no idea who this Heather Bradley is?"

"Just that she was kidnapped as an infant."

"And you think Sonya Daniels is Heather."

"Maybe. She looks like Don Bradley and favors Ann a bit." He shrugged. "I dropped some samples off at the lab, so I'm still waiting for the results."

"What's your gut feeling?"

"My gut says she's Heather Bradley and the kidnapper knows she's back."

Chapter 9

Sonya rolled over and pulled the covers over her head. Then smelled coffee and sat up. She could hear Missy in the kitchen, humming a tuneless melody. Her entire body ached. She touched her throat and grimaced. The stitches felt hot and uncomfortable, but nothing a couple of ibuprofen tablets couldn't handle.

After a quick shower and an abbreviated morning routine, she made her way into the kitchen.

Missy sat at the table, her steaming mug and Bible in front of her. She looked up and smiled. "Morning."

"Hey."

"Coffee's over there."

"Thanks."

Sonya poured herself a cup and popped two pieces of bread into the toaster.

"Are you going to tell me what happened last night or keep me in suspense until I simply burst?"

Sonya gave a small laugh, then quickly sobered. "How long did the police stay at the hospital questioning people after I left?"

"Forever. Now, what happened?"

When Sonya finished her recap of the day's events, Missy stared wide-eyed, jaw hanging. Sonya sighed. "So now I don't know whether I should stay here or not. I probably need to figure something else out."

"Absolutely not."

Sonya looked at her friend. "I appreciate your willingness to let me stay, but I won't put you in danger."

"I'm not giving you a choice. You're staying right here." She got up and walked to the window and looked out. "And cool. We have our own personal bodyguards."

"Missy, I don't think you understand. This person wasn't playing around. He put a bomb under Brandon's car."

Missy frowned. "I know. I get that, but I still think you'd be safer here with me than off on your own somewhere. Just stay, okay?"

"I wouldn't necessarily be on my own, but—"

"Good. Then it's settled."

Sonya blinked. "Missy—"

"Now, what are you going to do all day?" She narrowed her eyes at the wound on Sonya's neck. "You should probably rest. Have you taken your antibiotic?"

Sonya sighed. "Yes, I took it this morning. And I'm meeting my neighbor for lunch to talk to her about anything my mother may have said to her before she died."

"Well, sounds like a plan. I'm going to babysit my four-year-old niece while my sister goes to have her hair done. Will you text me throughout the day and let me know you're all right?"

Sonya's heart warmed. It was nice to have someone who cared. "Sure. And thanks."

"No worries."

"But the minute it looks like you're being targeted because of your association with me, I'm out of here, okay?"

"Okay. Now hush and let me finish my quiet time."

Sonya smiled and took a sip of her coffee, fixed her toast with the apple butter she found in the fridge and went into the den. Having a quiet time sounded like a wonderful idea.

At eleven-thirty, Brandon pulled up in front of Missy's house. He waved to Peter, who'd stayed most of the night and insisted on taking the morning hours until Brandon's arrival. Now he'd go home to sleep and be ready for more duty if Brandon needed him later.

He opened the door to step out at the same time Sonya opened the front door. She must have been waiting for him. He climbed out and went around to open the passenger door for her. "Good morning." He noticed the hint of vanilla when she stepped close to him. The sun picked up the red highlights in her hair. Hair that looked soft and silky and made him itch to run his fingers through it.

"Hi. Thanks for picking me up."

He balled his fingers into fists and told himself to stop. She was off-limits. For now. "No problem."

"I'm guessing you checked under your car this morning?"

He gave a short laugh. "Trust me, I went over it with a fine-tooth comb."

"Good."

"And when we go to pick yours up, I'll do the same."

His statement silenced her for a brief moment. Then she rubbed her forehead. "I didn't even think about that."

"That's what I'm here for."

She reached over and took his hand in hers and squeezed. "And I want you to know how very thankful I am for that."

Her words shattered part of the wall around his heart, and he tightened his hand around hers even while his mind screamed at him to put the distance back, push her away. He cleared his throat. "That's why you're paying me the big bucks, right?"

She slipped her hand away from his, and he had no trouble discerning her cooling attitude. "Of course." She paused. "Do you mind swinging by the Sandwich Factory? I told Mrs. Talbot I'd bring sandwiches."

"Sonya, I—"

She turned her head to look out the window, effectively cutting him off. He wanted to kick himself. He hadn't meant to hurt her, but in fear of his growing feelings for her, his desperate need to put some space between them, he'd done just that.

He pulled away from the curb and drew in a deep breath. More vanilla. And coffee. He wondered if she liked cream and sugar in it or drank it black.

"Thank you for arranging protection last night," she said, her tone neutral.

"You're welcome. I'm just glad the rest of the night was uneventful."

She blew out a breath and turned back toward him. "Me, too." Her frostiness had melted slightly, as though she'd made up her mind not to be mad at him.

"I'd stay and watch each night if I didn't need to be alert during the day. Peter's a night owl anyway. He can go home and sleep."

"So tell me about your family. There's Peter. And I know Erica's your sister. Any other siblings?"

"No." He heard his curt tone, but couldn't seem to help it. Talking about his family ranked number one on his least-favorite-things-to-do list.

This time his snappy reply didn't seem to faze her. "I got the feeling you were close to Erica."

"I am."

"And you give your brother a job when he needs one. But you don't like talking about your family."

So she'd noticed.

Relief filled him as he pulled into the parking lot of the Sandwich Factory. She shot him a thin smile. "I'll be right back."

"I'm coming with you." He didn't want her walking in alone. They'd told no one their destination, but he still wanted to stay close to her.

Together, they walked into the restaurant. She stood in line and Brandon watched her watch others. She'd become more alert, more aware of her surroundings since walking into his office two weeks ago. He was glad and pained at the same time. The line moved fast, and since she'd called the order in, they were back in the car within minutes. Sonya settled the bag at her feet.

Brandon glanced around, his senses sharp. Had they been followed? There'd been no indication anyone had been behind them, but he didn't let that stop him from being on the alert.

"Family's always been very important to me." She picked up right where she'd left off and he gave a silent groan. "The possibility of finding out that my parents aren't really my parents is scary. And incredibly hurtful. I have so many great memories with them. I just can't picture them doing anything illegal like adopting a kidnapped child."

He could imagine. He'd also hoped the whole family topic had been shelved. But it hadn't. Sonya was obviously still thinking about their previous conversation. Personally, he wouldn't mind finding out he had another set of parents somewhere, but didn't figure he'd voice that thought. "That's understandable."

He could feel her gaze boring into him. "What would you do if you were in my shoes?"

He didn't answer right away. In fact, he thought long and hard about it. She seemed to understand that he was thinking and didn't rush his answer. Finally, he said, "I would wait until I had all the facts before I made any decisions one way or another. If the DNA results come back that you're not related to Heather Bradley, then you can probably rest easy that you're not adopted."

"And if they come back saying otherwise?"

He sighed. "Then I suppose you'll have to deal with it, but until we know for sure, let's just focus on the facts."

"Which are?"

"Someone doesn't want us finding Heather Bradley and is willing to go to extreme lengths to keep us from looking for her."

"But who? Who benefits from us not finding her?"

"The only person I can think of is the person who kidnapped her."

"Agreed." She thought about it. "What about their adopted son? I mean, the Bradleys have a lot of money. What if he feels threatened? Like, if I'm proven to be

Heather, he'll have to split the inheritance." She shook her head. "He wouldn't, though. I don't care about their money. I just want the truth."

He nodded. "I thought about that. I've got my partner, Hector, looking into him in addition to anyone who was close to the family at the time Heather disappeared."

"Why do you think it was someone close?"

"Heather disappeared from the church nursery. Whoever took her is someone who fit in at the church and didn't stand out in any way. I read the report and all of the interviews done the day of the kidnapping. It was really pretty thorough. No one reported seeing anyone strange that Sunday. No one who made them stop twice for a second look."

"What about visitors?"

"The church was the largest one in town. They had visitors every Sunday. Visitors had the option to fill out a visitor card—or not. So even if we had a list of everyone who attended that day, there's no guarantee the person who took Heather filled anything out."

"No, the kidnapper wouldn't have wanted to leave any kind of trace. And if it was someone in the church, he—or she—would have known about the visitor cards."

"Right. So, Hector's looking into Mr. Bradley's business connections back then. See if anything makes a blip on the radar." He turned onto Mrs. Talbot's street and Sonya looked over at her mother's house. Now hers. It looked absolutely normal with no sign of the drama that had played out last night.

He parked the car and Mrs. Talbot stepped out onto her front porch, a wide smile of greeting on her lined face. She waved. "Come on in. I've got desserts all ready for after the sandwiches."

"Desserts?" he whispered.

"She's a baker. Trust me, you'll love anything she puts in front of you."

His mouth started watering before his foot hit the first step.

Sonya stepped inside the familiar foyer and her throat clogged with tears. As a child, she'd grown up about an hour and a half away, but her mother had always loved Spartanburg, having lived here until she met Sonya's father.

Throughout Sonya's childhood, they'd made trips to visit, always stopping to see Mrs. Talbot, who became like a grandmother to Sonya. Sonya's mother and Mrs. Talbot might have had a twenty-year age difference, but they'd been tight friends.

When the house across the street had come up for sale, shortly after Sonya had gone off to college, her father had purchased it and her parents moved home. Sonya finished undergraduate school, then graduate. One semester away from fulfilling her dream of becoming a doctor, she'd come home to take care of her mother.

A woman who might not be her mother.

Sonya introduced Brandon to the woman. Mrs. Talbot grinned. "So, you're Sonya's young man, are you?"

Brandon lifted a brow and glanced at Sonya. She knew her face was three different shades of red. "No, Mrs. Talbot, we're...friends," she answered before Brandon had a chance to say anything. No sense in going into everything right now.

"Well, if you're not smart enough to snag him, I might have a go at it." She winked at Brandon and turned toward the kitchen, fingers clutched around the sandwich bag. "Handsome thing like that, girl's got no sense if she's not going after that one...." She disappeared into the kitchen.

Sonya sighed and shook her head. "I told you."

Brandon grinned. "This is going to be interesting, isn't it?"

"You have no idea." He shut the door behind them, but not before she saw him take a look down the street, first to the right, then to the left. "See anything?"

The door snicked closed. "No."

"But you think someone followed us?"

"I don't know. I just want to be careful not to let my guard down."

She nodded. "I'm going to help Mrs. Talbot."

"I'm going to watch the street."

Sonya frowned. "All right." His vigilance hit home. The niggling thought that she might be putting the older woman in danger just by being in her house wouldn't leave her alone. Sonya decided they probably needed to eat and talk and get out as fast as they could without being rude.

Mrs. Talbot hummed as she worked, setting the sandwiches on her fine china. "Why don't you pour the tea, child?"

Sonya smiled. She'd always be a child to this dear lady. She did as instructed. "Do you mind if I ask you a couple of strange questions?"

"Strange questions?"

"About my mother."

Grief flashed across Mrs. Talbot's face. "No, I don't mind. I love talking about your mother. Goodness, I do miss that woman."

"I know." Sonya swallowed against the instant tears. "I miss her, too."

"Your father, too. He was such a good man. Loved your mother and you like I've never seen before. Would have done anything for the two of you."

"Yes, I know. Daddy was a wonderful man."

Mrs. Talbot cocked her head toward the den area, where Brandon was. "That one got potential?"

Sonya refused to blush. "He's helping me with something."

"What's that?"

"I found something in Mom's closet when I was going through her house, getting it ready for the estate sale."

Mrs. Talbot paused and studied her. "Something that has you troubled. What was it?"

"A baby bag with a birth certificate."

"Yours?"

"No. It belonged to a baby named Heather Bradley. Did Mom ever say anything about it?"

"No, she never did."

"You saw her in her last days. Did you notice how troubled she was?"

A sigh slipped from the woman's lips. "Well, truth be told, I did notice she seemed fairly agitated, but I thought she was just in pain."

She had been in pain, of course. "I think it was more than the physical pain of her disease. I think it was something else."

"Like what?"

Frustration filled Sonya. "Like something was on her mind and troubling her." She sighed. "I wish I knew."

"And I wish I could help you, honey, but I can't recall anything. She never said a word to me about anything that was troubling her. Other than leaving you, of course. She hated to leave you."

Sonya's throat closed and she fought the tears that wanted to flow.

Mrs. Talbot motioned toward the table. "Call your young man in here and let's eat."

Sonya nodded and took a deep breath. She wouldn't cry. She didn't have time for tears. If she could stay focused on the goal of finding out about the baby bag and Heather Bradley, she would be all right.

Throughout lunch, Sonya asked question after question and finally realized she wasn't going to get any more information from Mrs. Talbot. Although she had to admit watching Brandon gently field the woman's flirtatious comments was quite amusing.

He even thrilled Mrs. Talbot by flirting back a bit. Lighthearted and innocent, the woman giggled like a schoolgirl. Sonya thought it was charming and sweet and said a lot about Brandon's true personality. She found herself drawn even more to the man.

When Mrs. Talbot wasn't flirting, she enjoyed reminiscing and telling stories about Sonya's mother, but repeated that she had no idea about Heather Bradley or what her friend might have been so agitated about in the last few weeks of her life.

Brandon and Sonya left with promises to visit again soon. Sonya climbed into Brandon's car and shut the door.

He slipped in beside her. "She's quite a character, isn't she?"

"That's putting it mildly, but I love her."

"I can see why. I wonder if my siblings and I would have turned out different if we'd had someone like her in our lives."

His personal comment made her pause. "What do you mean?"

He flushed. "Nothing. It's not important."

She huffed. "Is it just me? Or do you shut everyone out?"

He stiffened. "I don't shut everyone out."

"Okay."

He drove for the next few minutes in silence. "I don't."

"Okay."

He tapped the wheel with his hands and hummed an eighties tune she recognized, but couldn't name. He stopped humming. "Do I?"

"Yes."

"Oh." Another long pause. "I'm sorry."

She shrugged. "I think it's just become a habit with you."

He didn't answer and she looked at him, ready to repeat the statement, but the look on his face stopped her. He was staring into the mirror, eyes narrowed, jaw tight. "What is it?" she asked.

"We've got company and I don't think it's the good kind."

Chapter 10

Brandon sped up.

"Who is it? Can you see?"

"No, but he's been on us since we turned out of your subdivision."

"You think he saw us leave Mrs. Talbot's?"

"I'm not sure. I don't think so. I think he was waiting at the entrance."

She turned to look out the back. "It's a brown sedan. Very nondescript."

The car continued to close in. Brandon sped up. The sedan backed off.

"Wish I could see the license plate."

Brandon pulled his phone from the cup holder and called in the description of the vehicle. The car stayed with them as he came to a red light. "I'm going to stop and see what he does. Duck down."

"But—"

"Just do it," he snapped.

Sonya flinched and unclipped her seat belt. She slid down half on the seat, halfway on the floorboard, her brown eyes never leaving his face. He swallowed. He'd been too sharp. In a soft tone he said, "There's a police cruiser just thirty seconds away. He'll be here before I stop at the light."

He hoped.

Brandon pressed the brake and slowed. The sedan stayed on his tail.

Closer. And the vehicle came to a smooth stop just behind his bumper.

Blue lights flashed almost immediately behind the sedan. The driver opened the door and shoved his hands upward.

And Brandon realized who it was. "You can get back up, Sonya. Sorry I snapped at you."

"Who is it?" she asked as she maneuvered back into the seat.

"Spike."

"Spike? What's he doing?"

Brandon threw open his door. "That's what I'm going to find out."

He walked back to the young man, who looked a lot more stressed than the last time he'd seen him just a couple of days ago at the restaurant. The officers from the cruiser had stepped out and approached Spike, hands on their weapons. Brandon waved them off. "Sorry, guys. False alarm."

The officer relaxed. "You sure?" Brandon thought he recognized the man who spoke. Jason Newman, a rookie, but one with promise.

"I'm sure. I've got this."

The officers climbed back into their vehicle and left. Brandon turned to Spike, who still had his hands in the air. "Get out of the car, man. What in the world are you doing?"

Spike stood, eyes lowered. "Looking for you."

"You couldn't use a cell phone like usual?"

He shook his head. "I couldn't pay the bill."

"Ah. Okay, then, a friend's phone?"

Another negative.

"Tell me why you're looking for me."

"My mama's sick and I can't afford her medicine."

Brandon got it now.

"Get in the car and follow me to the drugstore."

Spike's head jerked up and his gaze met Brandon's. "I ain't takin' no charity, dude. My mama would have a fit."

Brandon understood the pride behind the token protest. "You don't have to tell her how you paid for it."

Spike's eyes drifted over Brandon's left shoulder. "You're with her again."

"Yes."

He nodded. "Never mind."

"I trust her."

Spike paused. "For real or you playin' me?"

"For real."

"All right, then."

"You lead. I'll follow."

Brandon climbed back in the car and waited for the light to turn green. Their small drama in the street had backed up traffic, although once the other officers left, the cars had started to go around them.

Spike passed him and Brandon fell in behind him.

"What's going on?" Sonya asked.

"I'm doing a favor for a friend." He explained about Spike's mother. "She's got sickle cell and can't afford her medicine. I once told Spike, if he ever found himself in a situation where he needed help, to ask me. He doesn't have any money for the medicine."

"So you gave it to him?"

"No, I'm following him to the pharmacy to buy it for him."

"He's a recovering addict?"

"Yeah. He's been clean for about a year. The medicine's expensive. If I put that much money in his hands, he might be tempted to spend it elsewhere. I won't do that and he knows it." He felt Sonya's eyes on him and it made him a tad uncomfortable. "What?"

"You're a good man, aren't you?"

Now Brandon just felt embarrassed. "I don't know about good, but helping a kid when he needs it seems to be the right thing to do."

"Whatever you do for the least of these," she murmured.

He caught the words and gave her a smile.

Thirty minutes later, Spike had the medicine, three burgers, a large fries and a chocolate shake. He also had a full tank of gas and two bags of groceries, thanks to Brandon's generosity. It wasn't the first time satisfaction filled him after helping someone like Spike. Not from a sense of pride, but from knowing Spike would have a good night and his mother would have her meds.

Brandon hadn't had anyone do that for him when he'd been Spike's age, and he'd vowed if he ever found a way to help kids who couldn't help themselves, he'd do it.

His phone rang. "Hello?"

"Where are you, man?" It was Hector.

"On Calhoun. Why?"

"Can you come down to the station? We've got some video from one of your lady's neighbors. He called us and said he thought he got a picture of the guy who was sneaking around Sonya's house. Even has him at the trunk of your car. It's grainy and fuzzy and the guy has on a hat, so it's probably a long shot, but…"

His lady? What was it with everyone throwing him and Sonya together? First Mrs. Talbot with her "your young man" stuff, now Hector? But he was surprised to find he really didn't mind that much. He'd set Hector straight later. Maybe. "We'll be there in a few minutes." He hung up.

"What is it?" Sonya asked.

"Do you mind coming down to the police station? Hector got a picture from one of your neighbors' security cameras." He paused. "Who would have that kind of security?"

"Mr. Lehman," she answered without hesitation. "He's a retired police officer and his house is wired to the nth degree. He lives directly across the street from me. He has cameras pointed toward the street, which would cover my house. He also has them aimed up and down the street." She slapped her head. "I can't believe I didn't think to ask him about it."

"He called and volunteered it."

"Well, good. Maybe we'll finally see who it is."

"Hector said it isn't a very good picture."

"Well, it won't hurt to look."

Ten minutes later, they walked into the police station. Brandon waved back at those who acknowledged him, but led Sonya straight to his and Hector's desks. The station was a big open room. Desks and phones took up most of the space.

Hector looked up. When his eyes landed on Sonya, his brows lifted and he gave Brandon a thumbs-up. Brandon ground his molars and gave his partner a look that should have sent him scurrying. Instead, Hector grinned. Brandon noticed Sonya's lack of attention and sent up a silent prayer of thanks that she'd missed the communication between him and Hector. Her head swiveled on her neck and he realized she'd never been in a police station before. "It can be a little overwhelming. Just stick with me."

"Right."

She settled in the chair next to his desk. Brandon introduced her to Hector, who held her hand a few seconds too long, in his opinion. Hector loved women and women loved Hector. Brandon scowled when Sonya smiled prettily. But it wasn't flirty. He breathed deep and tried to resist the sudden flashes of memory. His ex-fiancée telling him she was seeing someone else. Then after they'd split, running into her with her new man at a restaurant and trying to pretend he was all right.

It had hurt.

But looking at Sonya now, he realized it didn't hurt as bad as it had a year ago.

"Bran?"

Hector's voice cut through the memories and he saw they were staring at him. "Oh, right. Sorry. I was thinking about something."

Hector made a humming noise in his throat and let his gaze bounce between Sonya and him. Then he said nothing more, just grabbed a photo from his desk and handed it to Sonya. "Anything look familiar?"

She squinted at the photo, tilted her head and sighed. "No."

"Didn't think you'd get much from it."

She pointed. "Look, there's a smudge—or something—on his right shoulder. Where his shirt slipped down a bit, you can see it. Is that a tattoo?"

Brandon leaned in. "Possibly." He looked at Hector. "Can we get that area enlarged?"

"We can, but it may blur it right out."

"Let's try."

"All right. It'll take a little while to get it back."

Brandon nodded. "I'll put a call in to the lab and request a rush." Hector laughed and Brandon shrugged. "Hey, it can't hurt."

"Brandon?"

He turned to see Mary Ann Delaney, one of the station's secretaries, waving at him. "Yes?"

"You have a visitor."

"A visitor?" He frowned. "Who?"

"Your mother."

Sonya saw him freeze. Saw him go totally still for a full five seconds as a woman with red hair headed toward him. She had a trim figure and green eyes that sparkled.

"That's your mother?" she asked.

"Yes."

"Wow, she's beautiful. She looks more like your sister than your mother."

His eyes shuttered and his lips thinned. "That's what happens when your mother's only sixteen years older than you are. She's in her mid-forties." His even, flat tone gave nothing—and everything—away.

"Oh." She cleared her throat. "Could you tell me where the nearest ladies' room is?"

He shot her a grateful look. "We passed it on our way in. There on the left." He pointed and she slipped inside before mother and son greeted each other.

Sonya decided to take advantage of the time and wound up retouching what little makeup she wore, and then she brushed her hair and washed her hands.

In the midst of drying her hands, the door opened and two female officers stepped inside. "Can you believe it?"

"She has some nerve showing up here."

"I heard she and her husband are still married, but they abandoned the children when they were younger. Now she's wanting to cozy up and make nice."

The two women talked as though Sonya were invisible.

"I don't see Brandon putting up with that for long. The last time she showed up, he was real quick to show her the door."

Sonya's ears perked up at Brandon's name.

"I don't know, Olivia." The woman paused to check her makeup in the mirror. Sonya was starting to feel like a fifth wheel. "Brandon's his own person. He's not going to let his mommy run his life, but it looks like she might be wearing him down."

"I didn't say she was trying to run his life. It just seems to me she's pushing for something that's not going to happen. I don't think she's wearing him down at all." The woman stepped into one of the vacant stalls, still talking.

Okay, that was it. Sonya couldn't stand here and listen to them spout their gossip any longer.

Olivia patted her nose. "I think she's just after him

because he's a success. He's slightly famous around here and she wants a piece of the status."

"What status?" Sonya blurted.

The officer paused in her reapplication of lip gloss and stared at Sonya as though seeing her for the first time. Sonya thought police officers were supposed to be observant. Honestly.

The officer said, "Excuse me?"

"Brandon is a friend and I don't think he'd appreciate your speculation on his family relationships. No offense, but it's not really your business unless he makes it so." She held up a hand to forestall the woman's words. "And your conversation wasn't my business, either. Sorry for butting in."

But she really wasn't.

She opened the door and stepped out without another word, heart beating so fast she was afraid it might leap out of her chest. She'd never done anything like that before in her life.

A small smile slipped across her lips. But she had to admit, it had felt good. And right.

The next words she heard wiped the smile off her lips.

"I said no, Mom. Now drop it."

Brandon's cold tone was enough to send shivers up her spine.

"But, son—"

"I've got work to do. Let me walk you out."

Sonya bit her lip as she watched Brandon take his mother's elbow and direct her toward the exit. Hector blew out a sigh. "One day he's going to have to forgive them."

"Who?" she asked.

"His parents." He snapped his lips closed then said, "But you didn't hear that from me."

"Seems like I'm hearing a lot of stuff today," she murmured.

"You're what?"

She glanced at him. "Nothing."

Brandon came back into the building and headed for his desk. Tension radiated from him and Sonya hated it for him. "Goodness, he has some real issues with his family, doesn't he?"

Hector shot her a sharp look. "If you grew up with his parents, you would, too."

"I wasn't being critical," she apologized.

He shrugged. "I was being defensive." He looked at his partner, who'd stopped to speak to another officer. "And he doesn't need my defense. He can handle it himself."

"He doesn't talk about his family much."

"No, he doesn't. It's a topic he avoids, and if you value your hide, you'll stay away from it, too."

Sonya simply watched the man she was starting to care way too much for. She wanted to know what his childhood had been like. She wanted to know how he'd risen up and become a respected citizen, a decorated cop. But that was for him to tell her. She might be curious, but she wouldn't listen to gossip. She wanted the facts from him.

He finally broke away and came back to his desk.

"Are you all right?" she asked.

He pinched the bridge of his nose and shook his head. "I'm fine. Personal stuff that shouldn't happen in the office. She knows I don't appreciate her showing up like that."

Sonya frowned. "Then why would she do it?"

"No worries, my friend," Hector said before Brandon had to answer. He waved the photo and changed the subject. "So we've got a suspect who has a mark on his shoulder."

"Right."

"Fuzzy enough not to be able to make it out, but we'll give the guys who like to play with photos a chance to clear it up a bit."

"Great." Brandon still looked as if his attention was elsewhere. Then he gave a visible shake and rolled his shoulders as though pushing off the stress his mother's appearance had put him under. "All right. Here's the deal—" His phone rang. He glanced at the screen then at Sonya. "It's Holt, my buddy at the lab."

"Oh, good," she breathed.

"Hello?"

He listened and Sonya strained to hear what Holt was saying, but couldn't catch a word. Brandon nodded. "All right, thanks for letting me know. And thanks for staying late to run the tests. We appreciate it."

He hung up and looked at Sonya. She gulped. "He did the DNA test, didn't he? And got the results?"

"He did."

"And?"

"You and Heather Bradley are a one hundred percent match," he said.

Chapter 11

Brandon watched her absorb the news. He couldn't say he was especially surprised. Not after seeing her next to Don Bradley.

Sonya pulled in a deep breath. "All right, so what does that mean? The parents I grew up with stole me?" Her jaw hardened. "I don't believe it."

"It could be they had no idea you were a kidnapped child. It could be you were a black-market baby. Someone kidnapped you and sold you to the highest bidder, so to speak." Brandon spoke gently. She'd had a shock. And while it looked as though she was dealing with it, he knew she was in for some rough times ahead. He found himself wanting to be there for her. He reached around the desk and took her hand. It trembled in his.

Tears hovered on her lashes, but didn't fall. "So. I'm

Heather Bradley. I guess the next step is to let the Bradleys know, right?"

"Yes." He picked his phone up from the desk. "I'll call Don and ask him if we can meet."

She nodded and sniffed. "Today. I want to do it today. If he has the time."

"I'd rather tell him in person. Over the phone seems pretty cold."

"Yes. In person is probably best."

Hector tapped his pen against his desk. "Do you want me to look into your parents' past? See if I can find any record of adoption or how they came to have you?"

Brandon saw a flurry of emotions cross her face, and then she nodded. "Yes. I've come this far. I might as well find out the whole story." She twisted the strap on her purse. "If I don't, I'll just wonder."

"I'll take care of it." Hector made a few notes. "Also, I would think you would want to do DNA tests with the Bradleys."

Sonya blinked. "Why?"

"For their peace of mind, for one thing. Just for extra confirmation."

Brandon dialed the number. Don picked up on the first ring. "Hello?"

"Hello, Don. Brandon Hayes here. I was wondering if you'd have some time to speak with us again."

"I'm at my office. Could you come here?"

"Of course. What time?"

"Anytime."

"We're on our way."

"You have some news, don't you?" He asked the question hesitantly.

"Yes."

"All right." Now the man sounded downright nervous. "I'll be waiting."

Brandon hung up. "All right, let's go."

Sonya stood. "I'm ready."

Hector held up a hand. "Hold on a sec." He had his phone pressed to his ear, listening. He nodded and hung up. "I ran down the Bradleys' son, Donald Junior. He's an accountant for Grand National Bank in Texas. He's been at a conference in San Diego for the past three days. He flies home tomorrow."

"Is he really there?" Brandon asked.

"He's there. He's one of the main speakers and hasn't missed a session."

"Then he's not the one after me," Sonya mused.

"Unless he paid someone," Brandon muttered. He looked at Hector. "Thanks."

"Sure thing."

Brandon escorted her down to where he'd parked the car and helped her in. She had her seat belt fastened by the time he climbed behind the wheel. "Are you all right?"

She let out a sigh. "I'm stunned, Brandon. My brain is whirling, and I don't know what happened or how my parents ended up with me. A kidnapped baby. I don't know why my mother had the baby bag and birth certificate in her closet or how it came to be there because I'd never seen it before that day. I don't know a lot of things, but I'm ready to find some answers."

He reached over to clasp her hand in his. Her strength and determination only made him admire her more. "You're a pretty amazing woman, you know that?"

She let out a low, humorless laugh. "No, I'm clinging to God with everything I have in me when all I really want to do is go home, bury my head under the covers and pretend this is all a bad dream." Tears floated to the surface again. And again she held them back. She lasered him with an intense look that shot straight to his heart. "I'm so glad I have you working on this with me, though. I really don't know what I would do without you," she whispered.

Her words rocked him, but didn't stop him from pulling her into a hug. "We'll get through this. I'm not going anywhere until you're safe and we have the answers you need."

"What if I never find them, Brandon? What if we just keep going in circles?"

He laid a light kiss on her lips, his desire to comfort her so strong it nearly strangled him. "Well, if you never find the answers, I guess that means I'm going to be around an awfully long time."

She flushed and he swiped a stray tear. "Thanks," she whispered.

"Welcome," he whispered back. Then let her go to start the car.

The twenty-minute drive to Don Bradley's office passed in a comfortable silence, both of them lost in their thoughts even though Brandon continued to keep an eye on their surroundings, alert for any hint of danger. But while his eyes roamed, his brain spun with his feelings for the lady beside him. She'd wiggled her way into his heart when he hadn't been looking. And that scared him. He hated to admit being afraid, especially since not much scared him.

His feelings for Sonya had him tied in knots. So what was he going to do about it?

Nothing.

She was a client.

Then you'd better stop kissing her. The thought taunted him. There was no way he wanted to lead her on, but the thought of her walking out of his life when all of this was over was simply unbearable.

He glanced at her. She had her eyes closed and her head against the window. Probably praying.

Maybe he should try it.

God? You know I believe in You even though I've been mad at You for a while now. Is it too late to ask for Your help? Not necessarily for me, but for Sonya. She really needs You. She believes You're there for her. She's hanging on to You. Could You just keep us safe? And help us figure out who wants us dead?

The prayer felt strange. And familiar.

He felt her gaze on him. "What are you thinking?" she asked.

"Nothing."

"Liar." The word lacked heat. It was a gentle rebuke that made him shoot her a rueful grin.

"Yeah. I wasn't really thinking. I was...praying."

That got her attention. Her brows shot up. "Really?"

"Yes."

"I didn't know you prayed."

He snorted. "I pray. Just not very often."

"Oh."

"I've been...mad at God. About a lot of stuff."

"Like your mom?"

He sighed. "Yes. Like my mom. And even my dad. But mostly my mom."

"Will you tell me why?"

He glanced at her again. The compassion in her eyes twisted his heart inside out. How could she do that to him with just one look? "I didn't have a horrible child-hood, if that's what you're thinking."

"Oh. Well, yes, that's kind of what I was thinking."

"My parents were teenage sweethearts. They got pregnant when my mother was sixteen. Instead of having parents raise us, we were all more or less like siblings. In the early part of our lives, my parents pretty much just ignored us. They partied. We were in the foster-care system a few times. Then they got us back after they took parenting classes and promised to party less." He narrated the story as though telling about someone else's life. It was the only way he could talk about it without the bitterness rising up to choke him. He looked at her. Felt her hand rest against his upper arm. He shrugged. "They started studying and going to school. Once we were old enough to be latchkey kids, we were. Mom became a nurse, Dad a mechanic. They worked all the time and we three kids fended for ourselves."

"But you turned out all right."

"We did. We had some good neighbors who kind of looked out for us. We even went to church with some of the other children in the neighborhood, catching a ride with whoever was going." He sighed. "It wasn't a miserable existence, but it wasn't ideal, either." He paused. "I wanted parents like some of the other kids had. The ones who came to the school plays and football games. I was quarterback and neither one of my parents ever made it to one of my games."

"Oh, Brandon, that's so sad."

"Exactly. And so now you know. I was angry for a long time. Then I pushed it aside and focused on making something of my life."

"And what about your mother? She came to the station today."

"Yes. My mother." He shook his head. "She's trying to make up for lost time, I guess. She wants me to come to dinner Sunday."

"Are you going?"

"No." He heard the flat, cold word leave his lips. It effectively ended the conversation. That, and the fact that they'd arrived at their destination. He turned into the parking lot and found a spot under a shady tree.

He opened the door and stepped out of the car. His window exploded and he heard Sonya scream his name.

Chapter 12

Sonya screamed again as the next bullet caught Brandon in his left shoulder. He went down. The few people in the parking lot took cover and grabbed for cell phones.

She scrambled across the seat to the open driver's door and grasped his hand to help pull him back into the car. He slammed the door, his fingers searching for the seat button to push it back as far as it would go.

"Are you all right?" she gasped, terror pumping the blood through her veins in double time. "Let me look at it."

"It's a scratch. Call 911."

Sonya saw that his color was only a couple of shades lighter than normal and his shoulder wasn't bleeding much. She found her phone and punched in the three digits.

"911, what's your emergency?"

"Someone's shooting at us." She gave the address, wondering if the woman could understand her shaky words.

"Units are on the way. Stay in a safe area if at all possible."

Another shot took out the back window.

Brandon muttered something under his breath but Sonya didn't catch it. He lifted his head and stared out the back. "I see him. Stay here."

"What?"

But he didn't answer. He shoved the driver's door open and bolted toward the large industrial-sized trash can for cover. A bullet dinged off the metal. Sonya debated whether to run after Brandon, go for the building or stay put.

He made it to the next building and used one of the concrete columns in front as a shield. Another bullet. And another.

And then he was across the street.

Sonya opened her door and waited.

No bullets came her way.

She looked out the back window and saw a figure on the second floor of the parking garage across the street lift his gun, turn and run.

Sirens sounded. She made the final decision not to let Brandon face the would-be killer alone.

She bolted from the car and followed in his footsteps.

Brandon had seen the man with the gun on the second floor of the parking garage. This time he wasn't getting away. Ignoring the throbbing of the wound in his shoulder, he raced into the garage, his weapon held in both hands, pointing down.

Footsteps sounded above him. He raced toward them. A woman with a baby started to get out of her car. Brandon used his left hand to flash his badge. "Get back in the car and lock the door, then get out of the garage."

She gaped at the badge and the gun, then obeyed without question, her face pale and scared. He heard her start the car. He waited until she was headed for the exit before moving to the ramp that would take him to the second floor.

Brandon could hear the sirens. He needed to call in his location and request backup, but he didn't dare stop yet. He came to the end of the ramp.

Stopped and listened.

Nothing. No more footsteps. His heart thundered in his chest and his adrenaline flowed, but he kept his breathing even, his focus on the sounds and even smells around him.

From the second floor, he heard the sound of a car cranking. The shooter? Or another innocent person getting ready to ride into the path of danger?

Pulling in a deep breath, Brandon rounded the corner, weapon ready. Tires squealed on the concrete and a black Honda headed for him. Brandon caught sight of the masked face behind the wheel. He aimed his weapon and fired at the front left tire.

The rubber exploded and the car spun.

Running feet sounded behind him and he whirled to find other officers on the scene. He flashed his badge and turned back to the car.

And the now escaping suspect. "Freeze! Police!" The man never stopped. Brandon raced to the edge of the garage and looked over. "Cut him off! Cut him off!" The shooter ignored the stairwell and went for the ramp on the other end of the garage. "He's coming your way on the ramp!" he yelled to the officer below him. The officer responded by changing his direction and heading for the ramp. Brandon gave chase. The officers behind him followed.

Cruisers were now on the ground level. And still the fugitive managed to elude capture. He disappeared into the thick forest of trees that led to the Goethe River. A wild rushing mass of water, thanks to the waterfall not too far away.

On a hunch, Brandon headed for the bridge. He snagged his cell phone with his left hand and called in his position and where he was headed. Backup would follow. His footsteps pounded, his wound throbbed and his breaths came in fast pants, mostly from the pain, some from the extended running. He was in good shape, but he figured he was pushing somewhere near six miles.

Where was this guy? *Who* was this guy who could run this far and this long without stopping? Brandon kept his phone on and shoved it in his pocket. He had his Bluetooth in his ear and gave breathless updates every few seconds. A helicopter thumped above him. "Let me talk to the chopper." Dispatch patched him through. "Where is he?"

"To your left. Keep going. He's almost to the bridge. Cruisers are headed that way. One will stop on either side and trap him on the bridge."

"What about the people on it?"

"There are two pedestrians."

Brandon put on an extra burst of speed. He had to get to the bridge and get those people off before the suspect realized he was trapped. Brandon knew the man had left the rifle in the vehicle he'd abandoned, but he didn't know if he had another weapon or not.

Brandon arrived at the bridge seconds after the fleeing man. The two pedestrians, who looked to be in their mid-twenties, stood still, watching the masked man before horror and realization hit them. Then the young man grabbed the girl's hand. "Run!"

They took off. The first cruiser screeched to a halt at the end of the bridge. The young couple scooted around it and dropped out of sight. The masked man stopped and spun. Saw Brandon and the cruiser blocking the way he'd just come. Brandon held his gun on him. "On the ground! Now!"

There weren't any weapons in sight, but that didn't mean he didn't have any. Brandon walked toward him. "You're trapped, dude. Give it up."

He didn't answer. Just backed toward the railing. Brandon approached with slow, even footsteps, keeping his weapon steady, ready for anything.

Sweat pooled at the small of his back and dripped from his face. He could only imagine how hot the mask was. The man's frantic eyes bounced from Brandon to the police officers who now approached, weapons drawn. "Come on," Brandon said. "You haven't hurt anyone yet. There's still a chance you could get off light."

"No way." He gripped the railing and Brandon realized what he planned. He lunged for him just as the man vaulted over the rail. Brandon reached the spot the shooter had just vacated and gripped the metal. He looked over in time to see the man hit the water hard and go under. Officers raced toward their vehicles, radios in hand, reporting the situation.

The chopper veered off and he knew they would do

their best to see where the man surfaced. Brandon placed his hands on his knees then winced as his shoulder reminded him of the rough treatment it had recently received.

"Brandon?"

He turned to find Sonya climbing out of another police cruiser. He walked toward her. "Hey, what are you doing here?"

"I couldn't stay in the car. I saw the man leave the parking garage. I hitched a ride with this officer, who was willing to help me once I explained that I was in the car the guy was shooting at." She paused and bit her lip. "I saw him jump."

"Yeah."

"You think he'll be all right?" The doubt in her eyes told him what *she* thought.

Brandon shook his head. "I don't know, but he'll have to surface at some point, and when he does, we'll grab him."

"The police are everywhere. Surely he won't get away this time."

"Let's hope not." He took her hand and turned her toward the car.

She gasped when she saw his shoulder. "Your shoulder. It's more than a scratch."

He looked at the wound. "It's bled more because I've been moving."

"Will you let me look at it?"

The officer who'd given her the ride spoke for the first time. "We have EMTs on standby. Hop in and I'll take you to one."

"Great." She gave Brandon a gentle shove toward the

police car. He hesitated with one more look toward the rushing river, then shook his head and gave in.

Sonya paced in the waiting room while Brandon was in the back getting patched up. Two officers stood guard over her at his insistence. As she paced, she touched the still-healing wound on her throat and thought.

She was missing something. Who would benefit from her death? The person who didn't want Heather Bradley found, obviously.

But why would someone not want the child found? What did it matter at this point if she was found or not? The only reason she could come up with was the adopted son. He didn't want her found because he felt threatened. But he had an alibi for the shooting. Then again, he could have hired someone.

"Sonya?"

She turned to find Don Bradley—her biological father—standing in the doorway. The officers moved closer. She nodded that it was all right and walked toward the man. "Hi."

"Is the detective all right?"

"He'll be fine. And I'm sure he wouldn't mind if you called him Brandon."

He gave a relieved smile. "I heard the shots and saw all the craziness from my office window. Then I saw Brandon take off after him—" He swallowed hard and shook his head. "I'm so sorry this is happening. I don't understand why someone wouldn't want Heather found."

"We don't, either."

He motioned for her to sit and she did. He eased into the chair beside her, then looked her in the eye. "You're

Heather, aren't you? That's what you were coming to tell me, isn't it?"

Sonya swallowed hard and gave a slow nod. "The DNA from the hair you supplied was a match. A hundred percent match."

"I see. You know, my wife's sister died shortly after you were born." His eyes shifted to the wall and she could tell his mind had gone to the past. "Those were hard days." His eyes reddened, but no tears appeared. "But we had you. You were the shining spot in my life." He reached over to grip her hand and Sonya let him. "I loved you with every fiber of my being—and then you were gone. And I felt I'd lost everything."

"I'm so sorry," she whispered.

He sniffed and blew out a breath, then stood and shoved his hands into his pockets.

Brandon appeared in the doorway and she rushed to him. "Are you okay?"

"Yes." He smiled and touched her cheek. "I'm fine. A scratch like I said." He saw Don and held out a hand. "Guess you heard the commotion."

"And then some." Don shook his hand. "Sonya just told me the news."

Brandon nodded. "I hated to tell you over the phone."

The man gave him a small smile. "When you didn't say it, I knew."

"I figured you probably did."

A woman entered the waiting room. Sonya recognized Brandon's sister, Erica. Brandon spotted her at the same time. Erica made a beeline for her brother. "Shot? Really? Again?"

Brandon hugged and shushed her. "Stop. It's barely there. Only needed five stitches and some antibiotics.

Already had the tetanus up to date and I'm good to go. Won't even need physical therapy."

Erica looked as if she was ready to add to her brother's pain. "Are you insane?"

He sighed. "Not last I checked. I'm fine, Erica."

"Where was Max or Peter or Jordan or Frankie? Or *someone?*"

His jaw tightened. "They can't babysit twenty-four-seven."

"Of course they can," she snapped. Sonya watched the two siblings snipe at each other a moment longer before Erica's shoulders drooped. "You just scared me."

Brandon softened at his sister's sincere worry. He wrapped his good arm around her. "I know. I'm sorry. I'll be more careful."

It was her turn to sigh. "No, you won't." She pulled away.

Sonya exchanged a glance with Don. He shook his head, a small smile playing on his lips in spite of the seriousness of the situation. Sonya felt a pang in the vicinity of her heart. Growing up, she'd always wanted a brother or sister, and now watching Erica and Brandon, she realized she still did.

"What's your son's name?" she asked Don.

"Grayson."

"How will he feel when he learns about me?"

"Thrilled. He grew up knowing he had a sister. He's always said he wished she—you—would turn up one day."

Sonya nodded. "Maybe soon we could meet. After the craziness is over. I don't want to put him in danger."

"Of course." He shook his head. "He used to pretend his nanny was his sister, but after we lost Heather—

you—having another girl just seemed…wrong some-how." He flushed. "Silly, I know."

"Nanny?" Brandon asked.

Don blinked. "Er…yes." He gave a little laugh. "My wife loves being a mother, but she also loves her social life." His lips twisted in a sad smile. "It was just easier to hire live-in help. With time off, of course."

"Of course."

Sonya knew exactly what was clicking through Bran-don's mind. "Did I have a nanny?" she asked.

His brows lifted. "Um…well…yes, as a matter of fact, you did."

"Was she the same nanny Grayson had?"

"No. I called to check on her one time and found she'd moved."

"Moved where?"

"I'm not sure. No one said."

"What's her name?"

"Rebecca Gold."

"You think she would talk to us?"

Don frowned. "Why?"

"She was Heather's nanny. I want to ask her if she saw anything suspicious the day Heather was taken."

"But she wasn't at church that morning."

"Are you sure?"

"Of course I'm sure. She didn't even go to that church." He paused. "You're not thinking she took Heather, are you?"

"The possibility crossed my mind," Brandon said.

"But the police talked to her and cleared her."

"Maybe they just didn't ask the right questions."

Chapter 13

Brandon's phone rang. Hector's number winked up at him. "Hello?"

"Are you all right? Heard you got nicked."

"I'm fine. And yes, thankfully, a nick is all it was."

"Your lady friend all right?"

Brandon glanced at Sonya, who appeared deep in conversation with Don Bradley. Her father. "She's hanging in there."

"You like her, don't you?"

Brandon snorted. "Do I *like* her? Are we back in high school now?"

"Fess up, partner."

Brandon turned serious. "Yes. I like her."

His simple statement seemed to throw Hector for a loop. Silence echoed back at him. Then Hector cleared his throat. "Well. Good. I…uh… Well, that's nice, Brandon. I'm happy for you."

Brandon smiled. He'd finally said something to make his partner go speechless. That was one for the books. "Keep me updated."

"Yeah. Yeah. And you learn how to duck a little faster, huh?"

"I'll see what I can do."

Brandon hung up and grimaced. His shoulder throbbed. Thankfully, it was the same side he'd taken a bullet in about a year ago. At least he still had one good arm. And this bullet hadn't even penetrated, just skimmed the surface. Still stung, though.

He walked over to Sonya. "Are you ready to go?"

"I guess so. The question is—are you?"

"I'm ready." He looked at Don. "I'm sorry for all the chaos looking into Heather's disappearance is causing. I hope this doesn't come back on you. What's your home security system like?"

The man shook his head. "My security system is state-of-the-art. After we adopted Grayson, Ann insisted. And I'm simply stunned with everything that's happened. It just doesn't make sense."

"It makes sense to whoever is trying to stop us." Brandon pulled the keys from his pocket. "I'm going to take Sonya home and get a little rest myself. We'll regroup and figure out a plan where to go from here."

"I want to talk to the nanny," Sonya said.

"I've got Hector tracking her down. As soon as we have an address, we'll pay her a visit."

Don stepped forward and took Sonya's hand. "I want to get to know you."

Brandon saw Sonya swallow hard. "I want that, too,"

she said, "but I don't think someone else is too excited about the idea."

"I don't care. We'll fight back together."

"No. I don't want to put you in danger. After this is over, we'll talk, okay?"

He looked at Brandon. "I want to help."

Brandon frowned. "I understand that, sir, but I don't really know what you can do at this point."

"What if Sonya comes to stay with us? My wife and I would love to have her. And I just told you we have a state-of-the-art security system."

"Oh, I don't know about that," Sonya said. "I'd have to think about it." She bit her lip and backed up a fraction.

Brandon wondered what was going through her mind. Sheer panic blossomed and she shot him a desperate look. He stepped over and put his arm around her. "We'll talk about it," he said. "It's actually not a bad idea, but give us some time to discuss it."

"Of course." The man shoved his hands into his pockets. "I didn't mean to push too hard."

"No, it's okay," Sonya said. She'd gathered herself together quickly and Brandon wanted to think his presence helped her do so. "Like Brandon said, I'll…think about it."

Don nodded and took a step toward the door. "I'll leave now." He shot a beseeching look at Sonya. "But please do think about it. I've lost almost twenty-eight years with you. I guess I just don't want to lose another minute."

Sonya said nothing more. She simply nodded.

He patted the front pocket of his blazer, then reached in and pulled out a small packet. "Before I forget. These are some pictures of our family. I thought you might like to see them."

Sonya took them. "Thank you. I definitely would like to look at them." She slipped them into her purse.

Don left.

Brandon turned to Sonya. "You don't have to stay with them, don't worry."

She gave a small shrug. "If I thought Mrs. Bradley wanted me to, I might consider it, but I'd never invade her home like that knowing how she feels about me."

Erica, who'd been standing by, observing and listening, turned to Brandon. "We've got resources, you know. If you need a safe house, it could probably be arranged."

Sonya shook her head. "No. No safe house." She pulled in a deep breath. "If I go into hiding, I'll never be able to come out." Her lips firmed and her chin jutted. "I'm going to stay in plain sight and just pray we catch him before he catches me."

Sonya wanted to recall her pseudobrave words. The harsh frown on Brandon's face said he didn't like them, either. But she couldn't take the words back and decided then she didn't want to. She knew if she disappeared, she'd never be able to have a real life again. Not as herself, anyway. She couldn't live like that. She had to find the truth and find it soon. She prayed that the Lord saw fit to let her live to do it.

Brandon escorted her from the hospital. She thought he looked pale and drawn. His shoulder had to be hurting him.

They stepped outside and Brandon came to an abrupt halt. "I don't have a car."

"No, but I do." Erica, who'd been following silently behind, smiled sweetly and swung her keys at them.

Brandon smiled. "Right. So is Max pulling protection duty tonight?"

Max, Erica's husband, didn't mind helping out when needed. And he was definitely needed tonight.

"Max and Peter." Erica led the way to her vehicle.

Sonya scanned the area. Was he watching? Was he wondering how they'd once again managed to elude him? Or had he drowned in the river? Was it all over?

They arrived at Erica's dark blue SUV, and Sonya saw Max parked next to Erica.

He rolled the window down as they approached. "Ready to roll?"

Brandon shook his hand. "What are you doing here?"

"Erica's the chauffeur. I'm the escort."

Sonya relaxed a fraction.

"I've also asked Jordan to be at the house when you're home tonight. You need to be able to rest without worrying about an intruder," Max said.

Jordan Gray. Sonya recognized the name. She hadn't met the other agency operative, but knew he was Brandon's roommate. The one who was marrying Katie Randall, a detective Brandon had worked with on occasion. When she'd first approached Finding the Lost, he'd given her the rundown on all of the employees.

Brandon motioned for Sonya to take the front passenger seat then opened the door. He looked at Max with a frown. "That's not necessary."

"Well, I think it is." Erica lifted her chin a notch and gave her brother a steely-eyed look. "And Jordan agreed with us. He'll be there when I drop you off. Peter is on the way to Missy's as we speak."

"And I'll be joining him shortly," Max said. Sonya listened to them go back and forth and leaned her head back against the headrest. It was all just too much. *I don't understand why this is happening, Lord, but don't let my faith waver now. When Dad died, I was devastated. When my mom died, I was ready to crumble. I begged You for peace, but didn't get it. I still don't know that I've truly accepted she's gone. That they're both gone. Please help me, Lord.*

The plea seemed to bring a measure of comfort. She didn't know if that was the Lord or if she just felt better after getting it off her chest. But she'd asked God for peace and now she felt better. She wasn't going to take that away from Him. *Thank You, Lord.*

Exhaustion swamped her.

Brandon's phone rang and she turned her attention to his conversation. "Who? Right. Okay, I'll ask him. Thanks."

"Who was that?" Erica asked before Sonya could get the words out.

"Hector."

"What did he want?"

"He's been investigating the Bradleys."

"And?" Sonya perked up.

"He said they came back clean. Squeaky-clean. No record of any kind."

"Oh, well, that's good, right?"

"Yes, it's great. He did mention that Mrs. Bradley's sister died shortly after Heather was born."

"Mr. Bradley mentioned that," Sonya said.

"Did he mention how she died?"

"No, just that it was a really hard time in his family. Heather was kidnapped—" Sonya simply couldn't refer to herself as Heather "—and his sister-in-law died."

"Apparently she fell down a flight of stairs and broke her neck."

Sonya gasped. "How awful!"

"Mrs. Bradley said she'd been depressed and had talked of killing herself, so they briefly wondered if it was suicide, but in the end it was ruled an accident."

"Suicide by throwing yourself down a flight of stairs?" Sonya scoffed. "That doesn't even make sense. Who does that?"

Erica pulled into Missy's drive and Brandon nodded. "I thought the same thing, but apparently there was no evidence of foul play."

"So it was just a tragic accident."

"Looks like."

Brandon's phone rang before he could climb out of the car. "Hello?"

"Me again," Hector trilled in a falsetto pitch.

"That's so annoying."

"I know. That's why I do it," Hector said in his normal voice. "I'll get right to it. We found your jumper or the shooter—whichever label you want to put on him."

"The guy I chased from the parking garage."

"Yep. He washed downstream and our guys pulled him out."

"Anything else?"

"Yeah. He left his weapon in the car. We're running ballistics on it even as we speak."

Even though Brandon and Hector both knew without a shadow of a doubt the guy was guilty, they needed hard evidence. Linking the gun and the bullets to him would prove he was the shooter.

"Have them check it against the one used in the park shooting," Brandon said.

Silence echoed back at him, and then Hector said, "Excellent idea. I'll have them do that as soon as we get off the phone."

"That's twice Sonya's been shot at. It wouldn't surprise me a bit if the bullets came from the same gun."

"But what about the other two women who were shot?"

"I don't know what the connection is. Why don't you do a little investigating on that, too?"

"All right. I'll see if Sonya has any link with those two and I'll call ballistics as soon as we hang up. What else?"

"Any information on Rebecca Gold?"

"Nothing yet. Still looking."

"Okay. Let's get back to the shooter, then."

"Right. Well, he's dead."

Brandon rolled his eyes. "I figured that. That was a pretty long drop off the bridge."

"Yeah. And the water's not more than four feet deep."

"Did he drown?"

"Broke his neck along with some other bones, but the neck injury killed him. He's definitely our guy from the photograph, though. The tattoo on his shoulder matches the one in the picture."

Brandon blew out a sigh. "Okay, what's his name? Did he have any ID on him?"

"No ID on him, but we ran his prints and he's in the system. Name's Buddy Reed."

"Should I know him?"

"No reason to. But he has a record. Armed robbery is his biggest offense when he was eighteen. It was a one-time deal and he got a slap on the wrist since no one was hurt. He seemed to get his act together and got his degree in sports medicine. Right now, he's a trainer at one of the local gyms. Or, rather, he was."

"Any experience with guns? Weapons?"

"Well, since he missed hitting you, I'm guessing not much. Then again, he had pretty good aim in the park if he's the same shooter." Hector paused and Brandon heard the rustling of papers. "But no, there's nothing other than the armed robbery. No military service, no guns registered in his name. I'm guessing the rifle he had was off the black market. The serial number was filed off. I'll keep looking into everything."

"Good. That would be great."

"You sound distracted."

Brandon blinked. "I'm just wondering if it's over."

"What do you mean? The shooter's dead. The danger's over, right?"

"Unless he was working for someone, and that someone just hires another killer when he learns of Buddy Reed's demise." Of course that was a possibility. "We'll keep the protection-detail plans for tonight and revisit it in the morning. Thanks for the info."

"My pleasure. See ya."

Click.

Brandon hung up the phone and turned to Sonya. She'd heard every word. "He's dead?"

"Yes."

"So is it over? I can go home?"

"Hector and I discussed the possibility that the guy could have been working for someone."

She blanched. "Oh."

"So, let's keep up the precautions and see where we are in the morning." The same thing he'd said to Hector.

She nodded. "Fine." But she couldn't help feeling massive amounts of relief. The man who'd shot at her was dead. She could sleep tonight. Maybe. If it hadn't been someone who'd been hired. If that was the case, then both she and Brandon were still in danger.

Chapter 14

Thankfully, the night passed without incident. Brandon woke to find his phone had no missed calls. His shoulder throbbed but wasn't painful enough to keep him down. In the bathroom, he popped three Advil tablets, showered, shaved and decided he was ready to face the day.

After a cup of coffee—or three.

In the kitchen, he found Jordan sitting at the table reading the morning paper on his iPad. "You get any sleep last night?" Brandon asked him.

"A little."

"You didn't have to play bodyguard, you know."

"I know, but you slept better knowing I was doing it, didn't you?"

Brandon let out a short laugh. "Yeah, actually I did."

"Then it was worth it. How's the shoulder this morning?"

"Sore."

"You need me for anything today?"

Brandon shook his head. "No." He glanced at his phone. "I'm waiting for Hector to get back to me on a few things. I need to know where Ms. Gold is and I want to know about the ballistics report. Once I have those two things, I'll be able to plan the next course of action." He poured himself a cup of coffee and added cream and sugar. "Other than that, I plan to send Max and Peter home and spend the day with Sonya, making sure she's safe." He took his first sip of the brew and closed his eyes with pleasure. Three more sips and he felt himself start to wake up.

"You don't think it's over."

Brandon looked at his roommate and lifted a brow. "Do you?"

Jordan shrugged. "I don't know. But I think you're doing the right thing."

"What's that?"

"Staying on guard, until you know for sure."

He nodded and slipped into the chair opposite Jordan. "Do you mind if I ask you something?"

"Of course not. You've never asked permission before."

Brandon smirked. "Right." He sighed. "How'd you know Katie was the one?"

"Ahhhh…"

"What's that mean?"

"Sonya."

Brandon flushed. "Yeah."

Instead of teasing him like he thought he would, Jordan turned thoughtful. "You know, when we first met, she was looking for Molly. Erica was a basket case and I wasn't exactly in a good frame of mind. But last year—"

he shook his head "—when Katie was in all that danger because she was looking for her sister and we were working together, something just sparked, you know?" He lifted a shoulder. "She was spunky and determined and—hurting. But she was a fighter and I really liked that about her. Like eventually turned to love."

"She and Sonya sound a lot alike."

Jordan nodded. "Then she's a keeper."

"It's looking like it."

"But?"

"But you know my history. And you know about Krystal. How do I know Sonya will be able to deal with my baggage? My family?"

"You don't. Until you trust her with it."

"Right. Easier said than done."

Jordan hesitated. "You know, it's not my place to lecture you, but your parents are trying to do the right thing. If you'd let go of all that anger, there's still time to build a relationship with them."

Tension immediately filled Brandon. "You sound like Peter."

"Sounds like Peter's getting some smarts." Jordan shut off the iPad and stood. "On that note, I'm going to go into the office."

"And I'm going to head over to Missy's."

"You want me to follow you?"

Brandon paused. "It's on the way, so why not? Keep an eye on my tail and see if you spot anything."

"Will do."

Brandon arrived at Missy's house with no tail in sight. As Jordan pulled away with a wave, Brandon wondered if he'd crossed the line onto the paranoia side. Max gave him a salute and left. Brandon knew he and Erica were having breakfast together. Peter lingered at the curb, so Brandon walked over to speak to his brother. He had the window down and was sipping on coffee he'd brought in a thermos. "How's it going?"

"It's been quiet." He lifted the thermos top posing as a cup. "Good thing I had this stuff or I would have been snoozing."

"But you didn't snooze, right?"

Peter's face darkened. "Of course not. You gave me a job to do and I'm doing it."

Brandon let his gaze linger on his younger brother's face. "Yeah. You are. And you're doing a good job, too. Thanks."

The darkness cleared and Peter swallowed. "It's the least I can do. You're giving me a second chance." He snorted. "Or maybe it's a third, fourth or fifth chance. I don't know. I've lost count at this point, I guess."

"I'm not keeping track. You're putting your life back together. That's all that matters."

"Are you coming to Mom and Dad's for dinner Sunday night?"

Brandon straightened and, at the mention of his parents, felt the familiar squeeze in the vicinity of his temple. "No."

"Why not?"

"You know why not." He kept his words low and even, not letting them explode like he wanted to.

Peter snorted. "They're trying, Brandon. They were young and on their own and didn't know what they were doing. Can't you find a way to forgive and move on?"

For a second, he almost relented. But the bad memories crowded out the moment. "I… I…can't. It's too late."

Peter sighed. "Don't you want a relationship with them?"

Brandon flinched. "No. Not really." As soon as the words left his lips, he realized they were a lie. He did want a relationship with his parents. He just didn't know how to get over the past. How did he let go of all the disappointment and hurt that had been such a part of his life? The pain that had shaped him into part of who he was today? He shook his head. "No, I'm not ready for that. Not yet."

"Will you ever be ready?"

"That's a question I can't answer right now."

"You know, in rehab we talked a lot about forgiveness—forgiving ourselves and asking forgiveness of others. Been going to church, too, and listening to sermons on the topic. It's been pretty eye-opening."

Brandon took a step back and planted his hands on his hips. He opened his mouth, but Peter lifted a hand to cut him off. "I'm not giving you a speech, just saying bitterness and an unforgiving heart can be as destructive as cocaine or meth. I may be the recovering addict, but you're the one who needs some rehab. Some heart rehab. Think about it." He cranked the car and drove off without another word.

Brandon let his brother's words rattle around in his brain for the next ten seconds. Then he turned to find Sonya standing behind him, face bright red, looking awkward and uncomfortable. She sighed. "I'm sorry. I didn't mean to interrupt. Or eavesdrop."

"It's a long-standing argument. Don't worry about it." He managed to get the words through his clenched teeth.

She chewed her bottom lip for a moment and he waited for the question. "Is he right?"

"No." His conscience shouted *liar,* but he ignored it.

"Hmm. Okay."

He motioned to his car. "Come on. I don't want you standing out here in the open."

"The shooter's dead, remember?"

"Right, but until we know for sure that this is over, I want you inside."

"Okay." She sighed and turned to go back into the house. He followed her, head swiveling left then right. He saw nothing that alarmed him, but wasn't dropping his guard. "Want to grab some breakfast?"

She eyed him and shrugged. "Sure. Are you feeling okay?"

"Food will take my mind off the aggravation."

"All right, then. Just let me get my purse."

"Hey, bring those pictures Don gave you, okay? I want to look over them."

"Sure." She disappeared inside.

Brandon's internal struggle didn't cease just because Peter had left and Sonya's all-seeing eyes were no longer on him. He stepped onto the porch and sat in one of the white wicker rockers. He let his gaze roam the street, probing into the shadows, watching for anything that looked as if it shouldn't belong. Even as he stayed alert and focused on his surroundings, Peter's words continued to ring in his mind. *Bitterness and an unforgiving heart can be as destructive as cocaine or meth.*

On an intellectual level, Brandon knew his brother was right. On an emotional one, he wanted to deny it. He remembered after Peter came home from rehab, one of the first things he'd done was ask his family for forgiveness. And Brandon had granted it without reservation. He wasn't bitter or unforgiving; he was apathetic.

Toward his parents, anyway. They hadn't needed him when he was younger, hadn't been supportive or even very caring. They'd been indifferent—and selfish. More focused on having a good time and partying than they'd been on raising kids.

It wasn't that he was even still angry with them. Was he? Brandon snorted. Yes, he was. He was angry, but he didn't need them. Or their sudden desire to be involved in his and his siblings' lives.

He flashed back to a day at the park. He'd been about eight years old. They'd had a family picnic, and he recalled laughter and his father pushing him on a swing, high-fiving him after his descent down the slide.

Brandon blinked. Where had that come from? Had he made it up? No. He remembered the park. He frowned. Were there other good memories he'd suppressed in his determination to hold on to his anger?

"I'm ready."

Her soft voice pulled Brandon from his thoughts. Casually dressed in a pink tank top and khaki capris, he thought she looked beautiful. Even the stitches covered by a small Band-Aid at the base of her throat didn't detract from her loveliness.

He rose and took her elbow to help guide her down the steps and over to his car. Warmth radiated from her and he swallowed. She was warm and compassionate, caring and generous. Everything his ex-fiancée had appeared to be on the surface. She'd enjoyed the status dating him had given her among her friends. Dating a police detective had been a big deal to her.

Until she'd gotten tired of the long hours. And the fact that he didn't make enough to support her in the lifestyle she wanted.

He wondered if Sonya would be able to handle it. As a nurse, she understood long hours and hard work. The irony of her profession hadn't escaped him. A nurse. Just like his mother. And yet, the two women seemed vastly different. He just couldn't picture his mother as compassionate.

Then again, he hadn't really been around her that much lately to make that judgment.

But he didn't think he could possibly be wrong.

Sonya wondered if Brandon could possibly be wrong. Wrong about it not being over. Ever since the shooter's death, things had been quiet.

Ominously quiet?

Maybe. She shivered.

He drove with precision. She watched him navigate the roads, clearly thinking deeply about something, yet attentive and aware of their surroundings.

He glanced at her and caught her watching. She flushed and looked away.

"Why did you become a nurse, almost a doctor?" he asked.

She blinked at the random question. "Because I care about people, about helping them." She shrugged. "And I like science and medicine. The human body is a fascinating, intricately designed machine. That intrigues me."

"Do you plan to go back to school and finish the classes you need to become a doctor?"

"Yes. As soon as I can." Sadness engulfed her. "My mother would want that. She felt so bad that I had to quit school to come back and take care of her."

"Did she have any brothers or sisters?"

"No, both she and my dad were only children."

Brandon pulled into the parking lot of one of the downtown cafés. As they walked into the building, he placed a hand at the small of her back to guide her. She shivered, feeling the warmth of his touch. First her elbow, then her back. He was comfortable enough with her to offer the simple touches. Innocent gestures that spoke of a growing closeness.

And she was comfortable enough to accept the touches—and the growing closeness. If only he could resolve his issues with his family. But he said he didn't date clients. Which was something she could understand. Didn't mean she liked it, but she could respect it.

She had a feeling he didn't like it so much himself. A small smile pulled at her lips at the thought. "You like this place."

He nodded. "I like their coffee. And just about everything else they serve here."

"Are you really still concerned that someone is still after me?"

"Not as concerned as I was before we found out the shooter was dead."

"But?"

"But I don't think it hurts to stay cautious until we know for sure."

Once they'd ordered, picked up their food and settled into a booth—facing the door, she noticed—Sonya said, "Do you mind if I bless it?"

He shifted, but didn't seem uneasy. He nodded and she bowed her head. "Thank You, Lord, for this food. For Your protection. Please let this thing be over. And thank You for putting Brandon in my life at just the right time."

When she lifted her head she found his eyes on her, warm and smoky. "That was a nice prayer."

Embarrassed, she shrugged. "That was a really nice thing you did for Spike and his mother."

"Spike's a good kid. He got into a lot of trouble two years ago, was hooked on meth and any other kind of drug he could get his hands on. I busted him during a drug sting."

"And now he thinks you hung the moon."

Brandon flushed and shrugged. "I gave him a chance."

"He reminded you of you—or what you could have been, didn't he?" she asked softly.

He jerked and took a sip of his coffee then a bite of his bagel. "Yes."

She nodded. "Why didn't you end up like Spike?"

He sighed. "I don't know." He tapped his fingers on the table, then seemed to make up his mind. "I mean, my parents weren't into criminal stuff—other than underage drinking—but I don't think they ever used drugs. At least none that I saw. They just weren't there. And while I was angry about it, I was still looking for something to connect with. That was sports. Football, basketball, anything to keep moving and not think too much. As much freedom as I had growing up, I knew if I got into drugs, I'd ruin my future."

"So you decided to make the right choices?"

"In a roundabout way. I wanted to play sports and couldn't do that if I was strung out or high. Once I got out of high school, I had a full ride to college on a football scholarship. I didn't want to mess that up. Throw in Erica's preaching and seeing what drugs had done to Peter—" He shrugged.

"So that's why you're so involved in Parker House. You want to give kids another alternative."

"Yes."

"You're a good, strong man, Brandon Hayes."

He flushed. "Thanks." Silence descended as they ate. Then Brandon's phone buzzed and he grabbed it. "Hector, just who I wanted to hear from. What do you have?"

"I've got an address on your nanny."

"Great. Text it to me, will you?"

"Already done. I also found out she's working as a nanny for another couple in Charlotte, North Carolina. Tomorrow's her day off."

"How'd you find that out?"

"I have my ways."

Brandon grunted. "Thanks." He hung up and looked at Sonya. "Feel like a road trip tomorrow?"

"Sure. Technically, I'm still on medical leave."

His gaze dropped to her throat. "How's it feeling?"

"Still sore, of course, but healing."

"Are you staying with Missy tonight?"

"Do you think I should?"

"Probably."

She gave a nod. "Then I will. Missy said I have an open invitation. The one good thing about this whole mess is that I think I'm making a lifelong friend."

"Nothing like looking on the positive side of things."

She rolled her eyes. "Well, it's better than the alternative."

"Did you bring those pictures Don gave you?"

She pulled them from her purse and handed them to him. "Why don't you slide around here so we can look at them together," he said.

Her heart tumbled over itself in eager agreement to be that close to him. She got up and slid in the booth next to him. He radiated warmth. Security. She scooted closer until her arm brushed his. She looked up at him and found him staring at her. His eyes dropped to her lips. Then he swallowed and fanned the pictures on the table. He cleared his throat. "So. Ah. Look."

Sonya leaned forward to see the first one. Don and Ann Bradley stood on the front porch of their house. Don held Heather, and Ann stood with her hand on the baby's head. They looked happy. "That must have been when they brought me home from the hospital." She sighed. "It's like staring at strangers. I can't bring myself to even think of them as my parents."

They continued to flip through the pictures. Sonya stopped and pulled one out. "Look. Who's that?" A woman held her, but it wasn't Ann—her mother—no, Ann. Sonya firmed her jaw.

She had a mother, and while that mother was dead, she'd have a hard time calling another by the name. "She looks similar to Ann. I wonder if that's the sister who died."

"Is anything written on the back?"

She flipped it over. "'Miriam and Heather.'"

"Miriam. I don't know that Hector ever said her name." He frowned and picked up the phone. "I'll call Don and ask him." He dialed the man's number and Sonya went through the rest of the pictures. It appeared that Heather had a couple of cousins, each who took turns holding her. "A happy family," she whispered.

Brandon hung up and she jumped. She'd missed the conversation. "What did he say?"

"He said it was Miriam, Ann's sister who died."

"The one who fell down the steps," she murmured. "Did they say how that happened exactly?"

"No, Mrs. Bradley—Ann—went to check on her sister and found her at the bottom of the steps."

"That's awful. Poor Ann."

He nodded then went rigid, his hard gaze on something beyond her right shoulder. "Brandon? What is it?"

"My parents."

Sonya turned and saw two people in their mid-forties heading their way.

The woman had her bright red hair pulled back into a loose ponytail. The man had on an auto-mechanic uniform. Grease stains dotted the gray material.

"Brandon. I'm so glad we ran into you," the woman gushed.

Brandon gave a brief nod. "We were just leaving." He nudged Sonya, who stood. Brandon followed. Pain flashed in Shelby's eyes, but she did her best to cover it with a smile. "Won't you introduce us?"

After a brief hesitation, he placed a hand on Sonya's back. "Sonya, this is my mother, Shelby Hayes, and my father, Brant Hayes."

Sonya smiled and held out a hand to each of them. "So glad to meet you."

Shelby gave her fingers a light squeeze then turned to her son. "Brandon, we'd love to have you come Sunday for dinner. Erica and Peter will be there and we've invited Jordan and Katie, too. Won't you come?"

"Probably not. I'm working a case."

The hope in his mother's eyes faded to a deep sadness. Sonya felt her heart wrench for the woman. "Of course," Shelby said. "I understand."

"Well, I don't," his father growled. "You gonna punish us forever? You're so perfect you've never made a mistake?"

"Back off." Brandon's low warning sent shivers up Sonya's spine. "This isn't the place."

Brant shook his head. "Come on, Shelby. Give it up. He's never going to let go of his anger."

Brandon's mother sighed and tears filled her eyes. "Why was it so easy to forgive Peter all the lousy things he's done over the years, but you can't find it in your heart to accept a plea for forgiveness from your parents? Can't you just give us a chance to prove we've changed?"

Sonya's heart ached at the coldness in Brandon's gaze. Yet beneath the chill, she thought she saw a glimmer of longing. He didn't answer, just took Sonya's hand and pulled her from the restaurant.

Once outside and in the car he said, "All right, we have a game plan. I'm going to head back to my office and get some work done."

"Which office?"

"Finding the Lost. I've got a couple days off from the force."

"Okay. Then just drop me at Missy's. It'll be good to hang out with her for a while."

"Fine."

She wondered if he would say anything about his parents. His tight jaw and narrowed eyes said he was still thinking about the incident. After thirty seconds of silence he shook his head and looked at her. "I'm sorry about that."

"It's okay, Brandon."

"No, it's not."

"I'm wondering about the question your mother asked you."

"Which one?"

"About why it seemed to be so easy for you to forgive Peter, but you can't give them another chance."

He flexed his fingers on the wheel. "I don't know."

His low, agony-filled answer made her heart ache anew for him.

"Your father is right. They're humans with faults just like all the rest of us. Keep trying to get past what happened when they were too young to be parents and focus on the fact that they want to right their wrongs."

He took a deep breath and she thought he might argue with her. He didn't. He simply stared out the window. Finally, he cleared his throat. "I'll pick you up in the morning?"

"That'll be fine." She let the subject go. If he wouldn't open up to her and let her help, he would have to work through the emotional baggage he carried by himself. She gripped his fingers. "I'm here if you need me, Brandon. I'll just be a nonjudgmental listening ear if you need it."

He gave her hand an answering squeeze. "I'll be looking forward to tomorrow."

The thought of spending the whole day with him tomorrow sent shivers chasing one another all over her skin. She only hoped they didn't have to spend the day looking over their shoulders and dodging people who wanted them dead.

Chapter 15

Thursday morning dawned hot and humid. Brandon picked Sonya up at eight o'clock sharp. He'd missed her after he'd dropped her off yesterday. Missed her a lot. He'd thought about her off and on all afternoon, her face appearing in his thoughts at odd moments even as he met with Erica and Jordan to discuss the other ongoing cases. He caught them up on Sonya and her case, then went home to rest. He hated to admit it, but his shoulder had been killing him.

Jordan followed him home and had spent the day playing bodyguard while Brandon grabbed some much-needed sleep. Max had taken the afternoon off to watch over Sonya and Missy.

Nothing happened during the night, and Brandon almost questioned whether he was just being paranoid in keeping such close tabs on Sonya now that the shooter was dead.

And yet, something niggled at him. He wasn't quite ready to believe that it was that easy. He felt in his gut that someone had hired that man to go after Sonya. And until that person was behind bars, Sonya was still in danger.

She stepped out onto the porch and he caught his breath. Which made him squirm. No woman had affected him like this. Not even his ex-fiancée.

She slid into the passenger seat and shot him a smile. "You've become quite adept at playing chauffeur over the past few days, haven't you?"

"I don't mind. I'm sorry it's necessary, but I don't mind." He ran a finger down her cheek. "Spending time with you is always the highlight of my day."

She shivered at his touch then blinked as though his straightforward bluntness had caught her off guard. He had to admit, it surprised him, too. "You're a very confusing man sometimes."

He felt his lips tilt higher. "Trust me, I'm not nearly as confusing as you."

"Why's that?"

"Because you're a woman. Women have the market on confusing."

She gaped at him. "I can't believe you said that. Are you stereotyping me?"

He swooped in and captured her lips with his for a brief moment. "Never," he whispered.

Her eyes locked on his. "Well. Good. I'm glad you cleared that up."

He leaned back. "But you're a client." Even as the words left his lips, he wanted to recall them.

"Yes. I am."

"And I don't get involved with clients."

She flushed and raised a brow, a tinge of anger darkening her already dark eyes. "Really? So you just kiss them."

He sighed and clasped her fingers in his. "No, I'm sorry. Not for kissing you," he clarified quickly. "But you're right. I'm—attracted to you, Sonya, and it's sending my heart spinning. Frankly, I'm not sure what to do about it."

She blinked. "Oh. The fact that you're laying this out here is really out of character for you, isn't it?" she murmured.

He gave a low laugh. "Tell me about it. But—" he ran a hand through his hair and sighed "—I know life is short, but these last few days of eluding death have really hit home. I want you to know that I *don't* go around kissing clients—or any woman, for that matter. I want you to know I'm not playing games with your heart."

"But you're going to table your feelings until all of this is resolved."

"Yes. I think I have to. I need to focus on making sure that you're safe."

She nodded. "Okay. If that's what you have to do."

"But when this is over—"

"I get it, Brandon."

He tilted her chin toward him. "I hope so. I really do." Then he let her go and pulled away from the curb.

Well, if Brandon's heart was spinning, Sonya decided hers was playing copycat. The man had her emotions all over the place. And yet, she appreciated his honesty.

She also had to admit she'd let her imagination swing toward shopping for white dresses and pretty flowers.

Every once in a while and when she'd needed a distraction from the crazy danger. But he was right. This wasn't the time in their lives to be thinking about that. Worrying about staying alive should be priority.

But later, when all of this was over…

The drive to Rebecca Gold's house took a little over an hour with Brandon watching the mirrors the whole time.

She and Brandon made small talk the rest of the way, dancing around the topic of relationships and kissing. That was fine with her. She needed her emotions to settle down.

When he pulled into the drive, she took in the residence. A brick ranch house in a nice middle-class area with a beautifully manicured yard. A white Toyota Camry sat in the single carport.

"Did you call her and tell her we were coming?" Sonya asked.

"No. I didn't want to give her a heads-up. If she was involved in the kidnapping in any way, I was afraid she'd run."

"What makes you think she was actually involved?"

"I don't. Just speculation. But in thinking that it was someone close to the family, after the parents, she's the next logical suspect."

"I wondered if she might have been involved. For the same reasons." Sonya opened the door and climbed from the vehicle. She shivered in spite of the hot sun blazing down on her. She walked around to Brandon's side.

"Let's try the front door."

Sonya walked up the steps and knocked. Brandon stood at her back, turned away from her, watching the street. She knocked again.

Nothing.

"She's not here, I guess," Sonya said.

"Her car is in the carport."

"Maybe she's taking a walk."

"Maybe." He looked doubtful. "Let's go around to the back."

Sonya followed him around the side of the house. The grass was sod, making a smooth green path to the back. Carefully tended flowers bloomed along the edges, and she could clearly see someone enjoyed her yard work.

A small patio led to a back door. Brandon started to knock, then paused. Sonya stepped closer. "What is it?"

"The door's open."

"And look at those flowers." She pointed to the other side of the porch. "They're crushed like someone stepped on them."

He stooped, resting one knee against the top step. "There's blood on the porch."

She looked to see what he was talking about. A brown patch marred the surface, then another one and another. "Are you sure it's blood?" she asked.

"Looks like it. Dried blood looks the same in just about every situation. And this one looks to be in the form of a shoe print."

She could think of a number of reasons for the open door and crushed flowers, but the blood worried her. With the way things had been going lately, she decided being on guard now might save them some trouble later.

Brandon must have felt the same. He pulled his weapon. "Stay behind me."

Sonya didn't argue. Brandon used his elbow to nudge the door open farther.

Just as he did, something slammed into it, causing

wood fragments to fly everywhere. Brandon cried out and went down. Sonya hit the floor of the porch, terror racing, survival instincts kicking in.

She felt Brandon snag her arm and roll her into the house. He slammed the damaged door behind them and pulled out his phone. He pressed it into her hand. "Call 911."

Blood dripped from his forehead. He had a gash on his cheek. Sonya realized his face had protected hers.

She froze for a split second, then dialed the number.

The operator came on the line. "What's your emergency?"

Sonya sat up. "Someone just shot at us. They're outside in the trees, shooting at the house." She rattled off the address. She turned to find Brandon at the window, pressed to one side, the curtain parted. Her gaze landed on the couch and she bit back a scream. Her muffled whimper caught his attention. She nodded to the couch and he blinked. Into the phone, Sonya said, "There's a woman who needs help. Actually, I think she may be dead."

Brandon left the window and went to the woman, felt for a pulse, looked up and shook his head.

Sonya approached the body and dropped to her knees. She handed Brandon the phone and mimicked his actions in feeling for a pulse even though she knew she wouldn't find one. The blood on the woman's torso said she'd met a violent death. Sonya looked into the open, staring eyes of the victim and felt her throat tighten. "Someone shot her," she whispered.

"And not too long ago," Brandon said. "The blood isn't dry."

Brandon identified himself to the 911 operator and

requested the necessary personnel for the crime scene. He handed the phone back to Sonya and let his eyes roam the house. Tension quivered through him and he went back to the window and held his weapon ready.

Sonya shivered and swallowed hard, the hair on her neck spiking. Goose bumps pebbled her skin.

He moved the curtain one more time. "I don't see anyone, but I didn't hear or see a car drive away."

"Whoever shot at us may have just run or had a car parked somewhere else."

"Yes." Brandon stepped toward the kitchen and rounded the corner in a smooth move. Then checked the pantry.

All the while Sonya could see him keeping an eye on her, too. "What is it?" she asked.

"I don't know. We don't dare go out yet, but I don't want any surprises in here, either."

"Surprises?"

"There are two glasses on the counter and a water bottle. The glasses could belong to Ms. Gold and her killer, and she could have poured the water from the bottle. Or the bottle could belong to a third person." He glanced around again. "If the shooter left someone behind…"

"Oh."

Sonya watched as he moved from the kitchen to stand to the side of the entrance to the hallway. She knew if she hadn't been there, he would have probably gone into the back rooms, but because of her presence he was waiting for backup.

That was fine with her. She rose and snagged her purse from where she'd dropped it when they'd tumbled into the house. It took only a moment to locate the small first-aid kit she carried. Packed with only the bare necessities, it still had a good-sized bandage. "Let me stop the bleeding on your head."

He swiped the bottom of his shirt across the wound. "Not yet."

He still wasn't convinced they were the only ones in the house.

She glanced back at the victim and felt sorrow squeeze her heart. Ms. Gold was in her early sixties. A woman who might have held some answers to Sonya's kidnapping. Answers that seemed to be lost forever now. But it wasn't just that. Ms. Gold probably had had quite a few good years left, and someone had stolen those from her. It wasn't fair.

"How long do you think she's been dead?" Brandon asked.

Sonya swallowed hard. "I don't want to touch anything or destroy any evidence, but..." She crouched down beside the dead woman and lifted her arm. It moved easily. "She's not in rigor. I'd say she's just recently been killed." She swallowed. "Like, in the past hour or so."

"Or past ten minutes," he muttered.

"I'm not a medical examiner, so it's just an educated guess, but rigor usually sets in within four hours of death."

"The fact that someone just shot at us tells me that if we'd gotten here a few minutes earlier, we might have interrupted the killer."

"And saved this poor woman's life." Tears squeezed her throat. She blinked and coughed to get rid of the knot. It didn't help much.

"I don't think her killer surprised her," Brandon said. Again, his gaze moved around the room.

Sonya saw what he did. "No sign of a struggle or forced entry."

He shot her a surprised look and she shrugged. She'd picked up a few things by hanging around him.

He nodded. "Exactly. I'm guessing she let the person in and was shot before she could think about what was happening." He aimed his weapon at the hallway. "This place needs to be dusted for prints. My guess is, if Ms. Gold knew the person she opened the door to, the person wasn't necessarily wearing gloves."

"So the killer might have touched something."

"Yes."

A sound from the back made her jump. A muscle in Brandon's jaw spasmed. Never taking his weapon away from the hallway, he pointed to Sonya and motioned her to the kitchen door.

Sonya heard the 911 operator on the phone requesting her attention. She lifted a brow, stood and moved in the direction Brandon indicated. She put the phone to her ear. Brandon backed toward her. Fear swirled in her stomach as she realized he thought someone else was still in the house.

Chapter 16

Brandon felt exposed. As if he had a big target on his back or his forehead and the killer was laughing at him as he took his time deciding when to pull the trigger. And Sonya...how was he going to keep her safe? He heard her whispering on the phone with the 911 operator.

She backed into the kitchen as a police car pulled up. Brandon kept his weapon trained on the hallway. The back door off the porch was still open. "Stay here." Officers were on the way. They'd have a plan and Brandon needed to be in on it. "Hand me the phone, please."

When she did, he identified himself to the dispatcher and gave his badge number. "I need to know the plan."

"Patching you through to the responding officers."

He heard the click on the line. All the while, he kept his gaze on the hallway entrance. No more noises had come from the back of the house, but that didn't mean he was ready to drop his guard.

A voice came on the line. "Officer Tim Miller."

"Officer Miller, this is Detective Brandon Hayes. Right now, this is your playing field. How do you want to do this?"

"Is the house clear?"

"Just the den and kitchen area. The victim is on the couch in the den."

"So you haven't yet cleared the bedrooms?"

"Right. We're holed up in the kitchen."

"We've got officers approaching now. Others are canvassing the neighborhood."

Brandon's blood hummed.

Ten minutes later, there'd been no more strange sounds and no more flying bullets. Two officers approached the back door, back-to-back and weapons drawn. Three more cruisers had arrived. Brandon opened the door and they entered.

Brandon flashed his badge and focused in on the officer whose name tag read Tim Miller. Miller eyed him. "You're Hayes?"

"I am."

Miller's gaze flicked to Sonya. "Stay with her while we clear the house."

Brandon itched to be a part of it, but he wanted Sonya safe more than he wanted to go looking for anyone who may be hiding. So he stayed and kept his weapon nearby while the officers cautiously headed down the hall.

"Clear!"

"Clear!"

The shouts came from the bedrooms.

Seconds later, Miller came into the room holding a

white-and-gray cat. "I think this may have been the noise you heard."

Brandon felt some of the tension leave him.

"Who knew?" Sonya asked.

His gaze snapped to hers. "What?"

"Who knew we were coming here? Ms. Gold is dead because we said something about coming to see her. So who did we tell and who did those people tell?"

Brandon pulled in a deep breath. "I don't know, but we're going to figure it out."

Exhaustion didn't begin to cover how Sonya felt. The shooting and the subsequent questioning by the police had taken their toll. Finding Ms. Gold dead had been a horrifying experience and all she wanted to do was go to bed. But the thought of going home—or even back to Missy's—had terrified her. Then, of course, there was the depressing fact that they no longer had any leads to figure out who'd kidnapped her all those years ago. She tried to push the thoughts aside and focus on her present situation.

Brandon had brought her to his house, planted her on the couch in his den and told her to nap while he fixed dinner. She'd closed her eyes, but knowing he was there—sensing him walk back and forth between the deck, where he grilled, and the kitchen, from where tantalizing smells emanated—stirred her appetite and she couldn't sleep. Instead she'd drifted, enjoying how, despite the danger, being with him made her feel safe.

Safe. She'd almost forgotten what it felt like. The sound of his approaching footsteps lifted her lids. He came out of his kitchen drying his hands on a towel. "Dinner is served."

She rose, walked into the dining area of the kitchen and gaped. Two steaks sat in the middle of the table along with two baked potatoes and a bowl of salad. "How did you do this so quickly?"

He laughed at her expression. "I've been a bachelor a long time. It was either learn to cook or starve."

"I'm deeply impressed."

He flushed. "Don't be. It was really easy."

"Well, thank you. I'm honored you'd cook for me."

He held out a chair and she slid into it. "I heard you order your steak medium well at one of the restaurants we went to, so this one is yours." He stabbed it with a knife and placed it on her plate.

"Perfect," she murmured.

He cleared his throat. "I suppose you want to say a blessing?"

"I'd love to." She bowed her head. "Thank You, Lord, for the food and for continuing to keep us safe. Amen."

"Amen."

She looked up and found his thoughtful gaze on her. "What?"

"Through all of the troubles you've had lately, you haven't lost your faith or blamed God."

She shrugged. "Why would I blame Him? He didn't kidnap me or shoot at me."

"But He could have stopped it."

She sighed. "Of course He could have, but He chose not to. For whatever reason, He's decided to allow this trial in my life at this time, and I'm not going to blame Him for it. I'm just going to ask Him to get me through it. Just because I have some trouble in my life doesn't mean He's not God anymore." She took the bowl of salad and transferred some to her plate, then chose the ranch dressing. As she poured it over her salad, she said, "It doesn't mean I like it, but—" she lifted a shoulder "—it is what it is and I'm going to trust Him to see me through."

"And if you die?"

"Then I die. Again, I don't want to die, but if I do, I pray something good comes from it that turns people to Him."

He frowned. "You're just like them."

"Who?"

"Erica and Max. Jordan and Katie. They all would have the same attitude you have."

She gave a small smile. "It's part of being a believer, a part of who I am."

"Not all believers have that attitude."

"No, I guess they don't. I'm not saying it's easy, but faith is a journey. I think when things are going well, it's easy to have faith. When things are going bad, you have to decide how you're going to react. Are you going to trust God or not?"

"I wish it was that simple for me."

"It's not simple. It's a choice."

"What about how you feel?"

"What do feelings have to do with it? You can't trust your feelings. Feelings can lead you to do or say things you shouldn't. Trust what's true and what's right because whatever is true and right is of God."

He simply stared at her, his mind spinning. "I've never thought of it that way before."

"Maybe you should."

"Maybe I should."

Her smile tipped into a frown and she looked around. "Speaking of Jordan, where is he?"

"Playing watchdog. He knew I was bringing you here, so he's guarding the perimeter."

"Oh, poor thing. It's really hot out there. I hope he's got some shade."

"And a vehicle with good air-conditioning. And you don't have to feel too sorry for him. I made him one of these steaks for later."

She nodded and took a bite. "Delicious."

"Thanks." He looked distracted then blurted, "But don't you *ever* doubt?"

She hesitated and thought about that. Then shook her head. "No, not about who God is or that He's in control."

"Then what?"

"Sometimes I doubt that my faith is strong enough. I get frustrated on occasion and want to whine or throw a temper tantrum and demand my way, but ultimately, it comes down to accepting that this is what it is right now and doing what I can to stay strong in the midst of it."

"Don't you hate the person who's doing this to you?"

"Hate him? No. Want him to stop? Most definitely. And yes, I'm angry and want to see justice done, but I'm not wasting my energy hating someone. What's the point in that?" He stared at her long enough to make her uncomfortable. She wanted to squirm. Instead, she took a few more bites of the steak. "You're a very good cook."

He blinked and looked down at his own plate. "Oh. Thanks." He lifted his head and caught her gaze once again. "You're amazing."

She flushed. She knew she did because she could feel the heat in her cheeks. How did he do that to her? She never blushed. "Well. Thank you."

"You make me want what you have."

Her heart flipped. "You already believe in God, Brandon."

"I know, but I've been mad at Him for a long time."

"Because of your parents."

"Mostly."

"And the fiancée?"

"Mmm-hmm. Yes." He continued to stare into her eyes.

"What?" she asked.

"I'm thinking that my fiancée leaving me could be the best thing that ever happened to me and I just couldn't see it until now."

Now it was her turn to stare.

He laughed, then shrugged. "I'm learning that there's more to just believing in God. There's the whole faith thing, trusting Him and believing that He has a plan in all of this."

"Exactly. It's not easy, but it's very…freeing, I guess is the word."

"Freeing?"

"Yes. You know. To have an absolute. To believe what God says is true. When you look at life through that filter, it keeps everything in perspective."

For the next few minutes, they ate in silence. Sonya's phone rang and she snagged it from her pocket to see Mrs. Talbot's number on the screen. "Hello?"

"Is this Sonya?"

"Yes, ma'am."

"Well, good. I hope I'm not catching you at a bad time."

"Not at all. What can I do for you?"

"You know when you were here asking all those questions about your mother?"

"Of course."

"I got to thinking about it and seems like I do recall her mentioning something about a phone call she'd gotten not too long before she passed."

Sonya sat up straight. "A phone call. From who?"

"She didn't say, just that she had to make a decision about something and was torn as to what to do. I didn't think much of it. I guess I thought it had to do with planning her funeral. And it may have. But I thought of it and wanted to tell you."

"Thank you so much. I'm glad you did."

"Hope it helps you figure out whatever it is you're figurin'."

"Me, too," Sonya said. "Me, too."

She hung up.

"What was that all about?" Brandon asked.

She told him. "You think it's important?"

"Maybe. Let me think about it."

"I wonder who called her."

He set his fork and knife on the edge of his plate. "Why don't we find out?"

"How?"

"Give me your mother's number and I'll get her phone records. We'll go through the numbers and see who called her the last couple of weeks before she died."

Sonya rattled off the number and he placed a call to whoever it was that could get him the information he needed.

He hung up. "So, let's get you over to Missy's and settled in."

"I think I'll go to Mom's house instead." Sadness gripped her. "One day I suppose I'll have to start calling it my house."

"Do you plan to keep it?"

"I might as well. It's paid for and I have some lovely memories of when I used to visit. We'll see."

"Looks a little small to raise a family there," he said.

She lifted a brow. "Well, since I don't have a family to raise, it's not a problem."

"What about later? Say if you meet someone, get married and start having kids?"

Sonya swallowed. She didn't want to read anything into his words, but she almost couldn't help it. "When—if—I get to that stage, then I suppose my husband and I would have to talk about it and decide what to do."

"So you'd be willing to move?"

She gave him a sad smile. "It's just a house, Brandon."

He stood up and carried his plate to the sink. She looked at her mostly eaten steak and half the baked potato and realized she was full. "I'd be willing to move, yes." Then she frowned. "But I want to be there tonight. I've been thinking that if she left the baby bag in the closet, there may be other things that I've missed."

"But you've cleaned out the house, right?"

"Most of it. But I haven't touched my mother's furniture. You know, her drawers."

"Just the closet?"

"Yes. And not all of that. I stopped when I found the bag."

"What about the attic?"

"No." She grimaced. "I don't like going up there. Anything in the attic wouldn't be worth looking at anyway, I don't think."

"You never know."

"And besides, what would I be looking for? I've already found the bag, and that was in the bedroom closet."

"So what are you thinking?"

"Whenever Mom got a phone call, she would write down important things on a small tablet she kept in her end-table drawer. I want to see if she wrote anything about that call that seemed to upset her."

"Good thinking. Come on. I'll take you."

"Now?"

"Why not? I want you safe, Sonya, and the only way that's going to happen is if we figure out who wants to hurt you. If you don't want to go to Missy's, then I'm going to make sure you're safe at your mother's."

"Right." She put her plate in the sink. "Don't you want me to help you clean up?"

He laughed. "Naw. That's what my cleaning service is for." He grabbed his keys. "Let's go. I'm impatient to see if we find something." He paused after he opened the door. "Stay here until I check the car out."

"You're going to look for a bomb, aren't you?"

"It only takes one time to make a man a little paranoid."

Chapter 17

Brandon pulled into her drive and looked in the rear-view mirror. Max had pulled to a stop across the street. He waved and Brandon gave a relieved sigh. Frankie couldn't pull guard duty tonight, so Brandon had had to come up with a plan B. Having contacts and friends that could help out at a moment's notice wasn't something he took for granted, but it was definitely something he appreciated.

His phone rang and he grabbed it while Sonya pulled her things together. It was Holt from the lab. "Hello?"

"Hey there. Somehow I got to be the designated caller."

"About?"

"Ballistics."

"Ah, yes. You want to tell me how, with your love of weapons, you didn't go into that part of forensics?"

"DNA opened up first, but I'm qualified to work ballistics, too. I just don't advertise it in case they decide they need to do some cutbacks or move people around. I'm happy where I am."

"Right. So what do you have for me?"

Sonya had stilled in the passenger seat and looked at him.

Holt said, "The bullets outside Mr. Bradley's office came from a Savage model 16FCSS Weather Warrior series bolt-action rifle. It's a .308 Winchester caliber twenty-two-inch free-float and button-rifled barrel with—"

"Just the facts," Brandon drawled. "And in English." He knew if he let him, Holt would go on and on about the rifle and never get around to the actual reason he'd called.

Holt quieted then cleared his throat. "Right. The bullets fired at you guys in front of Mr. Bradley's office from the rifle your shooter left behind and the ones fired at the people in the park where Sonya was jogging were a match."

Brandon let out a low whistle. "I was right."

"Yep."

"So why shoot the other women if he was after Sonya?" Brandon mused out loud.

Sonya frowned. Little lines formed above the bridge of her nose and he wanted to reach out and smooth them. Instead, he curled his fingers into a fist and concentrated on Holt's words.

"I wondered that myself. The only thing I could come up with was that he wanted to cover up the fact he was after Sonya."

"He wanted her to be a third victim in a random

shooting," Brandon muttered. "The police would investigate and come up empty on any connection between the three women and chalk it up to a crazy."

"That's my theory."

"It makes sense. Thanks, Holt."

Brandon hung up and interpreted the rest of the conversation for Sonya, but it looked as though she'd gotten the gist of it. Her face paled and she swallowed hard. "Those women in the park were shot because he was after me," she whispered. "And one died because—" She pressed her fingers to her lips and a tear slipped down her cheek.

"It's only a theory, Sonya. We don't have any proof."

"But it makes sense," she said. "I didn't have any connection to either of those women. None." She sniffed and swiped at her eyes.

He was almost ready to take her in his arms when she slammed a fist against the dash. "I still don't hate whoever is doing this," she said, "but I sure do want to see him in jail, where he belongs."

"Let's go inside." He climbed from the car and saw Max watching them with a look of concern. Brandon waved that all was fine and followed Sonya to the front door.

She paused, key in the lock. "I still haven't picked up my car from the hospital."

Brandon reached around her and unlocked the door. He knew he was big enough to block any bullets headed her way, but he wasn't in the mood to get shot again. He ushered her inside and shut the door behind them.

Sonya dropped her purse on the foyer floor on her way into the den. She paced from the mantel to the sofa and back. "I want this over with. I want my life back."

"I know. And we're making progress. It's just going to take time."

She touched the wound on her throat and then her fingers slid over the butterfly bandage on his cheek where the flying wood from the door had gashed him. "I'm tired of us getting hurt, tired of being afraid you—or someone else that I care about—is going to get killed because of me."

Brandon's fingers gripped hers. "I'm glad you care about me." Heat suffused her cheeks, but she refused to look away. She did care about him and wanted him to know it. "But," he said, "this situation isn't your fault. You're not responsible for the actions of whoever is doing this."

She sighed. "I know it's not my fault in that I'm not the one going around hurting people, but if I hadn't started looking for Heather Bradley, none of this would be happening and Ms. Gold would probably still be alive."

He grimaced. "Maybe she would. But if I understand things correctly, her death didn't take God by surprise."

Sonya stilled. "No. That's true. It didn't. None of this has taken Him by surprise."

"So let's focus on what we need to do to end it."

Sonya took a deep breath and nodded. "Okay."

"Now, where's your mother's room?"

"This way."

Sonya opened the door to her mother's bedroom. She'd saved this area for last, knowing it would take all of her strength to get through the memories, to wade through the grief and accept that her mother was gone from this side of heaven. The only thing that made the grief easier to bear was the fact that she would be re-united with the woman she loved one day for all eternity.

Hopefully, later rather than sooner as the person try-ing to kill her seemed to be determined to make happen.

She went to the end table and pulled out the drawer. Papers, pens, hair ties, face cream, a fingernail file.

Her notepad.

Sonya pulled it from the drawer and sat in the chair at the vanity table next to the door. She flipped through the yellow legal pad. Notes about doctors' appointments, things her mother had wanted to tell Sonya.

Tears welled at the sight of the handwriting. Bran-don's hand settled on her shoulder and she sniffed. "Sorry."

"It's okay."

She nodded and flipped through the pages. "I don't see anything," she whispered. "This was a dumb idea."

"It was a great idea," he countered. "It's never—" His phone rang and he pulled it from his pocket. Sonya started over at the beginning of the notepad, hoping she'd missed something. And she did. Two pages stuck to-gether. With a gentle tug, she separated them and stared.

"'Blackmail,'" she read aloud. "'Sonya.'" Just the two words written one on top of the other.

"Stay put, Spike. I'll be right there." Brandon hung up. "What did you say?"

"The word *blackmail* and my name underneath. Look." She turned the notepad so he could see it.

"Why would your mother write that on her notepad?"

"I have no idea."

"You think her agitation could have been because someone was blackmailing her?"

The thought sent knives of pain through her heart. "There was nothing to blackmail her about."

"How much money did she leave you?"

Sonya shrugged. "About a hundred thousand in savings bonds. And the house is paid off."

"So not an exorbitant amount, but enough that could be attractive to someone who didn't make but twenty or thirty thousand a year."

"I guess." Sonya swiped a stray tear and saw the frown between his eyes. "What's wrong?"

"Spike's been arrested."

"For what?" she gasped.

"Trespassing and resisting arrest are the charges. Apparently Spike was snooping around your house, looking in windows and such. A neighbor called it in. An officer drove by and saw him, tried to ask him what he was doing, and Spike panicked and ran. The officer chased him, caught him and took him downtown."

"When did all that happen?"

"Right before we got here." He held his phone up. "Spike just got his phone call."

"Then go. You need to help him. I'll just stay here and see if I can find anything else." She sighed. "I need to go through her stuff anyway."

"Are you able to do it?"

"I'm able." She gave a small smile. "The memories are good. I just miss her."

He pulled her into a hug and squeezed. "You're going to be all right, Sonya."

She leaned back and looked up at him, ignoring the pull on the stitches. "When you say it like that, I believe it."

"Good." He placed a light kiss on her lips, a quick

touch that offered comfort and expressed his concern for her. She also sensed a passion carefully held in check. She shivered and relished the moment.

When he pulled back, she asked, "That was lovely, but what about the no-kissing thing?"

He stopped and frowned. "Oh. Right. I must have been out of my mind." He ran his thumbs over her cheeks and gave her one last hug. "We need to talk, but it'll have to wait. I'll be back as soon as I take care of Spike. Max is right outside."

"All right. Thanks."

Brandon left and she locked the door behind him. They needed to talk? About? The kissing thing, probably. She went back to her mother's room and looked around. She sighed and went to the dresser. She opened it at the same time that her cell phone rang.

She snagged the device from her pocket and recognized the Bradleys' number. "Hello?"

"Am I speaking with Sonya?"

The female voice took her aback. "Yes, this is she."

"This is Ann Bradley."

For a moment, Sonya couldn't get her throat to work. Finally, she said, "Hello, Mrs. Bradley."

"I overheard Don talking to someone on the phone. He said that you're definitely Heather."

"Yes, ma'am. That's what they said."

"Well, I… I've been doing some thinking. Even a little praying."

"I see. About?"

"You, of course."

"Oh."

"And I've decided that I want to welcome you into

the family. That is…if you're even interested in being a part of our family."

Sonya swallowed hard. "I want to know you. I do. But I really want to know why I was kidnapped and who would do such a horrible thing."

"Do you think you can get past that? What if you never find out?"

Sonya thought about that for a minute. "Then I suppose I'll have to accept it and move on."

"Do you think you can do that?"

"I don't know. I suppose I would always wonder."

"Would you come to my house so we could talk?"

Sonya considered it, then thought about Max outside. "I really shouldn't leave. Someone still wants me dead."

"I could send a car for you."

"No, but…"

"But what?"

"I would tell you that you could come over here, but being around me can be dangerous. I have someone watching the house, but it's still not safe. I think we'll just have to wait until this is all over."

"I'll take my chances. Will you let your guard know I'm coming?" Sonya paused, undecided. A sigh filtered through the line. "Please, Sonya, I need to talk to you."

"All right, I'll let Max know. He'll probably ask for some identification."

"I'll have some."

"See you soon." Sonya hung up and felt her stomach swirl with a mixture of anticipation and dread. Inviting her birth mother into the house of the woman who'd loved and raised her for almost thirty years seemed almost wrong. But Sonya had been stolen from Ann Bradley and that wasn't her fault. She missed her mother, she always would, but that didn't mean she couldn't get to know the woman who'd given birth to her.

She called Max and told him the plans.

Brandon found Spike in the holding cell. He'd have to stay there until he could have someone bring the money for bond. Brandon wanted to know more before he decided to pay it himself. He didn't think Spike would be able to afford it and he knew his mother couldn't. He looked the teen in the eye. "What were you doing at Sonya's house?"

Red crept into the boy's cheeks and he shrugged.

Brandon sighed. "Come on, man. Talk to me."

"I wasn't going to break in and I wasn't going to hurt her if she was there."

"Okay, I believe you."

Spike's head snapped up. "You do?"

"Yes." Brandon did. Mostly. But he kept that niggling of doubt to himself and refused to let it show on his face.

Spike's shoulders slumped. "If I tell you, you will laugh your head off."

"Laugh?"

Spike nodded.

"Try me." Brandon couldn't imagine what was going through his young friend's mind.

"I was…" He mumbled the last part of the sentence.

"Say it again. Clear so I can understand you."

Spike lifted his head and his dark eyes bored into Brandon's. "I was trying to be like you. I was doing what a detective does. You know, check things out, seeing if your lady was all right. Keeping an eye on the place. Only someone saw me and called the cops."

Brandon pinched the bridge of his nose. All the time

and effort he'd put into helping Spike had paid off. And Spike had just laid the biggest compliment ever on him. Brandon blew out a breath. "Well, dude, I'm not going to laugh."

"You're not?" Skepticism showed.

"Nope. But I am going to get you out of here."

"How?"

"I'm going to pay your bail. How else?"

For the first time since Brandon had met Spike, he thought he saw a sheen of tears appear. Spike blinked and looked away. "Aw, man, you don't have to do that. I deserve to be here."

"For what?"

"For being so stupid."

"You weren't being stupid. You were being a kid." Probably for the first time in his short life. "All right. Hang tight. I'll be back."

"Yo, Hayes, you got a minute?"

Brandon turned to find Hector waving at him. "Yeah. Coming."

"I'll be at my desk."

To Spike, Brandon said, "I mean it. I'll be back."

Spike nodded and leaned his head back against the cell's wall. Thankfully, he didn't have any cell mates, and Brandon would see to it that he didn't.

Brandon hurried to find Hector. He found his partner and seated himself across from him even as he pulled out his phone and shot a text to Max. How is she?

Just fine. Quiet. Mrs. Bradley's coming for a visit.

Now, that was interesting. He looked at Hector. "Hang on a sec while I finish this text to Max."

"Sure." Hector went back to his computer.

Brandon sent a reply. Did she say why?

No, just that Mrs. B. wanted to see her. To talk.
OK. Keep me updated. Hope to be back soon.

10-4.

Brandon set his phone on the desk in front of him. "Okay, I'm finished for now. What's up?"

"I've found out something rather interesting."

"What's that?"

"You know how you were all skeptical about the death of Mrs. Bradley's sister?"

"Yes."

"I decided to dig into her death a little further. The M.E. did rule her tumble down the stairs an accident, but there was one little detail that you don't know."

"What?"

"She'd just had a baby not too long before her death."

Brandon froze as his mind clicked through this new information. "When was the baby born?"

"I don't have an exact date, but the M.E. noted in the chart, 'a recent birth, probably within the last couple of months.'"

"But no one's said anything about her having a baby. Where's the child?"

"She gave it up for adoption."

Brandon lifted his eyes to lock on Hector's. "Are you thinking what I'm thinking?"

"I'm thinking there's a lot more to this story than we know."

Brandon nodded. "What if Heather Bradley—Sonya—is really Ann and Don's niece?"

"Why keep that a secret?"

"Why don't we ask him? You got his number handy? I've got it on my phone somewhere…." He started scrolling through the list.

Hector pushed the file over to him and Brandon flipped through it until he came to the personal-information section, where he found Don Bradley's number.

The man didn't answer. Brandon left him a message asking him to call him back.

He looked at Hector. "Okay, so Sonya said her mother got a phone call she was concerned about. Said it agitated her. We requested her phone records with Sonya's consent. Where are they?" He asked the question almost absently as he moved files and papers to see if they'd been buried.

Hector reached into the bin on the corner of his desk and handed them to him.

"Thanks." Brandon started going through the list of numbers, looking for anything that might pop out at him. Fortunately, the list was short and he had a good idea of the time frame he needed to look at. He started at two weeks before Mrs. Daniels's death.

He pulled his keyboard toward him and opened the software that would allow him to input a phone number and trace it back to the owner.

Ten minutes later, he stopped and stared. Hector looked up. "What is it?"

"Why would someone from the Bradley household be calling Sonya's mother before Sonya even knew anything about the diaper bag and birth certificate?"

Chapter 18

Sonya opened the door to Mrs. Bradley and waved at Max, who gave her a two-fingered salute. "Come in."

Mrs. Bradley followed her into the den. "Would you like anything to drink?"

"No. Thank you." Mrs. Bradley twisted her hands together in a nervous gesture and took a seat on the couch under the window.

"What made you decide to call me?" Sonya asked.

Mrs. Bradley sighed. "A lot of different things. The main one being that if you're really Heather, then I can't ignore that."

"The DNA test was very conclusive."

"Yes, I know."

"Is that why you're here?"

"I came to find out what you want."

Sonya bit her lip. Then sighed. "I really don't want

anything. At least not from you. All I wanted was to find out who Heather Bradley was. I wanted to find out why my mother would have her birth certificate and baby bag in her closet. So I hired someone to find out." She stood and paced to the mantel, then back. "Then some-one tried to kill me." She held her hands up, beseech-ing. "Now I'd like to find out who wants me dead. Is that too much to ask?"

"But who?" Mrs. Bradley leaned forward and some of her resistance seemed to fade.

Sonya eyed the woman who was her mother. "You tell me. It's only when we started poking into your fam-ily that the assaults started."

Mrs. Bradley pursed her lips. "I can't think of a soul who would do such a thing."

Silence dropped around them like a scratchy blanket. Sonya shifted. "Look, if this is making you uncomfort-able, we don't have to do this. I know you don't want to believe I'm your daughter and that's okay."

"You're not my daughter."

"Even though the DNA test proves I'm Heather?"

"Yes, even though."

"I'm confused. If I'm not your daughter, then why does the DNA prove I'm Heather?"

Mrs. Bradley hesitated then rubbed a hand across her eyes. "Sonya, I believe you're Heather. And you were supposed to grow up as Heather Bradley, but I didn't… give birth to you. We adopted you."

Sonya froze and let that statement sink in. "Okay." She shook her head. "Can you please explain?"

Mrs. Bradley nodded. "It's a rather long and crazy story, but you're actually my niece. We adopted you from my sister."

"The one who died?" Strangely, Sonya felt nothing. No shock, no sorrow, nothing. She wondered if she had maxed out on emotional overload.

"Yes."

Sonya swallowed hard. "Did she really fall down the stairs?"

Mrs. Bradley teared up. "Yes, I think she really did. The carpet was messed up at the top and she was always warning me or guests to be careful." She gave a sad shrug. "I'd been by to see her that morning and she was fine physically. Emotionally was another story. Anyway, later that afternoon she was dead."

"So she was my birth mother," Sonya whispered.

"Yes."

"Who's my birth father?"

The woman shrugged. "I don't know. She never told me. All she said about him was that he was married and they weren't going to see each other anymore. And he didn't want the baby."

"So you adopted Heather. Me."

"Yes."

Sonya's head started to throb.

Brandon's phone rang. "Hello?"

"This is Don Bradley. You called?" The short clipped words took Brandon by surprise.

"I did. You sound busy. Is this a bad time?" Brandon tried to be gracious even though the man had called him.

"No." Don cleared his throat. "No. Sorry. I just had a rough meeting. What can I do for you?"

"We've come across some more information and need your input."

"What is it?"

"I'm just going to come right out and ask. Was Heather your niece and not your daughter?"

Silence rippled across the phone line, and Brandon almost wished he'd gone to see the man in person. Then a heavy sigh filled his ear. "Why do you ask?"

Brandon told him what Hector had discovered.

More silence. "I see."

"What do you see?"

"Sometimes when you keep a secret for so long, you start to believe the lies you told."

"What lies, sir?"

"I'm just not sure I see the point in—"

"A simple DNA test comparing Sonya's to your wife's sister's will be all it takes to find out. We're also going to want a DNA test to compare yours and your wife's to Sonya's."

"Why would you need ours?" The man's wariness came through loud and clear.

Brandon was bluffing. He had no grounds to stand on to ask for a DNA sample, but if he had the DNA from all parties involved, maybe he could get some answers for Sonya. "To find out who she's related to without question. Would you be willing to come in and offer a sample?"

Another heavy sigh. "I don't need to offer a sample. I guess the truth always finds a way to surface, doesn't it?" He paused. Brandon wondered if he was going to speak again. Finally, the man said, "Yes, she's my daughter." He hesitated again. Again, Brandon waited him out. "But," Don finally said, "she's not my wife's."

Brandon got it. "You had an affair with your sister-in-law."

"I did."

"I see."

The man sighed. "It wasn't an ongoing thing. It was actually a one-time thing. Ann was at the gym like always. Miriam stopped by and we talked, had a few drinks. She started crying about being lonely—" The pause drew out and Brandon could almost picture the man gathering his thoughts.

"And?"

"I went to comfort her and she kissed me."

"And you didn't push her away."

"No," he said flatly. "I didn't push her away."

"So when she came and told you that she was pregnant with Heather?"

"I freaked out. But," he sighed, "Ann and I had been trying to have a baby forever. Once I calmed down and thought about it, I realized this might be our chance." Another pause as though he was searching for the words. "Each month that went by without a positive pregnancy test sent Ann deeper and deeper into a depression. She dealt with it by spending more and more time at the gym, working out, getting fit, eating healthy. She thought if she kept her body in perfect shape, then it would happen. She'd get pregnant."

"But she didn't."

"No. And now I had a baby on the way with her sister."

"What did she say when you told her?"

"We didn't tell her. Miriam went to Ann and told her she was pregnant, but refused to tell her who the father was, just saying he was married, but wasn't in the picture anymore. She said that she couldn't raise the child by herself and would Ann and I be willing to take the baby."

"And Ann said yes."

"Not at first. She was afraid Miriam would change her mind, but Miriam didn't want the baby. She made that clear. She said she was too young to be a mother and if Ann wouldn't take it, she was going to see an adoption agency. I pressured Ann that we should do this and Ann finally agreed."

"Did Mrs. Bradley ever find out that the baby was yours?"

"No. Miriam would never say anything. She knew Ann wouldn't forgive her for that. Ever. And Miriam needed Ann." He snorted. "Or at least the money Ann poured into her."

"You resented the money she gave her sister?"

"Well, her father had cut her off for a reason. She'd made some pretty bad choices. Her parents had had enough of it and refused to give her any money."

"But Ann did."

"Yes."

Interesting. Brandon asked, "So she gave you the baby."

"She did. She had a home birth and a midwife. She just handed Heather to Ann when it was over. My lawyer took care of everything else. It was a private adoption with very little paperwork. But everything was straight up and legal."

"Who did she name as the father? The father would have had to agree to the adoption."

"Not if you claim you don't know who the father is."

Everything sounded as if it had been done legally, just as he'd said.

"So who would benefit from having Sonya out of the picture?"

"Now, that I don't know." He cleared his throat. "And

I would very much appreciate it if you would keep all of this confidential. I don't want Ann to find out. Ever. It would devastate her." Another slight pause. "And our marriage. My life would be over. Do you understand what I'm saying?"

"Unfortunately, I do understand, but I honestly can't make any promises. But I won't mention it unless I have to."

The man's silence conveyed his unhappiness with Brandon's answer, but Brandon wasn't going to make promises he might not be able to keep.

Brandon hung up with Mr. Bradley and flipped back to the front of the file. They'd put every scrap of information about the case into one place. He turned over page after page after page. And stopped when he came to the pictures of the car with the rifle. The one the shooter had used in the parking garage. The forensics team had gone through the vehicle with a fine-tooth comb and had photographed everything.

One picture stopped him.

"Hey, Hector."

"Yeah?"

"This guy worked at Gold Star Gym, right?"

Hector looked over his shoulder. "Yes. So?"

"So I've seen this emblem before." He pointed to the gold star on the man's identification badge.

"Where?"

"On Mrs. Bradley's gym bag."

"Oh, boy."

Brandon had another thought. "Check and see if Mrs. Bradley showed up for her appointment with her trainer at the gym the day Ms. Gold, the nanny, was killed. I'm calling Max and telling him to get inside with Sonya."

Hector got on his phone while Brandon called Max. When Max got on the line, Brandon said, "I don't have time for details. Just get inside with Sonya. Mrs. Bradley looks good for the one who's been trying to kill her. Be careful. Hector and I are on the way."

He stood as Hector hung up the phone. The grim look in his eyes didn't bode well. "What is it?"

"She never showed up. In fact, she hasn't been to the gym for the past two days. And guess who her trainer was?"

"Our shooter?"

"The one and only."

Sonya's phone rang and she flinched. "Excuse me a moment, please."

"Of course," Mrs. Bradley said.

She grabbed the device. "Hello?"

"Sonya, this is Brandon. Are you all right?"

Her heart thudded at his voice and his face came immediately to mind. "Yes, I'm fine."

"Max texted me that Mrs. Bradley was coming by. Is she there yet?"

Sonya glanced at her visitor. "Yes, we were just talking. I've learned some pretty interesting things."

"Okay, don't react to what I'm going to tell you, all right?"

Sonya swallowed, but hoped she kept her face expressionless. "Okay."

"I've asked Max to come inside with you. It looks like Mrs. Bradley is the one who hired someone to kill you."

Sonya couldn't help the small gasp that slipped out. She glanced at the woman who was watching her, head tilted, eyes narrowed. She quickly turned away. "Okay. Why do you think that?"

"The shooter was her trainer at the gym. He had a bit of a shady past and we think she hired him to kill you. And, Sonya—"

"Yes?"

"Don Bradley just told me that he and Ann adopted you from Ann's sister."

"I know," she whispered. "Right before your call, Ann revealed I was Miriam's daughter. But she never learned who my father was."

"Sonya..." Brandon hesitated. "Don Bradley *is* your biological father. He had an affair with Ann's sister." Sonya gasped. Her knees weakened.

"I know it's a shock," Brandon said, his compassion ringing through the line. "I'm heading that way now."

Sonya felt a small kernel of fear start to replace her shock. "That's fine."

There was a knock on the door. Sonya crossed the room and glanced out the window. "Max is at the door."

"Let him in," Brandon said. "I'm already in the car. I'll be there in less than ten minutes. I've also got backup on the way."

Sonya reached for the lock and wondered if Mrs. Bradley would try to stop her. She unlocked the door and twisted the knob. Mrs. Bradley didn't move.

Max stepped in and shut the door behind him.

Now the woman stood. "What's going on?"

Max eyed her. "That's what we want to know. Why are you trying to kill Sonya?"

Mrs. Bradley gaped. "What? Try to kill her? Are you out of your mind?"

The door burst in. Max started to turn and a gunshot rent the air. Max went down. Sonya screamed.

Chapter 19

Sonya dropped to her knees beside Max, who lay face-down. He groaned and tried to roll, then dropped back to the floor. "Max!"

A hard grip on her upper arm yanked her to her feet. The gun in her face sent terror racing through her. She lifted her eyes to the man behind the weapon and gasped.

Don Bradley.

"What are you doing?" Sonya cried.

"Taking care of things." He turned to his wife.

The woman stood pale and shaking, her brown eyes wide, blank.

Shock.

"Get in the car." Don shoved her toward the door and Sonya almost tripped over Max.

"What about Max?"

Another hard shove in the small of her back sent her

stumbling toward the door. "Hopefully, he'll die where he is." He aimed the weapon at Max. "Another bullet ought to take care of that."

Sonya whirled and hurled herself at him. "No!" She slammed into the arm that held the gun and Don went to his knees as he lost his grip. The weapon skittered across the hardwood floor and hit the edge of the brick fireplace.

Sonya dived for the gun. "Ann, run!"

A hard grip wrapped around her ankle and yanked. She lost her balance and rolled. Don regained his footing, grabbed the gun, aimed it at her and pulled the trigger.

The loud crack echoed. Sonya felt the bullet whiz past her face and froze. Don approached and shoved her up against the wall, fingers wrapped around her throat. "Get. In. The. Car."

Stars whirled in front of her eyes and darkness flirted at the edges of her mind.

Then she was free and gasping in air. Her already bruised throat throbbed in time to her heartbeat. His fingers tangled themselves in her hair as he dragged her to the door.

Ann still stood staring, eyes wide and blank.

Don shoved with the gun. "Get in the car, Ann. The backseat. I'm going to take care of this."

Ann walked out the door.

Pain ratcheted through her head, her throat, her neck. Everywhere. He pulled and she had no choice but to follow. Within seconds, Ann slipped into the backseat and Don opened the driver's door. "Crawl over."

The black BMW was large and roomy, and Sonya had no trouble slipping into the front passenger seat. All the while aware of the gun pointed at her. She glanced in the rearview mirror, the side mirror. Where was Brandon?

She looked at the clock. The entire incident in her house had taken less than five minutes.

Don held the gun in his left hand while he started the car with his right. "Just had to butt in," he muttered. "You just couldn't leave the past in the past, could you?"

She stared at him. "All I wanted to do was find Heather Bradley."

"And all I wanted was for her to stay gone."

Brandon pulled to the curb behind Max's car. Sonya's scream and subsequent click of the phone disconnecting had sent terror shooting through him.

Blue lights at the end of the street flashed the impending arrival of other officers. Brandon reported in his position, knowing the dispatcher would inform the other officers nearby.

Ann Bradley's vehicle was parked in Sonya's driveway. Max's car still sat at the curb. "Why isn't Max answering his phone?" Hector muttered.

Worry beat at Brandon. He wondered the same thing. Max hadn't answered his phone for the past seven minutes.

Jordan's brand-new SUV pulled up the rear.

Brandon climbed from his car and heard Hector's door slam. He pulled his weapon and held it close as he approached the front door. He rapped his knuckles on the wood.

No answer. "Sonya?"

Jordan motioned he would check the garage.

Hector stayed close. "You think she's in trouble?"

"She screamed. Then the phone cut off."

"Could have been a mouse."

"That would be good news."

"Yeah, I don't think so, either."

Jordan returned. "Garage has a vehicle in it." Brandon rapped on the door again, then twisted the knob. Unlocked.

He stepped inside. "Max!" He strode to his friend, the bloodstain on his back sending another bolt of fear through him. "Call for an ambulance."

Jordan was already on the phone by the time Brandon dropped to his knees to feel for a pulse. Faint, but steady. Relief made him shudder.

Then he spotted a cell phone wedged under the side of Max's abdomen. He pulled it out and held it up. "It's Sonya's," he told Jordan.

"That's not good."

Hector and two uniformed officers returned to the den. "All clear," Hector said. "How's he doing?"

"He needs a hospital," Brandon said.

An officer waved at Brandon. "We just got a 911 call from a neighbor on this street. A Mr. Tobias. Shots heard."

"Did he see anything?"

"No, said he was in the back of the house and thought it might have been a car backfiring, but then he decided to check it out. By the time he got to the window, he saw a car at the end of the street, but couldn't make it out."

Brandon ran a hand through his hair. "How am I supposed to find her?" He paced, thinking.

"Officer? Hey, let me through!"

Brandon turned. "Who are you? Do you know something about what happened?"

"I'm Sonya's neighbor across the street. Paul Lehman.

There was a guy who took Sonya and another woman. He had a gun."

"You saw him?"

"Yeah. He shoved them in a big black BMW and took off. Sonya was one of those women, but I didn't recognize the other one."

That stopped him. "A man?"

"And two women."

"Sonya dropped her phone, so that's not going to help us. And you say he had a gun?"

"Yes, but he was trying to hide it. By the time I went to get my own weapon, he was gone."

"Do you have a weapon on you now?"

"No, I'm not stupid. Once I saw they were gone, I locked it back up."

Brandon thought of Max. "Whoever he is, he's definitely not afraid to shoot someone."

An ambulance screeched to a halt and two paramedics headed for the house, directed by one of the uniformed officers.

"I don't suppose you got a plate?"

Mr. Lehman grimaced and shook his head "No, sorry. Not all of it, anyway. I think the first letter was an *H*. I couldn't get close enough to see it by the time he was pulling away."

Brandon squeezed the man's shoulder even as his anxiety skyrocketed. "I want to know who was here."

"We'll start questioning the other neighbors," Hector said. "And I've already put a BOLO out on a black Beemer."

"Can we get the helicopter?" Jordan asked.

Brandon pulled his phone out and called Christine, his sergeant. In terse, precise sentences, he filled her in on the situation. "I'm running out of time. He's got her and another woman, presumed to be Mrs. Bradley, in his car. I don't have a clue who he is or where he'd take them."

With only a slight pause, she approved the helicopter request.

All they needed now was to find the black BMW with three people. He started praying.

Sonya gripped the door handle as Don sped down the highway. In the rearview mirror, Sonya could see Mrs. Bradley slumped in the backseat.

"Why are you doing this?" Sonya whispered.

"I spun some pretty good half-truths and lies to your boyfriend, but it's only a matter of time before they figure everything out."

"Figure everything out? What do you mean?" His knuckles whitened on the steering wheel and Sonya moved her fingers to the door lock. "You said you wanted me to stay gone. Do you know who kidnapped me when I was a baby?"

"Yes."

"Because you set it up?" She took a shot in the dark even as she noticed they were on I-85 and going north.

He flinched and Mrs. Bradley gasped. Sonya took another look in the mirror and noticed the woman sitting upright and paying attention. Some of the shock had worn off and her eyes appeared clear. And narrowed. Sonya didn't think Don had noticed. He moved into the left lane to pass a slower vehicle. The needle on the speedometer inched up. Suddenly, things started clicking for Sonya as her mind put a few more pieces together. "You killed Ms. Gold, didn't you?"

"You were going to talk to her."

"And she's the only other person who knew the truth."

"Yes," he said.

"She took me, didn't she?"

"I paid her to walk into the nursery and walk out with you. That's the one thing she managed to do right in this whole thing."

"Were you blackmailing my mother?"

He snorted. "No. Rebecca was. She'd broken into the lawyer's office and gotten your mother's name as the adoptive parents. She figured out that you didn't know you were adopted and threatened to tell you. From what little I gathered, your mother didn't want you to know."

Sonya closed her eyes. Her mother wouldn't succumb to blackmail. She'd been going to tell her. Sonya now knew exactly why her mother had been so agitated before she'd died.

"What did Ms. Gold hope to get by blackmailing my mother?"

"Money, of course."

"Why after all this time?"

"I have no idea. I should have killed her long before I did."

His cold-blooded statement sent chills racing up her back. "I'm still not clear on why you didn't want me. You adopted me from your sister-in-law. Why would you do that if you only wanted me to disappear?"

"Because my wife insisted. And I had to do whatever it took to keep Ann happy." He glanced in the rearview mirror. "Right, Ann? Had to keep you happy." His lip curled, and the disgust Sonya saw on his face made her swallow. "When I paid Rebecca to take you from the nursery, I told her I didn't care what she did with you, just to get rid of you."

Sonya flinched. "So she put me up for adoption."

"No, she sold you to some lawyer who found two people desperate enough for a baby to part with their life savings."

"My parents," she whispered.

"Yes."

Sonya knew why he was being so forthcoming. He wasn't planning to let her ever repeat this crazy story. Her mind frantically worked, trying to figure out the best way to deal with him while looking for a way to escape. *Keep him talking. Keep him talking.* "Who was the man who tried to kill us? You hired him, right?"

"He was Ann's personal trainer. He was always looking for a way to make some quick and easy cash."

Sonya clenched her fingers into fists. "Where are you taking us?"

"I haven't figured that out yet. Now be quiet and let me think."

She ignored his order for quiet. "How did you know to come to my house?"

"Ann said she was going to go see you. I followed her. After the phone call with your boyfriend earlier, I could see he was putting it all together. Hopefully, I've fed him enough lies that he'll be confused for a little while. Long enough for me to put a plan together, anyway."

"You're going to kill us," she whispered. "You're going to kill your wife?"

A strangled sound came from the backseat.

Don shot her a fierce look. "I'm not going to kill my wife." He glanced in the rearview mirror. "We're going to take an overseas trip. Finally find a little place in the

Caribbean and have a nice quiet life. Doesn't that sound good, Ann?"

"Yes, dear." Her monotone voice worried Sonya, but Don didn't seem to notice. He gave a small satisfied smile.

"But you're going to kill me," Sonya stated.

The smile slipped from his face. "Your presence could ruin everything. You simply know too much. Especially now."

The man wasn't thinking straight. "I got a phone call before you got there. Brandon told me they suspect that Mrs. Bradley is the one who wants me dead. You don't think they won't be looking to talk to her, do you?"

He stilled, a muscle jumping along his jawline. "What makes them think she had anything to do with it?"

"You just told me that the man you hired was her trainer. It didn't take them long to connect the two."

"So they figured that out, did they?" he murmured. "That idiot. I told him how to cover his tracks and he ignored me. Just goes to show you that in order to get something done right, you usually have to do it yourself." He pulled into the back of his office building. "Get out my door. There's no one down here this time of day. We're going to use the service elevator and go up to my office."

Sonya frantically searched for an escape route, a weapon she could use on the way in, anything. The gun pressing into her lower back discouraged her from trying anything immediately. "I can't believe my own father would do this to me. I'm your blood child. What threat am I to you?"

"Shut up." He pressed her toward the entrance. Ann hadn't moved from the backseat. He looked at his wife.

"Come on, Ann. I need you to come with me. This will all be over soon enough."

Without hesitation, Ann climbed from the vehicle and followed them into the building. Confusion swept over Sonya. Why would he bring her here? It seemed like the most obvious place for Brandon to look for her.

Then again, he didn't yet realize that Don was the one behind everything. "Does your wife know you had an affair with her sister?"

The gun whipped around and caught her on the side of her head. "I said shut up!"

Pain ricocheted through her. A scream escaped and darkness threatened. She fought it off even as her knees buckled and she went to the ground.

When her vision steadied, she saw Ann staring at her husband, her face devoid of color. Don had his attention on her. "It's not true, Ann. She's lying. She'll say anything right now."

Sonya lurched to her feet and turned to run while he had his eyes and his weapon turned away from her.

She took two steps before a hard hand twisted in the back of her shirt and jerked her to a halt. She barely kept her feet when he yanked her around and shoved her toward the door. She slammed into it and leaned against it, praying she wouldn't pass out.

She noticed the security camera in the corner of the building and looked straight at it. Don gave a low laugh. "I've already thought of that camera, Sonya. It's no problem to erase the video. Now go."

Chapter 20

Hector's phone rang and Brandon shot him a look. His partner answered and listened while Brandon tapped the dashboard, impatience eating through him.

As soon as Hector hung up, Brandon pounced. "What?"

"The chopper spotted a black BMW entering the parking garage where Don Bradley works."

Brandon blinked. "Don Bradley? What does he have to do with this?"

"Maybe he's the one who took them?"

"But why?"

"Who knows? Maybe he's got his own reasons."

"But would he dare take them to his office? It's too simple, isn't it?"

"I'd say we're going to have to check it out."

"What if it's a decoy?" He paused then checked his

weapon. "Call for backup to head that way. I have a very bad feeling about this."

"His business is textiles, right?"

"Yes."

"If you wanted to get rid of someone without a trace and you owned a textile business, how would you do it?"

Brandon shuddered and a wave of nausea swept over him as he thought. "Textile companies use acid for various things. I'd say there's probably enough in the building to hide a murder."

Hector flinched and stepped on the gas. Brandon prayed even as he got on the phone and formulated a plan. He filled his boss in. "I need help here, Christine. I need blueprints of the building. I need a way to clear the building without letting Don know we're onto him. I need a SWAT team and a hostage negotiator. Send them all and send them fast."

"They're on the way."

"And I am, too."

Ignoring the intense throbbing at the base of her skull, Sonya pressed her palm hard against the door. If he was going to kill her, someone was going to find out she'd been here and she was going to leave evidence behind.

Her throat ached at the thought of dying and never knowing if she and Brandon could have had something wonderful. She hated the pain her death would cause him.

But maybe he'd figure it out soon.

She prayed for Max. She prayed for them all.

She'd seen Mr. Lehman looking out his front window. He'd seen her get into the black BMW, and she knew once Max was found, a full-on investigation would kick into play.

Once inside the building, Don directed her down a long hall past several other doors. They turned, right, then left, and by the time he finally stopped and let go of her hair, she knew she'd have a hard time finding her way back should she manage to get away from him. He gave her another hard shove toward a door marked with a hazardous symbol. "Step to the side."

"What are you doing, Don?" Mrs. Bradley finally spoke, coming out of her shocked stupor.

Don jumped and stared at her as though he'd forgotten all about her. Sonya's nerves twitched and she shifted. The weapon swung back to her even as he addressed his wife. "I have to take care of things." He handed her his keys. "I want you to go up to my office and wait for me."

She ignored the keys. "Take care of what? What about Sonya? Why does she think you're going to kill her?"

"I'm not going to kill her," he soothed her. "Sonya and I have business to take care of. Then we'll join you."

"What kind of business? Why do you have a gun? You shot that man at Sonya's house. Why?"

"Will you stop asking questions and do what I asked you to do?" His shout echoed through the area. His wife flinched and narrowed her eyes.

Then her shoulders slumped and she turned without another word.

"No, wait!" Sonya cried. "You can't do this!"

Ann paused, but didn't turn.

Don ignored her and simply reached over to punch in the code to the room. The door opened.

He shoved the gun into her rib and moved her inside.

Sonya frantically scrambled for an escape plan. Ann followed her inside.

"What are you doing? I told you to go upstairs." Ann stared at him. Don shook his head. "Fine. Fine. I'll just have to deal with you, too."

She didn't offer a response, but didn't leave, either.

Don moved behind his desk and picked up a key. "Now, it's time to end this once and for all."

"What are you going to do? If you're going to shoot me, shoot me!" Sonya knew at such close range, her chances of ducking were slim, but if he started shooting, maybe the noise would bring someone running.

"Shoot you? Of course not."

She stared at the gun and wondered if he'd lost his mind. "Then what?" she whispered. Why had he brought her here if he didn't plan to kill her? Confusion swept through her.

"You'll see. And I promise, it's relatively painless."

Brandon and Hector arrived at the parking garage only seconds ahead of the other officers. "There's the black BMW."

"You think it's his?"

"No idea." Brandon walked over to the vehicle and placed a palm on the hood. "It's hot. Hasn't been here long."

"First letter on the license plate is an *H*. Let's get a search going. We'll have to lock down the building. No one in or out."

Brandon nodded, his brain spinning, fear for Sonya wanting to short-circuit his thoughts. When Hector finished giving orders and putting the plan into motion, Brandon eyed the door with the combination code. "He wouldn't take them through the building, where anyone would see them."

"The basement?"

"Where does that door go?"

Hector tapped a few keys on his phone. "I had the blueprints emailed to me." More tapping. "Looks like it does go into an area that's sealed off. A hazardous area."

"That's where we need to go. I need the code. Who would have it?" he muttered. Then looked up. "The security officer. Where is he?"

Within seconds, they had the man at the door, punching in the code.

Sonya kept her fear under control. Barely. Mrs. Bradley had once again lapsed into a catatonic state. She'd backed up to the wall and slid down to sit on the floor. Now she stared, a blank, empty stare that said she'd suffered too much and had mentally checked out.

Sonya felt horrible at having exposed Don's affair with his sister-in-law in such a blunt way, but she'd been desperate and hoped the knowledge would spur the woman into helping her.

Instead it had sent her into a place in her mind that Sonya wasn't sure she'd ever come back from.

Don kept the weapon on her. The room they'd entered had a sign on the door that read Authorized Personnel Only. He shoved her toward one of the two matching steel chairs. "Sit down." She sat. With the gun still trained on her, he glanced into the other room toward his wife. "Ann!" The woman didn't move. Didn't blink. With a curse, he shook his head. "She's always been weak. Weak but loaded."

"So you married her for her money?"

"Of course not. I loved Ann. I would have done anything for her. But when she couldn't have children, she changed."

"So why not just leave her? Why kidnap the only child she'd ever have and send her deeper into depression?"

"Because the child was mine. And her sister's. And if her sister ever said a word, I was done." His steady hand never wavered and the gun never moved from her as he backed toward a file cabinet and opened the second drawer with his free hand. "You see, I signed a prenup. If Ann ever decided to divorce me, I would get nothing."

"And if Miriam ever said anything, Ann would divorce you without hesitation," she whispered. He blinked but didn't answer. He didn't have to. "You killed Miriam, didn't you?"

Don pulled a large hunting knife from his desk drawer.

Fear crawled through her. "What are you going to do with me?" Relatively painless or not, she wanted to know.

He set the knife on his desk and pulled out a roll of duct tape. Sonya knew he'd just confirmed what she'd known all along. He might not plan to shoot her, but he did plan to get rid of her.

"You don't have to kill me." She felt the quiver in her voice, but was glad it didn't come out in her words. She wanted to be strong. To believe help would come.

But help might be a long way off. She was going to have to rescue herself. *Lord, I need You to help me stay calm and think clearly. But I wouldn't mind some help if You could please send Brandon. Let him figure out where we are.*

"Yes. Yes, I do." He approached, duct tape in one hand, weapon in the other.

The coldness in his eyes made her shudder. "What does it matter now?" she cried. "You didn't want Ann finding out that you had the affair with her sister. Well, now she knows. What else is there that you don't want anyone to find out? What threat am I to you? Let me go and we'll forget this ever happened." She cast a glance at the still-open door. Don was either too preoccupied or too cocky to bother with shutting it. Ann hadn't moved. If she could make it to the outer door, she had a chance.

"Don't even think about it. I can't let you go. He'll find out and I'll be on the streets." She almost didn't catch the low muttered words.

"Who'll find out?"

"It doesn't matter now."

"Who?" she pressed.

"My father-in-law," he shouted. "The dictator." He moved toward her with the tape. Sonya stood and whirled to stand behind the chair.

Don stopped and blinked as if he couldn't believe she'd actually just defied him. The gun lifted. "I was trying to do this the nonmessy way, but—"

Sonya gripped the edges of the chair and in one smooth seamless move lifted it and crashed it into his outstretched arm.

Don screamed and the weapon clattered to the floor.

Sonya bolted through the open door.

His curses behind her filled the air as she ran, not knowing where she was going, but praying it was toward safety.

* * *

"Did you hear that?" Brandon lifted a hand.

"It was faint, but it sounded like someone yelling," Hector said.

"This way." Brandon moved down the hall, made a turn and came face-to-face with another hallway that branched off into two directions. He stopped. "Which way? It's a maze down here."

Hector glanced at his phone. "The blueprints aren't much help. Unless we know exactly where they are, I don't know which direction to take." He lifted his head. "You hear anything else?"

"No." Brandon listened. "Wait. Footsteps?"

"Maybe, but from where?"

Brandon shook his head. "I can't tell." Frustration filled him. Which way? "We can't just stand here." The officers shifted behind him. He turned. "Fan out. Split up. Check every room, every closet. I think we have the element of surprise, so be quiet and be careful. He's armed. Go." They went, their footsteps making little sound on the hall tiles. He looked at Hector. "Let me see those blueprints again, will you?"

Hector handed him the phone. Brandon moved his finger across the screen then zoomed in on the area where they now stood. "Okay, there's a large area. Looks like a warehouse type space. Over here are offices—"

Officers headed back their way, guns held, faces grim. "All clear back this way."

Brandon handed the phone back to Hector and motioned toward the next hall. "Then we go this way."

"Stop!"

Brandon froze. "You hear that?"

"Yeah. That way."

* * *

"I said stop!"

Sonya heard his furious shout as she raced down the hallway, her tennis shoes slapping against the tiles. A glance over her right shoulder sent terror shooting through her. Don followed right behind her, eyes full of fury, burning holes into her back while his right hand gripped the hunting knife. Fear spurred her faster.

She turned a corner, then another. She had no idea where she was. A large door at the end of the hallway beckoned. With an extra burst of speed, she reached it and yanked on the handle.

Locked.

And then he had her.

He wrapped his fingers around her upper arm and glared down at her. "You have to know the code," he snarled.

Sonya kicked out and caught him in the knee as she spun from his grip. With a howl of pain, he struck out and landed a hard fist against her cheek.

Pain blinded her for a brief moment. Long enough for him to punch in the code and shove her through the door.

She stumbled and fell to the floor. "Leave me alone!" Scents assaulted her. The smell of vinegar nearly over-powered her. Her gaze darted even as her brain pro-cessed the new environment. A large open area with a high steel ceiling. Blue barrels filled with whatever chemicals were used in the textile industry.

And no other exit that she could see.

Don yanked her to her feet and pushed her toward a set of steel steps that led to a second floor. A match-ing steel balcony ran the length of the fifty-yard wall.

He had no weapon but the knife, she realized. He

hadn't taken the time to grab his gun before coming after her. But he was strong. Much stronger than she. And the knife was wicked-looking and sharp.

Her face throbbed. Her head ached and nausea churned in her belly. "Why are you doing this? They'll find you and figure it out and you'll go to jail for murder. Stop now and you won't spend the rest of your life in prison!"

"Shut up!" He gave her another shove. She fell against the step. Pain shot up her shin. He grasped her hair once again and twisted. She cried out and her vision dimmed.

"Move!" She winced at his shout. Dizziness hit her and she fought it off.

Sonya regained her footing and took the stairs slowly, her brain spinning, her body aching. Barrels of acid below, the unknown above. At the top of the stairs, with his hand still gripping her hair, he paused as though to get his bearings. She realized he was undecided about what to do.

The acidic vinegar smell nauseated her, and her head pounded, begging for relief. Tears leaked from her eyes and prayers slipped from her lips.

A sound from below pulled her captor to a halt.

"Sonya!"

Brandon's frantic cry had never sounded so sweet.

Chapter 21

Brandon stared up at Sonya, trapped by Don Bradley, who shielded himself with her body, a knife at her throat. Her throat that had just begun to heal from the last time she'd been held in a similar position. "Don't come any closer. Get out! Get out!"

Hector moved behind him to his left, and other law-enforcement personnel swarmed behind him.

Brandon stepped forward, his eyes locked on the man and not the woman he realized he'd give his life for. "Let her go, Don."

"Not a chance. I'm not going to prison, so just back off and let me get out of here."

"Where do you think you can go that you won't be found?"

"I have money. I have resources. I'll manage or die trying. Now move! Get them out!"

Brandon saw movement behind Don. Someone had found another way in. He frowned. He didn't remember another entrance or exit on the blueprints.

But there was an elevator that came from up above. Officers must have utilized it.

But shooting Don in the back risked the bullet passing through and hitting Sonya. He had to talk this man down.

Sonya's terrified eyes followed him as he took another step toward the duo. "What are you going to do, Don?"

"I don't know! I have to think. How did you find me? How did you know I'd come here?"

Brandon ignored his questions. "You didn't plan this, did you? You're going by the seat of your pants." He took another step. And another.

"Stop! I'll kill her." He pressed the blade tighter, and Sonya's eyes widened as she went up on her tiptoes. "See that acid down there? I don't even have to cut her. I'll just throw her in it. Now back off!"

Brandon froze as he saw exactly what the man was talking about. Three barrels of acid, lids removed, were directly under the steps where Don had Sonya. All he had to do was give her a shove and she'd land in one of them. He shuddered. "Please, Don. Think of your wife. Ann's been through so much."

"Ann," he spat. Then his anger faded and sadness etched itself in the grooves of his face. "I used to love her, you know. But then she changed, became so sad. And I couldn't do anything to make it better."

"That must have been terrible." Brandon interjected as much sympathy as he could muster. He just needed to distract the man long enough to get Sonya away from him.

"So awful he turned to my sister and had a child with her." Ann's quiet voice came from behind Don.

He spun, the knife dropping slightly as he pulled Sonya around with him.

A shot rang out and Don's right shoulder took the bullet.

Sonya screamed as the knife scraped across her already wounded throat. Don flung her against the rail and she went to her knees. He fell beside her, his eyes bright with pain. His hand reached for her and she rolled.

Over the edge.

For one weightless moment she hung suspended. A scream welled and terror filled her. Her fingers grasped, scrambling for a hold.

"Sonya!"

Brandon's cry echoed as she gripped the edge of the steel landing. Her feet dangled over the barrel of acid.

Behind Don, who lay bleeding and writhing against the pain, she saw Ann on the ground, hands cuffed. Brandon's wide eyes appeared above Sonya's and his fingers locked around her wrist. Don gave a roar as he surged up and brought the knife around, aiming it at Brandon.

"Watch out!"

Another shot rang out and Don dropped. Officers raced to him, kicking the knife away and cuffing him.

Brandon gave a grunt and pulled on her wrist. She swung a leg over the landing and rolled into his arms. Sonya held on while tremors racked her.

"It's okay. You're all right. I've got you," he whispered.

Chaos reigned around them while he held her. After

a moment, she gained a semblance of control. "Is he dead?"

She didn't recognize her weak, shaky voice. But she wanted to know the answer. Pulling away, she looked around his shoulder and saw Don staring at her. Two officers stood over him, weapons drawn and pointed at his head. He blinked. "You didn't have to do this," she whispered.

"I didn't know what else to do," he rasped. "Ann would have divorced me. I thought getting rid of you would shut down the questions." He swallowed. "I couldn't lose it all."

"And yet, that's exactly what you've done."

He closed his eyes and fought for his next breath.

She saw Ann being led away by two officers. Paramedics entered and headed for Don. Brandon pulled her to her feet. Her knees wobbled and she leaned on him, grateful for his support, his nearness.

"Come on." He placed a kiss on her forehead and tightened his arm around her shoulders. "Let's get out of here. We can do our statements soon enough."

Sonya followed him, her mind in turmoil. "I want to see Ann."

"She's been arrested for shooting her husband."

"He was going to kill me. She should get a medal."

"She's lucky she wasn't shot, too. I wonder how she got the gun."

"It was Don's," Sonya said. "I managed to knock it out of his hand when I ran."

"But he still had the knife."

"Yes."

"I guess she knew a shortcut to where he was holding you. I don't remember seeing it on the blueprints."

"It doesn't matter now."

Once outside, the police let them through. A paramedic raced up and Brandon let her go long enough to get her throat looked at and rebandaged. The paramedic ushered her into the back of the ambulance. Sonya explained the original injury and the woman shook her head. "You've had a rough time of it, no doubt. The good news is, no stitches required for this new injury. Looks like the knife hardly touched you."

Sonya nodded her thanks. "It's really only a graze. It stung, but didn't really cut me." *Thank You, Lord.*

She looked for Brandon and found him a few feet from the ambulance. "What about the other bumps and bruises? You should go to the hospital and get checked out."

"No. I'll pass. I have enough medical knowledge to know Don didn't do any lasting damage."

"Thank God for that." He helped her down and led her over to his car, where Peter and Jordan stood. Peter grabbed his brother in a bear hug. "Are you all right?"

"Yeah, I'm fine. Or I was until you hugged me and set off the throbbing in my shoulder again."

Peter grimaced and stepped back. "Sorry."

"I'll live."

Jordan hugged Sonya. "Glad you're all right."

"Me, too. Thanks." Sonya shuddered and Brandon squeezed her fingers. "How's Max?" The man had never been far from her mind or her prayers.

"He's going to be fine," Jordan said. "The surgery to remove the bullet went well and he's already fussing about being stuck in the hospital. Erica's practically sitting on him to keep him from checking himself out."

Sonya breathed a sigh of relief. "Good. I'm so glad this is all over. Mostly at least."

"What do you mean?" Brandon asked.

"I still have some questions." She gave a light shrug, then winced at the movement. "I don't suppose they matter, but I would love to know why all this happened now. Why would Rebecca Gold wait so long?"

"She might not have been able to find you," Brandon said. "Didn't you move quite a bit?"

"Yes. A lot."

"So maybe once she got up the nerve to try to do the blackmail scheme, she couldn't find you until recently."

"Maybe."

"So Ms. Gold tracked down Sonya's mother and gave her the bag and birth certificate as proof she knew they had adopted Sonya," Peter said.

"That's why Mom was so agitated at the end," Sonya whispered. "She wanted to tell me, but couldn't find the courage to do so."

"And then we mention tracking down the nanny in front of Don Bradley and he has no choice but to find her first and kill her."

Sonya shuddered. "It's all so needless."

Commotion behind her caused them to turn. Paramedics wheeled Don Bradley from the building. He had an oxygen mask on his face, an IV in his arm and leg irons clamped around his ankles. Straps held his arms to the gurney.

Sonya blinked and tried to register the fact that the man whose blood she carried had wanted her dead. Had, in fact, killed others to keep his secrets. He'd had no desire to reunite with the child he'd given up so many years ago. It hurt, but Sonya realized she was much better off. Her parents had been wonderful and raised her to be strong in the Lord.

If she'd grown up as Heather Bradley, she'd be an entirely different person. "Thank You, God," she whispered.

Peter clapped his brother on his shoulder. "See you Sunday at Mom and Dad's?"

Brandon seemed to waver, and then his face hardened. "No, not yet."

Peter sighed and without another word turned on his heel and headed for his car.

Brandon pulled her aside, leaving the others talking and speculating about the day's events. "It's over."

She nodded. "I know."

He leaned over and kissed her. "I want a chance with you, Sonya."

"And I want one with you, Brandon. With all my heart that's what I want."

He pulled back and looked at her, wariness in his eyes. "I hear a 'but' at the end of that sentence."

She bit her lip and fought the tears that wanted to fall. "Tell me how I can help you get past the bitterness you feel toward your parents." She stroked his cheek. "Tell me how to help you."

"Why is this so important to you?" A muscle ticked in his jaw.

"Because I'm not perfect," she said.

He blinked. "I know that. I'm not, either."

"But you expect your parents to be. Will you expect me to be, too?"

He frowned. "What are you talking about?"

"Your parents made mistakes. Bad mistakes. Mistakes that haunt you today, but they've asked for forgiveness. They've asked for a second chance. What about when I mess up and make a mistake? One that makes you angry or hurts your feelings? Are you going to hold a grudge and refuse to forgive me?"

"Sonya, of course not."

"Then let it go, Brandon. Because until you do, I can't be with you."

Brandon stared as the woman he thought he might very well love walked away from him. But her words still rang like gongs in his ears.

Two days later, Brandon sat at his desk at Finding the Lost, staring out the window, contemplating the last words Sonya had spoken to him.

Was she right? Of course she was.

"You going to let her go?"

Brandon jerked and spun his chair to find Jordan in the doorway. Jordan's mild words sliced across his heart.

"No. No, I'm not."

"So what are you going to do?"

"I'm going to talk to Peter and see if he'll help me with my rehab."

At Jordan's raised brow, Brandon gave a sad chuckle. "I'll explain later. Right now, I have to find my brother."

He left Jordan smiling after him as he grabbed his keys and raced from the building.

Twenty minutes later, he knocked on Peter's door.

When Peter opened it to find Brandon on his doorstep, he raised a brow. "What are you doing here?"

"Looking for you."

"I'm not hard to find. Come on in."

Peter grabbed a bag of chips from the coffee table and held them out to Brandon. "Lunch?"

Brandon grimaced. "How did you do it?"

Peter didn't have to ask. He set the bag of chips aside and sank onto the sofa. "It wasn't easy, but I have a mentor. Someone who prays for and with me."

Brandon dropped into the recliner and noticed it was new. "That's enough to keep you away from the drugs?"

"Yes. It doesn't matter what time it is, day or night, if I call, he answers."

"And does what?"

Peter gave a self-deprecating smile. "Talks me off the ledge. Makes me laugh. Meets me for coffee. Whatever it takes to help me walk away from the temptation."

Brandon swallowed hard. "I'm sorry."

Peter frowned. "For what?"

"I'm sorry it wasn't me. I should have been there for you like that and I wasn't."

Peter shrugged. "No. It was better to have a stranger do it. If you had been the one telling me some of the stuff Nick has, I would have hated you, turned my back and never talked to you again."

"Oh." Brandon thought about that. "Then I'm glad it wasn't me."

Peter gave a short laugh. "No, we're better off just being brothers and friends."

Brandon sucked in a deep breath. "Well, as my brother and friend, would you help me understand how you forgave them?"

Peter sighed. "Get comfortable. This is going to take a while."

Brandon lifted the footrest and crossed his arms. "Where do I start?"

"With a 'want to' attitude."

Brandon thought about that. "Okay. I want to. I really,

really want to." And he found he did. Not just because of Sonya, but for himself. He was tired of the anger and the bitterness. He wanted a life of hope and forgiveness. He wanted the life God had planned for him right from the start. A life that included Sonya. His throat tight with emotion, he nodded. "Yeah. I'm ready."

Two months later

Brandon sucked in a fortifying breath and knocked on his parents' door. Eating crow wasn't on his list of favorite foods, but he knew he was doing the right thing. That made it a bit tastier. He smiled as he thought about his brother. Peter had taken joy in encouraging him and praying with him. And surprisingly Brandon had, too. And now it was time to talk to his parents.

The door opened and his mother stood before him, her mouth formed in a perfect O.

"Hi, Mom."

The surprise didn't leave her expression, but at least she was able to find her voice. "Brandon." She stepped back. "Will you come in?"

He hated the hesitation in her voice. "Thanks." He stepped inside and looked around. It wasn't the home of his childhood, but one he'd been to occasionally over the past ten years they'd lived in it. "Is Dad here?" He'd thought he would be, but sometimes his father took an extra shift at the garage.

"Yes. He's in the den watching television."

"Do you mind if I talk to you two?"

Curiosity, wariness and hope all flickered in her eyes. "Of course you can."

He followed her into the den. His father, who hadn't

even turned fifty yet and still had a head full of dark hair, sat in his recliner. He looked up when Brandon entered. Shock made him blanch. "What are you doing here?" He glanced at his wife, then back to Brandon. "If you're here to cause us more pain, just get out."

Brandon winced. "I'm not, I promise."

His father picked up the remote and clicked the television off. He frowned. "Then what?"

"I came to say I'm sorry—and to ask you to forgive my stubbornness, my hardheaded selfishness." His pulse pounded. Had he waited too long? Was it too late?

His mother gasped and walked around him to sink onto the couch. "Don't play with us, Brandon. My heart can't take it."

Brandon sighed and his heart tightened as he realized how terribly he'd hurt these two people. Yes, they'd hurt him, but they were actively working on becoming better people. They were trying to atone for their past mistakes. "I'm not playing. I've been talking to Peter over the past two months and listening to him. Actually listening. He's filled me in on all the changes you guys have made and the fact that you're sincere about wanting to put this family back together."

His mother slipped her hand into his and looked into his eyes. "We're serious, Brandon. We know we were wrong in the past and there's nothing we can do to change that. But we're still young." She gave a sad smile. "Younger than we should be to have a kid your age, but we want to be a part of your life if you'll let us. Please don't let it be too late."

For the first time in years, Brandon hugged his mother. She clutched his shoulders and began to sob. Brandon felt his own tears start to flow and realized

Sonya was right. He'd needed to do this as much for himself as he did for his parents.

Another arm slipped across his shoulders. He lifted his head and found himself staring into his father's tearful, red-rimmed, joy-filled eyes. "Thank you, son."

Brandon nodded. "So we're going to start over? No hard feelings, no bringing up the past. Just a fresh start."

"A fresh start." His dad smiled. "A family reunion."

"Of the best kind." Brandon cleared his throat. "I want to spend time with you guys, but there's a woman I need to go see."

"Sonya," his mother whispered.

"Sonya," Brandon agreed.

"Tell her she's welcome to join in the family reunion, too," his dad said with a watery grin. "On a permanent basis."

Brandon laughed, feeling as if he'd just shed a hundred-pound weight from his shoulders. From his soul. He headed for the door. "I may just do that."

Chapter 22

Two months. Sonya crossed the day off on her calendar. She hadn't heard from Brandon in two months. The longest months of her life.

She'd awakened early for a Saturday morning and now sat at her table sipping her first cup of coffee for the day. She'd worked six days straight this past week and had the next three days off. She actually dreaded them.

She didn't normally work so much, but with Brandon's sudden absence in her life, she needed the work to take her mind off the fact that she missed him terribly.

Lord, I lift him up to You again. I don't understand how my heart could be so entangled in another's this fast, but please continue to show him how much he needs to forgive and how much You love him. And as impossible as it seems, how much I love him.

She'd known him all of a month the day Don Bradley had kidnapped her from her home, but what a month that had been. She'd fought for her life and lost her heart to love in the process.

Her doorbell rang and she debated whether she felt like answering it or not. When it rang a second time, she set her cup on the table and rose.

At the door, she peeked out.

And gasped.

Brandon stood on her front porch.

When he rang the bell for the third time, she swung the door open. "What are you doing here?"

He stepped inside and kissed her. Hard. Then sweet and gentle. Sonya kissed him back, the past two months of loneliness and missing him expressed in her heart-felt response.

When he lifted his head, she saw a sheen of tears glistening in his gaze. "I've missed you."

"Well, that was some kind of hello." She grinned. "I've missed you, too."

He tapped her nose with his index finger. "I'm glad. Do you mind if I come in?"

"Please do." She stepped back and he shut the door behind him. "Come on into the kitchen. I've got coffee."

He followed her and seated himself at the table. "You were right."

She blinked at him. "About?"

"Forgiveness."

"With your parents."

"Yes, and Krystal, my ex-fiancée."

"You've been hurt, Brandon. It's only natural you'd build up some walls and reservations."

"But I don't want them anymore. They're not worth holding on to. Those walls were hurting every relationship I have. Thanks to you, I finally realized what I was doing. Thanks to Peter, I think I've managed to get rid of those walls."

Joy swept over her. He looked lighter. Happier. And at peace. "You've forgiven your parents, haven't you?"

He nodded. "They're good people. They were just too young to have so much responsibility. And they didn't have a lot of help. On my mother's side, my grandparents disapproved and refused to help and my father's parents had already passed." He shrugged. "My mom and dad did the best they could. They're actually pretty amazing if you stop and look at how far they've come and everything they've *overcome.* They beat the odds and are still together. Once I stopped judging, I was able to start seeing things from another perspective. One of compassion and understanding."

Tears filled Sonya's eyes. "I'm so glad."

"We're human. We're not perfect. I'm definitely not, but I believe you're just right for me." He swallowed hard. "I don't know where we're headed, but I want to find out. I know I don't want to spend another day without you in my life."

Sonya flung herself into his arms. "I'm so glad for you. For me. For *us.*" She laughed.

He laughed with her. "I've got to be honest with you, Sonya. I want to see you in a white dress, surrounded by flowers and friends, walking toward the front of the church. If you get what I mean." He flushed and shuffled his feet. "If that's not what you want, or not what you want with me, please tell me now."

"I want it, Brandon. I want it more than anything. With you. Only you. These last two months have been horribly lonely without you."

He hugged her tight again. She pressed her nose into the warm skin of his neck and inhaled. His musky scent filled her senses and she felt at peace. She was home. He was the reason God had led her to Finding the Lost. "I love you, Brandon. I know it's fast, but I do. I really do."

"Since when does love have a time limit?"

She giggled. "I like your reasoning."

"So do you think we can do the dating thing for a little while?"

"Absolutely. At least for a week or so."

He threw his head back and laughed, then wrapped his arms around her to pull her close. He placed his lips on hers and Sonya couldn't wait to see what the future held. She thought of how pleased her mother would be that she'd met such a wonderful man. Her father would give his stamp of approval, for sure.

And for Sonya, that was enough.

Enough to make her smile.

Epilogue

Thanksgiving
Eighteen months later

Brandon lifted his head after saying the blessing and looked around the Thanksgiving table. A wave of emotion flowed over him and he knew he had a lot to be thankful for. His bride of one year glowed as she passed the mashed potatoes to Max.

Brandon sent a prayer of gratefulness heavenward as he did every time he looked at her. He still had a hard time believing she wore his ring on her finger, but she did. The gold band on his left ring finger fit snugly. He'd already gotten used to wearing it. Took pride in wearing it.

Erica held her newborn son while Max began to heap

his plate with food. "Are you hungry, dear?" Erica asked, a hint of teasing sarcasm in her tone.

Max flushed. "Not any hungrier than your dad over there." He transferred the spoonful of dressing to his daughter Molly's plate, then lifted a brow as though asking if he had her approval now. Erica laughed.

Brandon's father had helped himself to a large chunk of turkey. "I'm not shy. I'm starving. I skipped breakfast so I could fill up here."

Brandon grinned and Sonya winked at him. He could see the joy in her gaze along with something else. Curious, he looked closer but couldn't put his finger on it.

Peter looked healthy and happy and joked with Spike. The two had hit it off from the moment they'd met. "So, bro, have you managed to beat Spike yet?" Brandon asked, coating his question in teasing innocence.

Peter's smile slipped into a scowl. "Let's not go there. He only wins because he cheats."

"I do not," Spike protested. The grin on his face said he wasn't too upset about the accusation. They both knew the truth. Brandon had hopes Spike would get a basketball scholarship to college. Spike's mother looked on with an indulgent smile.

Ann Bradley sat quietly on the other side of Sonya. She hadn't said much since the day she'd shot her husband. When he'd been killed in a prison-yard fight, she'd withdrawn even more into her protective shell. But she loved Sonya and seemed happiest when they were together.

Sonya passed him the bread without taking any. He looked at her and his heart skipped a beat. She looked pale. Her lip curled and she slapped a hand over her mouth. She exchanged a look with Erica. "Excuse me," she mumbled. She jumped up and raced from the suddenly quiet dining room.

"Sonya!" He bolted after her, but thought he could hear Erica laughing. Why would his sister laugh at Sonya's obvious distress?

He reached the hall bath and knocked on the locked door. "Hey, are you okay?" The sound of her being sick made him wince. "Oh, baby, do you think you picked up a virus?"

The door swung open. She turned back to the sink to rinse her mouth. Tears leaked down her cheeks. She grabbed a toothbrush and toothpaste. "No, it's not a virus." She gave a hiccuping laugh and brushed her teeth.

He waited for her to finish. "It's not? Then something you ate?"

She turned and patted his cheek. "I haven't eaten yet."

"You've been working hard all morning getting everything ready. Your blood sugar is probably low." He gripped her fingers and pulled her into the hall, ready to lead her back into the kitchen. "That's probably the problem."

"Actually, this problem is going to take about seven more months to solve."

"Seven—" Confusion, then realization, flashed in his eyes. He gave a whoop, then pulled her into a crushing hug. When he released her, she saw the tears in his eyes. "I'm going to be a dad?"

"Yes."

"And you're going to be a mom?"

"That's generally the way it works." She grinned.

He laughed and hugged her again. "Sonya, how long have you known?"

"Just for a little while. I'm about eight weeks along, I think. I have a doctor's appointment on Monday."

"A doctor's appointment? You *are* a doctor." She'd finished up her last semester just after their wedding.

She laughed. "I'm not that kind of doctor."

"Well, I'm going with you."

"Of course you are. That's why I scheduled it on your day off."

He grinned and his eyes danced. The last time she'd seen him so giddy had been on their wedding day. "God is good."

"He sure is," she whispered. "Even in the bad times."

He pushed a lock of hair back behind her ear. "It took some bad times to bring us together."

"Exactly."

His finger reached out to trace her lips. "I remember the first time I saw you, I wanted to see you smile."

"It was hard to find a smile during those days." Her lips curved up. "It's easier now."

"I love you, Sonya."

She wrapped her arms around his waist. "And I love you. We're going to have a great life together. You, me and the baby."

"Babies," he said.

She giggled. "Let's get through this one first."

"Absolutely. But know this. No matter what the future holds, as long as we're together, we'll be fine."

"Hey, are you guys all right?" Erica asked. She'd come into the hallway without either of them noticing.

Max and Molly appeared behind her, then Peter. Then Ann and Brandon's mother and father.

Ann Bradley. Her aunt. She'd pleaded self-defense to shooting her husband and had won. Frankly, Sonya didn't think the prosecution had tried very hard to build a case against her. And now she was a part of the family.

Their growing, rapidly expanding family.

Brandon grinned at his sister. "How would you like to be an aunt?"

Erica blinked, then grinned. "I'd love it!"

"I'm going to be a grandma again?" Brandon's mother pushed her way through the growing crowd to hug Sonya. His father did the same. "Oh, my goodness. This is wonderful."

Sonya looked into her husband's moist eyes. "It's the best thing ever." She clapped her hands. "Now, let's eat. I'm starving!"

Laughter filtered back to her as everyone headed back to the kitchen. Sonya couldn't help the tears that dripped from her cheeks. Sheer happiness filled her, and she offered a prayer of thanksgiving to the One who'd made it all possible.

And she smiled.

* * * * *

Laura Scott is a nurse by day and an author by night. She has always loved romance and had read faith-based books by Grace Livingston Hill in her teenage years. She's thrilled to have published over twenty-five books for Love Inspired Suspense. She has two adult children and lives in Milwaukee, Wisconsin, with her husband of over thirty years. Please visit Laura at laurascottbooks.com, as she loves to hear from her readers.

Books by Laura Scott

Love Inspired Suspense

Justice Seekers

Soldier's Christmas Secrets
Guarded by the Soldier

Callahan Confidential

Shielding His Christmas Witness
The Only Witness
Christmas Amnesia
Shattered Lullaby
Primary Suspect
Protecting His Secret Son

True Blue K-9 Unit: Brooklyn

Copycat Killer

True Blue K-9 Unit

Blind Trust
True Blue K-9 Unit Christmas

Visit the Author Profile page at Harlequin.com for more titles.

PROOF
OF LIFE

Laura Scott

Give thanks to the Lord for He is good;
His love endures forever.

—1 Chronicles 16:34

This book is dedicated with love to my son Jon. I hope you know how proud I am of the kind and generous young man you've become.

Chapter 1

Crime-scene investigator Shanna Dawson paused on the threshold to gather her bearings. The dilapidated four-room house reeked of stale beer, cigarette smoke, greasy fast food and the rancid horror of death. As a CSI, she was more accustomed to the latter than the former.

The interior of the house, located a few blocks from Carlyle University, a private college outside of Chicago, was a pigsty; fast-food containers, smelly clothes, dirty dishes and empty beer cans were strewn everywhere. Talk about a CSI's nightmare.

For a moment she imagined the kids who lived there. The victim, Brady Wallace, was a young college student who shared the place with three other guys. Yet despite the mess, she imagined this was the type of place the so-called popular kids would gravitate to for parties. A college student's version of fun and excitement.

Not hers, though. During her four years of college she'd never been invited to student gatherings. The party scene had never appealed to her. She was too serious, too introspective to indulge in lighthearted activities.

Fun hadn't been a part of her world in a long time.

Suppressing a sigh, she got to work. There was so much evidence to collect, she'd easily be here for hours. As she walked through the foyer and into the living room, she overheard two cops arguing.

"This is a homicide investigation, Murphy. Campus police don't have jurisdiction over homicides."

"I know. But this incident occurred on my turf. Give me a break, Nelson. The victim is my brother."

"Half brother," the detective corrected.

"Brother just the same." The campus cop, Murphy, was stubborn. After a long moment where it seemed the homicide cop wasn't going to give in, Murphy sighed and scrubbed a hand along his bristly jaw. "At least give me the courtesy of keeping me informed of the details of your investigation."

Murphy snagged her attention, mostly because he was the victim's half brother and because he didn't look much like the local campus cops she was used to. And not just because of his tall, broad-shouldered good looks. His body appeared to be pure muscle, and he wore his wheat-blond hair military short. His face wasn't handsome in the traditional sense but bore deeply worn grooves of experience, as if he'd carried the weight of the world on his shoulders. His green eyes held the shadows of a deep pain she could relate to. She was inexplicably drawn to him, as if he might be a kindred soul, but she forced herself to turn away, examining the crime scene.

Brady Wallace's body was lying on the floor, in the

walkway between the living room and the kitchen. His bright red hair was matted with blood, the left side of his skull concave where it had been crushed. A heavy marble rugby trophy was lying on the floor beside him, the four-by-four-inch base covered with hair and blood. She imagined microscopic evidence would confirm the blood and tissue matched the victim's scalp.

The position of the body was distinctive. Why was he lying on the floor, in the walkway between the living room and kitchen? Had he run from his attacker? Or had he been on his way to the kitchen for something to eat when someone clubbed him from behind?

And who could hate a college student enough to kill him?

Brady was young, barely twenty. The callous waste of a young life always upset her. She'd grown up believing in God, but over the years had drifted away from the church and her faith. And at times like this, when she faced the hard edge of death, she really couldn't understand God's plan. What had this kid done to deserve death? She couldn't imagine. Feeling slightly sick, she glanced back over at the two cops who'd fallen silent as they'd registered her presence. She forced a professional expression on her face as she faced their curious stares. "Who found the body?"

"One of his roommates, Kyle Ryker." Murphy's face was bleak as he scanned the room. "Four boys live here—the victim, Brady Wallace, and three others— Kyle Ryker, Dennis Green and Mark Pickard."

"They must have had a party last night," she murmured with a wry sigh. Saturday nights were big party nights, so she shouldn't be surprised. "I'd hate to think the place always looks like this."

Murphy grimaced and lifted a shoulder. "It's not much better on any other day. But you're right—they did have a party, one that apparently lasted until the wee hours of the morning. According to Kyle, Brady was alive at four in the morning, when Kyle went upstairs to crash for what was left of the night. When Kyle came down to get something to eat from the kitchen about nine-thirty, he tripped over Brady's body."

As Brady's half brother, Murphy obviously had a personal stake in solving this crime. She felt a tug of sympathy. She knew better than anyone how difficult it was to deal with the violent aftermath of a crime that hit too close to home.

"I'm Detective Hank Nelson." The older cop, wearing the ill-fitting polyester suit coat, quickly introduced himself. "And this is University Campus Police Officer Quinn Murphy. I'll be taking the lead on this homicide investigation."

She understood the implied order and gave both men a brief nod. "Shanna Dawson, crime-scene investigator. My boss, Eric Turner, will be joining me shortly. If you gentlemen wouldn't mind stepping outside, I'd like to get to work."

The two cops exchanged a long look as if debating their right to stay, but in the end they both turned and headed for the door.

"Officer Murphy?" she called, before they could both disappear.

He turned toward her, his eyebrow raised questioningly. "Yes?"

"I'd like to talk to you later, if you have time." She knew Detective Hank Nelson would do the full investigation into all aspects of Brady's life, but she was curious to know more about Brady. Her methods might be somewhat unorthodox, but the more she understood the victim, the better job she'd do with her investigation. As the victim's brother, Murphy would be a great source of information.

"Of course." He came over to hand her his campus police business card. "Call me when you're finished processing things here."

"I will." She pocketed the card and watched him leave. When she was alone, she picked up the camera around her neck and began to record the initial evidence of the crime scene.

Quinn Murphy would mourn his half brother's passing, but at least he had the comfort of knowing what happened. Maybe not the who or the why, but the rest. All some families knew was that a loved one had disappeared. They never knew if their loved one was dead or alive, at peace or living in some awful situation, praying for salvation and longing for home.

Shanna took a deep breath and let it out slowly, shaking off the painful memories of the past. She'd made it her mission over the years to bring families closure. To bring the comfort of knowledge. The peace of acceptance. Today she'd collect every possible clue, piece together as much of the puzzle as she could until she discovered who killed Brady Wallace and why. She'd do whatever was possible to help Brady's family begin to heal.

Even though there were many wounds that never could.

"It's going to take us forever to dust for prints," her boss pointed out in exasperation. "The kids had a party on Saturday night, and there were probably at least fifty people in and out of this place. How on earth are we going to isolate anything useful?"

Eric was right—this was a long shot for sure. "The police are interviewing the roommates, trying to get a list of party attendees together. I believe this is personal, likely someone with a grudge against Brady." She glanced around the filthy room, imagining how the events might have played out. "I have a hunch this kid knew his attacker. To have this happen after a party doesn't come across as premeditated, but more like a crime of opportunity, as if Brady was in the wrong place at the wrong time. Using the trophy to bash in his head could have been a simple act of rage or revenge. I'd like to start by dusting Brady's bedroom and the living room for prints."

Eric let out another sigh. "It just seems like a lot of effort for very little payoff. But you're right, the logical place to start is the bedroom and crime scene."

She nodded and went back to work. Her back ached from being hunched over for the past several hours, but she ignored the discomfort, concentrating on finding the proverbial needle in the haystack.

As she worked, her mind drifted to Quinn Murphy. Had he broken the distressing news of Brady's death to the rest of his family? Considering Brady had a different last name than him, she assumed they shared a mother rather than a father. Did Brady have other siblings? Were they huddled close right now, drawing love and support from each other?

She dragged her mind from things that didn't concern her, satisfied when she managed to find a few isolated prints on the rugby trophy, as well as other parts of the room. She did better up in Brady's room, where there was less clutter. Her boss grimaced but helped her collect the beer cans to check for prints. By the time they were finished, they'd probably have more suspects than they'd know what to do with.

Suspects that may or may not lead to the identity of the killer, since there was no guarantee Brady's murderer had left prints at the scene. Still, they didn't have much else to work from. Hair fibers were as much of a nightmare as dusting for prints because of the number of people who'd been in the house, not to mention that Dennis Green's cat shed like crazy in a house that had rarely if ever seen a vacuum.

Running all the fingerprints and hair fibers would take time, so she sent the strips and samples off to the lab for the techs to start working on, prioritizing the ones from the trophy and Brady's room. At the very least, they'd discover if any of the partygoers had criminal records.

Outside, she paused at her car, glancing down at Quinn Murphy's card, debating whether to talk to him now or to go home first to shower and change. She was hungry, having worked the crime scene for almost eight hours straight.

Home first, she decided. Then she'd contact Quinn.

She pulled up to her house, pausing at the mailbox on her way into the driveway. Sometimes she became so lost in her active cases that she forgot to pick up her mail. Today was Sunday, but had she picked it up yesterday? She didn't think so. When she opened the box, she found it was jammed full. As she pulled everything out, a small white envelope with her name printed on the outside, with no postage stamp or return address, made her heart pound heavily in her chest.

Another note. The third in the past two weeks.

She stared at it for a long minute, wishing it was nothing more than a figment of her imagination. But of course it wasn't. She headed inside the house. Even though she was tired and hungry, she used her own kit to dust for prints. She wasn't surprised not to find any.

She hadn't found prints on the previous two notes, either.

Trepidation burned as she opened the envelope flap. Slowly she withdrew the single piece of paper. The message was brief: "I'm coming for you."

Four little words. She dropped the card, struggling to breathe normally as fear clogged her throat. So far, each of the notes she'd received bore a different message.

Guilty as charged.

I'm watching you.

I'm coming for you.

Her knees went weak and she sank into a kitchen chair, struggling not to let fear overwhelm her. Who was doing this? And why? She wanted to think it was some person's strange idea of a joke, but the sinister tone of the notes wasn't easily shrugged off.

Which is exactly what the creep intended. He wanted to scare her. He wanted her to panic. Only a coward would send anonymous notes in the first place. And since she didn't have any men in her life, hadn't so much as had one significant long-term relationship, this had to be connected to her job.

She'd gone through all of her most recent cases, trying to figure out which one may have caused someone to fixate on her. The most likely case was one that had wrapped up two weeks ago, garnering her some media attention. Shanna usually preferred to work behind the scenes, but in this case, the investigation of a well-known cardiac surgeon's murder had cast her reluctantly into the limelight.

The trial had been difficult but her evidence had been solid, and in the end her testimony had caused the jury to find the surgeon's ex-wife, Jessica Markoviack, guilty of murder. But Jessica couldn't be the stalker, since she was currently serving a life sentence in an all-female state prison.

A friend of Jessica's, perhaps? If she remembered right, Jessica had a boyfriend, a guy named Clay Allen who hadn't been involved in the murder, at least according to the evidence. But that didn't mean he wasn't capable of doing the deed. She needed to go back through her case notes, to refresh her memory of the guy's background. He was a viable suspect, someone who had a reason to carry a grudge against her.

Fear gave way to anger as she rose to her feet. Maybe it was time to bring the police into this. The first two notes had been creepy but not outright threatening.

I'm coming for you.

She ground her teeth and turned her back on the note. She'd call the police, even though she knew there was little they could do. Hadn't she already tried to trace the origin of the white cards herself? There was nothing special about them, they were commonly stocked in every office supply store in the area.

Leaving the white card smudged with dark fingerprint powder on the table, she headed down the hall to the bathroom. First she'd shower, and then scrounge around for something to eat. It was only seven-thirty, and she still wanted to interview Quinn.

Focusing her attention on Brady's death would help her to ignore the eerie feeling of someone watching her, no doubt already planning his next move.

Quinn Murphy read through the extensive list of names of all the kids who'd attended Brady's party. The letters blurred and he had to blink to focus.

He rubbed his eyes, forcing himself to stay awake, even though he'd been up for the past thirty-six hours straight. There were already forty-one names on the list, and he was certain there were more that had been forgotten. Kids who'd come only for a few minutes, or those who blended into the woodwork to the point no one ever remembered.

Had the murderer stood back, watching? Waiting for the right moment to strike? He had no way of knowing. Wishing there was at least one solid lead to go on, he picked up the list again. Brady's girlfriend's name was glaringly absent. Anna Belfast had gotten hysterical when he'd told her about Brady's death. No college student, even one in the theater program, could be that good of an actress.

Anna won the lead role of Hannah in *Seven Brides for Seven Brothers* and had done a performance at the theater starting at seven o'clock the night of the party. She'd been irritated that Brady hadn't come to see her and claimed she'd refused to go to his party afterward, choosing to attend a cast get-together after the show instead.

Her alibi was solid, confirmed by several other theater students. Although the suspicious part of his mind insisted there was likely time for her to come to Brady's party after the cast get-together had broken up. Had Anna come to the party to find Brady with another girl? Her roommate, Maggie Carson, also had a role in the play and claimed Anna had come home right afterward, but there was a chance Maggie had lied to cover for Anna. Or Anna could have slipped out even later, after her roommate fell asleep.

Sweet little Anna didn't seem to be the type to bash Brady in the head, but her on-again, off-again relationship with his little brother was enough to keep her on the suspect list.

They didn't have the official report confirming the time of death, but the coroner at the scene had estimated it to be somewhere between five and seven in the morning.

His phone rang, startling him out of his thoughts. He frowned. The number wasn't one he recognized, but he answered it anyway. "Murphy."

"Officer Murphy, this is Shanna Dawson. I'm sorry to call you so late, but the crime scene took much longer than normal to process."

"I'm not surprised." He could easily believe that going through the party mess had taken several long hours. He glanced at his watch and realized it wasn't as late as it felt—just eight-thirty.

"If you're still available, I'd love to talk to you. But if you'd rather wait until tomorrow, I'd certainly understand."

He pursed his lips, thinking fast. The polite thing to do would be to wait until morning. Shanna had to be as exhausted as he was. But he also knew he wouldn't sleep, couldn't rest until he'd done everything possible to find Brady's killer.

"Tonight is fine." He didn't want to let her off the hook, and there was always the chance she'd give him some details on what they'd found. "Where would you like to meet?"

There was a slight pause before she responded, "I'll meet you at Karly's Kitchen on Dublin Street."

"Sounds good. I can be there in twenty minutes."

"Thanks."

He actually made it in fifteen, but Shanna must live even closer because he found her already seated at a booth, nursing a cup of coffee. He slid in across from her, glancing up as the waitress approached. "I'll have some coffee, too, thanks."

Shanna's face was pale and drawn, as if she'd taken Brady's death as personally as he had. With her wavy dark hair, alabaster skin and wide blue eyes, she reminded him more of a kindergarten teacher than a CSI. Maybe it was the air of innocence clinging to her. He'd thought most law-enforcement types became hardened by the brutal evidence of violence, but Shanna's personality didn't seem to have that distinctive hard edge.

She summoned a smile. "How are you?" she surprised him by asking. "Is your family doing all right?"

Amazed that she cared enough to ask, he sat back in his seat. She couldn't know he wasn't really a part of the family, not in the way she'd meant. His mother had pretty much abandoned him when she'd divorced his father, but over the years he'd made an effort to mend the rift between them, especially once his father died. No matter what, though, he was still an outsider. His mother had found a new life with her second husband, James

Wallace, and his half-siblings, Brady and Ivy, were the joys of her life.

And now Brady was dead.

He'd given his mother the news, taking the brunt of her anger and frustration as she railed at him. Knowing that she would have preferred if he was the one who'd died instead of Brady was difficult to ignore.

"I—my mother is taking Brady's death pretty hard, as you can imagine." He tried to soften his gruff tone. He didn't hold a grudge against Brady, even though the kid had been offered every opportunity possible to succeed in life. More than Quinn had been given, that's for sure. But Brady was basically a good kid.

As Quinn had gotten older, he'd understood how his very presence reminded his mother of her dismal marriage to his father. A fact that was indirectly his fault, since she'd only married his father because she'd gotten pregnant with him.

"I'm sorry for your loss." Shanna surprised him again by reaching across the table to touch the back of his hand in a simple gesture meant to offer comfort. "I'll do everything possible to find Brady's murderer."

"I know." He was impressed by her staunch dedication. And her empathy. Shanna looked young, barely twenty, although he figured with her training and experience she must be at least in her mid-to-late twenties. She was beautiful, her long wavy hair framing a heart-shaped face. The flicker of awareness annoyed him; he was here to help solve Brady's murder, nothing more. "Thanks."

She began the drill, asking about his half brother's life, going over all of Brady's friends and roommates. He gave her everything he knew, which wasn't all that much, since Brady had resented having his older half brother as a campus cop. Brady had kept his distance from Quinn as much as possible. Especially after Quinn had been the one to bust one of Brady's parties a month earlier.

If he'd known about this party last night, he would have busted it, too. And then maybe his brother would still be alive.

Just another reason to feel guilty. Although it wasn't like he was sitting around doing nothing. He'd been investigating a potential sexual assault on a young female student instead.

He pulled his mind to the matter at hand. He told Shanna everything he knew, although it wasn't anything different from what he'd told the detective. Still, working with Shanna as they reviewed the list of kids who'd attended the party made him feel as if he were part of the investigation instead of an innocent bystander.

At ten o'clock, she yawned so wide her jaw popped, and he realized he'd selfishly kept her up long enough. "It's late—we'd better go."

She nodded, signaling the waitress to bring their bill. He knew she intended to pay, but he took the bill from the waitress anyway. "My treat."

Shanna frowned. "You don't have to do that."

"Please, I want to." She couldn't know how much he'd needed to talk to her tonight, to be involved at least this much in the investigation. Besides, he couldn't get into the idea of allowing a woman to pay. Call it old-fashioned, but he didn't care. He stood, waiting for her to precede him out of the diner.

Outside, there were only a few other cars in the postage stamp-size parking lot. His SUV was on the far left end, but she turned toward the right, where a red Toyota Camry was parked next to a row of bushes.

"Thanks, Quinn," she said, formally shaking his hand. "I'll be in touch."

"Sure." Her hand felt small and fragile in his and he released it reluctantly. He followed, intent on making sure she got safely into her car. She only took a few steps though, before suddenly stopping.

She whirled around, coming back toward him. She grabbed his arm in a tight grip. "Do you see him?" she asked in a low, urgent tone. "Do you see the man standing next to my car?"

"Man?" He peered over her shoulder, not seeing any sign of a person, male or otherwise. Had her exhausted mind played tricks on her? "Relax, it's okay. I don't see anyone."

"Are you saying I imagined him?" The sharp edge to her tone made him lift a curious brow.

"No, I believe you. But I don't see him now. Maybe he disappeared behind those bushes."

Abruptly, she let go of his arm, swinging back to stare at her car. "He's gone. I can't believe I didn't get a better look at him."

Her tone was fierce and brave, but he noticed the slight trembling of her hands. He didn't blame her for being scared; there was no acceptable reason for a man to loiter around a woman's car at ten o'clock at night. Even if she had imagined the guy, he figured she was entitled after such a long day. "I'll walk you to your car."

"I'm fine." She started toward her car with a firm stride, but didn't protest when he caught up to her.

A small white card with her name printed on the outside was stuck beneath the wiper blade on the driver's side. Obviously, her mystery man wasn't her imagination after all.

She gasped in shock and stopped short, staring at the evidence.

"Don't touch anything," he ordered. "We need to call the police, see if we can get some fingerprints off this."

"Don't bother." Her tone was matter of fact.

"What do you mean, don't bother?" What sort of CSI expert was she? "Why not?"

"Because I've gotten several others just like it, and he hasn't left any prints yet."

Chapter 2

Quinn wasn't happy when Shanna insisted on driving home, but he followed right behind her as they went the couple of blocks to her house. She lived in a nice, if older, suburb of Chicago, where the houses were small and the lots even smaller, yet well-groomed. He gripped the steering wheel tightly, anxious to get to the bottom of this.

The brief glimpse of fear in Shanna's eyes tugged at him. He'd seen the same haunted expression in the young freshman's eyes last night, after the attack. His stomach squeezed. He didn't like the possibility of Shanna suffering a similar experience. Thankfully, the mystery man had only left a note and hadn't touched her.

Some people felt that campus police officers weren't the real deal, hiding from the true crime that stalked the city streets. He'd done his stint as a city cop for over six years. Now he preferred to proactively protect the younger, innocent college kids rather than taking criminals off the street, knowing there was always another cop eager to take his place.

He pulled into Shanna's driveway right behind her, and hurried out of his car to stop her from going inside. "Stay back. I want to check things out first."

She pushed his hand away. "I'm a trained law-enforcement officer," she protested.

"Yeah, but I'm armed." And he'd noticed she wasn't, at least not at the restaurant. She had carried a gun while she was investigating the crime scene as all CSIs were required to do. But knowing she was a trained officer didn't matter. For some reason, this woman raised his protective instincts to full alert.

She stared at him for a long minute and then took a step back, allowing him to take the lead. While she hovered behind him, he took the key from her fingers and ventured inside. The layout was a simple ranch design; the side door entered into the kitchen. The front door opened into the living room, and then there was a short hallway leading to the bedrooms.

The light over the kitchen sink was burning bright so he swept his gaze over the room, listening intently. His gut told him the place was empty, but he went through each room anyway, just to make sure.

When he finished, he headed back to the kitchen. Three notes were sitting in the center of the table. He leaned over, read them and then looked up at her askance. "Have you called the police about these threats?"

She winced and shook her head, her arms wrapped around her torso as if she were cold. "Not yet. I was going to, though. That last one came today. I mean, yesterday." She frowned. "Actually, I don't exactly know what day it came, because I sometimes forget to pick up the mail."

"So you received a note and still drove out to meet me tonight?" His fingers curled into helpless fists at her foolishness. "Are you crazy?"

Her shrug was nonchalant. "Working on Brady's case helped keep my mind off my problems."

A stalker wasn't just any old problem. He was tempted to snap at her, but realized Shanna was a trained law-enforcement agent, just like he was. She could take care of herself.

So why did he want to do that for her?

Because he was tempted to pull her into the shelter of his arms in a gesture of comfort, he forced himself to stay where he was, keeping a safe distance between them.

"Do you have any idea who's sending these?" he asked in a low tone. "A jilted boyfriend? Someone at work that you refused to go out with?"

She made a strangled sound. "No. I haven't been see-ing anyone, no ex-boyfriends. No one's been bothering me. My personal life is dull and uneventful. To be hon-est, I've already concluded the notes have to be related to one of my cases."

He shouldn't have been relieved to know there wasn't a man in her life, just as he shouldn't have noticed how vulnerable she'd looked when she'd admitted the boring details of her past. Why was such a pretty woman lead-ing a dull and uneventful life? Her personal life was none of his business, but he wanted to know just the same. He kept his voice firm. "You need to call the police."

"You're the police," she joked weakly.

"Shanna." He moved closer, lifting his hand to brush her hair away from her cheek. "You know I don't have jurisdiction here. You need to call this in, before this guy gets too close."

For a moment she simply stared at him with something forlorn in her gaze, but then she pulled back and straightened her shoulders. "Don't worry. I won't let him get to me."

He wanted to believe her. But that hint of vulnerability made him hesitate. Maybe because he was a pushover for a woman in distress. Yet she seemed just as determined to stand alone. A part of him admired her independence while another part of him was annoyed at her stubborn foolishness.

"Are you going to call the police?" he asked for the third time.

"Not right now. It's late. I'll wait until the morning. This isn't an emergency and there isn't anything they're going to be able to do about the notes tonight. Especially since I can't even give them a reasonable description of the suspect."

He knew she was right, but that didn't make it any easier for him to leave. He glanced around her small living room. "I don't like leaving you here alone."

"I'll be fine." The underlying steel in her tone finally convinced him.

"Okay, but do me a favor." He held her gaze, imploring her to listen to reason. "Close and lock every window."

She grimaced and nodded. "I like having the cool fresh air from outside coming through the windows, but I'll manage without for tonight," she reluctantly agreed.

He waited until she'd gone through every room, closing and locking the windows. Standing in the kitchen, his gaze continued to linger on the notes.

Who could have sent them? And why? Someone who liked to play games, obviously. Mind games. The thought caused a sick feeling to settle in his gut.

"All set?" he asked when she came back toward him.

"Yes. Thanks for following me home."

"You're welcome." He forced himself to walk toward the side door. "You have my cell-phone number. Promise you'll call if you need anything."

She smiled. "Don't worry. I'll be fine."

He told himself she was right. She would be fine. Outside he paused and listened, satisfied to hear the dead bolt click into place. He headed toward his car, glancing back to look at her house. She'd shut off most of the lights, except maybe the one in her bedroom, which he couldn't see from the street.

He slid behind the wheel and backed out of her driveway, intent on going home when he saw a car moving slowly down the street. Too slowly. Heart thudding in his chest, he pulled over to the side of the road, holding his breath as he waited. The car passed him by, turning into a driveway several houses down. The garage door opened, and the car disappeared inside.

"Idiot," he muttered to himself. He was exhausted, had been up for over forty hours straight, but he couldn't just go home.

Shutting off the car, he pulled the key out of the ignition and leaned his seat as far back as it could go. He cracked the windows so he could hear better, knowing he was going to spend the night here, watching over Shanna, despite her refusal to accept his help.

He was too tired to drive anyway.

Slouched in his car, he stared at Shanna's dark house, wondering about her. Why was she so alone when she lived in a nice neighborhood that seemed like the perfect place to raise a family? The pain shadowing her eyes hadn't all been from the notes, he was certain. Yet as much as he wanted to protect her, she seemed just as determined to brush off his help.

Rubbing his eyes, he briefly wished for peace rather than being haunted by the demons in his past. His dad had been a city cop for years. Hunting drug runners, witnessing armed robberies and murders, had taken its toll. His dad had turned to booze, ignoring the abuse he'd inflicted on his body until one day Quinn had come home to find his dad crumpled on the bathroom floor, lying in a pool of blood.

He'd called 911 but had already known it was too late. According to the coroner, his dad had been throwing up blood from some burst blood vessel in his esophagus, and had literally choked on it before he'd died.

The memory haunted him ever since.

Quinn had always avoided alcohol, but then he went a step further, giving up the stress of being a city cop to join the university campus police force. His mother had wanted him to get out of law enforcement altogether, claiming his dad's job had ruined their marriage, but he couldn't do it.

There was a part of him that needed to know he made a difference in the world, no matter how small and insignificant it may be.

His attraction to Shanna, though, forced him to remember all the reasons he veered away from relationships. He wasn't a safe bet, and not just because of his family history of alcoholism. He knew from firsthand experience that women wanted a man who came home every night. Men who weren't in danger. Men who didn't obsess over their work. Even as a campus cop, he'd been drawn on by gang members with guns more times than he could count. Most recently by two idiots who decided to rob the corner coffee shop.

Leslie had left him, just like his mother had left his father. Proving he was better off alone.

With a sigh, he let his head fall back against the seat rest, unable to prevent himself from closing his eyes. He'd stay here outside Shanna's place, making sure she called the police to report her stalker first thing in the morning. Once he was satisfied she'd taken steps to assure her safety, he'd go back to working Brady's murder investigation where he'd left off.

Finding out who'd killed Brady had to remain his top priority.

Shanna didn't sleep very well; the slightest noises kept waking her up. All because she'd let the creepy stalker get to her more than she'd wanted to admit.

At least she'd held it together in front of Quinn. He was too attractive for her peace of mind. Not handsome per se, but definitely ruggedly attractive. On top of that, he'd been nice, supportive. Not that she needed his help.

What she needed was action. Today she'd get a full investigation going on this note-writing guy, whoever he was. Stalking was against the law, as were threats. She'd find this guy and hand him over to the police the first chance she had.

With renewed determination, she took a quick shower and spent a few minutes blow-drying her hair before heading to the kitchen, intending to brew a pot of coffee.

As she walked past the entryway to the living room, she happened to glance through the large picture window overlooking the street. She froze, her heart leaping into her throat when she noticed the SUV parked directly across the street from her house. The car stood out because her neighbors across the street were elderly and didn't drive. Fearing the worst, she grabbed her cell phone and almost punched the numbers for 911 when she realized why the car looked familiar.

It was the same car that had followed her home last night. The vehicle belonged to Quinn. Flipping her cell phone shut, she crossed over to the picture window in time to see Quinn yawning and stretching his arms over his head. While she was staring at him, he glanced toward her house, capturing her gaze. For a moment, the strange connection between them seemed to shimmer in the air.

Had he really slept out there all night? She was touched by his chivalry but was determined not to read more into his actions than the situation warranted. Uncertainly, she opened the front door. Was she supposed to invite him in after the way he'd slept in his car to protect her?

He climbed awkwardly from the car, his limbs obviously stiff from the cramped seat. But then he came straight toward her, meeting her halfway. "Morning, Shanna. Did you sleep well?"

She tried to act nonchalant. "Better than you, I'd be willing to bet. Quinn, it was very sweet of you to sleep in your car, but I told you I'd be fine."

"I know, but I was too tired to drive," he said, glancing longingly over her shoulder. "Is that coffee I smell?"

"Yes." She felt bad about the exhaustion shadowing

his features. As uncomfortable as she was having him there, the least she could do was feed him. "Come on in, there's plenty to share."

He followed her inside, crossing the living room to the kitchen. He took a seat at her table, and she could feel his gaze on her as she filled a mug from the coffeemaker. She couldn't help feeling self-conscious with him there, maybe because she'd never had a man in her house. Ever.

She carefully set the mug on the table, thankful she didn't spill. "Ah, do you like eggs? Because I have to tell you, there isn't a huge variety of food to choose from."

"Eggs would be great." His stomach rumbled loudly, as if reinforcing his need for food. He flashed a sheepish grin and her heart did a funny little flip.

She squelched the reaction and quickly threw together scrambled eggs and toast. The sooner she gave him food, the sooner she could send him on his way.

When he'd finished the first cup of coffee, he came over to get a refill. His closeness was enough to rattle her, and she burned her thumb on the edge of the frying pan. She swallowed a yelp, thrusting her thumb under a stream of cold water. This was ridiculous; there was no reason to be nervous.

"Are you all right?" he asked.

"Fine." She forced a smile. "The eggs are just about ready."

"Thanks." He carried his mug over to the table, and she handed him a plate full of eggs and toast. They ate in silence for a few minutes before Quinn spoke up. "You're going to call the police when we're finished with breakfast, right?"

She barely refrained from rolling her eyes. The man sounded like a broken record. "Right."

As soon as she finished her meal, Shanna gave in and pulled out her cell phone. Considering she'd worked all day Sunday, she could afford to be a little late to work this morning. She had to look up the nonemergency number in the phone book and briefly explained her situation when one of the officers came on the line.

"They're sending someone over," she said, hanging up a few minutes later. "They asked me to leave the card from last night under the windshield wiper." She hadn't touched the note, figuring the cops would want to see exactly where the guy had left it.

"Good." Quinn sat back, sipping his coffee as if he wasn't in a hurry to leave.

"The police are on their way, Quinn. There's no need for you to stay." She carried her dirty dishes to the sink, cleaning up the remains of their breakfast mess. "You need to go home, get some decent sleep."

"How long before you get anything back from the lab?" he asked, ignoring her blatant hint urging her to go. "On the fingerprints and hair fibers?"

"We have lots of evidence to sift through. I'm afraid it will probably be awhile." She understood how anxious he was for news, any news. She'd been on his side of the waiting game. It had only been in recent years that she'd learned how patience was a virtue. "I promise I'll get in touch with you if we come up with anything."

He glanced at her. "You know I'm not really involved in this investigation, except peripherally. All of your evidence needs to go to Hank Nelson."

"I know." She wrung out the dishrag and turned toward him, resting her hip against the counter. "But you're the one who knows the students on campus, right? Hank has to keep you involved in the investigation to a certain extent. Maybe we do have to give all the evidence to the lead homicide detective on the case, but I see no reason why the crime lab wouldn't cooperate with the campus police, too."

He smiled and shrugged. "Hank probably won't like it, but I'll take anything you can give me."

His appreciation warmed her heart. After the way he'd slept in his car, just to protect her, this was the least she could do in return. Besides, the homicide had taken place on his turf. She'd expect the same consideration in his shoes.

Their gazes locked, and for a moment she felt as if she couldn't breathe. She didn't deserve to feel this attraction to him, but she couldn't look away. If she were honest, she'd admit she intended to keep him in the loop because she wanted to see him again, not just because of professional courtesy.

The ringing of her doorbell echoed through the house, breaking the moment. She swallowed hard and pushed away from the counter, crossing over to the living room to open the front door.

The officers who stood there had their respective IDs ready, which she carefully inspected before allowing Officers Kappas and Jones inside.

"Murphy?" Jones, the taller of the two, frowned when he recognized Quinn. "Haven't seen you since your old man's funeral." His gaze landed on Shanna, frankly curious. "I—uh—didn't know you were involved with anyone."

Funeral? Shanna glanced at Quinn in surprise, but then flushed when she realized the two officers assumed she and Quinn were a couple. "He's a friend," she said quickly.

The last thing she needed were rumors going around about her and Quinn. How embarrassing *that* would be.

"We were at Karly's Kitchen last night when Ms. Dawson saw a man loitering by her car," Quinn said, as if sensing her discomfort. "I didn't see him, but we found a white envelope with her name printed on the front in block letters, stuck under her windshield."

She was grateful Quinn cut to the chase, putting the interview back on track.

"Ms. Dawson has received other notes, as well." He picked up the three notes she'd left on the counter and handed them to the officers. "Shanna, when did you get the first note?"

"Two weeks ago." She explained how the first note had actually showed up in her mailbox down at the CSI lab. The message read "Guilty as charged," so she hadn't really thought too much about it. "I guess I figured the sender was just someone dealing with a lot of anger. The second and third ones, though, were in my mailbox here at home."

Her personal space. Her haven.

"You dusted for fingerprints?" Kappas asked.

"I'm a CSI—of course I dusted for prints. Didn't find any, though. I also tried to narrow down the source of the paper, but it's carried everywhere." She lifted her palms helplessly. "Really, this could be related to any one of my cases, although the one I just wrapped up, the Markoviack murder, is the most likely one."

"Did the man by your car look at all familiar?" Jones took over the questioning.

"I only caught a glimpse, but didn't recognize him at all."

"You mentioned this being related to one of your cases, like the Markoviack murder. Why does that one stand out in your mind?" Kappas asked.

She quickly explained about the last big case she'd worked on, how her evidence put Jessica Markoviack in prison. Both officers exchanged a look and agreed that Jessica's former boyfriend was a possible culprit.

"Where's the fourth note now?" Jones asked.

She glanced at Quinn. "We left it beneath the windshield wiper. My car is in the garage." Leading the way out the side door, to the detached garage where her Toyota Camry was parked, she gestured to the car.

The officers looked at the note, then used gloved hands to remove it from beneath the wiper blade. She took out her fingerprint kit and dusted both the note and the windshield for prints.

There weren't any, just like the previous notes.

Jones opened the flap and removed the note. They crowded around to see what it said. "Next time, you'll be alone," Jones read out loud.

"I don't get it," Quinn muttered. "How did he know you were with me?"

She couldn't suppress a shiver, fear congealing in the bottom of her stomach. "Because he's watching me."

Kappas and Jones exchanged a grim look. "I'll recommend increased surveillance of this neighborhood, ma'am," Jones said.

Sending a patrol car through every couple hours wasn't going to prevent this guy from trying to get her, but she understood they were doing the best they could. "That's fine."

"No, it's not," Quinn argued bluntly. "If this guy is watching you, he'll know to hide from the police. You need a bodyguard. Or at least a comprehensive security system."

"Maybe." She didn't want to admit his idea had merit. "I'll think about it."

Quinn looked as if he wanted to argue, but instead he turned toward the officers. "Anything else?"

"Ms. Dawson might want to find a friend to stay with for a while," Officer Jones said. "Being here alone is asking for trouble."

Friends? She almost laughed. The only real friend she had was Megan O'Ryan, and she'd recently moved to Crystal Lake, Wisconsin. Megan had just gotten married, and after everything her friend had been through, Shanna couldn't bring herself to dump her own troubles on Megan's shoulders. Megan had barely survived being strangled by a serial killer. Worse, the killer was someone they knew. Raoul Lee was a brilliant scientist. Now he'd spend the rest of his life in jail. The cops waited expectantly, so she nodded. "I'll see what I can do."

The officers left, promising to be in touch if they found anything.

"I'll follow you to work." Quinn's tone didn't leave room for discussion.

His persistence was starting to annoy her. But rather than arguing, she gathered her work stuff together, including her shoulder holster. She sensed Quinn's frustration as he stood watching her. Before she could get out the door, her cell phone rang.

She recognized Alan's number from the lab. Setting her laptop case on the kitchen table, she answered the phone. "Do you have something for me, Al?"

"Yeah, uh, we got a hit on one of the fingerprints found at your college frat house crime scene."

A hit on the fingerprints was good news. "Who is it?" she asked eagerly, glancing at Quinn. An identity would get them one step closer to finding the killer.

"Are you on your way here? Because I think we should talk in person." He cleared his throat loudly. "The news is going to be a bit of a shock."

His tap-dancing around the issue only irritated her. "Just tell me."

There was a pause. "Shanna, we have a set of fingerprints matching a child who's been missing for fourteen years."

A child? Missing for fourteen years? No. Oh, no. Her stomach twisted, and little red dots swam in her vision. She grabbed the edge of the kitchen table and pushed the word through her tight throat. "Who?"

"Your sister. Skylar Dawson."

Chapter 3

Shanna blinked, staring up at Quinn's anxious face looming over her. The kitchen floor was hard and unyielding beneath her back. Disoriented, she winced and lifted her head. "What happened?"

"You fainted." Quinn's gruff tone betrayed his concern.

"Fainted?" Embarrassed, she pushed up onto her elbows, her head throbbing. She must have hit her head on the floor.

"Let me help you up." Quinn put his arm around her shoulders, supporting her weight as she struggled to her feet. Her knees still felt wobbly, so she sat at the kitchen table.

"What happened?" Quinn asked, picking up her cell phone from where it must have skittered across the floor. "One minute you were saying something about the fingerprint results from the crime scene, and the next you collapsed onto the floor."

In a rush it all came flooding back.

Skylar. The pressure in her chest built to the point she could barely breathe. Her fault. It was her fault her little sister had been kidnapped fourteen years ago. Her fault that her parents had divorced, destroying what was left of their family.

"Shanna, breathe," Quinn commanded in a sharp tone.

Feeling dizzy again, she obeyed, taking a deep breath before she did something stupid, like fainting for a second time. After a few minutes the room stopped spinning.

Forcing herself to meet his questioning gaze, she knew she couldn't lie to him. Not now. Not about this. "The prints at the scene of Brady's death match those of my sister, Skylar."

Quinn frowned, perplexed. "Okay. Does your sister go to Carlyle University, too?"

"I don't know." She licked her dry lips. "Skylar was kidnapped when she was only five years old. Her case has remained unsolved. I haven't seen her in fourteen years. No one has."

Quinn's jaw dropped, and he sank into the chair beside her. "You're kidding."

"No. I'm not." The memory burned with a clarity that belied the passing years.

On Skylar's first day of kindergarten, her mother had insisted Shanna take her sister all the way inside the elementary school to meet the kindergarten teacher. She was older by five years, so Shanna had agreed. As they'd approached the school, she'd discovered a bunch of her friends were playing kickball on the older kid's section of the playground, farthest from the building.

"Shanna!" Toby Meyers, the boy she secretly liked, had waved and shouted to her from the game. "Hurry up, we're losing. We need you on our team."

Thrilled that he'd noticed her, and that he'd wanted her on his team, she'd dropped Skylar's hand. "Just go inside the building there, Skylar, okay? You'll see Mrs. Anderson, the kindergarten teacher, in the first classroom."

"But Shanna," Skylar protested, hanging back.

"Just go!" Impatiently, Shanna had given Skylar a little push and then turned away, rushing over to join the kickball game already in progress. Toby made room for her in the lineup to kick next.

She'd taken her turn, kicking the ball with all her strength, sending it sailing over the heads of all the kids. With Toby cheering her on, she'd rounded the bases, making it all the way home to score.

They hadn't won the game—the bell had rung and they'd had to quit—but Toby's cheering had echoed in her head for the next hour. Until the school principal, Mrs. Haggerty, had tapped her on the shoulder, taking her out of her fourth-grade class to the office.

"Shanna, when did you last see your sister?"

Skylar? Guiltily, Shanna realized she hadn't even thought about her sister since hurrying off to the kickball game. "This morning, when I walked her to school."

"Did you take her inside to see the teacher?"

Numbly, Shanna shook her head no.

"She's not in the kindergarten class." Mrs. Haggerty looked extremely worried. "Your mother is on her way here. I think we'd better search every classroom. Maybe Skylar got lost and is hiding somewhere."

Shanna felt sick, knowing her mother would be so angry that she hadn't taken Skylar all the way inside the classroom as she'd been told to do. Mrs. Haggarty had hurried away to begin searching for her sister, but she'd just sat in the principal's office, afraid to do anything, hoping and praying they'd find Skylar hiding as they thought.

But her little sister hadn't been hiding. Nobody had seen Skylar anywhere around the school. Shanna had been the last person to see her sister alive and well.

Now she was gone. And it was all her fault.

"Here, drink this." Quinn thrust a glass in her hands.

Blinking at him, she willed the guilt-laden memories away. She took the glass and drank, reveling in the cool water soothing her throat. "Thanks. I'm fine."

"No!" Quinn's tone was sharp. "You're not fine. You're pale, as if you're going to faint again."

"I won't," she protested. She refused to faint again; once was certainly bad enough. She needed to pull herself together. The reality of the situation finally sank into her brain. Her sister's prints were found at the scene. After fourteen years of not knowing anything, those fingerprints meant that Skylar was alive. Alive!

Closing her eyes, she bowed her head and probed the depths of her soul, dragging out the faith she shouldn't have given up on, praying for the first time in years. *Lord, thank You for showing me that Skylar is alive. And please guide me. Give me the strength and courage to find my sister.*

"Shanna?" Quinn's tone was anxious.

She lifted her head and forced a smile. "It's a gift,

Quinn. A true gift. After all this time, we finally found Skylar. I have to call my mother, to let her know the news." And her father. He'd flat-out refused to talk to her when she'd tried to get in touch with him a few weeks ago, but surely he'd talk to her now.

"Whoa, wait a minute." Quinn took her hand in his, halting her from surging to her feet. "Why don't we wait until we know what we're dealing with?"

"Are you kidding?" Shanna stared at him, tugging at her hand. "My sister is *alive*. Do you know how many years we've waited to know even that much?" She was ashamed to admit she'd thought the worst. That Skylar was lying dead and buried in an abandoned field somewhere. At any moment she'd expected the police to uncover her bones.

God, forgive me for losing faith. Forgive me for believing Skylar was dead.

"Yes, she's alive. But we don't know where she's been for all these years. And I highly doubt she's going by the name of Skylar Dawson. Besides, her fingerprints were found at a crime scene, which makes her one of the many suspects in Brady's death."

Skylar a suspect? No, it wasn't possible. But Shanna slid back into her seat, the sick feeling in her stomach persisting. No. There was no way she believed her long-lost sister was a murderer. "Skylar didn't hurt your brother."

Quinn's glance held a trace of sympathy. "Maybe not, but take a moment to think this through. What can you really tell your mother at this point? You don't know what name Skylar is using these days. We don't even have a photo yet. Why don't we go through the names of the kids who were known to be at the party? We can get their ID pictures from the school, and you can see if any of the girls look familiar."

She had to admit, his idea had merit. And she had enough vacation time to get out of doing the routine lab work. Besides, now that her sister's prints had been found, Eric would remove her from actively working the case.

"Maybe we can even get a younger picture of your sister to perform a computer aging process," Quinn continued. "Once you know Skylar's current name, you'll have really good news to tell your mother."

She bit her lip and nodded, knowing he was right to take things slow. But she wanted to find Skylar now. Her patience was nonexistent after fourteen years. "My mother has a computer age-progression image of Skylar—it's posted on the website for missing children. But first I still need to go to the lab. I need to find out exactly where Skylar's prints were found."

"I'll go with you." Quinn released her hand and rose to his feet.

She stood, taking her phone from his hand. Skylar's prints were found at a college house. How ironic to know Skylar was here at a local university, only twenty miles from home after all these years.

Did Skylar remember her? Or their parents?

She almost hoped not, because that would mean Skylar had suffered, missing her home and her family while being taken somewhere else.

Her stomach clenched as the worst-case scenario flashed through her head. She dearly hoped that Skylar's life since she'd been gone had been decent and good.

Not dark and twisted.

* * *

Quinn kept a wary eye on Shanna as he drove to the CSI crime lab. Her face was still pale, but she looked a little less fragile than she had lying cold on the floor of her kitchen. She'd taken years off his life when she'd fainted like that. Although, after hearing her long-lost sister's fingerprints were found at Brady's crime scene, he certainly understood why she'd reacted the way she did.

He couldn't imagine how awful it must have been to lose a younger sibling to a kidnapping, never knowing if she was alive or dead.

Dead. Like Brady. His fingers tightened on the steering wheel. Quinn knew he should be heading over to his mother's offering his support, rather than sticking close to Shanna's side, but he couldn't in good conscience leave her alone. Besides, staying with Shanna meant he might get more information related to Brady's case, which was what he wanted.

Satisfied with his decision, he turned his head from side to side, trying to ease the kinks from his neck. He wasn't interested in Shanna's mysterious past unless it had a direct bearing on Brady's murder. Although for the life of him, he couldn't see anything but a random connection. But if Skylar disappeared fourteen years ago, she would be nineteen now. Just a year younger than Brady. Interesting.

Pulling up in front of the state crime-lab building, Quinn glanced at her. "Is it okay if I come in with you?"

"Sure." She glanced at him in surprise. "We'll register you for a visitor pass."

Intrigued by what they might find out inside the crime

lab, he followed Shanna as she headed to her buddy Al, the fingerprint analyst.

"Shanna?" A tall, thin middle-aged man hurried over. "I've been waiting for you. I ran these prints first thing this morning. Come here—you have to look at this fingerprint comparison for yourself."

"I believe you," she protested, going along with him anyway. She peered at the computer screen for a long moment as if afraid to believe the truth. "You're convinced there's no way this could be a mistake?"

"None." Al went on to explain exactly which pattern in the fingerprint made them unique. "Despite the size difference between an adult and a child, they're definitely the same."

"What part of the crime scene did this print come from?" Shanna asked.

Al's glance slid from hers and he grimaced. "Now, don't be upset, but I found her fingerprints on both the rugby trophy and the desk in the victim's room."

She sucked in a harsh breath. Quinn crossed over to stand beside her, since it seemed she'd forgotten his presence. "Don't jump to conclusions," he warned. "There might be a legitimate reason for her prints to be on the trophy."

"True enough," Al chimed in. "We found a total of four prints on the trophy, one from the victim, one from your sister and two others. After we get all the kids identified, we'll start getting copies of their prints in the system, to see what matches."

Shanna nodded, although Quinn could tell she was badly shaken by the news. She asked, "Do you have anything else to go on? Any other fingerprint matches?"

"Not yet," Al admitted. "I started with the trophy

and the kid's bedroom, and so far, your sister is the only match I've gotten from the database, aside from the victim's, of course. Getting through the rest of the house is going to take some time."

"I understand." Shanna fell silent.

Al looked at her with sympathy. "I already informed Eric about this. He told you to take off as much time as you need."

Shanna nodded as if she were still in a daze.

"Do you need to do anything else?" Quinn asked, putting a hand on her arm. "Or do we have time to head over to the admissions office of Carlyle University to look at photo IDs?"

"The admissions office," she agreed. "Al? If you find anything else, please let me know."

"I will." The older scientist gazed at her with true concern. "If you need to talk, I'm here."

A slight smile flitted around her mouth. "Thanks. Let Eric know I'll be in touch later."

Clearly, Shanna was close to Al, and he found himself wondering about her family as they walked back outside to his SUV. She'd mentioned her mother, but not her father. "This news is really going to shock your family, isn't it?"

"Yes," she murmured, sliding into the passenger seat as he climbed in behind the wheel. "My mother always clung to the belief Skylar was alive, but my dad refused to even talk about her. My parents divorced a few years after Skylar's kidnapping, mostly because of my dad."

His heart squeezed in sympathy. "I know what it's like to come from a broken home."

"Maybe, but at least you know the breakup wasn't

your fault." The faint bitterness in her tone surprised him.

Her fault? He shot her a quick glance. "Shanna, I'm sure your parents didn't blame you."

Her gaze was bleak. "Yes, they did. Because it was true. Skylar's kidnapping was my fault." She turned away, staring out the window. "You were right to hold off on telling my mother. I want to find my sister first. I can't bear to raise her hopes for no reason."

He reached over to take her hand in his. "Maybe looking through the student IDs will help."

"I hope so," she murmured. "I need to be able to give my mother that much."

He didn't know what to say to that. His cell phone rang, and he juggled the steering wheel, going against state law by answering it. "Hello?"

"Quinn?" His mother's shrill voice echoed in his ear. "Where are you?"

"I'm following up on some leads from Brady's case," he told her, trying to ignore that she hadn't bothered asking how he was doing. His mother tended to live in a world that was centered on herself and her second family. Not the mistake of her first marriage. "What's wrong? Are you and James doing all right?"

"It's been awful to sit here not knowing anything. We've been waiting for you to bring us some news." Her tone was full of reproach.

"I wish I had some news to bring you, but I don't." He maneuvered the car around a turn with one hand, refraining from reminding her that Brady had been dead for just a little more than twenty-four hours. "Look, Mom, I have to go. I'm driving. After I go through the list of kids who were at Brady's party, I'll be in touch."

"Call us the minute you find anything. We have an appointment at the funeral home this evening, but we don't know when they're going to release Brady's body." Her tone grew thick with suppressed tears.

Guilt swirled as he realized he should be making the funeral arrangements for her. "I'll help you with the arrangements, Mom. I'll find out when they're going to release Brady's body, and I'll meet you at the funeral home when I finish here."

"All right. I'll let James know the plan." His mother hung up. Fighting a surge of helplessness that he couldn't do more, Quinn flipped his phone shut.

"I can look through the photo IDs myself," Shanna offered in a low tone. "Sounds as if you have a lot to do at home."

Selfishly, he didn't want to leave Shanna. Not yet. Not until he knew whether or not she'd recognized any of the photo IDs as potentially belonging to her sister.

"I have time. Let's go through the pictures first, see if anyone looks even vaguely familiar. For now we'll use whatever aged photo your mom has posted on the missing children website."

"Sounds good."

Quinn parked in a no-parking zone, using his campus police tag to identify his car, and walked inside the main registration office with Shanna at his side. It was busy for a Monday, but within moments they were granted access to the library and the database where the computer records of all the college students' information and photos were kept.

"Here's the list of partygoers," Quinn said, pushing the list in front of her. At least half the attendees were female. "Let's start with these first."

She nodded, and he typed in the first name on the computer. After a few seconds, the photograph popped up on the screen. Shanna stared at the image so long, he cast a concerned glance her way. "What's wrong?"

"Nothing." Shanna slowly shook her head. "It's just that other than Skylar's brown eyes, I don't even know what to look for. Her hair could be any length, any color."

"Brown eyes?" He raised a brow, peering at her. No contacts that he could see. "Yours are blue."

"Yeah. Skylar takes after my dad. He has brown eyes. Mine and my mom's are blue."

"I see. We could narrow the search function to just those girls with brown eyes."

"No." She put her hand on his arm, stopping him. "I'd like to see them all, if you don't mind."

He hesitated, but then nodded. His time constraints weren't hers. After all these years, Shanna deserved at least a couple of hours to get through the list. "Okay."

One by one, she paged through the list of girls who'd been identified as attending the party. A few times she toggled back and forth between the picture of how Skylar might look now and the actual student photo, but in the end she sat back, slowly shaking her head.

"None of them look familiar." Her dejected tone made him empathize with what she must be going through. "I thought…" She didn't finish.

"Hey, we've only gone through the party list. There are thousands of other female student pictures to get through." He didn't have time to get through the rest now, but he could come back later, after the visit to the funeral home.

"Maybe." Shanna lifted her tortured gaze. "Looking at these pictures is harder than I thought. I should recognize her. My own sister. The image should jump out at me, don't you think?"

"Try to relax," he soothed. "We still have time—"

"No! You don't understand! It's already been fourteen years. I have to find her, Quinn. I have to!"

Chapter 4

Shanna stared at Quinn, feeling the pressure building up in her chest, preventing her from breathing. At the same time, her pulse skyrocketed into triple digits. For a moment she was helpless, unable to fight the overwhelming sense of panic.

Fourteen years! She'd waited fourteen years to hear news about her sister, and she was so close. Her sister was here, somewhere on this college campus. She couldn't fail to recognize her now. *She couldn't.*

"Easy, Shanna, breathe," Quinn said in his low, hypnotic voice. "This isn't the time to have a panic attack."

Panic attack? What was he talking about? "I'm not!" she snapped. The flash of anger at Quinn helped loosen the tightness in her chest. But her breathing was still shaky.

His green-gold gaze held a note of sympathy. "It's

okay. You've certainly been through a lot over the past few hours."

She closed her eyes, feeling like the worst kind of basket case, and concentrated on breathing. Deep breath in, hold for ten seconds before exhaling slowly. She repeated the process several times, calming herself and realizing Quinn was right. She was having a panic attack.

Earlier today, she'd fainted for the first time ever, and now this. What in the world was wrong with her? She needed to pull herself together, or she wouldn't be any good to Skylar. She needed to remember she was a trained crime-scene investigator.

Not a victim. Not anymore. Her sister was alive. And she'd need every one of her investigative skills to find her.

"I'm fine," she murmured when he lightly rested his hand on her shoulder in apparent concern. She opened her eyes and lifted her head to glance up at him sheepishly. "I'm sorry. I'm not usually this much of a mess."

"Shanna, cut yourself some slack already, would you?" Quinn stared at her with mild exasperation. "First you have some creepy guy following you, and then you discover your long-lost sister is alive. I think you're entitled to lose control a bit."

For the first time in what seemed like hours, she cracked a small smile. "Thanks, Quinn. But that's not a good excuse. I'm not the type to fall apart like this."

He scowled in disagreement. "If that's not a good excuse, I don't know what is."

Slowly she shook her head. Suddenly, everything fell into place, crystal clear. "No, this is God's way of reminding me I can't succeed on my own. For years I didn't put all my heart, soul and faith in God, and now

I realize how wrong that was. It's about time I face the truth. I need to put my fears and my worries into God's hands. With His support and guidance we'll find Skylar." Even as she said the words, Shanna felt calmer. More at peace.

How could she have forgotten the power of prayer? How could she have abandoned her faith when she needed it the most? No wonder she'd started falling apart.

Quinn's eyes widened as if he were surprised by what she'd said, and then he physically pulled away and averted his gaze. "So, how about I drive you home?" He glanced up at the clock on the wall. "I need to leave now to meet my mother and her husband at the funeral home."

His withdrawal and the abrupt way he'd changed the subject was a response she hadn't anticipated. Clearly, Quinn wasn't comfortable talking about faith and God. Because he didn't believe in God? Or the power of prayer? While she could relate to a certain extent, hadn't she made a similar mistake over these past few years? She still found it unbearably sad that Quinn might not believe in God at all.

But she wasn't brave enough to broach the subject now. Not when he clearly had other problems crowding his mind. Like planning his brother's funeral.

"No thanks. I'm going to stay for a while," she said lightly, turning back toward the computer screen. "I want to make a dent in these photos."

"There's plenty of time for that tomorrow," he started, but she cut him off.

"No. I'm staying." She wasn't the weak woman who'd suffered from a panic attack just a few minutes ago. Already she felt stronger, more determined. With God's help and support she could do anything. She forced a reassuring smile. "Don't worry about me. I'll catch a cab home when I'm finished here."

He stared at her for several tense moments before letting out a heavy sigh. "I'd rather you wait for me," he protested. "How about if I come back here to pick you up after we're finished with the funeral arrangements?"

"I'm fine with taking a cab, Quinn. You don't need to go out of your way."

He scowled with frustration. "Wait for me," he repeated with more force this time. "I'll pick you up when you're finished here, okay?"

With only a slight shrug in response, she kept her gaze glued to the computer screen as she started with the female students at the beginning of the alphabet. Abbot, Carrie? Not a match. Abel, Rebecca? Not a match.

She knew exactly when Quinn left, the library door shutting quietly behind him.

Glancing back, she watched him through the glass door, fighting the urge to call him back. There was no need to keep dragging him into her problems. He should be with his family right now.

It would be in her best interest to remember that finding Skylar was her priority, not his.

Quinn drove west to the Life-Everlasting Chapel, the place his mother had chosen to handle Brady's funeral arrangements.

As he drove, Shanna's words about trusting God tumbled through his mind. For some odd reason, he was surprised to hear about her faith in God.

He hadn't been inside a church in years, since before his parents' marriage had crumbled. A happy memory from long ago crept into his mind. He'd been about four or five years old and had attended church with his parents. Afterward, they'd gone out for breakfast, and he remembered walking between them, holding each of their hands while they'd count to three and swing him up off the ground, making him laugh.

Good times that hadn't lasted, he thought wryly. Within a year, his world had fallen apart when they'd first separated and then divorced. He could still remember the bitterness of their fights, especially because he happened to be at the center of each disagreement.

He'd gone back and forth between his parents' homes for thirteen months, until his mother married James Wallace. Once she gave birth to Brady, Quinn began spending longer and longer time frames with his dad, rather than with his mother and her new family. Eventually, at the age of thirteen, he lived with his father full-time.

Quinn shook off the painful memories as he pulled up to the Life-Everlasting Chapel. Obviously, going to church as a family all those years ago hadn't prevented his parents' marriage from falling apart.

But then again, his father had chosen a path far from God, especially over the last few years of his life when he'd turned to alcohol for comfort. So maybe that wasn't a surprise after all.

His mother, his stepfather and Ivy were already seated inside, talking to the funeral director when he walked in. The place reeked heavily of roses, to the point he had to fight back the urge to sneeze.

He approached the table where his family was seated, feeling invisible when they didn't so much as glance in his direction after he took a seat across from them.

"Just wait here a few moments, and I'll gather everything together for you, all right?" The middle-aged bald funeral director stood, and then when he caught sight of Quinn, quickly introduced himself. "Arthur Crandon," he said in a low, respectfully hushed voice, even as he pulled a business card from his pocket.

"Quinn Murphy," he said in response. "Brady was my half brother."

"My condolences for your loss," Arthur murmured.

"Thanks."

When the funeral director left the room, his mother finally looked at him. "Well?" she demanded. "Do you have any news? Have the police found Brady's killer?"

"No, I'm afraid not." He glanced helplessly at his stepfather, James Wallace, who sat with a supportive arm around his mother's shoulders. "I don't have anything new to report right now, but the investigation is still ongoing. Hopefully we'll know something soon."

His mother's expression grew angry. "Tell me this, Quinn. What good is it having you on the campus police force if you can't keep my children safe?" she asked harshly.

Resentment swelled in his chest, but he wrestled it back with an effort. His mother's eyes were red and swollen from crying, as were Ivy's. The deep grooves in his stepfather's face and the dark circles under his eyes made him look much older, too. Quinn had seen enough grieving families to know that they often lashed out in anger.

Yet listening to his mother lashing out at him personally hurt more than he'd expected.

"I'm sorry," Quinn repeated. Time to change the subject. He looked at the paperwork Arthur had left on the table. "Is there something I can do? Do you need anything?"

"No, we've already made all the arrangements," his mother said bitterly. "And it doesn't matter anyway, since everything is on hold until after the autopsy." She made the statement another accusation, glaring at him again, as if it were personally his fault that Brady's autopsy wasn't completed yet. And guiltily, he remembered promising her he'd follow up, but he hadn't.

"I'll make some phone calls, see what I can find out about the timeline for releasing Brady's body for the funeral," he said, standing up and reaching for his cell phone. The autopsy should be either in process or almost completed, and hopefully the detective assigned to the case would know the details.

His mother turned to his stepfather and Ivy, effectively dismissing him. For a moment he stood awkwardly, realizing he was only making his relationship with his mother worse by staying. By trying to be a part of the family.

Because he wasn't part of the family. She'd made that clear over the years. Her new family, James, Brady and Ivy, had been the center of her world for a long time.

Once again, he suspected his mother would have preferred to be planning his funeral rather than Brady's. She'd resented him from the very beginning of the divorce, arguing over the forced joint custody arrangements.

Obviously, nothing had changed since then.

"I'll be in touch when I have news," he murmured helplessly before turning and walking back outside.

Taking a deep breath of fresh air to clear the cloying scent of roses from his nasal passages, he tipped his head back to stare at the crescent-shaped moon surrounded by bright stars in the sky.

If there was a God, he could sure use some help from Him now, he thought idly.

He took another deep breath and glanced down at his phone. After punching in the number for Hank Nelson, he waited for the detective to answer his call.

But, of course, there was no response—from either God or Hank Nelson.

He snapped his phone shut and decided there was plenty of time to do a little investigating of his own before he needed to pick up Shanna. He knew a little about his younger brother, and that one of his favorite hangouts was a small coffee shop located not far from his house.

His mother deserved answers, and he was more determined than ever to get them for her.

It was the least he could do, after the way he'd messed up her life.

Shanna rubbed at her burning eyes and gave up, pushing away from the computer screen. The images were so blurry, she couldn't trust herself to continue. What if she missed Skylar simply because of exhaustion and eyestrain?

No, better to head home and begin again tomorrow, when her vision would be fresh and crisp.

She stood and gathered her jacket and her purse. Spying her cell phone, she picked it up and then hesitated.

Should she call Quinn? Or not?

Glancing at her watch, she realized she'd been sitting in front of the computer reviewing photos for almost two hours. Was Quinn still busy making funeral arrangements? She had no idea how long something like that would take.

She glanced at the phone and scrolled through it. No missed text message or phone calls that she could see. So he hadn't called her. The flash of disappointment was completely illogical. Quinn was likely still in the midst of planning his brother's funeral.

There was no reason to bother him for something as simple and basic as a ride home when she could just as easily call for a cab. Quinn should be supporting his family during a difficult time like this.

She called for a cab and then went outside to wait for her ride. The crisp October air had turned cool and she burrowed down in her coat, seeking warmth. Just when she was about to go back inside the building to wait, her cab came around the corner and parked near the curb.

Glancing at her cell phone one last time to verify there were no calls from Quinn, she tucked it in her pocket and slid into the backseat of the cab. She gave the driver her address and then settled back for the short ride.

She lived on the southwest side of Chicago, and the ride from Carlyle University only took about fifteen minutes. She paid the driver in cash and climbed out of the cab.

Her house was completely dark, and Shanna realized she must have forgotten to leave the kitchen light on as she usually did. Was it only this morning that she'd found out about Skylar's fingerprints? Seemed as if the phone call from Al had taken place twelve days ago.

She paused at the mailbox and opened it cautiously, hoping there wasn't another mysteriously blank, threatening note inside. When she didn't find anything but a handful of junk mail, her shoulders sagged in relief.

Thank You, Lord.

The whispered prayer felt good, felt right after not talking to God for so long. She couldn't believe she'd given up on her faith. With a small smile, she tucked the junk mail under her arm and searched inside her purse for her house keys as she walked up to the front door.

Maybe it was time to try calling her father again. Not to tell him about Skylar—she wanted to have better news first. But she could keep trying to mend the rift between them. The crime scene she'd worked just after the Markoviack case was also related to a brutal murder. And the victim's sister kept going on and on about how they hadn't spoken in years, and now it was too late. She'd immediately gone home to call her father, leaving several messages, but her father hadn't answered her calls. She'd even gone so far as to show up at his apartment, but he'd looked out the window, saw her and then refused to answer the door.

She knew her father blamed her for Skylar's disappearance, but she'd hoped he'd eventually let go of his anger. Yet it was difficult to make amends when he wouldn't even give her a chance to talk.

When the victim's sister had confessed how they hadn't spoken to each other in over a year, Shanna had been able to relate. Because her father hadn't spoken to her in over ten years. And she was ashamed to admit she hadn't tried to get in touch with him until recently.

Maybe mending their relationship was hopeless, but it wouldn't be her decision to give up. Not this time. No matter what, she intended to keep trying.

With a sigh, she unlocked the front door and walked inside. She paused for a moment to allow her eyes to adjust to the darkness. A loud creak echoed through the house, and she froze in the act of reaching for the light switch.

Was someone inside?

Shanna stayed exactly where she was, straining to listen. But now, all she heard was silence.

Slowly, the tension in her muscles eased. The noise must have been her imagination. Or just the normal creaks and groans of an older home.

She swept her hand along the wall, searching for and finding the light switch. She flipped the lever up.

Nothing.

With a frown, she flipped it on and off again. Still no light flashed on.

What were the odds that both lightbulbs in both lamps would go out at the exact same time?

Probably about the same as finding her missing sister's fingerprints at a crime scene.

As she was about to make her way across the room, she smelled some sort of heavy aftershave just a fraction of a second before she heard another rustling sound.

Someone was inside! The stalker!

Instinctively she ducked to the side, toward the door, in a desperate move to escape.

But she was too late. She felt a hand clamp down onto her arm seconds before pain exploded in the back of her head.

Chapter 5

Quinn called Shanna's cell phone for the fifth time, frowning when, once again, the call went unanswered. Hadn't they agreed she'd wait for him? Granted, he'd stayed at the coffeehouse, which had been unusually packed with college kids for a Monday night, longer than he'd anticipated. But still, they'd had an agreement.

When he didn't find Shanna in the computer library, his annoyance grew. Why wasn't she answering his calls? The hour wasn't that late—if she had gone home, she could have at least told him her plans. Or answer her phone.

She acted as if there was no reason to fear the weirdo guy leaving threatening messages.

The itch along the back of his neck wouldn't go away, so Quinn headed to her house, on the southwest side of town. He pushed the speed limit, figuring he'd use his badge to get out of a ticket if he was stopped.

He pulled up in front of Shanna's house, scowling when he noticed the place was completely dark. Was it possible she'd really gone to bed by eight-thirty at night?

Or hadn't she gotten home yet?

He climbed out of his car and approached the front door, knowing that if she had gone to bed, she wouldn't be thrilled to find him standing there.

He hesitated, but then shook his head. Too bad. He wasn't leaving without talking to her. With a determined stride, he stepped up on the porch and knocked loudly on the door.

No answer. He knocked again, harder. When she still didn't respond, he tried the door handle. To his surprise, it wasn't locked. Warily, he pulled his weapon from his shoulder holster and flattened himself against the wall before pushing the front door open.

The door didn't open all the way, and it took him a moment to realize there was something in the way. Pale skin, gleaming in the moonlight. An outstretched hand.

Shanna?

With his heart pounding in his chest, he quickly dialed 911, knowing he needed backup—and fast.

"What's the nature of your emergency?" the dispatcher asked.

"I have an injured woman, and her attacker could still be on the premises," he said urgently, keeping his voice as low as possible. He quickly rattled off her address. "Send the police and an ambulance. Hurry!"

The dispatcher told him to wait outside for the police, but he ignored her. Setting his phone on the ground to keep the connection, he decided there was no way he was going to sit there and do nothing when Shanna was hurt. He had no way of knowing if the intruder was still inside, so he eased through the narrow opening, keeping his back to the wall.

The house was quiet, but that didn't mean anything. The person could still be inside, waiting for him. Quinn swept his hand up for the light switch, and the itch on the back of his neck intensified when the lights didn't come on.

Keeping his weapon ready, he slid down the wall and reached out to feel for a pulse. Overwhelming relief swept over him when his fingers found the faint beat of her heart.

Thank You, God.

The prayer flashing into his mind was a surprise, as was the calming sense of peace. He didn't have time to dwell on it, though. Instead, he continued to listen for any indication that the prowler was still around, knowing her house was an unsecured crime scene.

Every instinct he had screamed at him to get Shanna out of there. But he was afraid to move her. Keeping his weapon ready, he gently used his free hand to check for injuries.

Shanna was lying facedown, as if she'd tried to run for the door. And as he swept a hand over her hair, he found the sticky wetness at the base of her skull that could only be blood.

His stomach twisted with fear. *Please, God, keep her safe.* Wishing desperately for some light, he once again debated his options. Move her? Or wait for backup to arrive?

What could possibly be taking the ambulance so long

to get here? And the police? Hadn't those two cops promised to drive past Shanna's house on a regular basis?

There were no indications anyone was still in the house, but the perpetrator could be hiding. Waiting. He wasn't leaving Shanna's side. Not until he knew for sure she was safe.

The wail of sirens finally reached his ears, but he didn't relax until he could hear the thuds of police boots on the step.

"Quinn Murphy, campus police," he said, announcing his presence. "I'm here beside the injured victim, but I haven't been able to confirm the house is secure."

"Okay. The ambulance is here, but we're going to do a sweep of the house first."

Quinn understood the need for safety, and he continued his vigilance next to Shanna while the rest of the Chicago P.D. went through the house.

"Kitchen, clear!"

"Bathroom, clear!"

"Bedroom one, clear!"

"Master bedroom, clear!"

The officers went through the entire house, including the basement, and then suddenly, the living room lights came on. The bright light was so unexpected, Quinn winced and ducked his head, trying to blink away the sudden blindness.

Seeing Shanna in the light did not reassure him. Her hair was matted with blood. Too much blood.

"Someone turned the breaker off," one of the officers said when he returned to the living room.

When the EMTs arrived, Quinn reluctantly moved out of the way, giving them room to work. Shanna groaned when they gently logrolled her onto a backboard, and then lifted her up onto the stretcher.

"What happened?" she asked, wincing as she raised a hand to her head.

"You tell us," Quinn said, taking her hand in his, needing the connection. He could hardly relax; adrenaline still rushed through his bloodstream a million miles a minute. "Looks like someone hit you on the back of the head."

"Yes," she whispered, her blue eyes clinging to his. "Someone was in my house. I tried to get away..." her voice trailed off.

"It's okay," he said reassuringly. He was just so glad to see her awake. And talking, in spite of the copious amount of blood. "Don't worry, you're going to be okay."

"Quinn, I'm sorry," she said, as her eyelids fluttered closed. "I should have waited."

"Don't apologize," he said again. This wasn't the time to argue. Not when her face was still so pale, and the tension around her mouth and eyes indicated she was in pain. All that mattered right now was knowing she'd be okay.

But he couldn't deny being concerned about the extent of her head injury.

"Which hospital are you taking her to?" he asked, as the EMTs loaded her into the back of the ambulance.

"Hospital?" she squeaked, her luminous blue eyes opening wide. "I'm fine! Just give me a few minutes to gather my thoughts. I don't need to go to the hospital."

Now he was going to argue. Big-time. "You're going to the hospital, Shanna. End of discussion."

The EMTs gaped at his harsh tone, and then the one closest to Shanna's head glanced down at her. "He's right," the EMT said kindly. "You really need to be checked out. The doctors are going to want a CT scan of your head to make sure there's no internal bleeding."

"Which hospital?" he asked again, impatiently.

"Chicago Central. It's the closest."

"I'll meet you there." He watched Shanna for a few seconds, relieved when she gave up and relaxed back on the gurney. He closed the ambulance door and then turned back to the cops swarming around Shanna's house. "What did you find?" he asked.

"Nothing resembling a weapon," the older cop said grumpily. His name tag identified him as Officer Rawlings. "We'll have the place dusted for prints, but whatever he used to hit her on the back of the head, he took with him."

Quinn couldn't help but agree. "Anything else?"

"We found her cell phone." Rawlings raised a brow. "Looks as if you called her several times."

He glanced at her phone display, where she'd labeled his cell number with his name. "Yeah, well she wasn't supposed to come home alone." He was bothered by the way she hadn't waited for him. Didn't she trust him? He said he'd return. "She was supposed to wait for me. There's been some wacky guy following her, leaving threatening notes."

"Yeah, I saw a copy of the report." Rawlings chomped hard on a piece of gum. "Good thing for you. Otherwise we'd be taking you downtown for a chat."

Quinn felt his temper rise, and he had to take a calming breath before responding. These guys were only doing their jobs, even if they weren't doing them very well, at least in his opinion. "I'm not the assailant who's been stalking her. I was at the Corner Café Coffee Shop between six and eight tonight. Plenty of people can verify that I was there."

"Okay," Rawlings agreed mildly. "We'll check out your alibi. No reason to get your boxers in a bundle."

He let that one slide. "Have you figured out how the assailant got inside?"

"Yep. There's a broken window in the basement we think he used to gain entry. We suspect he tripped the breaker and then hunkered down to wait for Ms. Dawson to come home. I suppose you're going to want to see everything for yourself?"

He did, but he wanted even more to make sure Shanna was okay. "Later. Right now, I'm heading to Chicago Central."

Shanna kept her eyes closed as a halfhearted attempt to minimize the pounding in her head. Her stomach churned with nausea, but she didn't say anything to the EMTs, hoping the sick feeling in her stomach was from knowing someone had been inside her house, and not from a potential brain injury.

She owed Quinn an apology. He'd told her to wait for him but she hadn't, too proud, too stubborn to call him. The excuses seemed flimsy now. She couldn't believe he hadn't said those famous last words.

I told you so.

Of course, saying something like that didn't seem to be Quinn's style.

"Ms. Dawson, we've arrived at the hospital." The EMT loomed over her, fussing with the IV line that they'd placed in her arm. "How are you feeling?" he asked.

"I'm fine." Or at least she would be, once her mammoth-size headache went away.

She couldn't help wincing a bit when they jostled her, pulling the gurney out of the back of the ambulance. As they went in through the emergency department doors, she felt like a complete fraud when a group of staff members rushed over to greet them as if she were on death's door.

"Vitals stable, BP 110/60, pulse 98 and respirations 16," the EMT announced as they wheeled her inside. "She has an open laceration in the back of her head, and was found unconscious at the scene."

Good heavens, the EMT was making her sound far worse than she was. "I'm fine," she said, trying to make eye contact with one of the staff members.

But it was no use. No one was listening to her, too intent on doing whatever medical tasks they deemed necessary. One nurse hooked her up to a heart monitor, while another checked her blood pressure again. A third one tied a tourniquet around her arm. "Tiny pinch here," she said mere seconds before inserting the needle.

The pain in her head must be bad, since she didn't feel the needle in her vein at all.

"Hi there, my name is Dr. Lyons." A man old enough to be her father bent over her bedside and flashed a kind smile. "I'm just going to take a listen to your heart and lungs for a moment. Then we'll review the extent of your injuries."

The extent of her injuries? "It's just my head," she protested. But she needn't have bothered since no one was paying any attention. The kindly doctor put his stethoscope buds in his ears and listened intently.

Despite being completely surrounded by hospital staff, she'd never felt more alone.

She closed her eyes and tried not to feel sorry for herself. She should be grateful they were all intent on doing their jobs. The sooner she was medically cleared, the sooner she'd be able to go home.

"Shanna?" Quinn's familiar deep voice made her heart jump. She braved the light, opening her eyes to look for him.

"Sorry, sir, you can't be in here," one of the nurses said, putting an arm out to stop him. "No family allowed."

She had to smile when he scowled and flashed his badge. "Police. Ms. Dawson is a victim of a crime."

The nurse relaxed and waved him past. "You can't question her now, so stay out of the way until after we're finished examining her."

Quinn came closer, careful not to interfere with the medical team. "How are you holding up?" he asked in a low voice.

"Better now that you're here." The honest statement slipped out before she could stop it.

His features softened, and when the doctor stepped back he inched a little closer, managing to stay out of the nurse's way even as he reached over to take her hand.

Gratefully, she closed her fingers around his.

For a moment their gazes locked. Held. The depth of emotion in his expression startled her. Tears pricked her eyes, but she told herself they were because of her pounding head, and not just because she was so glad to see him.

"You're going to be fine," he said. And she wondered which of them he was trying to convince.

Within minutes, though, the staff members who'd hovered around her moved on to other tasks. Obviously, she wasn't hurt very badly, since only one nurse remained at her bedside.

"We're going to take you over to radiology in a few minutes, as Dr. Lyons has ordered a CT scan of your head to rule out a subdural hematoma."

A what? Sounded like something bad, so she didn't bother to ask. "Okay."

"I'd like to go with her," Quinn said. Now that everyone had dispersed, no one seemed to mind that he'd planted himself right next to her.

"Fine with me," the nurse said with a shrug.

"You don't have to stay," Shanna murmured. "It's my own fault that I'm even here in the first place."

Quinn's eyebrows levered up. "I hardly think it's your fault someone broke into your house and waited there for you to come home."

She shook her head and then winced as the slightest motion made the hammering in her head nearly unbearable. "No, I mean it's my fault because I didn't call you."

Quinn stared down at their entwined hands for a long second before raising his gaze to hers. "So why didn't you call me?"

"I thought your family probably needed you more than I did." Or at least, more than she should. But she didn't voice that part. "When you didn't call me, I figured you were busy with your family and forgot." Okay, now that just sounded pathetic.

He let out a heavy sigh. "No, Shanna. I wasn't busy with my family. The funeral arrangements were pretty much finished by the time I arrived."

Really? Then where had he been for the hours she'd

spent looking at photos? Before she could ask, a tech came over and began disconnecting her from the heart monitor.

"I'm going to wheel you over to radiology. It's right around the corner from the trauma bay. And the scan won't take long, just ten to fifteen minutes. Are you allergic to anything? Iodine? Shellfish?"

"Not that I know of."

"Great." The tech pushed her bed away and, true to his word, Quinn walked right alongside, holding her hand the entire time. Once she was taken into the scanner he had to step back. But as soon as it was complete, he returned and took her hand again.

This time, the radiology tech took her to a private room. "You've been cleared from a trauma perspective," one of the nurses explained. "We're waiting for the resident to come over to clean and stitch up your scalp laceration."

Didn't that sound like fun? Not. Still, she didn't complain. The resident showed up a moment later. "Good news. Your CT scan is negative, which means you have a minor concussion but no bleeding into your brain. The laceration you have back there is going to need a few stitches, though. Once we're finished with that, you'll be able to go home."

Her stomach lurched at the word *home.*

Stop it, she chided herself. She was lucky to have escaped with only a minor injury. And at least she had a home to go to. Closing her eyes, she offered up a quick prayer. *Thank You for sparing me from greater harm, Lord.*

She slowly turned over so the resident could wash and suture her head. She kept as still as possible, while he first shaved the hair away from the wound and then began to clean it. Her head pounded so badly, she couldn't bring herself to care when she saw long strands of her hair falling to the floor. Apparently, she was going to have a bald spot on the back of her head for a while.

Could have been so much worse.

"More good news, this only needed four stitches," the resident announced cheerfully. "I'm all finished. Just rest here for a few minutes while we get your discharge paperwork ready."

After she rolled over on her back, she caught Quinn's serious gaze. His hand tightened on hers. "You're not going back home alone, Shanna."

"You never mentioned how he got inside."

"Broke in through the basement window and tripped the fuse so the lights wouldn't work. Unfortunately, we didn't find what he used to hit you with."

The force of the blow had felt like a rock, but, honestly, it could have been anything. The thought of staying in her house alone wasn't the least bit appealing, but it would be inappropriate to have Quinn stay with her. "I was thinking about going to a motel for the night."

He looked as if he wanted to argue, but then nodded. "All right, that seems like a reasonable compromise."

"Why do you think he left me alive?" The question had been nagging at her, even though it was hard to imagine anyone hating her enough to hurt her. But why hadn't he made sure she was dead before he left?

Quinn blew out a heavy breath. "Best I can figure, the ringing of your cell phone scared him off. I started calling you, over and over again. Maybe he figured I was closer than I was."

His theory made sense. "Thank you for calling," she whispered. "You probably saved my life."

"I should have called you sooner," he said, his tone full of self-reproach. "So, really, it's my fault you're here. I got caught up in the investigation and lost track of time."

The investigation into Brady's murder? Her attention was diverted from her incessant headache. "Did you find something? Any evidence?"

"Not evidence, exactly," Quinn said slowly. "But one of Brady's roommates told me my brother hung out at the Corner Café Coffee Shop, so I went over there. I flashed his photo and just about everyone remembered Brady being there often."

"Really?"

"Yeah. Several kids told me he was always working on his laptop computer, using the free Wi-Fi services the coffee shop provided. I assumed he was probably doing homework of some sort. Until one person mentioned Brady's article."

She frowned. "Article? What sort of article?"

"I'm not sure," he admitted. "But I did a little digging and discovered Brady was taking a journalism course. He was also one of the reporters for the college's on-line newspaper."

She didn't quite understand why this news was so important. "So what does that mean? I'm sure there are a lot of kids who are journalism majors."

"Yeah, but this one kid I spoke to seemed to think Brady was hot on some story. Some story he was pretty secretive about. I'm just wondering if he stumbled into something he shouldn't have."

She stared at Quinn, unable to imagine what sort of information a college student could stumble upon that was bad enough to get him killed.

Chapter 6

Shanna seemed surprised by his revelation, but they were interrupted when the gum-chewing Officer Rawlings entered Shanna's hospital room. Quinn frowned. "Did you find something significant?"

"No." Rawlings crossed over to the other side of Shanna's bed. "Ms. Dawson, we'd like you to go through your home to inventory anything that might be missing."

"Missing?" Shanna's alabaster skin paled even more. "Do you think the intruder was trying to rob me?"

Quinn snorted his disbelief, but Rawlings ignored him. "We want to cover all possibilities. It doesn't look like much has been disturbed, but you'd be the best one to judge for sure. Here's my card. I'd like you to call me once you're finished."

Shanna seemed upset by the news. "All right."

Quinn took the card from Shanna's fingers and tucked

it into his breast pocket. "I'll be sure she makes a list if anything's missing."

Rawlings shrugged. "Fine." He turned to Shanna. "I need a statement from you, Ms. Dawson, and I'd rather get the details while they're fresh in your mind."

"Okay," she responded.

"Tell me what happened, starting with where you were before you went home." Rawlings pulled out a small notebook and a stubby pencil, glancing at her expectantly.

"I spent most of the day at Carlyle University. I called for a cab about ten minutes to eight at night. The cabbie arrived about five minutes later, and I probably got home around eight-fifteen or so."

Quinn tightened his grip on her hand. Five minutes. He'd missed her at Carlyle University by five minutes!

"Then what happened?" Rawlings asked.

"I came home and went in through the front door. I'm not sure why," she mused with a frown, "because normally I go inside through the side door."

"Hmm." Rawlings jotted something down in his notebook.

"I thought I heard something, but figured it was just the normal creaks and groans of an older house. I flipped on the light switch, but it didn't work."

"Then what happened?"

She hesitated, her fingers tightening around his. "I smelled him." Rawlings's eyebrows rose upward. "I know that sounds crazy, but he was wearing some sort of stinky aftershave. The moment I realized I wasn't alone, I tried to run, but he hit me on the back of the head."

Listening to Shanna reiterate the series of events wasn't easy. He should have been there with her.

"Anything else? Did you see him at all?"

"No. I only smelled him."

Rawlings shut his notebook. "Okay, if you think of anything else, give me a call."

"I will." Shanna's smile was strained.

Quinn waited until after Rawlings left. "If we went to the store to test samples of aftershave, would you be able to pinpoint what he smelled like?"

She wrinkled her nose. "Yes. I'm sure I'd recognize it."

Satisfied they might have at least one lead, he nodded. "Okay, plan on going tomorrow, then."

"I need to look at more photos of college students tomorrow," she protested. "We'll check out the aftershave later."

"There's no guarantee your sister is enrolled at the university," he pointed out.

"It's my best lead," she repeated stubbornly.

They were interrupted by the resident coming back into Shanna's room. "Here you go. Here's a prescription for a narcotic pain reliever, although it might be helpful to start with over-the-counter medication like ibuprofen first." He went through the list of discharge instructions, stressing the importance of coming back to the hospital if her symptoms got any worse.

"Sign here." The resident indicated the paperwork.

She signed and then swung her legs over the side of the bed. She swayed a bit, and Quinn reached out a hand to steady her.

"Which motel?" he asked as she slowly made her way outside. He steered her in the direction of his car.

"Quinn, I want to go home first."

Home? "I thought we'd reached a compromise."

Her face took on the all-too-familiar stubborn expression. "Home, so I can check for anything missing and pack an overnight case."

"Home first, then a motel," he agreed reluctantly.

She slid into the passenger seat and kept her eyes closed during the short ride back to her house. He glanced at her frequently, wondering if he should just ignore her desire to get whatever she needed and take her straight to the motel.

She had to be exhausted. Not that he blamed her. But the moment he pulled into her driveway, her eyes opened. "Are you sure you're all right?" he asked.

"As fine as I can be with a monster headache," she said with a wry smile. She pulled out her keys. "Guess I should get my locks changed."

"At the very least." He came around to help her out of the car. "I thought you were considering a security system?"

"I have to admit, that idea is sounding better and better." She went in through the side door this time, walking into the kitchen. He followed her inside, glanced around curiously. The interior of her house was neat, tidy.

"Give me a few minutes to look around and then pack my things," she said, moving down the hall, flipping lights on as she went, making her way toward the bedrooms.

Quinn stood in the kitchen, glancing around curiously. Had the intruder waited for her in here? Only to be disappointed when she came in the front door instead?

There weren't a lot of hiding places, though. The kitchen table was tucked into a corner, and the rest of the kitchen area was wide open, with the white cabinets mounted on two walls across from the entryway.

He walked over behind the door to mimic what the intruder might have done. The assailant had waited right here for her to come in, holding his weapon—a bat, or a club of some sort—ready in his hand.

How long had he waited? Ten minutes? Thirty? A couple of hours? The assailant had chosen to lie in wait for her, rather than to follow her.

Next time you'll be alone.

The last note she'd received mocked him, and he battled a wave of guilt. Next time, she wouldn't be alone.

Standing with his back against the wall, he imagined how the assailant must have heard Shanna come in through the front door. Waiting in the dark, having tripped the breakers in the fuse box, meant he must have felt along the wall, moving toward the opening to make his way into the living room.

Quinn took the path that made the most sense, and right at the entryway into the living area, a floorboard creaked under his weight.

Bingo.

The satisfaction was bittersweet. Thankfully, Shanna had come in through the front door. Because if she'd come in through the kitchen, her assailant might have killed her.

But because he'd had to move through the house, she'd heard him and smelled him, which caused her to run for the door. Maybe in the dark, the assailant had misjudged the distance and hadn't hit her as hard as he'd intended. And then Quinn had called her cell phone several times, one call right after the other, scaring the guy off.

The scenario he'd created fit. Only too well.

Grimly, Quinn turned and headed for the basement.

Rawlings had told him the guy had come in through a broken window. The least he could do while he waited was secure the house.

But when he flipped on the basement light, he was surprised to discover one of the officers on scene had already done the work. A board was nailed securely over the broken window, and the shards of glass had been swept into a neat pile.

Thoughtfully, he walked back upstairs. Glancing at his watch, he wondered what was taking her so long. "Shanna? Do you have everything you need?"

"Not yet," came her muffled reply. From where he stood, at the beginning of the hallway, he could tell her voice came from the bedroom closer to him, not the master bedroom, which was further down the hall.

He didn't think this was the right time to go through her stuff to make sure nothing was stolen. Rawlings was crazy if he thought this was the work of a burglar. He'd bet his entire pension that the stalker who'd left the threatening notes was the guy who'd waited patiently for her in the kitchen.

He headed down the hallway. "Shanna, we need to leave," he said, pausing in the doorway of the first bedroom. She used it as an office, judging by the rolltop desk and computer taking up one wall. He found her half-buried inside the closet. "What are you looking for?"

She didn't answer, but he could hear her mumbling to herself. "It's here somewhere. I know it is."

What was there somewhere? "Let me help you look," he offered, venturing farther into the room.

"You can't help me. I'm the one who put it somewhere

safe. Or so I thought." After another few minutes, she finally exclaimed, "I found it!"

He watched as she pulled a large box down from a shelf in the back of the closet, staggering a little beneath the weight. Before he could take it from her, she set it on the floor and dropped to her knees. Gently, she pried off the lid, and the first item he saw was a pink stuffed elephant.

This was what she was searching for? His stomach twisted. Maybe her head injury was worse than they'd thought. "Shanna, come on, we really need to get you to a motel room. I think you need to get some rest."

She lifted her gaze to his, and the tortured expression in her luminous blue eyes tugged at his heart. "I couldn't leave without making sure everything was still here."

Everything? A pink stuffed animal? And then he understood. "These are Skylar's personal belongings, aren't they?"

"Yes." Shanna rifled through the box. "Most of it is Skylar's—a few of her stuffed animals, her baby ring, her favorite blanket. But I also have my research notes in here from the investigation."

"Investigation?" His curiosity piqued, he came over to kneel beside her. He wished Rawlings had never given her the idea this could be the work of a burglar. "The police investigation?"

"Not exactly." She rocked back on her heels. "My own investigation. Skylar's kidnapping is what made me decide to go into CSI work in the first place, and I never gave up hope that we'd eventually find out what happened to her. I've continued to work on her case, on and off, for the past eight years."

* * *

Shanna knew Quinn was looking at her as if she'd lost her marbles. But what did he expect? Of course she hadn't given up on the cold-case investigation.

"Did you really think the person who broke into your house was here to steal this stuff?" he asked.

"Maybe." How could she explain her convoluted feelings? "Probably not, but I wanted to be sure."

Quinn's gaze was serious. "You told me the notes began to show up a couple of weeks ago, right?" When she nodded, he continued, "So I'm sure Brady's murder and finding your sister's fingerprints at the crime scene aren't connected to the assailant."

Logically, she knew he was right. "I know." She stared down at the box, the sick feeling in her stomach intensifying as she stared at Ellie, the elephant. Skylar's elephant. From what she could see, everything was still there.

"Unless…" Quinn frowned. "Have you been working on your sister's case recently? Interviewing people? Stirring up the past in a way that you're making someone nervous?"

She let out a heavy sigh. "No, I haven't done any investigating of my sister's case in months." And she was ashamed that she'd let her work cases sidetrack her from finding her sister.

Quinn's expression was full of disappointment. "Okay, then I really don't see how they could possibly be related. Why don't you put this stuff away for now? I think you need to get some rest."

Now that she had the box of her sister's belongings in hand, she was loathe to let it go. Losing the contents of this box would be like losing her sister all over again.

With a sigh, she picked up the folder containing her notes and a stack of newspaper clippings. Several items slid out onto the floor, and she reached over to gather them back together.

"Wait a minute," Quinn said, putting his hand on hers. He picked up the article closest to him and scanned the newspaper print. "This isn't related to Skylar's kidnapping. It's about some other child."

"Yeah, I know." When he still looked puzzled, she tried to explain. "There weren't many clues about Skylar's disappearance. I got a copy of the police report, and none of the people interviewed had seen anything. So I searched on the internet for other cases that were similar to Skylar's."

"Other cases," he repeated. "In the Chicago area?"

"Not just in the Chicago area," she explained. "But I did find about six other cases that all took place in an eighteen-month time frame and within a hundred-mile radius."

Quinn looked totally shocked. "That's incredible. I think you were clearly onto something, Shanna. But I can't figure out why the feds weren't involved?"

"They were for a while. They interviewed my parents. But other than that, I don't know that they found out much, probably because each case was slightly different." She pulled out several of the articles showing what she meant. "See this child here? His father disappeared at the same time, and the parents were divorced, so the crime was considered to be the result of the custody battle."

"But they never found the father or the child?" Quinn persisted.

"No." At his skeptical gaze, she shrugged. "I know

it's odd, but they figured the guy must have gone to Mexico, or maybe Canada."

"Interesting." He shuffled through the articles to pick up another one. "Wow, this child is just fourteen months old."

"Yeah, that one wasn't exactly like the other children. Most of the ages were between two and a half and five. My sister was one of the oldest children taken."

"The FBI must have a file on this," Quinn mused, his gaze sweeping over all the evidence she'd collected over the years. "Maybe now that we have Skylar's prints at the crime scene we should call them."

"You're probably right," she agreed slowly. With the FBI's resources, surely they'd have the ability to track down Skylar better than she could. If they were even willing to reopen the case. Surely finding Skylar's fingerprints gave them a good reason.

"I know I'm right." Quinn sat down on the floor next to her box, making himself comfortable. She smiled, realizing his cop instincts had gotten the better of him. Now that he knew there might be other missing children related to Skylar's case, he was intrigued by the information.

"Hey, this kid was taken from a shopping mall," Quinn said, a note of eagerness in his voice. "That's pretty similar to being taken from a school."

"I know. That was the case I spent the most time on because the cases were so similar." She leaned in to read over his shoulder, even though she had the details of the article memorized. "The only difference was that Kenny was a boy, and just a month shy of being four years old."

She remembered the case all too well. Kenny Larson was the child who'd been taken, nearly nine months before Skylar. The nearly four-year-old had been at the mall with his grandmother when they'd gotten separated. Thinking he was lost, his grandmother had frantically called the mall security, and they'd gone through every store. Finally, suspecting the worst, they reviewed every mall exit security tape but, despite their efforts, had not been able to capture a photo of the kidnapper.

She remembered because there was a long article about how the police had an image they were working with, a large group of people leaving the mall at the same time with a small boy in the middle of the group. But the image was so blurry and the group so large, that even with skilled enhancements, they hadn't been able to pinpoint the kidnapper.

"You know, maybe we should take this stuff with us to the motel," Quinn admitted. "If nothing else, we could spend some time reviewing the evidence, see if anything jumps out at us."

"We?" she echoed, pouncing on the pronoun. "Quinn, you're not staying in the motel room with me."

He merely raised a brow. "Are you telling me I can't check into a room right next to yours?" he asked carefully. "Because I'm pretty sure they'll give out rooms to anyone willing to pay for one."

She bit her lip, forced to admit she'd love nothing more than to have Quinn be in a motel room right next door to her. But she was already leaning on him far too much.

What would happen when Brady's murder investigation was over? And they'd found her sister? Each of them would end up going their separate ways.

Quinn was just being nice and supportive to her because he was a cop, and she happened to be in danger.

He'd held her hand throughout her brief hospital stay because he was a nice guy and he felt responsible for the attack. He wasn't attracted to her.

Not the same way she was attracted to him.

Besides, she wasn't in the market for a relationship. She wasn't very good at them, anyway. At least, according to Garrett, the one relationship she'd had during college.

"Obviously you can do whatever you'd like, Quinn," she said finally, raising her gaze to his. "But be honest. I'm sure you have other things you'd rather be doing, like following up on more leads related to Brady's murder."

He gave a careless shrug, but she could tell she'd hit a nerve. "In helping you find Skylar, I could also uncover a lead related to Brady's murder. And besides," he hesitated and then reached over to take her hand, "I need to know you're safe."

His confession touched her in the deepest recesses of her soul. When was the last time she'd ever felt as if someone was on her side?

Ducking her head to hide her blush, she quickly gathered the articles together. "Okay, then let's go."

In her haste, she moved too quickly, and several documents slid out of the folder. Feeling even more foolish for the slightest betrayal of her nervousness, she quickly gathered them back together. Her gaze landed on Skylar's birth certificate.

She froze, staring down at the date in complete disbelief.

"What's wrong?" Quinn asked, reaching over to lightly grasp her arm. "Is your headache getting worse?"

Slowly she shook her head. How could she have forgotten? The first of September was the day Skylar had disappeared. The date was burned into her brain, had haunted her ever since.

"Shanna, please. Tell me what's wrong."

She finally raised her tortured gaze to his. "I don't know how I missed this, but today is October 19th. Skylar's birthday."

Chapter 7

The tiny hairs on the back of Quinn's neck stood on end as he stared at Shanna in shocked surprise. Today was Skylar's birthday?

They'd just decided Shanna's stalker and Skylar's kidnapping couldn't possibly be related, but that was before this bit of news. Was it really a coincidence that Shanna was attacked by her stalker on the day of her missing sister's birthday?

Quinn didn't believe in coincidences.

"You're sure you haven't done any investigating related to your sister's disappearance in the past few months?" he asked again. His gut was clamoring at him, but there had to be a connection somewhere. "Because now that we know today is Skylar's birthday, I can't help thinking there must be some connection between your stalker and your sister's disappearance." It was the only possibility that made sense, even though the timing was off.

Her stalker had started sending notes a couple of weeks ago, and they'd just found her sister's prints two days ago. But the attack on Shanna occurring on Skylar's birthday seemed to be some sort of message.

One they couldn't afford to ignore.

"I'm absolutely sure," Shanna said firmly. "Honestly, Quinn, my job has been so busy over the past few months that I haven't had time." Her gaze dropped to the birth certificate in her hands and her mouth turned down at the corners. "No, that's not quite true. The real answer is that I haven't made time. I allowed my job to take precedence over my sister."

He hated the way she kept beating herself up over this. No matter what she thought, her sister's kidnapping wasn't her fault. "Without some new clue or piece of information to go on, what good would come from reviewing the same old evidence?" he asked reasonably. "Even the feds have pretty much given up the investigation, right?"

"Yeah, maybe," Shanna murmured, sliding the birth certificate back into the folder with the rest of the paperwork. "But giving up on Skylar isn't the answer, either."

He tried to ignore the twinge of guilt. Wasn't he allowing Shanna to distract him from finding Brady's killer? He could pretend that finding her sister might give him a clue to Brady's murder, but he knew that wasn't entirely true. For some odd reason, he wanted to help Shanna.

He did his best to drag his attention back to the matter at hand. "Look, Shanna, you can't change what happened in the past—all you can do is move forward from here. And now we have the best lead ever—your sister's fingerprint at a crime scene, linked to a university." *And a stalker who's watching you,* he added silently.

His words seemed to hit home as she straightened and nodded. "You're right, Quinn. I'd like to take all this stuff with me to the hotel. Going through the evidence again may spark a new idea."

"Sounds like a plan," he agreed. "And I can look at the evidence too at some point. Maybe a new pair of eyes will pick up something you've missed."

"Ah, sure." Again, she seemed flustered by his offer to assist. Because she thought he was becoming too friendly? During those hours at the hospital, she'd clung to his hand as if it were a lifeline. But now she avoided his gaze as she finally put all the items from Skylar's childhood and her investigation into the box. "We'd better get going," she said.

He shouldn't be surprised at how she pulled away. Hadn't he learned his lesson about relationships after the fiasco with Leslie leaving him? Quinn rose to his feet, taking the box from her hands even though it wasn't very heavy. "Do you have your overnight bag packed?"

"Yes. Give me a minute to get it, and I'll meet you in the kitchen."

He nodded and carried the box out to the kitchen where Shanna met him less than a minute later. He waited until she closed the door and locked it before storing the box and her overnight bag in the back of his SUV.

The ride to the hotel didn't take long, and he even took extra precautions, using a zigzag route to make sure they weren't followed. When he was satisfied no one could possibly have tailed them, he pulled into the parking lot. The chain hotel wasn't anything fancy, and at the last minute, he decided against staying there with her.

Keeping a measure of professional distance between them would be smart. Safe. Shanna was in the middle of a family crisis, and the last thing she needed was to worry about him crowding her. And that wasn't his intention. But surely they could be friends?

And besides, he needed to put more time and effort into investigating Brady's murder. What sort of man let a pretty woman get in the way of his duty? Not Quinn Murphy, that's for sure.

When he requested one room, not two, in the middle of the hallway, halfway between the elevators and stairwells, she glanced at him in surprise but didn't utter a single protest. And she insisted on using her own credit card to foot the bill.

"Thanks for the ride, Quinn," she said, reaching for her overnight bag. Was it his imagination, or was her smile strained? "I appreciate all your help tonight."

He didn't relinquish his hold on her overnight bag or the box of Skylar's things. "I'm not staying because I need to check on my mother. She's really been a wreck over Brady." The excuse sounded weak, even to him. "I'll walk you up to your room," he offered, grasping on to the flimsiest excuse to prolong their time together.

"There's no need," she protested. But he ignored her and walked over to the elevator, punching the button to open the door. She rolled her eyes and crossed her arms over her chest.

During the elevator ride, he racked his brain trying to think of something to say. Something to ease the sudden tension between them.

Something to reassure her that his intentions were honorable.

The elevator doors opened on the third floor, the highest floor of the midsize hotel, and he followed behind her as she walked briskly to her room.

She unlocked the door and pushed it open, so he could set her bag and box inside. She stayed at the door until he returned. "Thanks again, Quinn," she said.

"You're welcome," he murmured. On the threshold he paused, and then turned back to face her. "Shanna, I know we just met a few days ago, but I hope you consider me a friend. Please call me if you need anything, okay?"

"Of course I consider you a friend, Quinn," she assured him. Was that relief he saw reflected in her eyes? "And I really do appreciate everything you've done for me."

Ridiculous to be disappointed at how quickly she'd accepted his offer of friendship. "Anytime, Shanna." And when it came time to walk away, he simply couldn't do it. "How about meeting me here for lunch tomorrow to compare notes?"

A flicker of surprise flashed across her features. "You're off work again tomorrow?"

"Yeah. They gave me a week off, due to Brady's death." And here he was trying to figure out a way to spend more time with Shanna.

"Okay, lunch tomorrow would be great. Good night, Quinn."

It took every ounce of willpower he had to step back, rather than gathering her close for a hug. "Good night, Shanna."

He waited until she'd closed the door and slid the dead bolt home. Then he forced himself to walk away.

He had six days of vacation/bereavement time off work. It was about time he put forth a stronger effort to find Brady's killer.

And he vowed to start tonight. The customers at the coffee shop thought Brady was working on some "secret" article. There was no easy way to get a hold of Brady's computer tonight, although earlier, he'd put in a second call to Hank Nelson requesting a copy of all the files on Brady's hard drive.

But he could go back through his brother's previous college newsletter articles to see what sorts of topics Brady liked to write about.

And maybe focusing on Brady would make it easier to forget about Shanna, at least for a little while.

Shanna sat down at the desk inside her room and began to review her notes from Skylar's kidnapping. But her throbbing headache wasn't easy to ignore. When she realized she'd read the same paragraph three times and still couldn't remember a word, she shoved the notes aside.

It was no use. She couldn't concentrate.

Turning off the lights and climbing into bed helped to ease the pain a little.

She was exhausted. Mentally and physically exhausted. So why couldn't she sleep?

The image of Quinn's earnest expression as he asked if they could be friends flashed in her mind. She should be glad, relieved that he considered her a friend.

So why the hint of disappointment?

It wasn't as if she and Quinn had a lot in common. Other than maybe being estranged from their respective families.

But Quinn wasn't comfortable talking about God, which should be a huge hint that friendship was all that could ever be between them.

Look what happened when she'd tried to date Garrett? They'd started out as friends, but then he began pushing for a physical relationship when she wasn't ready, and in the end, they'd broken up and their friendship had been ruined.

She didn't want to make the same mistake with Quinn.

Shanna pushed Quinn's image out of her mind and tried to focus on her newly reawakened faith.

Dear Lord, please guide me on Your chosen path. Help me to find Skylar and please keep my sister safe in Your care. Amen.

The tension eased from her body, lightening the throbbing in her head. But it wasn't until, just as she was falling asleep, that it occurred to her—maybe God intended her to show Quinn the value of believing in God and the power of faith.

When Shanna woke up the next morning, she felt a hundred percent better. Her headache had subsided to nothing more than a dull ache, easily treated with ibuprofen, and her stomach rumbled with hunger, indicating the return of her appetite.

She splurged a little, ordering a light breakfast through room service, mindful of the lunch she'd promised to share later that morning with Quinn.

And after she'd eaten her yogurt parfait and toast, showered and dressed in fresh clothes, she went back to reviewing her notes. But reading through them with the knowledge that Skylar was alive today didn't help shed any light on the events around her kidnapping. Nothing jumped out at her as significant.

After a couple of hours, she sat back in disgust. Going over the scant information in the articles about other kidnapping cases she'd dug out all those years ago wasn't where she should be spending her time or her energy. She needed to be back at Carlyle University going through photographs of female students.

Looking for someone who resembled Skylar.

She glanced at her watch, considering whether or not to cancel the lunch plans with Quinn. If she called for a taxi now, she could easily be back at the university in thirty minutes or less.

But she'd slept later than she'd thought, and Quinn was due to arrive in forty-five minutes. Maybe it would be better for her to spend the time checking on how the processing of evidence was going.

Putting a call in to her forensic expert, Al, she waited on hold until he picked up the call. "Yeah?"

"Hi, Al," she greeted him. "Just wondering how things are going. Did you find any other fingerprint matches? Or anything on the hair fibers?"

"We did get a couple of fingerprint matches," he acknowledged. "But all from beer cans, not from the rugby trophy or the victim's room."

Prints off the beer cans didn't mean a whole lot, but at this point, she'd take what they could get. "Okay, give me the names of the matches."

"There is an Erwin Fink, who is in the system because of a shoplifting record as a juvie—he stole a CB radio. And a Bradley Wilkes, whose prints were in the system because he spent four months in the military. Before you start thinking the worst, he was honorably discharged after they discovered a medical problem with his heart that they didn't find during the routine medical screening."

Shanna wrote down the two names, hoping and praying they wouldn't be dead ends. How sad to hope they had some sort of criminal tendency that would make them the logical suspects in Brady's murder. "That's all? Just two matches?"

"Hold on to your horses, would ya?" Al said irritably. "I'm getting to the others. We did match up the three boys who live in the house to prints on beer cans, as well, which isn't a huge surprise. I think it's a little odd that we didn't find any prints of his roommates in the victim's room."

She didn't think that information was so surprising. Living together in a house likely meant they'd spend most of their time in the living room and kitchen, wouldn't they? Not in each other's bedrooms.

"But there are two other names that popped out of the system—Tanya Jacobs and Derek Matthews. I saved these for last because I think they're your best place to start. Both of these kids were in serious trouble last year, and it just so happens they both were busted at the same time."

Her pulse jumped with excitement as she jotted down the two names, underlining them with bold strokes. "At the same time? What for?"

"Drug dealing on campus." The note of satisfaction in Al's tone was unmistakable.

"At Carlyle University?" she asked in shock. Didn't students get kicked out of school for that sort of criminal activity?

"Interestingly enough, no, they were at a state-college campus in Milwaukee, Wisconsin. They were arrested last year, did only a few months of time before they were released again."

"I can't imagine they're enrolled in college. Wouldn't they do a criminal background check?" she asked. It was interesting that the two kids, male and female, came to Chicago together, once again hanging out with the college crowd. Were they in a romantic relationship? And was their intent to continue dealing drugs?

"Not routinely in the state of Illinois," he told her. "But I haven't checked yet to see if they are enrolled. Figured you could do that part. I knew you'd be interested in these two. Maybe your victim was somehow involved in the drug scene, too?"

Shanna found herself hoping not, for Quinn's sake. "We'll know after we get the autopsy results if he had drugs in his system, in addition to the alcohol."

"Yeah, the preliminary results were released this morning, but they won't have the tox screens done for another four to six weeks."

"I know." The lengthy time frame to receive complete autopsy results was annoying, to say the least. But a necessary evil, if you wanted to rule out any and all possibilities. "Thanks, Al. This gives us a place to start."

"I'll keep you posted if anyone else pops up," he promised.

"I'd appreciate it." She hung up and stared down at the two names of potential suspects: Tanya Jacobs and Derek Matthews.

Finally, they had a decent lead. Clearly the fact that these two were arrested together in Milwaukee last year, and now happened to both be at the same party where a young college student ended up dead, bore further scrutiny.

She could hardly wait to give Quinn the news.

Quinn drove up to the hotel fifteen minutes early. He was too excited by what he'd found to stay away.

In the lobby, he called her cell phone. She answered on the second ring. "Hi, Quinn."

"Hi, Shanna," he responded, knowing his goofy grin stretched from ear to ear. "I know I'm early, but I hope you don't mind."

"No, I don't mind. I have a breakthrough on the case that I'd like to discuss with you, anyway," she said.

His fingers tightened on his phone. She had a breakthrough, too? Maybe between the information they'd both discovered, they'd be able to wrap up this entire murder case sooner rather than later. "Great, I have some news, too."

"Okay, see you in a few minutes."

He snapped his phone shut and paced the foyer in front of the elevators, waiting impatiently. When the elevator dinged and the doors opened, he stepped forward eagerly, but then checked himself.

Back off, Murphy, he told himself. Friends. They were just friends, remember?

"Hi, Quinn," she greeted him warmly. He was surprised to see she had her overnight bag with her, but not the box containing Skylar's things. "I hope you don't mind, but I'm going to need a ride out to the university after lunch, so I can go back to reviewing the college ID photos."

"Of course I don't mind." He reached over to take the

overnight bag, surprised to find it felt heavier than last night. "Did you want me to run up and get Skylar's box?"

"No thanks, I managed to jam everything in the overnight bag," she admitted with a shy grin. "The box was bulky and awkward, so I just put everything in the bag and left the box up in the room."

"You're not planning to check out, are you?" he asked with a frown.

"Yes, I am. But let's fight about that later, okay? First I have something important to tell you."

He didn't want to let the matter drop, but he figured there would be time later to get into the issue. She wasn't safe at her house, that was for sure. But at the moment, he wanted to exchange information. "Let's get seated in the restaurant first, okay?"

She nodded. He approached the hostess and requested a booth in the back for privacy.

After they were seated, they quickly placed their order for burgers and soft drinks. Once the waitress left, Shanna leaned forward. "Okay, you first. Tell me what you found out."

"Remember how I told you that I spent a few hours at the Corner Café showing Brady's picture around?" When she nodded, he continued, "And several students claimed he was working on some sort of secret article for the college online newsletter?"

"Yes. Did you find out what he was working on?" she asked.

"Yep. I called Hank and asked for a copy of all Brady's files from his laptop computer, and he gave them to me. I started going through them and found the article he'd been working on in the weeks before his death."

"Don't keep me in suspense," Shanna urged. "Tell me what the article was about."

He hoped she wouldn't freak out too much when he told her. "I know this may be hard to believe, but his article was focused on adoption. Specifically, a private adoption agency that was located in Chicago."

She stared at him, her brow furrowed. "And why would an adoption agency be such a big secret?"

"From what I can tell, he was investigating the agency located here in Chicago because his roommate, Dennis Green, happened to be adopted through them. But that same agency, called New Beginnings, closed down and disappeared fourteen years ago."

"Okay," Shanna said slowly. "But I'm still not clear as to how this helps us."

"Shanna, think about the possibilities. What if Dennis Green was kidnapped for the purposes of being adopted? And what if Skylar was also kidnapped and then adopted out illegally through the same private adoption agency?" He held his breath, hoping he wasn't raising her hopes too high as far as their ability to find Skylar.

Chapter 8

Shanna stared at Quinn in disbelief. As much as she wanted to trust his theory, there were too many holes in his logic. "I'm sorry, but that theory really doesn't make sense. Most families want to adopt babies, right? Infants? Or at least kids under a year. I mean, come on, Skylar was five years old."

But even as she voiced the protest, she remembered how everyone thought her sister was younger than she actually was. With her honey-brown hair, big brown eyes and petite frame, Skylar had been adorable.

The old familiar guilt burned low in her belly. Her fault. Skylar's kidnapping had been her fault. And for years she'd feared Skylar had suffered horribly before she'd most likely been killed.

She hoped, prayed that Skylar hadn't suffered.

"I know, I thought the same thing at first," Quinn

said, interrupting her dark thoughts. "But from what I read, Brady's theory has some merit. Some families, those who really want a child, will go up a few years in age. Look at how adoptions abroad have expanded over the years. Those kids coming in from foreign countries aren't all infants. And those overseas adoptions take time, along with a significant amount of money. What if you wanted a child now, had the money and didn't want to wait a year or maybe longer to go through the normal process? Maybe these adoption agencies offered a quick turnaround for couples willing to take older kids."

Was he right? The possibility was mind boggling. "Still, I would think that if you were going to kidnap a child to turn around and adopt, why wouldn't you go for younger kids?"

Quinn lifted a shoulder. "Could be that they take what they can get. Parents keep closer eyes on smaller kids. They're either carried or pushed around in a stroller. But those old enough to move under their own power become easier targets."

She shivered because suddenly, Brady's theory made sense. Horrible, chilling sense. She thought about her sister, who might have looked like an easy target. Or the little boy who disappeared from the mall. But there were still a few gaps they needed to understand. "Why did Brady suspect New Beginnings in particular?"

"I think because they were only in existence for a total of five years," Quinn admitted. "But honestly, that's where his theory starts to fall apart. Just because a private adoption agency went out of business didn't mean the owners were breaking the law."

"No, but it's a place to start. I wonder if we should turn this information over to the feds?"

"We probably should, but maybe we need to investigate this link a little further. Right now, we have a lot of assumptions without any concrete proof. We could look at other private adoption agencies to see if there are any common threads."

The thought that other agencies could be doing the exact same thing made her blood congeal in her veins. "There have to be hundreds of private adoption agencies out there."

"I know," Quinn said with a grimace. "But we could try to narrow down our search to those private agencies that aren't in operation anymore. Or those that have only been around for a few years."

She couldn't help feeling the task would be hopeless. What they really needed was some sort of proof that at least one or two of the New Beginnings adoptions were illegal. And going back fourteen years wouldn't make that an easy task. "You really think that your brother was killed because of this article? Because someone found out that he was investigating this particular adoption agency?"

Quinn sighed and shook his head. "I don't know. It sounds far-fetched, doesn't it? But it's a lead, and we can't afford to ignore any potential link. Especially considering your sister disappeared fourteen years ago, as well."

He was right about that, she was forced to admit. The timing of the adoption agency shutting down and her sister's disappearance was almost too much of a coincidence.

Their food arrived just then, interrupting the conversation. Shanna bowed her head to silently give thanks for the food before she began to eat. She sensed Quinn's curious gaze, but when he spoke, he returned to their previous discussion.

"So what information did you come up with?" Quinn asked after digging into his meal.

She took a bite of her burger before answering. "Based on what you just told me, I'm not sure if my information is nearly as helpful. I spoke to Al this morning, and we have a few fingerprint matches. Two kids in particular, Tanya Jacobs and Derek Matthews. They were busted well over a year ago for drug dealing at a state campus in Milwaukee, Wisconsin. And both of their prints showed up on beer cans from your brother's party."

Quinn's munched a French fry, his expression thoughtful. "Well, that certainly adds an interesting twist."

Privately, she thought the former drug dealers were more likely candidates to have murdered Brady than some stranger from a nonexistent adoption agency. Yet she really liked the adoption-agency theory because she wanted, very badly, to believe Skylar had been adopted into a nice family.

"Yeah, I thought so," she agreed. "Here they are, hanging around a private college in Chicago, their prints found at the scene of your brother's murder. They may or may not be actual students—we can find that out easily enough. But even if they're not officially enrolled, we should get copies of their mug shots and show them around campus."

"Sounds like a good plan," Quinn murmured in agreement as he took another bite of his burger.

They both fell silent as they finished their meal. Shanna kept thinking about the other children who'd been kidnapped about the same time as Skylar. Was it really possible they were all part of some sort of illegal adoption ring? That they were adopted out to other families? Was this what had happened to Skylar?

And to Brady's roommate, Dennis Green?

Quinn noticed Shanna was lost in thought as they finished their lunch. He had a strong feeling his brother had been on to something with his investigation into the New Beginnings adoption agency.

But Shanna's question looped over and over in his mind. Did he really think the adoption article was directly related to Brady's murder?

His cop instincts didn't follow the logic. To think that someone actually linked to the agency, with something to hide, had discovered his brother's investigation and tracked him down to silence him forever was a total and complete stretch.

Logically, it made sense that two students with felony convictions for drug dealing were the more likely candidates for being guilty of a crime of opportunity. Shanna was right about that part; it wasn't as if someone had strategized long and hard about getting Brady alone to kill him. And if someone from the adoption agency was looking for him, it seemed as if they'd go that route, rather than clubbing his brother on the back of the head with a rugby trophy in the early hours of the morning.

Had his brother found out about their drug dealing? Had Brady kicked them out of the party, and they'd come back later for revenge? Or had some other student gone crazy while under the influence of drugs? Any of those scenarios was far more likely.

Shanna was right; they needed to start with the two

felons. Finding out if they were actually enrolled in classes or if they just liked hanging out with the college crowd.

"Are you ready?" Quinn asked when the waitress returned with their tab. He took it quickly, before Shanna could try to get all independent on him.

Her smile was a bit lopsided as she nodded. "Yes, I'm ready."

"You look upset," he said with a frown.

"Not at all," she countered quickly. "In fact, I'm glad that we've made so much progress in such a short period of time. I believe God is guiding us, Quinn."

He stared at her for a moment, remembering how she'd said the same thing last evening, before he'd gone to help his mother with Brady's funeral arrangements. And he'd also noticed that she'd bowed her head to pray before eating. He wasn't familiar with the kind of faith she mentioned, so he wasn't sure how to respond.

"Quinn, do you mind if I ask you a personal question?" Shanna's blue eyes were wide and serious.

"Of course not," he responded. After all, they were friends, right? Right.

"Do you believe in God?"

The blunt question took him by surprise. He'd expected some sort of question related to his previous relationships, or why he wasn't married. "Yes," he responded a little too quickly. "Why do you ask?"

"Because I've noticed you get quiet and try to change the subject every time I mention faith or God," she pointed out. "If you didn't believe in God, I could understand that you might be uncomfortable with the subject."

He shrugged, embarrassed that she'd read him so easily. For a moment he remembered the brief prayer he'd said when he found Shanna alive at her house, and the flash of peace. "I was brought up to believe in God, and my parents took me to church services when I was young. But I haven't been to church in years," he said honestly. "So I am a little uncomfortable with the topic, since I can't claim to be in a close relationship with God." And didn't have a clue where to start, even if he wanted to. Which he wasn't at all sure he did.

The smile that lit up her face nearly blinded him. "That's okay, Quinn. Believing in God is half the battle. He'll forgive you for straying if you want to start fresh. Maybe you need to just give Him a try?"

He stared at her for several long seconds, not sure if he appreciated the opportunity or was afraid of moving forward. Praying inside was one thing; talking out loud was very different. "I'll think about it," he said evasively. And hated himself when the bright light of hope in her eyes dimmed.

"That's all I'll ask," she said, with a smile that looked forced. "I think you'll be surprised if you can find a way to open your heart and your mind."

He wasn't so sure, but he nodded anyway. He signed off on the credit-card receipt and then stood. "Do you still want to go back to Carlyle University to go through student IDs?" he asked.

"Yes. I know there's no guarantee Skylar is a student, but I feel like I need to go through them all anyway, just in case."

He understood her need to be sure. "All right. But on the way, I'm going to stop at the police station to get mug shots of our two suspects, Tanya Jacobs and Derek Matthews."

"I'm interested to see those mug shots, too," she agreed.

For a moment he wondered if it was possible that Tanya Jacobs was actually Shanna's sister, Skylar. But just as soon as the thought entered his mind, he knew they couldn't be one and the same. Both sets of prints were found at the crime scene, which meant there were two different girls.

Relieved for Shanna's sake, he slung her bag over his shoulder and let her lead the way out of the restaurant. As they went through the lobby to go outside, their fingers brushed and he found himself wishing things could be different. That he had the right to hold her hand.

Friends, he reminded himself. He'd learned the hard way that when it came to women, friendship was all he had to offer.

But it occurred to him as they both climbed into the car that if there ever was a woman he'd want to have a relationship with, she would be exactly like Shanna.

Shanna stayed with Quinn as he inquired at the student-services desk if either Tanya Jacobs or Derek Matthews was enrolled in the university. She wasn't surprised when neither name showed up on the student roster.

"Guess I'll have to show their photos around, see if anyone recognizes them," Quinn muttered, "since the only address on file is the one from Milwaukee."

"Do you want me to help?" Shanna asked, even though she really wanted to finish up with the student IDs.

Quinn seemed to consider her offer, but then shook

his head. "No, thanks. I'll meet you back here in a couple of hours."

Shanna smiled in agreement and then went over to her usual computer workstation. She pulled up the student IDs, trying not to allow her thoughts to dwell on Quinn.

She was glad, very glad, that Quinn believed in God. Now she just needed him to open up to the concept of renewing his faith.

Earlier that morning, when the elevator doors opened and she saw Quinn waiting for her in the lobby, her breath had gotten stuck in her lungs. He'd looked amazing with his black jeans and his long-sleeved white polo shirt. She'd immediately realized that God had brought Quinn into her life for a reason.

Not just to help her find Skylar, but more importantly, so she could help him reconnect with his faith.

When lunch was finished, Quinn had agreed to think about it, and she told herself to be patient. So she sent up a quick prayer, asking God for guidance.

Turning her attention to the task at hand, she flipped through photograph after photograph, trying to see even the slightest resemblance to Skylar's age-progression photo. As she moved slowly through the alphabet of last names, she began to get discouraged. Leaving the *O*'s to start on the last names beginning with the letter *P*, she couldn't help wondering if she was wasting her time going through the photos.

There was no guarantee Skylar looked anything like the age-progression picture. But what else could she do? Now that she was more than halfway through the list, she didn't really want to stop.

Completely lost in the photos, Shanna started when,

over an hour later, Quinn came up behind her, putting a light hand on her shoulder. "How's it going?" he asked.

She closed her eyes and willed her heart rate to return to normal. "About the same," she said honestly. "So far no matches anywhere close."

He pulled up a seat beside her. "How many more until you finish the list?"

"Not very many. I'm already up to the *W*'s." She glanced over at him, thinking he seemed tired. "How did it go with the two mug shots?"

"Didn't come up with much. A couple of kids thought the two suspects looked familiar, but couldn't give me any insight as to when or where they saw them last." His tone sounded as dejected as he looked.

More dead ends. Seemed like they took two steps backward for every one step forward.

No, that wasn't fair. She was letting her discouragement get to her. She needed to have faith that God would show them the way.

"You know, if the two of them are involved in anything illegal, like selling drugs, other kids aren't going to be so quick to turn them in," she said.

"Yeah, I thought of that," Quinn said slowly. "But you would still think there are some honest kids who would come forward."

"But honest kids probably haven't interacted with them," she pointed out. "But maybe we're on the wrong track. Maybe we need to start with Brady's roommates. If Brady had spoken to either of the suspects, or argued with them, surely his roommates would have noticed."

"Yeah, I already tried to contact them. The Chicago P.D. has already questioned them and didn't come up with much, at least not according to Hank. And as of today, they were allowed to return to their residence. But when I went over there, no one was around. It would be pretty amazing if they'd already gone back to class."

Very true. But it was possible that going back to class was exactly what they needed to feel normal. Sometimes getting lost in the normal routine of her life was the only way she could cope with Skylar's kidnapping.

She glanced at her watch, wincing a little when her headache started to return. Time for more ibuprofen. "It's almost four o'clock. If they did go to class, they'll be done soon. Why don't you wait for me to finish here and then we'll both head back over?"

"Your energy level is amazing," Quinn said with a light chuckle. "Okay, you win. We'll work on this together."

She wanted to give her faith credit for her energy level, but decided not to push it. Quinn would find his way, and if God wanted her to intervene, He'd give her a sign.

Finishing the list of female students didn't take long. "Take a look at these five," she suggested, going back to the handful of student images that she'd saved. "Here's the age-progression photo to compare to. What do you think?"

"They're close," Quinn admitted. "But not really a match. Look at the shape of the eyes on this picture." He pointed to the first one. "They slant up, and Skylar's are definitely more round. There are some similarities on these other three, but this last one here is way off. The shape of her face isn't exactly right, either. Skylar's is more heart-shaped, like yours, and hers is oval."

He thought her face was heart-shaped? "Yeah, that was my thought, too, but I wanted to make sure I wasn't being too picky." With a sigh, she shut down the computer. "I guess we know that Skylar isn't likely a student here at the university."

"I'm sorry, Shanna," Quinn murmured.

"It's okay. Every bit of knowledge helps." And she was determined to keep her faith. "If Skylar's not a student, then she must have run into your brother somewhere here on campus."

"I hate to tell you, but Chicago North, an Illinois state campus, is located just six miles from here. The private kids often hang out with the state-school kids."

She grimaced. "I know—I already thought of that. Not just as a place to find Skylar, but as a potential link to our two suspects. Since they were enrolled at a state school in Wisconsin, I thought they might have gone the same route here."

"Let's finish up on this campus first, before we broaden our search too wide," Quinn cautioned.

"All right." But she silently vowed to start looking through the Chicago North student ID listing as soon as possible. There was no reason to suspect Skylar couldn't be a student on that campus. "Are you ready to visit Brady's roommates?"

"Yes." Quinn walked back out with her to his car and drove the couple of blocks to Brady's former residence. It wasn't easy finding a place to park, and they ended up several blocks away.

As they walked up, they ran into Kyle Ryker. "Kyle? Wait up," Quinn called.

The young man glanced at them, and for a moment looked as if he might run. But then he stopped in the middle of the sidewalk, giving them time to catch up.

"I already gave my statement to the police," Kyle said defensively.

"I understand how hard this must be for you," Shanna quickly spoke up sympathetically. "And we just have a quick question. Do you remember seeing these two people at the party Saturday night?"

She watched Kyle's eyes as Quinn handed over the photos. There were no telltale signs of recognition, and after a few moments he shook his head. "I'm sorry, but I don't recognize either of them. My girlfriend was over, and I didn't pay a lot of attention to the other kids Brady invited."

"You think Brady invited them?" Quinn asked.

"Either Brady or Dennis. Both of them were passing out flyers to the kids on campus. Mark and I weren't as keen on the thought of having another party. Especially after getting underage-drinking tickets from the last party."

"Thanks. I'd rather you didn't tell your roommates about these two until we have a chance to show them," Quinn said.

Kyle hunched his shoulders. "Fine with me. I already told the cops my theory about how Brady was playing with fire the way he kept flirting with that new chick all night at the party. Either Anna or one of her friends or even Anna's brother could have smacked him in the head."

She caught her breath and glanced at Quinn, his eyes mirroring her surprise. New chick? "Do you have a name?"

He shrugged. "Phoebe—but don't ask me her last name, 'cause I have no idea."

Phoebe? Shanna's heart raced. Was this the clue they'd been waiting for?

Chapter 9

Quinn eagerly grabbed his wallet from his back pocket and pulled out the list of students they knew for sure were at Brady's party. Quickly, he ran his finger down the neatly typed names.

No Phoebe.

He made a mental note to add her name, now that Kyle had confirmed she was there, as he folded the list and put it back inside his wallet. Then he glanced at the mug shots of the two drug dealers and held up the picture of Tanya Jacobs. "And you're sure this woman isn't Phoebe?"

Kyle studied the picture for a long moment. "Yeah, I'm pretty sure. I mean, they look a little similar I guess, but not a lot. Look, I gotta go." He moved as if to step past them.

"Wait." Shanna stopped him with a hand on his arm. "Can you tell us what Phoebe looks like?"

Kyle rolled his eyes, clearly annoyed with being detained. "I don't know. She's cute I guess, has long dark hair. But I didn't really pay much attention, 'cause my girl gets jealous, you know?"

"Is she tall? Short? Thin?" Quinn persisted. Surely if she were as cute as Kyle claimed, he could give them a little more information.

"Short and thin, in an athletic sort of way. I swear I don't know anything more. Except that Anna would be mad if she knew how much time Brady spent with her."

"Sounds like you don't like Anna very much," Quinn observed, hearing the distinct note of disdain in Kyle's tone.

"She thinks she's hot stuff, that's all. We don't generally hang with the same crowd. Are we finished now?" His impatience was palpable.

"Yes, thanks. You've been a huge help," Quinn told him. He glanced at Shanna, giving her a nod, so she dropped her hand from Kyle's arm.

"Yes, thanks, Kyle," she added sincerely. "Take care, okay?"

"Sure," he said half over his shoulder, picking up his pace until he was jogging to get away from them.

"What do you think?" Shanna asked when Kyle was out of earshot. "Is it possible your brother was killed because of some sort of love triangle?"

"I don't know what to think," he muttered. "Except that we have more suspects than we know what to do with."

"Usually it's the opposite problem, isn't it?" Shanna murmured.

"True enough. Phoebe wasn't on the list of party attendees, so at least we have another name to add. And there is a slight possibility that Phoebe is Tanya Jacobs. I hope we don't have to go through the entire list of all female students enrolled here at Carlyle again, looking for her."

"At least we can cross-reference her first name," Shanna pointed out. "And it's original enough that there probably won't be more than one."

She was right about that. "So do we head back to the chancellor's office before they close? Or continue looking for Dennis Green and Mark Pickard?"

"We can call first thing in the morning to find out about Phoebe. Let's just keep looking for Brady's roommates."

Quinn was glad Shanna's thoughts were in complete alignment with his. "Let's go then, see if the other two guys are home yet."

As Shanna fell into step beside him, he wondered how to convince her to return to the hotel later tonight. The threat of danger was diluted in the bright daylight, but it was less than twenty-four hours ago that he'd found her lying in her house, bleeding from a head injury.

No way did he want to risk anything like that again. Yet he wasn't sure she'd appreciate him sticking his nose into her business.

Unfortunately, they didn't have any more luck with Dennis or Mark. The guys didn't recognize the two mug shots as kids who'd attended the party, and of course they also didn't know the infamous Phoebe's last name, either.

"If you remember anything or run into this Phoebe, will you please give me a call?" Quinn asked, handing over copies of his business cards.

The boys took the cards with obvious reluctance. "Yeah, sure," Dennis said. Mark put his card in his pocket without even looking at it.

He knew he shouldn't be frustrated with the lack of information and cooperation from Brady's roommates, but he was.

"Not sure I believe they'll ever call," Shanna murmured as they turned and walked away.

Quinn agreed with her assessment. "Yeah, I guess talking to the cops isn't high on their list of fun things to do."

Shanna scowled. "You'd think they'd want to help find Brady's killer."

The same thought had occurred to him, as well. Maybe they'd given up too hastily on considering the roommates as potential suspects. Just because a group of guys lived together didn't make them best friends. Hadn't Kyle confirmed they didn't hang out with the same group of kids? Maybe as long as each guy held up their end of the financial side of things, like rent and utilities and food, nothing else mattered?

"Come on," he said, taking Shanna's arm. "Let's grab a quick bite to eat and then head over to the library."

"The library?" she echoed in surprise. "Why? I can't imagine that the kids who hang out in a library will have much interaction with drug dealers."

"No, probably not. And that's assuming that these two are still in the drug-dealing business. Earlier, when I called Anna to set up a meeting, she was in class. But she told me she'd be studying at the library tonight. Let's see if she recognizes either of these suspects as kids who've been hanging around Brady."

And maybe, just maybe, Brady's former girlfriend would know where to find the mysterious Phoebe.

Shanna ordered a salad, still full from the burger she'd had for lunch. She once again said a quick prayer before eating, and this time, instead of staring at her, Quinn bowed his head, respectfully waiting for her to finish before he opened his fast-food meal. He didn't say anything, though, just dug into his food with gusto. She watched in amazement, impressed by his voracious appetite. She wasn't used to how much food a man could put away, but then again, her experience with men was rather limited.

Garrett probably wasn't the best yardstick to measure other men by, since he'd gotten very frustrated with her early on in their relationship. She'd tried, but just hadn't been able to take their relationship to the next level. She'd cared about him as a friend, but nothing more. She'd thought maybe her feelings would change over time, but Garrett hadn't been interested in waiting around.

For some reason, she didn't get the impression Quinn would give up as easily. Not that she was looking to turn their friendship into something more.

"Should I offer a quarter for your thoughts?" Quinn asked, breaking the silence. "You seem pretty intent."

She almost choked on a piece of chicken from her salad. No way was she going to mention that she was thinking about Quinn. "Actually, I'm wondering about Phoebe, the girl your brother was flirting with at the party. Do you think it's possible she might be Skylar?"

"I actually doubt it, only because of Brady's article on adoption."

She frowned. "What do you mean?"

"Well, he mentions Dennis Green's adoption. Don't you think he might have mentioned Phoebe if he knew she was adopted too?"

"Good point," she said with a sigh. "I suppose it's possible Phoebe is adopted but doesn't know because her parents never told her?"

"I doubt her parents could get away with that, considering they wouldn't have any baby pictures of her—any pictures at all until she was five, right?"

"You're right. Again." She'd been so hopeful that they'd finally had a lead on Skylar. Best for her to remember there were roughly fifty people at the party, and Skylar could have been any one of them.

"Are you done?" Quinn asked when he'd finished his fish sandwich and fries.

She stared at her salad, surprised that she'd managed to eat most of it. "Yes, I'm finished."

As they left the fast-food restaurant, she noticed the sun was low on the horizon. She loved fall, with the brightly colored changing leaves and the cooler temperatures, but she wasn't thrilled with having shorter days. Quinn headed toward the last row where his SUV was parked, but she hung back. "Quinn, the library is only a couple of blocks away. Why don't we walk?" she suggested. "Maybe we'll pass some kids who fit the description of our two suspects."

"Good thinking," he agreed.

There were a fair amount of students milling around the campus, even at six o'clock in the evening. By mutual agreement, they kept their pace slow, giving them plenty of time to scan the faces of the students. When Quinn's fingers brushed hers, she took his hand, and then blushed when he glanced at her in surprise. "We might get further with questioning these kids if we don't act like cops," she said, by way of explanation.

His slow grin, and the way his hand gently and firmly cupped hers, made her chest tighten with awareness. Flustered, she averted her gaze and tried to focus on finding their suspects, which wasn't easy with Quinn holding her hand.

Poor judgment on her part, to pretend they were a couple as a way to blend into the crowd. She liked being with him a little too much.

"Hey, look over there," Quinn said in a low voice, gesturing to the right with their joined hands. "See that small group of kids next to the commons? Do they seem to be acting suspicious to you?"

She stared, trying to figure out what had caught his attention. "Not really, why? Am I missing something?"

"Could be nothing, or it could be some sort of drug deal going down," Quinn muttered. "Hard to tell from here."

She glanced at him, wondering what it must be like to see possible criminal activity on every corner. Obviously, he patrolled this area a lot in his job, on the lookout for anything suspicious. At least when she was called in to gather evidence, the crime had already been committed. But as a cop, Quinn's duty was to try to prevent crimes from happening, if possible.

She slowed to a stop, letting go of his hand to kneel down, pretending to tie her shoe. "Do you want to go over there?" she asked. "I can wait here."

"No, they're already breaking up and heading in different directions," he said. "And none of them look familiar. Maybe it really was nothing."

"Do you want to follow one of them?" she asked, not sure what he would normally do if he were alone.

"No, let's head over to the library. I think our time is better spent questioning Anna Belfast."

She hoped so. When she stood, he once again took possession of her hand.

They reached the library a few minutes later, and she glanced around curiously. There were more students in the library than she'd expected, and half of them were sitting on overstuffed chairs, working on laptops. The rest seemed to be studying from textbooks.

"Did Anna give you a hint as to where she usually studies?" she asked.

"No. But maybe we should split up, since we can cover more ground that way," Quinn said. "I'll make color copies of the mug shots for you."

"Except I don't know what Anna looks like," she protested.

"That's right. I forgot." Quinn headed over to two copy machines along the wall. He made the color copies and handed one set to her. "Okay, let's find Anna first, and then we can split up to question the rest of the kids."

She definitely liked that plan better. She followed his lead, wandering through the expansive library.

"Over there," Quinn said. "See the blonde sitting in the orange chair? That's Maggie, Anna's roommate. But I don't see any sign of Anna."

Before she could respond, Quinn walked over to the spot where Maggie sat.

"Hi, Maggie," he greeted her, smiling as if they were long-lost friends. "How are you?"

She looked up at him blankly, but then recognition

slowly dawned. "Well, if it isn't Officer Murphy," she responded in a cool tone. "What brings you here?"

"I'm looking for your roommate, Anna. Is she around?"

Maggie shrugged and glanced around rather pointedly. "She's not here that I can see. What makes you think I know where she is?"

"Because Anna told me you'd both be here studying for an exam. Didn't she mention that to you?"

Maggie frowned. "No, she didn't."

Shanna stepped forward, hoping maybe she could connect with Maggie on a woman-to-woman level. "Hi, Maggie. My name is Shanna Dawson. Can you tell me if you recognize either of these two people?" She showed Maggie the mug shots of Tanya Jacobs and Derek Matthews.

Maggie made a face and shook her head. "I don't know anyone who spent time in jail."

It was unfortunate they didn't have other photos of the two kids, since there was no disguising a mug shot. "They were arrested a year ago, and they're out now. Isn't it possible you've maybe seen them around campus? I mean, you wouldn't know they did jail time, right?"

Maggie's eyes narrowed, and she looked again at the two mug shots. "They still don't look familiar, although there are a lot of kids here. I only just transferred here this fall, so I don't know a lot of the students yet."

"I understand," Shanna said sympathetically. "But maybe if you do see them, you'll give us a call?" She handed over one of Quinn's business cards.

"I suppose I could do that." At least Maggie looked at the card, then back up at Quinn, before tucking it inside her purse.

"So you and Anna didn't come to the library together?" Quinn asked, turning the subject back to Brady's former girlfriend.

"No." When Quinn just stood there staring at her, she squirmed in her seat. "She did say she might meet me here later," Maggie finally admitted.

"We'll hang around for a while and wait for her, then," Quinn said.

"By the way, Maggie, do you know Phoebe?" Shanna asked before Quinn could turn away.

There was a flicker of something, recognition maybe, in her eyes, but she shook her head. "No, I don't."

"But you've heard her name, right?" Shanna persisted.

"Yeah, maybe. It sounds familiar, but I don't know her," Maggie insisted. "And if you don't mind, I really need to study. I can't afford to flunk this exam."

She glanced at Quinn, trying to read the expression in his eyes. Did he think Maggie was lying? Or telling the truth?

"Sure thing," Quinn said easily. "Good luck with your studying."

Shanna followed his lead, moving away from Maggie until they were out of earshot. "What do you think?" she whispered. "Is she being honest with us?"

"I think so," Quinn murmured. "Considering Kyle's comments earlier, could be that Anna heard about Brady's flirting with Phoebe through the grapevine. It's not a stretch to think she shared the news with her roommate."

Quinn's logic made sense. "So now what? Do we hang out here waiting for Anna?"

"Let's split up for a bit," he suggested. "And see if

anyone else recognizes either the photos of our two suspects or the name Phoebe."

"All right, let's meet back here in thirty minutes."

Shanna headed to the opposite end of the library from Quinn, showing several students the photographs. But no one seemed to recognize the two former drug dealers as anyone they'd seen around campus. And even worse, no one admitted to knowing anyone by the name of Phoebe.

She tried not to get discouraged, knowing from first-hand experience that key information was often discovered when you least expected it. Much of the evidence she collected in her role as a crime-scene investigator was from sheer determination and tedious attention to detail.

But she'd really been hoping for a break, especially in uncovering the identity of the mysterious Phoebe. Even though she agreed with Quinn's theory that Phoebe was likely not Skylar, she couldn't help feeling as if finding the girl would help crack their case wide open.

But then again, finding Phoebe could be nothing more than another dead end.

She returned to the center of the library, where she'd promised to meet Quinn. Maggie was still sprawled in her orange overstuffed chair, studying. She waited a few minutes to see if Maggie noticed her standing there, but she didn't.

Quinn walked up a minute later. "Any luck?"

"No."

"Me, neither." He glanced at his watch, then over to where Maggie was studying, a frown furrowing his brow. "Anna should be here by now."

"Maybe you scared her off?" she suggested.

Quinn sent a sideways glance in her direction. "She

doesn't have a reason to be afraid, unless she happens to be guilty of something."

"Some people just don't like talking to the police," she said. "And as Brady's girlfriend, she must know she's a potential suspect."

"Yeah, maybe." Quinn seemed uncharacteristically indecisive. "Should we wait here? Or head over to her dorm room?"

"Hey, look." She gave his arm a tug. "Maggie's packing up her books."

Quinn's scowl deepened, and he immediately headed over to the girl. "Finished studying already?" he asked.

"You're making me nervous, standing there staring at me," the girl said defiantly. "So I'm leaving."

"Have you heard from Anna?" Quinn persisted, blocking Maggie's path. "Or maybe I have that backwards. Maybe you called Anna, telling her not to come?"

Maggie's face went pale. "I didn't call her, and I didn't hear from her, either. Check my phone," she said, thrusting it at him.

"You could have erased the messages," he said after giving the screen a cursory look.

"I don't even know how to delete the memory," Maggie argued. "But have it your way." She waited for Quinn to step aside before heading out of the library.

Shanna wasn't surprised when Quinn followed the girl outside. Maggie had to have known they were behind her, but she didn't glance back even once.

"Guess we're going to Anna's dorm room, huh?" Shanna asked in a low tone.

"Might as well, since I don't have any other bright ideas as to where she might be."

Just then, Maggie, who was a few yards ahead of

them, lifted up a hand and waved frantically. "Anna!"
she called. "Over here!"

A dark haired girl turned to look, but must have seen
Quinn because she abruptly spun away, taking off at a
run.

"What is she doing?" Quinn muttered, breaking into
a jog to catch up with her. Shanna sprinted after Quinn,
while Maggie stood there, staring in shock.

The section of the sidewalk they were on disappeared,
due to some sort of construction, so they went out into
the road. As they came up to an intersection, bright
headlights blinded her from a car heading toward them.

She winced and slowed down, the lights intensifying
the dull ache in her head. She hoped the car would hurry
up and pass her by, but instead, the car picked up speed.

Realization dawned just a little too late.

"Look out!" Quinn shouted.

Chapter 10

Quinn grabbed Shanna's arm, wrenching her out of harm's way, the momentum bringing her solidly up against him. The last-minute motion saved their lives, as the car missed them by inches, hitting several of the orange construction barrels and sending them flying through the air.

He clutched her close, his heart lodged in his throat and a loud roaring echoing in his ears. The way her arms were clamped around his waist betrayed how frightened she was. Not that he could blame her.

Close. That was way too close.

Thank You for keeping her safe, Lord.

The whispered prayer came instantly to his mind, and he couldn't help but wonder if Shanna was right about having faith. Maybe he could learn something from her.

"Are you okay?" He managed to find his voice after

a long minute. The taillights of the car had already disappeared down the street, and he couldn't help feeling frustrated that he hadn't been able to get the tag number.

No way did he think this was some sort of accident. Not after the way Shanna had been attacked in her home the evening before.

"Yes." The sound of her voice was muffled by her face buried against his chest. He ran a reassuring hand down her back, thinking he could hold her like this forever.

But, of course, Shanna was too strong, too independent to lean against him for long. All too soon, she loosened her grip, lifted her head and took a step back. He reluctantly released her, although he kept a steadying hand on her arm, unable to break all physical contact with her.

"That guy shouldn't be allowed to keep his license," she said grimly, pushing her tangled dark hair away from her face.

"Shanna, it wasn't an accident. He headed straight for you," he said, his tone coming out harsher than he'd intended.

She glanced up at him in surprise. "Are you sure? Because for a moment I thought he was heading toward Maggie."

"Maggie?" Quinn spun around, sweeping the area with his gaze, searching for Anna's roommate. Then he saw her about ten yards away, sitting next to a grassy embankment beside two orange barrels lying on their sides. Quickly, he headed over. "Maggie? Are you all right?"

Maggie lifted her head, and the sight of her tear-streaked cheeks hit him hard. He knelt beside her, searching for signs of injury.

"I'm fine," she said, brushing her fingertips over her damp cheeks. "Just scared."

"I don't blame you for being scared," Quinn murmured. "You're sure you don't hurt anywhere?"

"I'm sure. I jumped out of the way," Maggie admitted. "But I didn't think he was trying to hit me. From what I saw, he was heading straight for her," she said, waving a hand at Shanna who'd come over to stand beside him.

"I'm so glad you weren't hurt," Quinn said.

"Me, too," Shanna agreed. "Maggie, did you recognize the car at all?"

"I couldn't even see the car with the bright headlights blinding me," she admitted.

"I know. I think he had the high-beam lights on," Shanna said. "I couldn't see what sort of car he was driving, either."

"I'm pretty sure it was a dark green Honda Accord," Quinn said. "But I only caught a glimpse once I realized the idiot driver was trying to hit you." Replaying the sequence of events in his mind, he couldn't say for sure which woman was the primary target, since Maggie had been just a short distance from Shanna. It was pure luck that he'd noticed and had time to yank Shanna out of harm's way.

He was ashamed to admit he hadn't even thought of Maggie.

But no matter what Shanna's or Maggie's impressions were, he firmly believed this was the work of Shanna's stalker. The guy must be following her, since their decision to go to the library had been made on the spur of the moment.

"But I don't understand. Why would he try to hit one of us?" Maggie asked.

"I feel like I should apologize to you, Maggie, because I was probably the real target," Shanna said. "Some creepy guy has been stalking me."

Quinn was surprised at how Shanna took the blame. Obviously, after thinking about it, she logically knew she must be the target. But what about her impression that he'd aimed for Maggie? Unless in the darkness, he'd momentarily mistook Maggie for Shanna?

"You have a stalker?" Maggie echoed in horror. "That's awful. So he really was trying to hit you?"

"I'm afraid so," Shanna said. "I'm so sorry."

"That's okay," the young student murmured. And Quinn sensed Maggie was somehow relieved by the news.

"Maggie, why did Anna run away?" he asked, bringing the conversation back to the events prior to the attempted hit-and-run.

Maggie's expression turned guarded. "I don't know what you mean."

Quinn's patience thinned. "Stop it," he said with a touch of annoyance. "Be honest. You waved at her, and the minute Anna saw me, she took off running. Tell me what's going on. Is she afraid to talk to me for some reason?"

Maggie's shoulders slumped, and Quinn sensed he finally got through to her when she reluctantly nodded. "Yes. She is afraid to talk to you. She's afraid you're going to try to prove she hurt Brady. And frankly, I'm tired of being dragged into Anna's problems."

Quinn couldn't help the surge of satisfaction. "She never planned on coming to the library tonight, did she?"

"No, she didn't," Maggie admitted. "I'm sorry."

"That's okay," Shanna said soothingly. "It's not your fault."

Quinn didn't necessarily agree since Maggie willingly tried to protect her roommate, but he kept quiet, sensing Shanna had a better chance of getting through to Maggie than he did.

"You don't have to keep protecting Anna," Shanna continued. "Loyalty is one thing, but breaking the law is something completely different."

"I wasn't lying about Anna being in the dorm the night of Brady's party," she said earnestly. "Anna isn't perfect, but she wouldn't murder anyone. Especially not Brady. She loved him."

Quinn wasn't sure he believed that, either. "I heard she got mad at Brady and that she has quite the temper."

"She might get mad easily, but I've never seen her hit or be violent with anyone, ever," Maggie protested.

There was always a first, but he didn't mention that. For some reason, he couldn't help feeling Anna held a key to the mystery surrounding Brady's death. "Tell me the truth, Maggie. Anna was mad at Brady, wasn't she?"

"She was mad he'd planned a party on the night of her last performance," Maggie admitted. "But that's all. She was annoyed more than anything, certainly not angry enough to hit him in the head."

"Are you sure she wasn't upset with Brady because he was flirting with other girls?" Shanna persisted.

At first, Maggie shook her head, but then she shrugged. "That might have been part of the issue with the party," she allowed. "I mean, he knew Anna couldn't come to the party due to the performance, right? So maybe she did wonder if there was another girl. Anna didn't confide in me that Brady might be cheating on her, though."

Cheating with the infamous Phoebe? Quinn wished he knew for certain. "Okay, thanks for your help," Quinn said. He stood and held out a hand to help Maggie up. "Now, how about we walk you back to your dorm room?"

"Sure," Maggie murmured, taking Quinn's hand and allowing him to assist her. "But I have to tell you, I doubt you'll find Anna there."

"We just want to make sure you get home safe," Shanna said quickly.

They walked across campus, heading for Dorchester Hall, where Maggie and Anna lived. Once inside, they took the elevator to the seventh floor.

"Room 724?" he asked, as they stepped out of the elevator.

"Yes, this way," Maggie said, taking the first corridor to the right.

He and Shanna waited patiently as Maggie pulled out her key and unlocked the door. She pushed it open and then waved a hand. "See? Told you she wouldn't be here."

Quinn poked his head inside the room, verifying that it was indeed empty. Both girls had their beds raised up off the floor on stilts to give them more space to sit underneath. Clothes jammed the closets, spilling out onto the floors, so there was no way to hide in there, either. The dorm room was messy but definitely empty.

"Thanks Maggie," he said, moving back outside. "I'm sure it won't do any good, but tell Anna I'd still like to talk to her, okay?"

"Try to reassure her that we don't believe she hurt Brady," Shanna interjected. "But we do want to know more about Brady's friends. Because someone at his party struck him in the back of the head and killed him. Anything more she can tell us might help."

"I'll tell her," Maggie said. "I'm not sure it will help any, but I'll try to convince her to cooperate."

"That's all we can ask," Shanna said. "Take care, Maggie."

"Bye," Maggie said, before closing the dorm-room door.

Quinn let Shanna lead the way back to the elevators. It was too late to go looking for Anna any more tonight. Besides, he had an almost desperate urge to get Shanna somewhere safe.

"That was an interesting night," she said as they rode the elevator down to the lobby.

Interesting wasn't the word he would have used. But he noticed she usually downplayed the danger she was in.

"Shanna, will you do me a favor?"

She hesitated for a moment. "Maybe. What kind of favor?"

"After everything that's happened, will you please let me take you back to the hotel tonight?"

For a moment, she grimaced as if she might argue, but then she slowly nodded. "All right, Quinn. I'll go back to the hotel for another night."

He didn't bother to hide his relief. "Thanks, Shanna." He was glad she didn't try to fight him on this issue.

And as they walked through the Dorchester Hall lobby and headed outside, he decided that this time, nothing was going to prevent him from staying in a room at the hotel with her.

Nothing.

* * *

Shanna couldn't believe it when Quinn asked for two hotel rooms side by side. She didn't have her same room, since she'd checked out earlier that morning. "There's no need," she tried to tell him, but he clearly wasn't listening.

"Thanks," he said to the clerk behind the desk, as he took both room keys and then slung her duffel bag over his shoulder.

"You don't even have any luggage," she tried pointing out, catching up with him as he strode toward the elevators. "Quinn, be reasonable. You made sure no one followed us. I'm perfectly safe here."

"I'm not leaving you," he said flatly.

His protectiveness was sweet, but she couldn't help feeling guilty. She knew she was keeping him from investigating his brother's death. And yet he'd asked her to come here for the night, as a favor to him.

There had to be something she could do to help him.

He paused outside the first room, handing her the key and waiting while she unlocked the door. "Thanks, Quinn," she said, when he finally handed over her bag. She swung the bag inside the room, setting it on the floor with a thud.

"You're welcome," he said, bracing his arm on the door frame and staring down at her for a long moment.

His gaze was mesmerizing, making it impossible for her to look away. She sensed he wanted to say something, but then he surprised her by bending to press his mouth warmly against hers.

Her lips clung to his, and she reveled in the sensation, remembering those moments when he'd held her close in his arms. But the kiss was over too quickly, as he broke away and took a step back. "Remember, I'm right next door if you need anything," he said gruffly.

Unable to speak, she could only nod and watch, bemused as he took the few steps to get to the next door down.

"Good night, Quinn," she finally managed, after he unlocked his door and waited rather obviously for her to go inside.

"Good night, Shanna." Only after she shut and locked her door did she hear the click of his door closing.

And she couldn't help admitting how incredibly safe she felt, knowing Quinn was right on the other side of the wall.

The next morning her phone rang, waking her from a sound sleep. "Yes?" she answered groggily.

"Shanna? Would you like to meet me for breakfast?" Quinn asked.

She blinked away her fatigue, thinking he sounded far too cheerful considering the early hour. "Uh, sure. Could you give me about a half hour to get ready?"

"No problem," he assured her. "Meet me downstairs in the restaurant, okay?"

"Sure." She hung up the phone and pushed her hair out of her eyes, yawning widely. She'd struggled to fall asleep last night, her mind dwelling on Quinn's kiss. Reliving the moment. Wondering why he'd kissed her. Wondering if he'd kiss her again.

Pathetic. She needed to stop thinking about Quinn and the feelings she was beginning to have for him and keep focused on trying to find Skylar.

It took her a little longer to get ready, making her a few minutes late when she finally arrived in the restaurant. Quinn didn't seem impatient; he was just sipping a mug of coffee and reading the paper.

"Sorry," she murmured, sliding into the seat across from him in the booth.

"No problem." He folded the paper and tucked it away. "I'm sorry, Shanna, but I'll need to drop you off somewhere this morning. I have a few errands I have to run for my mother."

"Oh, sure. Of course." Flustered, she glanced at the menu, but then brought her gaze back up to meet his. "We can skip breakfast if you need to get going."

"No, please. Order whatever you'd like."

Quinn seemed anxious to leave, so she decided to order a simple bowl of oatmeal. Quinn surprised her by choosing the same thing.

"Is everything okay?" she asked after the waitress left.

"Yes, it's fine," he answered. "But my brother's body is being released today and my mother needs some emotional support."

"I understand." And she truly did. After the way Skylar's kidnapping ripped her family apart, she knew only too well the impact of a terrible tragedy. Thinking of Quinn's mother made her wonder if she should try, once again, to talk to her father. After all, he couldn't keep ignoring her forever. Could he?

Maybe once they found Skylar, he'd find it in his heart to forgive her.

When their food arrived, Shanna bowed her head and prayed. "Thank You, heavenly Father, for this food we are about to eat. And guide us on Your chosen path while keeping us safe in Your care. Amen."

"Amen," Quinn echoed.

Startled, she opened her eyes and looked at him. She hadn't even realized she'd spoken out loud until he'd responded. "Sounds as if maybe you've found your faith after all," she said.

Quinn slowly nodded. "I haven't prayed in a long time," he admitted. "But I've found myself thanking God for saving you, both last night when you narrowly missed being hit by that car, and the night before when I found you lying unconscious in your doorway. Praying has given me peace. And I can't help but think God really is watching over you."

She was touched by his admission. "God is watching over all of us, not just me. He's watching over you, too, Quinn. He's always with us, even if we're not always paying attention."

A ghost of a smile played along his features. "I hope so."

"I know so," she argued lightly. "Trust me."

"I do trust you, Shanna," he said seriously. "Very much."

The waitress interrupted then, asking how their food was and they assured her the oatmeal was fine.

"Where would you like me to drop you off?" Quinn asked, as he prepared to pay the bill.

"My house."

He narrowed his gaze. "Shanna, I'm not so sure that's a good idea."

"I need a change of clothes and I need my car. There's no reason you have to drive me around everywhere I go."

"There is a reason for me to drive you around." Quinn's expression turned stubborn. "For one thing, we know this guy has followed you, so he knows what car you're driving. And a red Camry will be easy to find and follow. For another, I think it's better if we stay together, so he has less of a chance to find you alone."

She knew attempting to get her car was a long shot, but she'd wanted to give it a try. Quinn was going out of his way to be nice, but she still couldn't help feeling guilty. "Surely you have better things to do than cart me around."

"Nope."

She sighed and gave up, realizing that if she kept arguing he'd be delayed even more. "Okay, then for now drop me off at Carlyle's admissions office. Later, you're going to have to take me home so I can get a change of clothes."

"What are you going to do at the university?" he asked as they left the restaurant and headed out to his SUV.

She waited until he'd stored her overnight bag in the back and climbed into the driver's seat. "I'm going to search for Phoebe."

"Okay." Quinn started the engine and backed out of the parking space. "Promise me you'll keep me posted on whatever you find."

"I will."

The ride from the hotel to the university didn't take long. When she reached for her bag, Quinn's brows rose in surprise but he didn't say anything other than promising to call her once he was finished before he drove away.

Shanna returned to the computer station she'd begun to consider her own, and began searching for students with the first name Phoebe.

Nothing.

She stared and tried again, using Phoebe as the last

name. Still nothing. She unzipped her bag and dug out the articles related to the other children who'd gone missing around the same time as Skylar.

Her gaze settled on the Kenny Larson story, the four-year-old who'd been kidnapped from the shopping mall. To refresh her memory, she read through the article and then turned back to the computer.

After finding the website dedicated to missing children, she pulled up Kenny Larson's page, just to make sure nothing had changed and that he hadn't been found.

Unfortunately, Kenny Larson was still listed as missing. So she clicked on the age-progression photo. For several long minutes, she stared at the picture, trying to figure out why the face looked familiar.

Then suddenly she knew. Dennis Green. Her heart leaped as she quickly pulled up his university ID. Seeing the two photos side by side, there was no mistake. They were one and the same.

Dennis Green was really Kenny Larson.

Chapter 11

Numb with shock, Shanna stared at the two matching photographs. Looking closer, she could see they weren't exactly the same—age progression could only do so much—but the similarities were uncanny. In her mind, there was no denying Dennis Green and Kenny Larson were one and the same.

The evidence proving that Brady had been onto something when he'd begun his investigation into the New Beginnings Adoption Agency was chilling.

Why hadn't she considered sooner the possibility that Dennis Green was one of these missing kids? Keeping her gaze locked on the photos as if they might disappear, she reached with trembling fingers for her phone.

Tearing her gaze away just long enough to dial Quinn's number, she held her breath as she waited for him to answer.

Sharp disappointment stabbed deep when the call went straight through to voice mail. She took a breath and let it out slowly. "Quinn? It's Shanna. Call me when you have a minute. It's important."

She hung up without saying anything more.

Now what? Staring at the proof before her that at least one missing child had ended up adopted by another family, she wasn't sure how to proceed from here.

Except that they absolutely had to get the FBI involved. Certainly, the federal government had far better resources to begin investigating deeper into the New Beginnings Adoption Agency. And Kenny Larson's family deserved to know their long-lost son was alive and safe.

They'd gone off on the wrong track, thinking that Brady's death was related to some sort of presumed love triangle. It could be that the mysterious Phoebe was nothing more than some girl who'd flirted harmlessly with Brady during a party.

But then, why had Anna acted so strangely? In her experience, innocent people didn't shy away from the police.

She glanced at her phone impatiently, willing Quinn to return her call. Because now that they had this link, she desperately wanted to see Brady's notes related to the adoption agency. Kenny Larson had been found, but Skylar, along with dozens of other children, was still missing.

For a moment, she considered calling her mother with the news. Surely, once the FBI became involved, they'd be able to track down all the adoptees from New Beginnings and solve many of the crimes. They'd find Skylar now, even without knowing her fingerprints were at the crime scene.

But tracking down the rest of the missing children through the link of the New Beginnings Adoption Agency didn't solve the mystery of who killed Brady.

The shrill ringing of her phone startled her, and she reached for it eagerly. "Quinn?"

"I just picked up your message," he said. "What's going on? Are you all right?"

"I'm fine," she hastened to assure him. "Can you get here soon? I want to show you what I found."

"You found Phoebe?" he said, his voice rising with excitement.

"No. But I'm looking at proof that Brady's roommate, Dennis Green, is Kenny Larson."

"Kenny Larson?" Quinn echoed in a puzzled tone.

"Remember the four-year-old who was taken from the shopping mall about nine months before Skylar's disappearance?" she asked. "They're the same person, Quinn. I think your brother was on to something with his investigation into the New Beginnings Adoption Agency."

"Stay right where you are. I'll be there in less than fifteen minutes."

Quinn snapped his phone shut and glanced over at his mother. She looked as if she'd aged ten years in the four days since Brady's death. His heart ached for her, yet at the same time, he couldn't help wondering if his mother's grief would be more tolerable if she had the same level of faith Shanna did.

"There's been a break in the case, Mom. I have to leave."

Fevered hope flared in his mother's tired, red-rimmed eyes. "A break in the case? You've found the person who killed my son?"

"We've found another piece of the puzzle," Quinn corrected, unwilling to raise his mother's hopes too high. He glanced at his watch to verify the time. Her mother's husband, James, would be home in less than an hour. "If you think you'll be all right here until James gets home, I'd like to go and see where this clue leads us."

She blew her nose and sniffled loudly. "All right, but call me as soon as you know *anything*."

He wasn't going to call her unless he had irrefutable proof, but he nodded and leaned over to give her a kiss on the cheek. "Bye, Mom. I love you."

"Bye, Quinn." There was a distinct pause before she added, "I love you, too."

Hoping he'd made a little headway in the troubled relationship with his mother, Quinn jogged out to his car, feeling more elated than he had in a long time.

It occurred to him as he drove quickly back to the university that one way his life seemed to be taking a positive turn was because of Shanna.

And maybe more so, as a direct result of renewing his faith and renewing his relationship with God.

Thank You, Lord. Please keep my mother, her husband and Ivy safe in Your care.

The silent prayer made him feel much better. He parked outside the university admissions office and hurried inside to find Shanna. His heart thudded loudly in his chest when he saw her rise up to greet him.

Acting instinctively, he embraced her in a warm hug. Time seemed to freeze momentarily as her arms tightened around his waist, hugging him back.

He could have held her like this forever, but after a long moment he forced himself to release her and step back. "Show me what you found," he murmured huskily.

"Look at this," she said enthusiastically as she resumed her seat in front of the computer screen. He sank into a chair beside her as she refreshed the image.

Two side-by-side photos took up the entire computer screen, and he immediately agreed with her assessment. The age-progression image of Kenny Larson was remarkably similar to the college ID photo of Dennis Green.

"This is huge, Shanna," he said, awed by her discovery. "We have to take this to the authorities. The police first and then probably the FBI."

"I know. I didn't want to call Detective Hank Nelson without showing you first."

He glanced at Shanna, surprised by her apparent loyalty. When had the two of them become a closely knit team?

Since the first night when they'd had coffee together and he'd followed Shanna home, he slowly realized. Somehow, after that first encounter, they'd worked together and managed to accomplish amazing results.

The proof of those results was staring them in the face.

"Thanks," he murmured. "I appreciate you including me in this. I think we should make a copy of this evidence, both on a flash drive and on paper, and take them down to the Chicago P.D."

"Good idea, except I don't have a flash drive."

"I do." He pulled out the one he'd used to download all of the files from Brady's computer. He quickly inserted it into the university computer and copied the photos. Then he printed them on a color printer. The paper wasn't photo paper, but the image was good enough, in his estimation, to convince Hank to contact the feds.

"All right, let's go," he said as he disconnected the flash drive.

Shanna gathered her files and newspaper articles together and stuffed them back into her duffel bag.

He held the door for Shanna. "I'm parked over there," he said, gesturing with one hand to where his SUV waited two blocks down the street.

"I see it," Shanna said, heading in that direction.

He stayed behind her, his gaze sweeping the area, looking for any sign of her stalker. Granted, it was the middle of the day, rather than the dark of night, but he couldn't help thinking that this guy was still following her.

Last night, they'd been walking along the road when he'd come after her in his car. It could have been a coincidence that he saw her along the road and drove straight for her on impulse, but then again, the stalker could just as easily have tagged his car the night he'd found Shanna unconscious and had been following his car ever since.

Either way, he wasn't taking any chances.

She tucked her overnight case in the backseat before opening the passenger door. He swept his gaze across the area once again, and paused when he noticed a familiar couple standing on the street corner near the commons. The two drug-dealing felons. On the exact same corner, where he'd noticed the small group of kids gathered last night.

"Shanna, get in the car and lock the doors. I'll be right back." He spun on his heel and headed over to where the group of kids appeared to be in deep conversation.

When he heard the door of his SUV close, he relaxed, knowing Shanna was safe. Quickening his pace, he kept his gaze locked on the kids.

His instincts were on high alert. He'd bet his last paycheck that a drug deal was going down right there in front of the commons, in broad daylight.

He was maybe ten yards away when the familiar face of their suspect, Derek Matthews, lifted and looked directly at Quinn. Their eyes locked and, suddenly, Derek broke away from the group, taking off on foot in the opposite direction.

"Stop! Police!" Quinn shouted, sprinting after Derek. Luckily, the area around the commons was crowded with students, slowing Derek's progress.

"Stop! Police!" Quinn yelled again, hoping, praying one of the kids would help out. And suddenly, one of the students did exactly that—stuck out a leg and tripped Derek so that he stumbled and fell, falling face-first onto the concrete.

Quinn picked up his pace, catching up with Derek before he could jump back up to his feet and take off again. "Don't try it," Quinn advised. He knelt on Derek's back, forcing him to stay down as he wrenched the young man's hands around his back. "Derek Matthews, you're under arrest for evading a police officer and fleeing the scene of a crime."

"What crime?" Derek asked loudly in protest. "I didn't do nuthin'."

"Then why did you take off when you saw me?" Quinn demanded, patting the suspect's pockets. "Hmm, what do we have here? Is that marijuana and a pipe?"

"It's not mine," Derek claimed. "I borrowed these jeans from a friend."

"Yeah, right. Tell it to the judge," Quinn advised. If he had a nickel for every time he'd heard that excuse, he'd be a rich man. "Now you're under arrest for possession. And that's a parole violation."

Derek let out a stream of curses that Quinn ignored. Thank goodness he had his badge, cuffs and gun handy, or this could have ended very differently. After making sure Derek was securely contained, he flipped open his phone to call for back up.

Before he could dial, though, the wail of sirens filled the air and a campus police car squealed around the corner, lights flashing. Shanna must have called them when he'd taken off after Derek.

Then he frowned and glanced behind him. Sure enough, Shanna was standing about twenty yards behind him, her phone in her hand. He wanted to yell at her for leaving the safety of the car, but the arrival of two fellow police officers distracted him.

"I'm pretty sure there was a drug deal going down outside the commons," Quinn told Craig and Skip, the two guys who'd responded to Shanna's call. "This guy took off from the scene. I found drugs in his pocket, and his fingerprints have been discovered at the scene of Brady's murder. Not to mention he has a felony record for drug dealing in Wisconsin."

"Well, well, well," Craig drawled. "Looks like you've earned yourself a trip down to the cop shop."

"I didn't do nuthin'," Derek mumbled weakly, as if he sensed returning to jail might be imminent. "I wanna lawyer."

"Can you afford one? Or should we put a call in to the Public Defender's office?" Quinn asked.

The pained expression on Derek's face made it clear how he felt about the Public Defender's office, but he gave a resigned sigh. "I can't afford one."

"Then we'll call someone for you." Quinn didn't like how lawyers managed to get reduced or eliminated charges for criminals, releasing them back onto the streets, but in his heart he believed in the justice system. So Matthews would get his public defender.

"Murphy, you'll need to come downtown with us," Skip pointed out as he hauled Derek Matthews to his feet. "We'll need a formal statement regarding exactly what you saw."

Quinn glanced over to where Shanna still stood on the fringes of the group and gestured for her to come over. "That's fine, but Ms. Dawson is coming with me."

"Did you see anything?" Craig asked Shanna.

"Just how the group of kids scattered when they realized Quinn was about to bust them."

"We'll take your statement, too, just in case," Craig decided.

Quinn stepped back, giving room to Skip and Craig to take their suspect to the caged police cruiser. He took Shanna's hand in his as they walked back to his SUV. "I wish you would have stayed inside with the doors locked," he said.

"I know, Quinn. But when you took off after Derek, I saw Tanya Jacobs run straight for me, so I took a picture with my cell phone. I thought it might help if we could prove that both of them were there together."

"Good thinking," he praised her. "And I'm glad you didn't try to follow her."

"I was going to," Shanna admitted. "But then I decided I should back you up instead."

Back him up? There she went with that partner mentality again. Except she was a crime-scene investigator, which meant she was far removed from the type of action he faced every day. And his gut twisted at the thought of Shanna being anywhere near the danger he was accustomed to.

"Shanna, why is it that you keep forgetting there's some crazy stalker following you?" he asked, trying not to let his frustration show. "I can't help feeling that guy is going to strike out at you when we least expect it."

"I couldn't leave you to face Derek alone," she stubbornly repeated. "What if he'd had a gun?"

He stared at her, not sure what to say. He'd never met a woman like Shanna. One who was strong, stubborn, determined, yet didn't carry the hard edge that he'd noticed in many female cops.

The ride to the campus police headquarters didn't take long. They'd process Derek Matthews's paperwork there first, before sending him downtown.

Inside the station, there was the usual amount of chaos. He noticed Shanna looked around with keen curiosity. Before he could take her someplace to sit and wait, Hank Nelson strolled over.

"Holding out on me, Murphy?" he asked, a glint of anger in his eyes.

"No, sir. At least, that wasn't my intent. I'd like to fill you in on everything we've discovered so far. But first I need to give my statement regarding the drug bust."

Detective Nelson scowled and crossed his arms over his chest. "I'll wait."

He glanced over to find Craig, but he was still busy with their suspect. Skip was already taking Shanna's statement so he crossed over to his desk and booted up his computer to write down his version of the events.

Officer Craig arrived about ten minutes later, just

as Quinn was finishing. He printed the document, then quickly went through everything verbally.

"What made you recognize the suspect?" Craig asked, when Quinn finished.

"His prints, along with Tanya Jacobs's prints, were found at Brady's crime scene," he admitted. Shanna had finished with Skip and came over to stand beside him.

"That's interesting," Craig murmured. "Okay, thanks. If we have more questions we'll let you know."

"Sounds good." He stood and looked at Shanna. "Detective Nelson wants to talk to us."

She grimaced a bit and nodded. "Yeah, he told me. We're supposed to meet him in the interview room, wherever that is."

"This way," he said, taking her arm. Hank stood there, still scowling, when they both took seats on the same side of the table.

So this is what it felt like to be interviewed like a suspect, he thought wryly, when Hank closed the door and dropped into a chair across from them.

He glanced at Shanna, whose expression radiated guilt, and took the lead. "Maybe we need to start at the beginning."

"Yeah. Why don't you?" Hank asked snidely.

So Quinn went through everything—Shanna's stalker, Brady's notes regarding the New Beginnings Adoption Agency, how Dennis Green was adopted through that agency, discovering Derek's and Tanya's fingerprints at the crime scene, looking for Skylar and the mysterious Phoebe, the two attacks on Shanna by her stalker and finishing with their theory that Dennis Green and Kenny Larson were the same person.

Shanna pulled out the computer image they'd printed

at the university and slid it across the table toward Hank. "We thought at first that Brady's death was related to some sort of love triangle between Anna, Phoebe and Brady, but now we're thinking the New Beginnings Adoption Agency could be the common factor. They handled Dennis Green's adoption, placing a kidnapped child with a new family. Who knows how many other kidnappings could be related? My sister, Skylar, was kidnapped nine months after Kenny Larson. Can it be just one big coincidence that her fingerprints have shown up at the scene of Brady's crime, when Brady's roommate was kidnapped and adopted, too?"

Hank hadn't spoken more than a couple of terse sentences during their long explanation of what they'd discovered. Quinn sensed the detective was still angry, but after Shanna's passionate question, he sighed heavily.

"I'm still mad at both of you, but you're right. This isn't a coincidence. If we're dealing with kidnappings that happened fourteen and fifteen years ago, then I need to get the FBI involved."

"I promise, we really were planning to come to you with this information," Quinn said. "The drug deal going down at the corner of the commons distracted me."

Hank tossed them both a look full of skepticism.

"Honestly, we were," Shanna spoke up earnestly. "I know we need the FBI to help find Skylar, and you must realize how badly I want to find my sister."

"Okay, okay," Hank said, throwing his hands up in the air. "Quit groveling already. I'll make the call to the feds, but you both have to promise me to stay out of this from now on. We can't work this case in a vacuum."

"But—" Shanna started, and he grabbed her hand

under the table and squeezed it as a warning to keep quiet.

There was a sharp knock at the door and Hank turned around. "Yeah?" he called.

The door opened and Craig poked his head in. "Murphy, you're not going to believe this. We matched Matthews's fingerprints to one of your open cases."

One of his open cases? "Which one?"

Craig pushed the door open and tossed some papers onto the table in front of Quinn. "Remember that robbery at the Corner Café a few months ago?"

"Yeah. I remember." The night was etched in his mind as one of the few times in his job as a campus cop that he'd been forced to fire his gun. "The suspect got away, and we found his escape vehicle, which happened to be stolen, a few miles from the café."

"Yeah, and when we recovered the gun and the car, we found a partial print on the steering wheel. The print matches your drug-dealing suspect, Derek Matthews."

Quinn frowned. "Matthews has a record. We didn't match him earlier?"

"We did, but we'd canvassed the area without anyone claiming to recognize him," Craig explained. "Now that he's been brought in for possession, we can hold him on the armed-robbery charge, too."

Quinn was glad of that, since the young girl behind the counter at the café, who'd looked tough with her purple-streaked hair and her eyebrow piercing, had been badly shaken after the robbery. He remembered far too clearly how she'd broken down and sobbed on his shoulder.

"He's going back to prison for sure this time," Craig said with satisfaction.

"That's good," Quinn murmured. Glancing down at the police report, a familiar name jumped out at him, and he stared down in amazement. The name of the victim, the girl with the purple-streaked hair who'd been robbed at gunpoint by Derek Matthews, had the same first name as their mystery girl.

Phoebe Fontaine.

Chapter 12

Quinn dragged his gaze from Phoebe's name on the police report to look at Shanna. He wanted to let her know he might have found their mystery girl, but truthfully he wasn't even sure Phoebe was still working at the Corner Café. Although with a last name, they should be able to find a last known address.

He didn't say anything out loud, though, because while he understood Hank's desire to take the lead in the investigation, he wanted to follow up on this lead himself. They'd already given Hank everything they had, including Kyle's claim that Anna was jealous of how Brady was supposedly "flirting" with a girl named Phoebe.

Hank was going to get the feds involved, which was good because the FBI had a better chance of following up on all adoptions handled through the New

Beginnings Adoption Agency. And with Dennis Green matching the photo of missing four-year-old Kenny Larson, there was a good chance his brother's murder was linked to his proposed newspaper article.

For some reason, he wanted to give Shanna a chance to see Phoebe first, meet with her, talk to her. They'd already decided that it was hardly likely that Phoebe was really Skylar, but he wanted to make sure before he turned the information over to Hank and the feds.

"Quinn? Anything else you want to add?" Hank asked.

He dragged his attention back to the current discussion. "I'm sorry, what was the question?"

Hank gave an exasperated sigh. "We're going to start following up on the Dennis Green/Kenny Larson angle, and call the feds to see where they want to go from here. Do you agree with the plan?"

His approval wasn't necessary; Hank could really do whatever he wanted, but Quinn appreciated being allowed to participate. "I think it's a good plan," he said, glancing at Shanna. "We desperately want to find Shanna's missing sister, Skylar."

"And we want to know who killed Brady," Shanna added.

"Don't worry, the more pieces to the puzzle we uncover, the more likely we'll find the missing links," Hank assured her.

"If you don't need anything more from us, we'd like to get going," Quinn said, rising to his feet. "We've missed lunch, and I don't know about Shanna, but I can't think clearly on an empty stomach."

Hank's gaze narrowed suspiciously, but then he

slowly nodded. "We're finished here, but if anything else happens I want you to call me ASAP."

"We will," Shanna assured him.

Quinn took her hand as they strolled outside, crossing the street to the parking lot where he'd left his car. After they were both seated inside, he started the car and looked at Shanna. "I think I found Phoebe."

Her blue eyes widened in shock. "What? When? How?"

"She works at the Corner Café, or at least she did at the time of the robbery." He backed out of the parking space and then took a right-hand turn, heading toward the café. "Phoebe Fontaine was the girl working behind the counter the night Derek Matthews tried to rob her."

"Thank You, God," Shanna whispered reverently. "I've been praying we'd find her."

"Shanna, don't get your hopes up too high," he cautioned as he took a left at the next stoplight. "We don't know that Phoebe is adopted, and we certainly don't know that she's Skylar."

Shanna nodded quickly, but he could still see the frank hope reflected in her eyes. "I know, Quinn. Trust me—I do realize that this is a total stretch. But what if she is Skylar? What if today is the day I'm going to find my missing sister?"

Luckily, he managed to find a parking spot just a couple of blocks down from the Corner Café. He turned off the engine and twisted in the seat to face Shanna. "I'll be thrilled if you do find your missing sister. Before we go inside, though, you need to know how Phoebe looked the last time I saw her."

Shanna's smile evaporated and she clasped her hands together tightly in her lap. "What do you mean how she looked? Is she in trouble? On drugs? In an abusive relationship? What?"

"No, Shanna, she was physically fine, from what I could tell. Shaken after being held up at gunpoint, but fine."

She let out an audible sigh of relief. "Well, what are you talking about then?"

"Just that she doesn't have the sweet, girl-next-door look. Phoebe has dark hair heavily streaked with purple and an eyebrow piercing."

Shanna hiked her eyebrows upward. "So what? Do you think I care if she has purple hair or facial piercings? If she's my sister, I'll accept her no matter how she looks."

He grinned with relief. "Okay, then. Let's go."

Shanna was so excited, she wanted to sprint at full speed rather than walk calmly beside Quinn as they followed the sidewalk to the Corner Café.

She took several deep breaths, reminding herself that it was far more likely that Phoebe wasn't Skylar. But even a one percent chance was better than nothing.

They walked inside the café, which was surprisingly crowded. Going from the bright sunlight outside to the darker interior of the café momentarily blinded her. She stood for several seconds until her eyes adjusted to less light.

"Do you see her?" she asked in a low tone, searching for anyone with purple-streaked hair. Although for all they knew, Phoebe could have changed to blue or green streaks, or none at all. If she'd turned blonde, would Quinn still recognize her?

"Not yet, but let's find a seat first," Quinn answered, sweeping the area with his gaze.

Shanna noticed two girls rising to their feet from a small table near the back of the café. She darted around several students standing and talking to snatch the vacant table.

Quinn followed her but didn't sit down. "What would you like?" he asked. "Are you hungry? They have some muffins and other baked goods for sale, too."

"Coffee and a muffin would be great."

Quinn stood in line, and she watched the two girls behind the counter closely, searching for any possible similarities to Skylar.

It wasn't easy to get a good look though, since there were so many people milling about the café, and the two counter attendants kept turning their backs to fill orders. She should have offered to go up for the coffee and muffins.

Quinn returned five minutes later with their order. Before she could open her mouth to ask, he shook his head. "No, Phoebe isn't working right now. She's due to come in at four o'clock."

"Four o'clock?" she echoed with a stab of disappointment. "That's over an hour from now."

"I know," Quinn said as he sat down in the chair across from hers. "But we're probably better off waiting here. Unless you have a better idea?"

"No, I don't have a better idea," she admitted.

Quinn quickly unwrapped his muffin and then hesitated, glancing up at her. "We should pray first, right?"

She laughed, the tension easing out of her chest. She should know better than to try and rush God's plan.

She'd find Skylar when God intended, and not before. "Yes, we should."

He reached over to take her hand and then bowed his head. She held his hand and closed her eyes, praying in a low voice just loud enough for Quinn to hear. "Dear Lord, thank You for providing us food to eat, and please keep us safe and show us the path You want us to take. We also ask that You continue to keep Skylar safe in Your care. Amen."

"Amen," Quinn echoed.

"Next time, it's your turn to provide the prayer," she teased as she removed the cellophane from her muffin. They weren't freshly baked, but she was so hungry she didn't care. And the muffins were surprisingly good.

"I'll try," he said hesitantly. "But I still have a lot to learn."

"You'll be fine." She paused, glancing around the café. "We probably should have told Hank we were coming here," she murmured before taking a sip of her coffee. "I don't think he's very happy with us."

Quinn shrugged. "Look, Shanna, we don't know that Phoebe has anything to do with Brady's murder or the mystery surrounding your sister's disappearance. As soon as we know something, I promise to call Hank. Besides, we did tell him about Kyle Ryker's accusations regarding Anna being upset with Brady for flirting with Phoebe, remember?"

"Yes, but we didn't tell him Phoebe works here at the Corner Café."

"We didn't know that for sure until we came and asked for her," Quinn pointed out. "She could have easily quit her job here after being held up at gunpoint."

"True," she admitted with a frown. "I wonder why

she stayed? This can't be the only job around. And since she's not enrolled in any classes, she wouldn't be limited to something on campus. And surely her parents would have encouraged her to find something different, don't you think?"

"Yes, assuming her parents knew about the incident."

"I suppose you're right." She didn't want to think about Phoebe being estranged from her parents. Guiltily, she realized that the main reason she didn't want to believe Phoebe was estranged from her parents was because she believed Phoebe could be Skylar.

"Don't look now, but Anna and Maggie just walked in," Quinn said in a low, urgent tone.

She almost turned to look, despite his warning not to. Keeping her gaze on his, she leaned toward him. "Should we go over to talk to them?" she asked.

"I don't want to scare Anna off again, but I would like to talk to her," Quinn admitted.

From the corner of her eye, she could see both girls, Maggie and a brunette who she assumed was Anna, standing in line at the counter. "If we're going to talk to them, we should head over by the door so Anna can't take off running again."

"Exactly what I was thinking," he admitted. "Let's wait until they've placed their order."

The next three minutes passed with excruciating slowness. It was hard not to stare at Maggie and Anna, so she kept her eyes locked on Quinn's.

Finally he rose smoothly to his feet, and she quickly followed him as he made his way through the cramped maze of tables to the front door.

Once Maggie and Anna had their respective coffees, they turned to walk toward the door. The shocked expression on Maggie's and Anna's faces and the way they stopped abruptly was almost comical.

Maggie was the first to recover, but the terrified expression on Anna's face tugged at her heart. What on earth caused the girl to be so afraid? Instinctively, Shanna stepped forward in an attempt to reassure her. "Please don't panic, Anna. We just want to talk to you. I promise you're not in trouble or anything. We just have a few questions."

"Just talk to them, Anna," Maggie urged with obvious exasperation. "They'll find you eventually anyway."

"I already gave my statement to the police. I don't have anything more to tell you," Anna argued with a dark scowl. "Why can't you just leave me alone?"

Something was off; the fear radiating from the girl was nearly palpable. "What's wrong, Anna? Is someone bothering you? What are you so afraid of?"

Anna didn't answer, but the slight flicker in her gaze gave her away.

"We shouldn't talk here," Quinn pointed out, as a few café patrons were beginning to watch them with interest. He stared at Anna. "We can do this the easy way or the hard way," he said conversationally. "We can go outside and talk in private, or I can arrest you now and we can talk down at the station. Your choice. And know this—if we go outside and you take off running, the latter option automatically takes precedence."

"Come on, Anna," Maggie urged. "Let's just get this over with, okay?"

"Fine." Anna angled her chin stubbornly and waited for Quinn to hold the door open before moving past them to go outside. For a moment, the girl's stubbornness reminded Shanna of how she was at that age.

Could Anna be Skylar? The hair color was right, as
was the age. Her pulse kicked into high gear at the possibility.

But once they were outside, standing alongside the
brick building of the café, she realized Anna's eyes were
a greenish hazel, not brown. No colored contacts, either.
Her heart sank like a rock.

"So what do you want to know?" Anna demanded.
Her spunk in the face of her earlier fear was admirable.

"You come to this café often?" Quinn asked casually.

Anna shrugged. "Sometimes, why?"

"You must know Phoebe then, right?" Quinn asked
again.

Anna's mouth thinned. "No, I don't know her. I heard
she works here, but I could care less about that."

"Really? You didn't care that Brady spent so much
time hanging out here?" Quinn pressed.

"Not really," Anna said, although the guarded expression in her eyes made Shanna think the girl did mind,
very much. "I don't care what you've heard. I know
Brady loved me."

Love? A pretty strong word for a twenty-year-old.
"I'm sure he did care about you," Shanna said with a
smile. "Which is why it makes perfect sense that you'd
be upset to find out he was flirting with someone else."

Anna refused to acknowledge the obvious. "You can
believe whatever you want. I don't care."

"So what happened last night?" Quinn asked, changing the subject. "Why did you take off running when
you saw us?"

"I wasn't in the mood to be interrogated," Anna shot
back. "Why is it so hard for you to understand I just
want to be left alone?"

"Anna, why don't you tell them?" Maggie asked in a low tone. "He's a cop. Maybe he can help."

Shanna glanced at Quinn, who looked as puzzled as she felt. "Anna, what's wrong? What's going on?"

"Nothing," Anna said, shrugging off Maggie's hand.

"Some old guy was bothering her," Maggie announced. "That's why she's been trying to stay low-key."

A chill snaked down Shanna's back. Could the old guy bothering Anna be the same guy who'd been stalking her? And if so, why?

"It's nothing," Anna insisted. "I haven't seen him in a week. It was probably just my imagination anyway."

"Can you give me a description?" Quinn asked, a frown furrowing his brow.

Anna shrugged. "Not very tall, about five feet ten inches with gray hair."

"Could you work with a sketch artist, maybe?" Shanna suggested.

"No, I didn't really get a good look at him. Besides, I told you, I haven't seen him in a while."

"Where do you work?" Shanna persisted.

"At the Olive Grove restaurant," Maggie supplied on her friend's behalf. "She's a hostess there during the week."

"Lately, I've only been working a couple of shifts each week," Anna admitted. "Because of the rehearsals and the play."

"You're sure you can't give us any more description of the guy following you?" Quinn asked.

"I'm sure."

Shanna caught Quinn's gaze and shrugged. She didn't know what else to do to encourage the young woman to open up.

"Can I go now?" Anna asked. "My coffee's getting cold."

"Yes. But Anna, if you see that old guy following you again, will you please call me?" Quinn took out his wallet, extracted a business card and handed one to Anna. "Please? I don't want you to get hurt."

Anna took Quinn's card with obvious reluctance. "All right," she agreed slowly. "If I see Creepy Guy again, I'll call you."

"Thanks," Quinn murmured.

Shanna watched thoughtfully as Maggie and Anna hurried away. "Do you think it's possible we have the same stalker?"

"Anything is possible," Quinn responded grimly. "But it's weird that he'd leave you notes and break into your home to attack you while doing nothing more than following Anna around."

"She has hazel eyes," she said, a hint of sadness in her tone. "So she can't be Skylar."

"I know." Quinn put his arm around her shoulders, surprising her with a quick embrace. "Don't worry, I just know we're going to find Skylar."

She raised her gaze to his. "I hope so," she whispered.

For a long moment he gazed down at her, and she sensed he wanted to kiss her. She held her breath, surprised by how much she wanted it, too, but then the moment was gone.

"It's past four," Quinn said, dropping his arm and stepping away. "Let's go meet Phoebe."

She nodded, trying to hide her disappointment. Surely meeting Phoebe, seeing if she was actually Skylar, was more important than Quinn's kiss?

Of course it was.

Back inside the café, they walked up to the counter. The place had emptied out; there was no line. "Could we please speak to Phoebe Fontaine?" Quinn asked.

"Sorry, but Phoebe called in sick," the young girl behind the counter said. "She sounded terrible."

Sick? Shanna frowned and glanced doubtfully at Quinn.

"Okay, thanks for letting us know," he said pleasantly. He turned and headed for the door, and she quickly followed, swallowing the hard lump of disappointment.

"I'm so upset," she said as they walked back toward Quinn's SUV. "I really wanted to talk to her."

Quinn flipped open his cell phone and punched in a number. "Hi, Skip. Do me a favor and pull up Phoebe Fontaine's address for me."

By the time they reached the car, Quinn had Phoebe's address. As much as she felt bad bothering the poor girl when she was sick, Shanna didn't protest when he drove the few blocks to a rather run-down apartment building.

"Phoebe lives here?" she asked, trying to hide her dismay.

"Apartment 217," Quinn said, climbing out from behind the wheel.

They walked up to the main door, and Quinn frowned when he tugged on it. "I can't believe it's not locked," he muttered.

There was a small foyer with mailboxes lining one wall. The door leading to the rest of the building was locked. He pushed the intercom button above number 217 and waited.

No answer. Shanna stepped up and pushed the buzzer a second time, holding the button in longer. But still there was no answer.

"I can't believe it," Shanna murmured.

Quinn rubbed a hand over his chin. "I guess we'll have to come back tomorrow."

She stared at the silver mailbox with the name Fontaine printed neatly above it. "Maybe not," she said, as an idea formed. "What if I dusted her mailbox for fingerprints? If we're able to match Phoebe's prints to the ones we have on file for Skylar, we'd know for sure that they're the same person." Shanna gazed at Quinn, barely able to contain her excitement. She was so close to proving Phoebe was really Skylar, and she didn't want to wait one minute longer than she had to in order to prove it.

Chapter 13

"I doubt you'll get anything useful," Quinn protested.

She lightly grasped his arm. "Please, Quinn? What can it hurt to *try?* I can't bear not knowing for sure."

He glanced down at her and then smiled slowly. "All right, Shanna," he agreed. "Why not?"

"Great." She was overwhelmed with relief. "Take me back to my place—I have everything I need at home."

Quinn nodded, and they left the apartment building where Phoebe lived to walk back to his SUV.

"Don't get your hopes up too high," he cautioned as he drove toward her house. "We have no proof whatsoever that Phoebe is Skylar."

"I know," Shanna murmured. And she did know the odds were against them. At the same time, she couldn't completely quell her excitement. She knew God was helping her, showing her the way. And if the fingerprints weren't a match, then she'd know to keep moving forward.

When Quinn pulled into her driveway, she gripped the door handle, ready to bolt into the house.

"Hold it," Quinn commanded, hitting the locks so she couldn't jump out of the car. "You're not going inside until I make sure it's safe."

"All right," she said, handing over her keys. "But please hurry." Holding back wasn't easy, but there wasn't any point in arguing. The faster Quinn determined no one was hiding inside, the quicker she'd get her supplies and head back to Phoebe's apartment.

"Stay inside the car with the doors locked," Quinn instructed. She waited until he'd climbed out from behind the wheel before hitting the door locks.

Quinn went inside and she held her breath, fidgeting impatiently in her seat as she waited for him to return. After a long, agonizing ten minutes, he finally opened the door and gestured for her to come inside.

"Doesn't seem like anyone's been in since you were here last," Quinn admitted as he held the door open for her. "The air is a bit stale."

She wrinkled her nose, agreeing with his assessment. Surely by now, the stalker had given up watching her house, especially given that she hadn't been back to stay since the night of the attack.

In her closet, she found her fingerprint kit right where she'd left it, tucked in a corner in the back. She brought it out and walked back to the kitchen. "Quinn, I really need to take my car back to the university campus. This investigation is heating up, and I don't want to be without my own vehicle."

"No, absolutely not." The stubborn expression on Quinn's face made her want to sigh.

"Quinn, we can cover more ground on this investigation if we each have our own cars." She knew she was fighting an uphill battle, but she had to try. "Besides, I'm sure the stalker has given up watching my house and my car, since we purposefully haven't used them in the past few days."

"What about the attempted hit-and-run?" Quinn asked skeptically.

"We don't even know that I was the target," she pointed out. "And he probably got lucky catching sight of me walking along the street. I'll be safer in a vehicle."

Quinn stared at her for a long moment. "I'll only agree on one condition."

"What's that?"

"We switch vehicles for now. I'll drive your car and you can drive mine."

At least he'd attempted to compromise, meeting her halfway. "Agreed. Thanks, Quinn."

"You're welcome," he responded grudgingly.

They swapped car keys, and Shanna waited on the street in Quinn's car until he'd pulled her car out of the driveway and closed the garage door behind him.

He went ahead, and she followed behind as they drove back to Carlyle University. Finding two parking spaces next to Phoebe's apartment wasn't easy, but Quinn didn't say anything about it as they walked up to the apartment building.

Shanna eagerly began to unpack her supplies, but Quinn once again pushed the buzzer for Phoebe's apartment. She froze, holding her breath, but just as earlier, there was no answer.

"If she's sick, why isn't she here to answer the door?" he muttered under his breath.

"Maybe she went home to visit her parents," she mused, brushing the silver metal door with fingerprint powder. "She's still young—maybe she's looking for some TLC from her mother while she's not feeling good."

"Maybe," Quinn responded, although he didn't look convinced.

She worked on the mailbox door, but after a good ten minutes, she tossed the brush down in disgust. "You were right, Quinn. There are way too many prints on this door to find anything useful."

"It was worth a try," he said consolingly.

She didn't want to admit defeat. Taking a soft cloth from her kit, she wiped down the door, using force to make sure that all the current smudges were eliminated. "Maybe when she returns home, she'll check her mail and I'll be able to find an isolated print." Tonight. She'd come back later tonight.

Quinn's cell phone rang before he could respond. "Hi, Hank," he answered. "What's up?" There was a long pause, and then he met her gaze. "Yeah, she's here with me. I'll let her know, thanks."

She lifted a brow. "Let me know what?"

"That Special Agent Marc Tanner from the FBI wants to talk to you. Actually, to both of us."

She shouldn't have been surprised. Hadn't Hank told them he was getting the feds involved? "That was fast," she murmured.

"Yeah and they're waiting down at the police station, anxious for us to tell them everything we know," Quinn said.

She glanced regretfully at the shiny silver mailbox and then forced herself to turn away. She would come back after their meeting with the feds. "Well then, I guess we shouldn't keep them waiting any longer."

Quinn pulled up into the police station general parking lot and waited for Shanna to park his SUV in the empty spot next to him. He tried to tell himself that Shanna was perfectly safe in his vehicle, rather than driving around in her own, but knowing that logically didn't prevent him from offering a quick, silent prayer.

Dear God, please keep Shanna safe in Your care.

He found the prayer comforting, and knew that Shanna deserved the credit for his newfound faith. The way her blue eyes sparkled bright with excitement made her look more beautiful than ever.

Once again, he wondered what would happen between the two of them once they'd found Shanna's sister and Brady's killer. The case had brought them together, but once it was solved, would they each go their separate ways?

He knew that being a cop made having a relationship nearly impossible, but now that he'd met Shanna, he didn't want to lose her.

She's not yours to lose, he reminded himself sternly. But he still took her elbow as they walked up the stairs and into the station.

Hank stood beside a tall, young man with chocolate-brown hair and clean-cut features. For a moment, he glanced down at Shanna, hoping she didn't find the guy attractive. She must have sensed his gaze because she glanced up at him and smiled nervously.

"Thanks for coming in so quickly," Hank said by

way of greeting. "Special Agent Marc Tanner, this is Officer Quinn Murphy and crime-scene investigator Shanna Dawson."

"Nice to meet you," Shanna said, stepping forward to take Agent Tanner's outstretched hand. "Skylar Dawson is my younger sister."

"Ms. Dawson. Officer Murphy." Agent Marc Tanner shook hands with both of them briefly and didn't waste any time on small talk. "If you'll come this way?" He indicated the room they'd occupied just a few hours earlier.

The way Shanna clasped her hands tightly in her lap betrayed her nervousness. He put a hand on her back, trying to reassure her. They took two seats across the table from Agent Tanner.

"Officer Murphy, I understand you have some information regarding the New Beginnings Adoption Agency?" Agent Tanner asked.

"Yes. My brother, Brady Wallace, was doing a story on adoption for the university online newspaper. According to his notes, his roommate, Dennis Green, had asked my brother to assist in finding his birth mother."

"Brady Wallace is your half brother, correct?" Agent Tanner asked.

Quinn tried not to let his annoyance show. "Technically, yes, we have different fathers. But Brady was my brother in every way that counts."

Agent Tanner looked surprised by his curt reaction. "I wasn't implying otherwise, Officer Murphy, just making sure I understood the difference in your last names."

He forced himself to relax. "Brady was looking for the New Beginnings Adoption Agency because that's the paperwork Dennis Green apparently had regarding his adoption. But the agency was only in business for five years. According to Brady's records, the agency shut its doors fourteen years ago."

"Interesting timing, wouldn't you agree?" Tanner asked. When Quinn nodded, the FBI agent continued, "Do you mind sharing all the information your brother uncovered for his article? He could have some information there that might seem innocuous but could in reality be a great lead."

"I don't mind at all, but honestly there isn't a lot of concrete information in his notes." Privately, Quinn had thought his brother hadn't exactly used the unbiased eye of a journalist on the subject. But Brady was only a journalism major, not a full-fledged investigative reporter. "Most of the stuff he wrote down was nothing more than theory and speculation. Although he was trying to find other private-adoption agencies that were in the area, too."

This caused Agent Tanner to lean forward eagerly. "Do you have names of any other adoption agencies?"

He shook his head. "Sorry, but no, my brother didn't list any by name."

"I see." Disappointment flared in Tanner's eyes. "Well even so, I'd appreciate access to everything your brother has."

"I'll make sure you get a copy of this," he said, pulling out the jump drive.

Shanna had been quiet up until now. "Agent Tanner, do you have any leads on Skylar's disappearance? Is it possible she was also adopted out through the New Beginnings Adoption Agency?"

The FBI agent's gaze softened a bit. "Not yet, but you need to know, finding your sister's fingerprints at the crime scene injected life into a very cold case, Ms. Dawson. To be honest, we assumed your sister was dead."

Shanna blanched but nodded her understanding. Quinn leaned forward, placing a reassuring arm around her shoulders. "We'll find her, Shanna," he murmured. "Knowing your sister is alive, is all that matters right now."

She nodded, but leaned against him anyway, as if needing some of his strength. He found he enjoyed being there for Shanna.

And maybe, just maybe, once they solved this case, she'd let him stay a part of her life.

The thought was a little scary, considering he'd given up any hope of ever having a relationship. But the alternative, life without Shanna, was even worse, so he squelched the niggle of fear.

"Obviously, we were hoping you had a few leads related to Skylar's kidnapping," Quinn said.

Agent Tanner was silent for a moment. "We do have an adoption agency that we're looking into right now that's located in Atlanta, Georgia. In fact, that's where I was when we got the call from your Detective Nelson. The name of the agency in Georgia is Sunrise Adoption Agency."

Shanna glanced up at Quinn hopefully, but he only shook his head. "Never heard of it, I'm afraid."

"Me, neither," Shanna said sadly.

"The founder of the agency is a guy named Geoff Wellington," Tanner continued. "And interestingly enough, the owner of the New Beginnings Agency was a man by the name of George Worth."

"The same initials, huh?" Quinn glanced at Shanna,

who wore a hopeful expression. "Do you think these two could be the same guy?"

"We have photos of each man, and they don't look as if they're the same guy. But that doesn't mean that a ring of thieves hasn't figured out how to use fake names and identities, switching off as agency founders so no one links them together."

Quinn had to admit the theory made some sense. Criminals spent almost as much time covering their tracks as they did perpetuating actual crimes.

"So they really could be the same agency?" Shanna asked.

"This new agency has only been in business for eighteen months, so it's entirely possible that they keep reinventing themselves every few years," Tanner explained. "We've had our eye on them because within the past six months, two children within a fifty-mile radius of Atlanta have gone missing. And there were also two others, one from North Carolina and one from Alabama, who went missing. We suspect they're trying to widen the range of abductions to remove any potential links between the kidnappings."

Shanna reached over to grasp Quinn's hand tightly. "Four more? You have to stop them, Agent Tanner. Before any more children go missing."

"That's the plan, Ms. Dawson," he said with a hint of dryness in his tone. "But we're also trying to link this founder to the other agencies that are no longer in business. We're pretty sure that Geoff Wellington is an alias. He didn't exist, from what we can tell, until three years ago. And interestingly enough, George Worth disappeared right after New Beginnings closed down."

Quinn had to believe the feds were on the right track.

"More evidence, although circumstantial, that they might be one and the same man."

"That's my thought," Tanner agreed.

"Is there anything we can do to help?" Quinn asked. He didn't want to be left out of the investigation, and he especially didn't want Shanna left out. She had more to lose. He wanted to bring justice to Brady's murderer, but she wanted to find her sister. Live siblings took priority over deceased ones.

"Not at this time. Trust me when I tell you we're following up on all leads," Tanner said kindly. "In fact, I'm going to interview Dennis Green next."

"I'm sure Hank told you we believe Dennis Green is really Kenny Larson, the child who disappeared from the shopping mall fifteen years ago," Shanna interjected. "I have the age-progression photo next to Dennis Green's university ID photo to prove it."

Agent Tanner's face darkened, as if he was embarrassed. "Yes, Detective Nelson did give us your photos. Nice piece of detective work, Ms. Dawson. Between finding your sister's fingerprints at Officer Murphy's brother's crime scene and discovering the link between Dennis Green and Kenny Larson, you've really helped us rejuvenate this cold case."

Quinn beamed with pride. Because he, too, thought Shanna had made remarkable strides in a case that was fourteen years old. "Maybe you should offer her a job," he joked.

Tanner didn't laugh or even crack a smile. "Maybe we should," he admitted grimly. "The agent in charge of this case retired a few years ago, and I can't say I'm overly impressed with his efforts."

"Interesting," Quinn murmured. He bet there was

plenty of finger-pointing going around at the FBI head-quarters now that a lowly college journalism student and a crime-scene investigator had broken their case wide open.

"I'd ask you to both stay in touch with me, especially if you find out anything further," Tanner continued, sliding two business cards across the table.

"Of course," Shanna murmured.

He pocketed Tanner's card and then removed his arm from Shanna's shoulder, immediately missing the warmth of her skin and the vanilla scent she wore. "We'd appreciate you keeping us in the loop, too, especially if you find out anything about Shanna's sister."

Tanner's smile resembled a pained grimace. "Guess that's the least I can do after the way you've helped us out."

He and Shanna shook the agent's hand again before leaving. Outside, he noticed a young man with a sullen expression on his face sitting beside Hank Nelson.

Recognizing Dennis Green from his photo, he gave his brother's roommate a brief nod before making his way to the door. Shanna followed much more slowly, hardly able to tear her gaze away from the boy she believed to be Kenny Larson.

"Are you okay?" he asked in a low voice as they walked out to their respective vehicles.

"I just can't help thinking how happy his family will be to see him," she admitted slowly. "But he already has a life, and adopted parents who love him. He wanted to find his birth mother, but discovering he was really kidnapped must be a shock. I'm just realizing how difficult it will be for him to reconcile his two identities."

He knew she was talking about Skylar more so than

Dennis Green. "Shanna, don't think the worst. Not yet. Skylar is alive, which is more than you've hoped for over the years, isn't it?"

"Yes, it is." She stopped beside his SUV, glancing up at him. "I'm sorry, Quinn. I don't know what's wrong with me. I should be happy that Skylar is alive and well. If she doesn't want me in her life, then I'll learn to live with that."

Would she really? He wasn't at all convinced. "I'm sure that in time, Dennis Green and Skylar will come around."

"I know," she said quickly. But there was a faint glitter of tears in her eyes.

"Shanna," he murmured, hating to see her upset. "Don't cry. Please don't cry."

"I'm not," she protested, even as she sniffled.

Unable to stand her suffering for another second, he drew her into his arms and lowered his head to capture her mouth in a gentle kiss.

Chapter 14

Momentarily surprised by Quinn's kiss, it took a second for her to respond. This kiss was different, more deliberate than the first one. When she felt him begin to pull away, she quickly wrapped her arms around his neck to stop him, holding him close and trying to tell him, without words, to stay.

He obliged her by kissing her again, and her brief sadness over Skylar was quickly replaced by overwhelming feelings for Quinn. He tasted wonderful, and she'd been dreaming about this moment since the first time he'd kissed her.

All too soon, the lingering kiss was over and she clung to his shoulders, worried her boneless legs wouldn't hold her weight.

"Shanna," he murmured again, his face buried in her hair and his arms wrapped tightly around her waist.

She loved the way he said her name. The way his heart pounded in his chest beneath her ear made her feel good to know he was as affected by that kiss as she was. "I hope you're not looking for an apology."

She laughed weakly and shook her head, wishing they could stay like this forever. "No, Quinn. I'm not looking for an apology." In fact, she wondered what he'd think if she asked him to kiss her again.

"We'd better get going," he said with true regret, but he didn't move. Clearly he was waiting for her to decide where to go from here.

She didn't want their embrace to end, but they were standing in the middle of the parking lot, and besides, she really did want to go back to Phoebe's apartment building to see if there were any fingerprints on the surface of the mailbox. Prints that didn't belong to the postman, that is.

"I guess we'd better," she agreed, loosening her grip. Strength returned to her limbs as her heart rate slowed to normal. The moment she pulled away, he released her.

His gaze searched hers and she smiled, feeling her cheeks turn warm. Her fair skin made it difficult to hide her feelings.

"You're so beautiful, Shanna," Quinn said in a low, rough tone. "I don't deserve someone as good and kind-hearted as you."

She thought that was an odd choice of words. "That's funny, because I was just thinking we deserved each other."

A shadow darkened his green eyes, and he turned to open the driver's side door of his SUV. "Where are you heading off to?" he asked, completely changing the subject. "I have to make a copy of Brady's notes for Agent

Tanner, but then I can meet you back at the coffee shop, or Karly's Kitchen if you want to grab something to eat."

She wanted to ask why he didn't think he deserved happiness, but sensed he wasn't going to open up about the topic here and now. Maybe later they could eat dinner and talk. "Karly's Kitchen is probably a good idea. We already know Phoebe isn't returning to the Corner Café tonight. How about we meet in an hour? I'm going to check Phoebe's mailbox for fingerprints first."

"Shanna." The exasperation in his tone was clear. "Don't set yourself up to be disappointed."

She knew he was only trying to help, but she didn't appreciate the way he kept bursting her bubble. "If that happens, it's my problem, isn't it?" she said curtly as she slid behind the wheel. She reached over to close the door, but he hung on to it.

"I'm sorry," he said with a sigh, sensing her annoyance. "I really do hope you're right and that you find something significant."

She couldn't help thinking Quinn was the type of man who hedged his bets. The type who didn't get his hopes up so he wouldn't be disappointed. Maybe because he'd been hurt in the past? "I'll see you in an hour, okay?" she said, forcing a smile.

He hesitated, and then stepped back and released the door. Quinn stood watching her as she started the car and then backed out of the parking spot.

Leaving him standing there felt strange. She hadn't been left alone much the past few days. With Quinn driving her around and helping her, she'd gotten used to his presence.

About time she stood on her own two feet. Quinn wasn't going to be with her forever. Once they'd found

Skylar and the person who'd killed his brother, they'd likely go their separate ways.

She lightly touched her lips, still tingling from Quinn's kiss. Maybe they wouldn't go their separate ways. Maybe this time, he'd kissed her as a way to tell her he wanted to keep seeing her even once this investigation was over.

The thought made her smile.

And even the sharp disappointment, fifteen minutes later, of not finding any fingerprints on Phoebe's mailbox didn't wipe the smile off her face.

Quinn couldn't get Shanna's voice out of his head as he used his computer at work to make a copy of Brady's notes for Agent Tanner.

That's funny, because I was thinking we deserved each other.

For a moment his heart had leaped with excitement, before it crashed to the pit of his stomach. That was easy for her to say, since Shanna didn't know everything about him. She didn't have a clue how close he was to making the same mistakes his father had made.

He dropped off the removable storage disk for Agent Tanner and then decided to go back to the coffee shop to chat with Brady's friends before heading over to meet Shanna.

There was no point wishing his life had been different. But he did wish that he could be the man Shanna thought he was.

Lost in thought as he walked up to the Corner Café, he almost missed the flash of purple hair. As soon as he realized the girl ahead of him might be Phoebe, he broke into a run.

Thankfully, she was just as oblivious because he caught up to her easily enough. "Phoebe?" he asked urgently.

She turned around in surprise, her gaze narrowing with suspicion when she saw him. "Leave me alone!" she cried.

"Wait! Please, don't run." Keeping one hand up where she could see it, he reached into his breast pocket to pull out his badge. "You're not in any trouble, I promise. I just want to ask a few questions, okay?"

She didn't run, but stood glaring at him. And then she sneezed twice in a row.

"Bless you," he said automatically.

"Thanks," she muttered, sniffling loudly and digging in her pocket for a tissue. "Better stay back—I'm full of germs."

"Is that why you called off your shift?" he asked, tempted to call Shanna but worried he might scare Phoebe away if he did.

"Yeah." She blew her nose loudly. With her puffy eyes, red nose and purple hair, it was hard for him to tell if Phoebe bore any resemblance to Shanna—if she could possibly by Skylar. "Have you ever tried serving customers when your nose is running like a faucet and you keep sneezing and coughing? Mega gross."

He chuckled, enjoying her self-deprecating sense of humor. "I completely understand. Look, I know you're not feeling well, but a friend of mine wants to meet you and ask a couple of questions if you don't mind."

Her gaze turned wary. "Is this about Brady?"

"Yes." He kept his tone light, casual, so she wouldn't take off. "Did you know Brady Wallace?"

She nodded, her eyes filling with pain. "He came into the café all the time. We became close friends."

It was on the tip of his tongue to ask just how close they were, but he kept his questions nonthreatening for now. "I'm sure his death must have been hard for you."

"Very," she said in a low whisper. "I cared about him a lot."

Her sorrow seemed genuine. "Did you attend his party that night?" he asked. His phone was in his pocket, and with a casual movement, hoping she wouldn't pay attention, he opened the device and sent a quick text message to Shanna. Phoebe at café.

"Yes. For a while." She hunched her shoulders as if the memory was painful. "I didn't stay long because I knew Anna was coming over after the play."

The slight sneer in her tone gave him a clue that Phoebe wasn't a fan of Brady's girlfriend. "Were you hoping Anna and Brady would break up?"

Phoebe ducked her head, hiding behind her purple-streaked jet-black hair. "Can't hurt to hope he'd finally see past the fakeness to her true colors, right? She wasn't that good of an actress."

A shiver of unease slid down his spine. Was it possible their initial love-triangle theory had some merit after all? Both Anna and Phoebe seemed to care for Brady. Had one of them bashed him on the head?

He found himself hoping and praying neither girl was a potential murderer.

"What time did you leave the party?" he asked.

She shrugged and then sneezed again. "Probably around nine-thirty or ten. That's what time Brady thought the play would be over."

The time Brady thought Anna might come? "So Brady was trying to keep the two of you apart?"

She avoided his gaze. "Only to avoid another scene."

"What happened?"

"I was working Friday night—the night before the party—and Brady was at the café working on his article. I sat with him while on break, and of course Anna showed up. She went crazy, yelling and screaming at Brady. My manager came out, threatening to call the cops, so Anna left. Brady went after her."

He winced a little at her resigned tone. "I'm sure that was difficult for you, considering how much you cared about him."

"A little," she allowed.

He was about to ask another question when a familiar SUV suddenly pulled over to the curb beside them. Despite the no-parking zone, Shanna jumped from the vehicle and approached them.

"Phoebe?" she asked in a rush.

The girl looked taken aback. "What do you want?"

Quinn put his hand on Shanna's arm, trying to warn her to go slow. He hadn't even asked whether or not Phoebe was adopted. "Phoebe, this is my friend, Shanna Dawson. Remember I told you she wanted to ask you a few questions?"

Phoebe took a step back, shaking her head. "Look, I'm done with this scene. I don't know who hurt Brady, and I'm sick. I need to go home. Maybe we can do this some other day, okay?"

"No, wait!" Shanna said urgently. "Please, Phoebe, just give me five minutes?"

The girl with the purple-streaked hair let out a heavy sigh. "Okay, what do you want to know?"

Shanna hesitated and glanced up at him, as if unsure how to proceed. Since he'd established some sort of rapport with her, he asked the question he knew was burning first and foremost in Shanna's mind. "Phoebe, were you helping Brady with his adoption story?"

Her eyes widened in surprise. "How did you know?"

"Were you adopted, too?" Shanna asked.

"Yes, I was adopted. And Brady did want to include me in his story. I wasn't really that anxious to participate, though. I mean, yeah, Dennis wanted to find his birth mother, but I didn't."

Shanna paled. "You didn't?"

"No. Why would I want to find some woman who didn't want me?" Phoebe asked in a hard tone. "One set of parents constantly fighting was bad enough. I wasn't anxious to add another parent into the mix."

Shanna stared at Phoebe in dismay. From the moment she'd faced the girl, she was convinced Phoebe was Skylar. She was adopted, for one thing, but the big brown eyes and the heart-shaped face bore an eerie resemblance to the age-progression photo of Skylar.

"What if I told you that your mother didn't give you up at birth?" Shanna asked, keeping her voice steady with an effort. "What if I told you that you were kidnapped as a five-year-old child and adopted by someone else illegally?"

Now it was Phoebe's turn to pale, her red nose standing out starkly against her features. "No. I don't believe you."

"I'm not lying about this. There's an FBI agent working on the case right now. I—we believe you might be my sister, Skylar Dawson."

"I'm not your sister," Phoebe said now, her tone carrying a hint of panic. "My parents told me I was adopted as an infant."

"So you don't remember this?" Shanna pulled out the stuffed elephant triumphantly. "Ellie the elephant was your favorite toy. You took her everywhere with you."

Shanna thought there was a flash of recognition in her sister's eyes, but then Phoebe was shaking her head vehemently. "No, I don't. I'm not listening to any more of your garbage, either. Leave me alone, do you hear me?"

Phoebe spun away and Shanna moved to follow, but Quinn stopped her with a hand on her arm. "Don't," he advised in a low tone. "Give her some time, Shanna."

She watched Phoebe hurry away, heading in the direction of her apartment. "But she's Skylar. She looks just like the age-progression photo I have. I know she's Skylar!"

"It's highly likely," Quinn agreed. "And I'm sure we'll get her fingerprint match to prove it. But that doesn't mean she's going to welcome you or your parents with open arms, Shanna."

She closed her eyes and ran an unsteady hand through her hair. Quinn was right. Skylar's expression had mirrored that of Dennis Green as he'd waited to be interviewed by Agent Tanner.

She'd found her long-lost sister, but clearly Skylar wasn't interested in the family she'd been taken from fourteen years ago.

"Don't torture yourself over this, Shanna," Quinn said. "You found your sister alive and well. Isn't that what matters most? And given time, she might come around."

"I hope so, Quinn," she murmured. Reaching into her

pocket, she pulled out the age-progression photograph and showed it to him. "See what I mean? Once you look past the purple hair and the eyebrow piercing, you can see they're the same person."

"The resemblance is difficult to ignore," Quinn agreed. "So we'll let Agent Tanner know, and he'll take over from here. Who knows, maybe she'll believe someone in authority, like the FBI, rather than the two of us."

She nodded, trying not to be disheartened. Quinn was right, though. God had helped her find Skylar, and there was nothing more she could do to change Skylar's mind about her family.

She'd leave that problem in God's hands, too. *Please, Lord, help Skylar to realize how much we love her, care about her and miss her. Amen.*

"Are you ready to eat?" Quinn asked.

Shanna shook her head. "I'm not hungry, and if you don't mind, I want to see my mom."

"You don't have proof yet that Phoebe is Skylar," he pointed out reasonably.

"I have the proof I need," she said, holding up the age-progression photo. "Did you see the way she looked at the stuffed elephant? Phoebe is Skylar, all right. And my mother deserves to know she's alive."

Quinn looked as if he wanted to argue, but then he stepped back. "Okay, will you call me afterwards?"

"Sure," she replied, somewhat absently. She was glad he wasn't going to try to stop her from doing what she knew in her heart was right. Impulsively, she gave him a quick hug. "See you later."

"Take care," he said, hugging her back.

Smiling for the first time since she'd received his text message, she walked around to get into his SUV.

The ride to her mother's house didn't take long. Her mom had stayed in the house after her parents had split up, and Shanna knew her mother refused to move because she secretly hoped her sister would somehow find her way back home.

Her father hadn't moved far, either; his auto-repair shop was close to the Carlyle University campus.

When she knocked on her mother's front door, she looked surprised to see her. "Shanna, what are you doing here?"

"I found Skylar," she blurted.

Her mother swayed and grabbed the edge of the door for support. "What? Did I hear you correctly? You found Skylar?"

"Yes, Mom. I did. Can we sit down for a minute? I'll tell you the whole story."

Her mother opened the door, and the two of them headed for the kitchen. Glancing around at the house she'd grown up in, she felt the familiar pang of nostalgia.

But this time, there wasn't any guilt. Yes, she should have walked Skylar inside the school building, but her sister's kidnapping wasn't totally her fault. Based on what Agent Tanner had revealed, there was a ring of criminals who preyed on innocent and vulnerable children.

Her mother made a pot of decaf coffee while Shanna filled her in on everything that had happened, from the moment she'd found Skylar's fingerprints at Brady's crime scene to finding and talking to Phoebe Fontaine.

"And you're certain this Phoebe is really Skylar?" her mother asked, cradling her coffee mug in her hand.

"We'll get the fingerprint match to prove it, but based

on your age-progression photos and her subtle reaction to Ellie the elephant, I'm sure."

"I can't believe it," her mother murmured. "After all this time, we finally know that Skylar is alive."

"I know, it's nothing short of amazing, isn't it?" Shanna asked. "And now that I've told you, my next stop will be to tell Dad. I know he's mad at me, but surely once he realizes Skylar is alive he'll find a way to forgive me."

"I don't think that's a good idea," her mother said when Shanna stood.

She stared at her mother. "Why not? I've been trying to talk to Dad for a few weeks now, but he wouldn't listen. But he has to listen if I tell him I found Skylar."

"I think Larry will take the news better coming from me," her mother argued.

"But that's the whole point, Mom. I want to mend this ridiculous feud between us. I know Dad blames me for Skylar's kidnapping, but at least I've avenged some of the wrong I did by finding her."

"You don't understand, Shanna," her mother said, twisting her hands in her lap anxiously. "There's another reason your father won't talk to you."

There was? Shanna slowly sank back into her chair. "What is it, Mom?"

Her mother paused for so long, Shanna feared she wouldn't tell her, but then finally, she raised her tortured gaze. "Early in our marriage, I had an affair. And when I discovered I was pregnant with you, the man I was seeing took off, returning to college a hundred miles away from here. I know what I did was wrong, and the fact that we were having some marriage problems isn't a good excuse. And of course my cheating with another man certainly didn't help. Larry was angry and upset, but after some extensive marriage counseling, we agreed to stay together and try again."

An affair? Her blood turned cold as the knowledge sank deep. "Are you saying what I think you're saying?" she hoarsely asked.

Tears filled her mother's eyes. "Yes. I'm sorry Shanna, but you're not Larry's daughter by blood."

Shanna didn't know what to say.

Her mother's voice dropped even lower. "But Skylar is."

Chapter 15

Shanna stared at her mother in horror. She wasn't her father's biological daughter? Skylar was?

No wonder Skylar looked so much like her father and Shanna didn't.

And that bit of news certainly explained why he'd been so bitterly angry, blaming her for Skylar's kidnapping.

Memories from the past swirled in her mind. The way her father had doted on Skylar from the moment her baby sister was born. The way he'd gone all out for Skylar's birthday, hiring a clown and even offering baby elephant rides because elephants were Skylar's favorite animal.

She hadn't been jealous of her sister, at least not that she remembered. But maybe subconsciously? No, she refused to believe she'd let Skylar go into her kindergarten class alone because subconsciously she wanted something to happen.

Please God, help me make sense of this. Please?

"Forgive me, Shanna," her mother cried, tears filling her eyes. "I thought God had forgiven me, but after Skylar's kidnapping, I realized that God was trying to teach me a lesson, making me atone for my sins."

"Oh, Mom," Shanna murmured, going over to give her mother a hug and a kiss. "Of course I forgive you. And I'm sure Skylar's kidnapping wasn't God trying to punish you. Everything that happened was a test of your faith to make you stronger."

"Maybe," her mother replied uncertainly, sniffling and then reaching for a tissue to blow her nose. "Larry certainly didn't keep his faith. Instead he turned his back on church, God and me. He moved out and started divorce proceedings. I gave him the divorce because that's what he wanted, but deep down, I consider myself still married to him. I keep hoping that someday we'll be a family once again…."

To hear her mother admit that she still hoped for a reconciliation with her father—Skylar's father, rather—was almost as surprising as finding out she wasn't her father's daughter. "Oh, Mom, I'm sorry. So sorry. Skylar's kidnapping was my fault, and you've suffered so much as a result."

"No, Shanna. Don't say that! Skylar's kidnapping was not your fault. I told you that back then, and I firmly believe it now. If it's anyone's fault, it's mine. I could have taken Skylar to her first day of kindergarten. But instead I left the job to you. And Larry constantly reminded me of that bad decision over and over again."

"Maybe it's not either of our faults," Shanna pointed

out, giving her mother another hug before going back to her seat. "Bad people kidnapped small children to make money through illegal adoptions. We couldn't know that they'd targeted Skylar. And let's look on the bright side. God brought Skylar back to us, so we have a lot to be thankful for."

"You're right, Shanna."

"And now we can tell Dad, er Larry, that Skylar has been found. Maybe this is what he needs to let go of the past once and for all."

"I hope so." Her mother tried to smile. "But I think it's best if you let me be the one to tell him the news, okay? I'm not sure he'll listen to you long enough to hear anything you'd tell him."

"Okay." Shanna stared at the scarred wood table, gathering her courage to ask about her real father. "Mom, would you please tell me who my biological father is?"

There was a pause before her mother answered. "His name was Randal Hanson, and he was my high-school sweetheart. Larry and I were married young, too young, and he was gone all the time, working during the day and taking classes at night to finish his associate's degree. I ran into Randal during spring break, when he was home from college."

Randal Hanson. Did he live far away? Shanna knew she had some vacation time coming, and she wondered if it might be a possibility to visit the man who'd fathered her.

"When I discovered I was pregnant, I called Randal in Boston to tell him the news. He panicked because he was already engaged to another woman." Her mother looked as if she might start crying again. "So he told me

I was on my own, because he was still going to marry his fiancée at the end of the summer."

"I'm sorry, Mom," she said helplessly. What a horrible situation for both of them.

"Don't be—it's my fault. And, Shanna, before you start making plans to go looking for Randal, you need to know he passed away three years ago from cancer."

Passed away? No! For a moment, a wave of anger overwhelmed her. How dare her mother wait until now to tell her the truth? Waiting until after her biological father died so she could never get to know him? Why hadn't her mother told her all those years ago?

She ground her teeth together. Holding back the scathing words that threatened to spill out was one of the hardest things she'd ever had to do.

"Randal did care for you, Shanna," her mother continued, as if clueless to how angry Shanna was. "In fact, he put money into a college fund when you were born. That's how we paid for your tuition."

She managed to nod, unable to trust her voice, trying to rein in her rioting emotions. At least her biological father had cared enough to help her get a good education. Even though he'd left her mother to fend for herself.

Paying for her college had been nice, but she'd rather have met her biological father in person instead of getting the money.

"Shanna?" Her mother reached over to put a hand on her arm. She managed, just barely, not to shake off her touch.

"I'm fine," she finally said. "It's just—a lot to absorb." No wonder Phoebe had reacted so negatively to the news of her kidnapping. It wasn't easy having your illusions shattered.

"I understand," her mother agreed. "And I'm sorry Larry was so unkind to you."

She shrugged. He'd been bitterly angry, but her mother's husband hadn't been unkind in a physical way. "At least everything makes sense now." She rose to her feet, anxious to leave before she said something she regretted to her mother. "I have to go, but I'll be in touch soon, okay?"

"Sure, dear." Her mother didn't seem to sense anything was amiss as she headed for the door. "Goodbye, Shanna."

"Bye, Mom." She brushed a quick kiss on her mother's cheek and then bolted out the door, desperate for the safety of Quinn's SUV.

Inside, tears blurred her vision and she swiped them away, wanting nothing more than to get away from here.

Shanna drove without paying much attention to her surroundings, her brain rehashing every shocking bit of news her mother had told her.

Her cell phone rang, and she glanced down at the display. Quinn's name flashed on the screen.

She ignored the call, letting it go to voice mail. She couldn't talk to him. Not right now. Not until she'd come to grips with everything she'd just learned.

Not until she'd found a way to forgive and forget.

Quinn placed a call to Agent Tanner. "I have some news," he said when Tanner picked up the call. "We found Phoebe Fontaine and she admitted she was adopted. Not only that, but when Shanna pulled out a stuffed elephant, Phoebe seemed to recognize it. We believe that Phoebe is Shanna's missing sister, Skylar Dawson."

"Very interesting. Where are you?" Agent Tanner asked abruptly.

"At the Corner Café, near the commons. Why?"

"Stay there. I want to talk to you in person. Give me fifteen minutes."

"All right," Quinn agreed, his curiosity peaked.

He waited in the café, wishing Shanna was with him. He hadn't agreed with her decision to run to her mother's with the news about Phoebe. Not without a firm fingerprint match. And especially not when Phoebe clearly expressed no interest in meeting her birth parents.

"Hey, Murphy," Tanner greeted him as he plopped into a seat beside him in the coffee shop. Quinn was impressed—the FBI agent had gotten there in just over ten minutes. "Interesting turn of events."

"Isn't it?" Quinn didn't need more caffeine, but he sipped his coffee anyway.

Tanner leaned forward eagerly. "I'm going to head over to visit Phoebe as soon as we're finished here. Her prints will prove she's Skylar."

"She wasn't exactly in the mood to cooperate," Quinn said slowly.

"I can get a court order to test her fingerprints. Or we can simply arrest her."

Arrest her? That seemed like overkill. "She'll cooperate," Quinn said. "She was surprised when Shanna confronted her, but given time she'll come around."

Tanner stared for a moment and then changed the subject. "I wanted to talk to you because as I reviewed Brady's notes, I wasn't convinced his murder is actually related to his article. I mean, he just didn't have enough information to make anyone want to kill him to keep him quiet. And how would anyone involved in the New

Beginnings Adoption Agency know that he'd stumbled on to them?"

Quinn cradled his coffee and let out a sigh. "You could be right. But then that means we're back to the theory of a love triangle." And now, more than ever, he didn't want Skylar to be a suspect.

"I know. So tell me what information you have regarding Anna Belfast," Agent Tanner asked.

Quinn lifted his brows. "Anna is a sophomore at Carlyle University, just like Brady. She was dating my brother, a fact that was confirmed by several others, including Brady's roommates. Anna was in the Thespian Club, landing the lead role in *Seven Brides for Seven Brothers*. She's in the theater arts program, and her roommate is Maggie Carson. The two of them work as hostesses at a local restaurant called Olive Grove. That's about all I know. Why?"

"Detective Nelson wanted me to tell you that Anna Belfast was admitted to the hospital two hours ago. Apparently, she was mugged on campus."

The tiny hairs on the back of Quinn's neck stood on end. Mugged? In a flash, he remembered how Shanna had looked lying on the floor of her house, her head bleeding. And now Anna was a victim, too? He shook his head. "That's a strange coincidence."

Tanner let out a harsh laugh. "Murphy, you and I both know there aren't any coincidences. Your first instinct regarding the love triangle was right on target. Unfortunately, Anna Belfast is still unconscious, so we can't question her about what happened. Luckily, the doctor is hopeful she'll recover."

Quinn didn't like where Tanner was going with this new turn of events. "There's no way Phoebe hurt Anna," he protested. "She really was sick—you can't fake a cold. Her nose was red and stuffed up, and she was coughing and sneezing the whole time we talked. Not to mention she's a tiny thing, short and skinny. She wouldn't have the strength to hurt anyone."

Tanner sat back in his seat as if he was enjoying Quinn's discomfort. "Phoebe wasn't working today. In fact, you happened to come across her here when she should have been home resting, right? I'm betting she's stronger than she looks. And how much strength does it take to lift a rock or a brick to hit someone in the back of the head? Phoebe has the motive and the opportunity. Not to mention her fingerprints were found on the rugby trophy."

"No. I don't believe it." Although he couldn't fault Tanner's logic. Hadn't he thought Phoebe might be guilty in the beginning, too? "There were two other unidentified sets of prints on the trophy, and one of those could easily belong to the killer." Knowing Shanna would be crushed at this turn of events, he instinctively pulled out his phone to call her.

"Wait," Tanner said quickly. "Before you make any calls, I have one more piece of interesting information to tell you."

He forced himself to wait, setting his phone carefully on the table before glancing up at Agent Tanner. Suddenly, he wasn't at all certain he liked the guy. "Like what?"

"We did manage to match another set of prints from the rugby trophy."

Quinn braced himself. "You did?"

"Anna Belfast's fingerprints were also found on the trophy from your brother's crime scene." For a moment Tanner's face held distinct satisfaction. "Which makes me believe the three of them—Phoebe, Anna and Brady—were definitely involved. And with Anna in the hospital, Phoebe, aka Skylar Dawson, is the obvious and most logical suspect."

Shanna drove aimlessly for almost twenty minutes before she realized she was close to her home. Feeling safe in Quinn's SUV, she turned down her street and pulled into the driveway. She turned off the engine and sat for a few minutes, trying to pull herself together.

Wishing she'd been given a chance to meet her biological father wasn't going to get her anywhere. Why was she so focused on him? Because she hadn't felt truly loved by the man who'd raised her?

It wasn't as if Randal had stayed around to be a part of her life, either. So what if he'd paid for her college tuition? He'd likely made the gesture out of guilt more than anything. Certainly, he hadn't done it out of love.

And at least now she knew why Larry, the man who'd raised her, hadn't loved her, either.

So why did she feel so betrayed?

She rested her forehead against the steering wheel, trying desperately not to feel so sorry for herself. Self-pity wasn't an admirable trait.

Her mother loved her. God loved her. And Quinn cared about her. Maybe she needed to focus on all the good aspects of her life, instead of whining over missed opportunities.

Help me to forgive and forget, Lord. Give me the strength to move forward with my life, rather than wallowing in the past.

A sense of calmness came over her and she lifted her

head, already feeling better. She thought about finding Quinn, but then realized that while she was here at her house, she may as well go inside to get some new clothes since she'd been wearing her current ones for a couple of days. When they'd stopped here earlier for her fingerprint kit, she'd been so excited about finding Phoebe that she'd forgotten to pack more clothes.

Using her key, she unlocked the side door and pushed it open. Remembering how Quinn had gone in first, she waited a moment before walking inside.

The musty smell of a closed house made her relax. For once, coming home to an empty house was a relief, especially when everything looked exactly like it had earlier in the day. She tossed her purse and keys on the kitchen table and then walked down the hall to her bedroom.

She riffled through her closet, pulling out a couple of casual outfits, but then tossed them aside in favor of long, sweeping skirts, secretly hoping Quinn would like how she looked.

Vain, she thought with a sigh. What was wrong with her? First wallowing in self-pity and then vanity. This wasn't like her at all.

She needed her life to get back to normal. Or at least as normal as it could be now that Skylar had been found.

She gathered two blouses, a sweater, another pair of jeans and a long flowing skirt before heading back to the kitchen. She'd left the overnight bag in the back of Quinn's SUV.

When she saw a bearded man standing in the middle of her kitchen, she let out a scream.

Her stalker!

"Shut up!" he said fiercely, taking a threatening step toward her.

Instinctively, she clamped her mouth shut and took a step back, clutching the clothes tighter to her chest. She stared at the man, looking past the scruffy beard to recognize him. "Dad?" she asked hesitantly.

"Shut up!" he said again, harshly. "I'm not your father."

No, he wasn't. Larry Dawson, the man who'd raised her, wasn't her father. But he was Skylar's father.

"I know," she said calmly, trying to judge the distance between where she stood and the front door. Because he was in front of the kitchen door, she didn't have many escape options. She debated whether or not to run back to her bedroom, but it wasn't as if the door had a lock. He'd catch her before she could open a window and escape.

"I told you I'd find you alone," Larry said, stabbing her with a look of pure hatred. "I should have made sure the job was done right the first time."

The first time? So he'd been the one to hit her on the back of the head. And then she smelled the sick scent of his aftershave. She'd never made time to go to the store to figure out the brand.

Stiffening her spine, she tossed the clothes aside and held up her hand beseechingly. "Please don't do this. I have something to tell you. Your daughter, Skylar, is alive."

His expression didn't change one bit. Instead he took another step forward, and she resisted the urge to back away. If she went any farther down the hall, she'd end up trapped.

"Didn't you hear me?" she urgently demanded. "There's no reason to hurt me. I found Skylar! She's alive and I know she's anxious to reunite with you."

That last part was a lie, but she didn't think God would mind, given the circumstances.

"I know where Skylar is," Larry said with a sneer. "I know more than you do about her life."

Her mouth dropped open in surprise. He'd found Phoebe and recognized her as Skylar? No, she found that hard to believe.

Larry must have seen the doubt on her features, because he went on. "She goes by the name of Phoebe and works at the Corner Café Coffee Shop. The café is only two blocks from my auto-repair shop. I stumbled upon her over four months ago, and knew the first time I looked into her eyes that she was my daughter. Skylar."

Four months ago? Why hadn't he called the authorities? Because he'd wanted to reunite with her first? And suddenly missing pieces of the puzzle fell into place. "You killed Brady. Because you knew Phoebe—er, Skylar was falling for him."

"That young kid didn't deserve her," Larry said. "She ran back to the coffee shop, crying on my shoulder about how Brady forced her to leave the party because Anna was due to arrive. So I went back to Brady's party and waited for the right moment."

Shanna sucked in a harsh breath. Had he really just admitted to killing Brady? He'd bashed a young man in the back of the head for a daughter who didn't remember him?

"Skylar is never going to be hurt by anyone, ever again," Larry continued. "I'm always going to be there to protect her. Always."

Sensing he was distracted, she took a chance and rushed across the living room, heading for the front door.

Her hand clasped the doorknob and she eagerly tugged it open.

But Larry caught her from behind, yanking her painfully backward. She sprawled on the floor, staring with horror at the only father she'd ever known.

"You'll never escape," he said in a low voice, hovering over her. "Never!"

Chapter 16

Shanna shivered with fear, feeling sick as she realized the man who'd raised her truly hated her enough to kill her.

Dear God, please help me! Save me!

She dug her heels into the carpet and used her elbows to try crawling backward, away from him. If only she'd called Quinn to let him know she was here. The last time she'd been attacked, Quinn's phone calls had saved her. But tonight, her phone was in her purse on the kitchen table. Even if Quinn called her, Larry wouldn't hear the phone. He wouldn't know that Quinn was looking for her.

This time, she was on her own.

A firm hand grabbed her around the ankle, halting her progress. Belatedly, she realized Larry was wearing latex gloves. He must have worn them the night of

Brady's murder, too. No wonder he hadn't left finger-prints on the rugby trophy.

"Oh, no. Not this time," he said with a sneer. "This time I'm going to finish the job right."

"Why?" she asked desperately, trying to find some-thing, anything, to use as a weapon against him. At the moment all she had were words. "What point is there in killing me now?"

"I lost my daughter because of you." The wild glint in his eyes convinced her that his thought process was far from lucid. He was clearly lost in a world all his own. "And you couldn't leave me alone, could you?" He mim-icked her with a high tone. "Daddy, please let me in. I just want to talk to you. Please, Daddy?"

She swallowed hard, remembering the messages she'd left on his voice mail and how she'd called out to him through his front door. She'd wanted desperately to mend the rift between them.

But that was before she'd discovered the truth. That he'd never loved her because she wasn't his biological daughter.

"I'm sorry. I'll never call you again," she vowed, still trying to instill some logic into his warped brain. "I promise to never call you or contact you again."

"You think it's that easy?" he demanded, his face twisted in a mask of anger. "Now that you've found Phoebe you'll fill her head with all sorts of sisterly no-tions. No, there's only one way for this to end. Once you're gone, Phoebe will continue to come to me for help the way she has been for the past few months. Her adopted parents don't care—they're losers. They fight all the time and kicked her out when she was eighteen.

I'm the one who'll support her. I'm her real father. Her only father. Me!"

With his hand clamped around her ankle, she couldn't crawl backward any further. Desperately, she reached behind and realized she was up against the end table next to her sofa.

"I'll go away and never contact Phoebe—er, Skylar again," she said. "I promise. There's no reason to hurt me."

"You deserve to die for what you did," he muttered. He lifted his hand, a heavy glass picture frame in his latex-gloved grip.

"No!" she cried. She lunged upward and grabbed the cord of the lamp sitting on top of the end table, knocking it down at the same moment he brought the heavy picture frame toward her head. She ducked, and the picture frame whizzed past her ear, hitting her hard on the shoulder.

Pain zinged down her left arm, leaving her impaired. But she was strangely calm as she picked up the lamp with her right arm and swung it at Larry's head. God must have been with her because she hit him square in the face. He howled and reared backward, blood spurting everywhere from his mashed nose.

Without his hand holding her ankle, she was able to scramble to her feet. She held up the lamp, prepared to swing again, when Quinn came barreling through the living room from the kitchen.

"Leave her alone!" he shouted, rushing Larry and tackling him around the waist. The two of them hit the floor with a horrible thud.

"Quinn!" Shanna helplessly watched them roll around on the floor, each vying for the upper hand. Of course

Quinn was younger and stronger, so it didn't take long for him to pin Larry down.

Within moments her father gave up the fight.

"Lawrence Dawson, you're under arrest for attempted murder," Quinn said harshly, pulling a pair of handcuffs out of his back pocket. He slapped one of the handcuffs around her father's wrist and then flipped him over so he could cuff the other wrist behind him. "You have the right to remain silent..."

As Quinn went through the rest of the Miranda rights, Shanna closed her eyes and lowered the lamp to the table, suddenly overwhelmed with emotion.

Thank You, Lord. Thank You for sending Quinn. Thank You for sparing my life.

Quinn hauled her father to his feet and then walked him over to a kitchen chair, forcing him to sit down. She followed more slowly as Quinn stepped back, keeping a wary eye on his prisoner.

"He admitted to killing Brady," she said, rubbing her sore shoulder, "because your brother treated Phoebe badly. He recognized Phoebe as Skylar and has established a rapport with her. He's been trying to protect her!"

Quinn's expression darkened, but he nodded. "I shouldn't be surprised. I believe he tried to kill Anna Belfast, too."

Her eyes widened in surprise. "Anna? What happened?"

"She was mugged on campus. She's in the hospital with a concussion and has just started to wake up. I eventually remembered how Anna said some creepy old guy was following her. Once we're able to take her statement, we'll add that violation to the list. Don't worry, he's going to have so many charges filed against him, he'll go to jail for a long time."

The wail of sirens could be heard growing louder and louder. Quinn had obviously called for assistance. "How did you know I was here?" she asked.

He looked at her for a long moment, his expression grim. "I don't honestly know, but when you didn't answer my phone calls, I suspected something was wrong. I thought maybe you were upset after visiting your mother, and if so, the most logical place for you to come would be here." His questioning gaze was full of reproach, and she knew he'd wished she'd called him.

She wished she had, too.

"I'm so glad you came when you did," she murmured, wanting to rush over and hug him.

But the sirens pulled into her driveway, and seconds later four armed cops came in through both doors.

"I have the suspect handcuffed," Quinn said loudly. The officers pulled up short, looking disappointed that their firepower wasn't needed.

Of course, the police wanted a statement from her, so she went through the entire chain of events, from the information she'd learned from her mother to coming home and finding him standing in her kitchen.

When she got to the part where he'd tried to hit her on the head with the heavy glass picture frame, Quinn abruptly stood up and came to stand beside her. He placed a reassuring arm around her shoulders.

"I hit him in the face with the base of the lamp," she explained, leaning on Quinn for strength. "I think I broke his nose."

Quinn muttered something under his breath that sounded like, "He's lucky that's all you broke."

She frowned at him before turning back to the officer. "Quinn came in before I had to hit him again."

The officer looked at Quinn, who took up his side of the story. "I tackled him, cuffed him and read him his rights."

The brevity of Quinn's explanation made her smile. "Quinn arrived just in time."

"Okay, I don't think we need anything else at this time," the officer said, rising to his feet. Two of the other cops had already dragged her father out to the squad car. She was glad because she couldn't bear looking at him and seeing the seething hatred reflected in his eyes.

Quinn walked the cop to the door, and when they were finally alone again, he turned to face her. "Are you sure you're all right?"

She nodded, rolling her shoulder experimentally and trying not to wince at the pain. "I'm fine. Maybe a little stiff and sore, but nothing that a dose of ibuprofen won't fix."

Quinn stared at her for a long moment. "Why didn't you call me?" he finally asked. "I was right about you being upset after visiting your mother, wasn't I?"

She sighed and nodded, feeling foolish. In hindsight, her reasons for coming here alone didn't make much sense. "Yes, I was upset. My mother told me she had an affair. Larry isn't my biological father, and that's why he never forgave me for Skylar's kidnapping. All these years, he's hated me because I was here and Skylar wasn't. It all makes so much more sense now that I know the truth."

"I see." Quinn tucked his hands in his pockets as he came closer. "But that still doesn't explain why you didn't call me."

"I should have called you, Quinn," she said softly. "I was upset with my mother because she'd kept my biological father a secret all this time. And since he died three years ago from cancer, I'll never have the chance to know him. Meet him. See him…"

"Hey, it's okay." Quinn took her hand, gently tugging her to her feet. "Don't cry, Shanna. I'm here for you."

She wrapped her arms around his waist and buried her face in his chest. That he was here for her was amazing. Didn't he realize his brother's death was indirectly her fault? "I know," she said in a low, muffled voice. "It's stupid of me to be so upset. I don't even know that my biological father would have wanted any sort of relationship with me, even if he was still alive. But I was so angry at my mother, even though I knew it was wrong."

Quinn stroked a hand down her back, holding her close. After a few minutes, she lifted her head to gaze up at him. "I'm so sorry, Quinn. Your brother died because of me. Because of Skylar's kidnapping."

"Shanna, don't. That man's actions are not your fault." For an instant his expression turned fierce, but then it was gone. "Just knowing he'll spend the rest of his life in jail is enough for me."

She tried to smile. "God always wants us to forgive those who act out against us, so I will forgive him. But I have to admit, after everything he's done, I'm glad I don't share any of his genes."

Quinn's expression turned grim, and he immediately released her and stepped back. "It's getting late. I should leave."

What? She stared at him, trying to figure out what she'd said wrong. "I feel like I need to apologize. Are you still upset with me? Because your brother was killed by the man who raised me? Or because I didn't call you? I'm sorry, Quinn. Please forgive me."

He turned away, as if he couldn't bear to look at her. "No need to apologize, Shanna. As you said, God always forgives our sins, and I promise I don't hold any sort of grudge against you. But I really do need to leave." He looked around the kitchen, everywhere but directly at her. "I'm sure you'll be all right alone here now that Larry is in custody."

Quinn was pulling away from her, and Shanna instinctively knew that if she let him go now, she'd lose something infinitely precious.

"Please don't go," she begged. "Talk to me, Quinn. Tell me what's bothering you."

He hunched his shoulders, and she thought he was going to simply walk away until he slowly turned back to face her. Stark regret flickered in his green eyes. "Did I mention my father was a Chicago cop?"

She shook her head. "No. I know your parents are divorced, but you haven't said much about your father."

Quinn let out a harsh laugh. "No, I haven't. Because it's not a pretty story to tell. My parents divorced when I was young, and of course they shared joint custody of me, so I went back and forth between them. But once my mother met James and remarried, she didn't have as much time for me. So I ended up staying with my father for longer and longer periods of time. Soon, I was living with my father full-time."

Shanna couldn't help a flash of anger toward Quinn's mother. What sort of woman abandoned her own child? Especially since she sensed that living full-time with his father hadn't been a good thing for Quinn.

The way he stood in her kitchen, so isolated and

alone, made her heart ache. She walked toward him, putting her hand on his arm. "I'm sorry. Sounds like your childhood left a lot to be desired."

"Yeah, you could say that." He paused, and she was glad he didn't pull away from her touch as he continued, "My father drank. A lot. At first he managed to drink only on his days off work, but then he was drinking more often until I knew he was likely drinking on the job. I called his partner and best friend on the force to let him know. Luckily, they took him off the streets before he could hurt anyone."

Thank goodness, Shanna thought.

"But being off the streets only made him drink more. They did their best to get him into a program, and he played along for a while, but he always went back to drinking. And then it was too late. One night I came home from work to find him lying on the bathroom floor in a pool of blood."

She sucked in a harsh breath. "Oh, Quinn."

"The doctor told me he had esophageal varices, distended blood vessels in his esophagus, and one of them blew. He ultimately bled to death. I called 911, but he was gone before the paramedics arrived."

Suddenly, she understood what she'd said wrong. She'd been glad she didn't share Larry's genes, but Quinn certainly shared his father's. "Quinn, listen to me. Just because your father drank too much doesn't mean you'll make the same mistake."

"How do you know?" Quinn challenged. "Being a cop is a high-risk job. Some women can't handle knowing we're constantly in danger. My mother couldn't. And neither could Leslie."

A stab of jealousy speared her heart. "Who's Leslie?"

"No one special," he said quickly. "We dated for a while, that's all. I thought maybe one day our relationship would turn serious, but she couldn't put up with my career so she found herself a nice, safe accountant."

The relief was overwhelming. At least he wasn't still in love with Leslie, who was nuts if she thought some accountant was a better catch than Quinn Murphy.

"Good for Leslie. But I don't want a nice, safe accountant," she said boldly. He visibly reacted to her statement, throwing his shoulders back and straightening his spine. "There's nothing wrong with your chosen career, Quinn. I work in law enforcement, too, you know. Granted, as a crime-scene investigator I'm not often in danger, but we are trained for the possibility."

Quinn stared at her for so long she felt her cheeks grow warm. Was he thinking of a graceful way out? Had she been too forward? Too bold?

"Shanna, I know I said this once before, but I don't deserve you."

She let out the breath she'd been subconsciously holding. "Quinn, do you believe in God?"

He looked surprised by the abrupt change of subject. "Yes, Shanna, I do. You've helped show me the way back to my faith. In those long moments when you weren't answering your phone and I knew you were in danger, I prayed over and over for God to keep you safe. I also prayed for the strength to get to you in time."

She smiled, thinking Quinn's timing was just about perfect. "I prayed, too, and obviously God listened to both of our prayers."

"I know I still have a lot to learn," he admitted. "But I was hoping you'd continue to teach me, showing me how to keep my faith."

"Okay, well here's your first lesson. God loves you, Quinn, just as much as He loves me. Just as much as He loves all His children, His followers. He loves you, He watches over you and He answers your prayers, right?"

Quinn nodded hesitantly. "Right."

"So if God loves both of us, how is it that you aren't worthy enough to be with me? Are you implying you know better than God?"

Realization dawned in his eyes. "No, of course not."

She smiled up at him. "Remember when I told you we deserved each other? I really meant that, Quinn. I feel so lucky to have met you. Having you at my side through all this, helping me find my sister, saving me from harm, has meant the world to me."

"Shanna," he murmured, lifting one hand and tucking a stray lock of hair behind her ear. She turned her cheek so that it rested against the palm of his hand. "I'm the lucky one. You have no idea how much I care about you."

"I think I do have an idea. Because I feel the same way, Quinn," she said simply. "And I'm hoping that even though we've solved your brother's murder and found Skylar, you'll still be a part of my life."

"I want that, too, Shanna." Quinn's voice was low, husky. "More than you'll ever know. But I'm afraid. What if I change into the man my father was?"

"I suppose anything is possible," she said, although she couldn't imagine Quinn ever doing that. "But let me ask you, did your father believe in God? Did he live his faith every day? Did he pray for help with his illness?"

"No." Quinn's expression lit up with hope. "And I'm sure if he had believed in God, his life would have turned out very different."

"Of course it would have," Shanna agreed.

Suddenly, Quinn swept her into his arms, burying his face in her hair. "Shanna, I love you so much!"

Tears of happiness sprang to her eyes and she clutched him close, her heart soaring. "I love you, too, Quinn."

And she knew, deep down, that together they made a great team.

Epilogue

One month later

Quinn whistled happily as he walked up Shanna's driveway. The diamond ring he'd purchased burned a hole in his pocket, and he planned to propose marriage tonight. He felt good knowing that he'd found two important pieces of his life that were missing before, God and Shanna.

Before he could knock at the door, Shanna opened it, greeting him with a warm smile. "Hi, Quinn. How was your day?"

"Good," he responded, and he wasn't lying. During the past four weeks, they'd made a pact to share both the good and the bad about their respective jobs. He gave her a quick hug and a warm kiss that went on longer than it should. Finally he huskily asked, "And how was your day?"

"Fair," she murmured with a sigh. "We spent hours going through the crime scene but didn't find much of anything useful."

"Do you want to talk about it?" he asked, dropping his arms and taking a step back so he could breathe properly. Shanna's scent tended to cloud his brain. The sooner she married him, the better.

"No, it's fine." Shanna smiled as she headed into the kitchen. "I hope you like pot roast, because that's what we're having for dinner."

He'd tried to tell her she didn't need to cook for him, but she'd insisted. Watching her work in the kitchen, he decided not to wait until after dinner. "I love pot roast, but will you come and sit in the living room for a minute?"

She flashed him a concerned look, but did as he asked. "Quinn, is something wrong?"

Her worry made him smile. "No, everything is just right." Once she was seated on the sofa, he went down on one knee and took her hand in his. "Shanna, I love you. I thank God every day for bringing you into my life. Would you please marry me?"

Her eyes rounded, and her mouth dropped open in shock when he presented her with the simple diamond ring. "Oh, Quinn! Yes! Yes, of course I'll marry you! I love you, too."

She leaped off the sofa and he stood just in time to catch her as she threw herself into his arms. He kissed her again, reveling in the moment. "Soon, Shanna. Marry me soon," he whispered.

"I will," she promised, her eyes bright with tears.

The doorbell rang, interrupting their special moment. Shanna scowled. "I hope that's not a salesman," she muttered. He was proud of the way she looked through the window first, before opening the door.

"Phoebe!" Shanna exclaimed, opening the door wide. "Come on in."

"Uh, hi," Phoebe said nervously. Quinn noticed that the purple streaks in her hair had been dyed back to match her natural color, although the eyebrow ring remained. "I—uh—is this a bad time?"

"No, of course not." Shanna darted a warning glance in his direction as she quickly closed the door behind Phoebe. "Please come in. You remember Quinn, right?" When Phoebe nodded, Shanna continued. "How are you?"

"Fine." Phoebe looked distinctly uncomfortable, and Quinn was about to make himself scarce when she suddenly said, "I remember Ellie the elephant."

Shanna's eyes softened and filled once again with tears. "I'm so glad to hear that."

Phoebe went on, as if she needed to get everything off her chest. "I remember Ellie the elephant and I remember the night I had a nightmare and you rubbed my back, talking to me until I fell back asleep."

"Yes, I remember that, too," Shanna whispered. "Oh, Skylar—I mean, Phoebe. I missed you so much when you were gone."

"I'm sorry I didn't remember you sooner," Phoebe said urgently. "But if it makes you feel better, I didn't remember my father, either. All those weeks he came into the café to talk to me, I just thought he was a lonely old man."

Quinn had wondered how Phoebe had taken the news

of her father's arrest. "You're not to blame for his actions, Phoebe," he said quickly.

Phoebe sent him a grateful smile before turning back to Shanna. "Agent Tanner has questioned me twice, but I just don't remember anything about the kidnapping. I guess I subconsciously blocked those moments from my mind."

"Please don't worry about it." Shanna jumped up and went over to kneel before her sister. "I'm just so glad you're alive. And healthy. That's all that matters."

"You need to know I won't ever be Skylar again," Phoebe said slowly. "I've been Phoebe too long."

"That's okay. I like the name Phoebe," Shanna said reassuringly. "It suits you."

There was an awkward silence, as if neither knew what else to say. "Phoebe, Shanna never stopped looking for you," Quinn said. "And if she hadn't kept the information from her ongoing investigation, we never would have found you."

"Thanks, Shanna." Phoebe abruptly threw her arms around Shanna in an exuberant hug. "Thanks for never giving up on me."

"Never," Shanna murmured.

"I hope we can be friends," Phoebe said, releasing Shanna and wiping away her tears. "I'm still getting used to all this, but I want us to be friends."

"Of course we can," Shanna agreed. "I'll always be here for you, Phoebe. No matter what."

Quinn caught Shanna's gaze and smiled at her, silently thrilled to see the two sisters united at last.

His family.

* * * * *

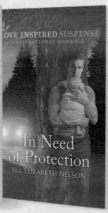

Love Harlequin romance?

DISCOVER.

Be the first to find out about promotions, news and exclusive content!

Facebook.com/HarlequinBooks

Twitter.com/HarlequinBooks

Instagram.com/HarlequinBooks

Pinterest.com/HarlequinBooks

YouTube.com/HarlequinBooks

ReaderService.com

EXPLORE.

Sign up for the Harlequin e-newsletter and download a free book from any series at
TryHarlequin.com

CONNECT.

Join our Harlequin community to share your thoughts and connect with other romance readers!
Facebook.com/groups/HarlequinConnection

HSOCIAL2021

HARLEQUIN

Heartfelt or thrilling, passionate or uplifting—Harlequin is more than just happily-ever-after.

With twelve different series to choose from and new books available every month, you are sure to find stories that will move you, uplift you, inspire and delight you.